R.C. PERRY

From The Ashes

A Kingdom of Beasts and Starlight

First published by The Valerian Press LLC 2025

First edition

ISBN (paperback): 979-8-9985872-1-4
ISBN (hardcover): 979-8-9985872-2-1

This book was professionally typeset on Reedsy.
Find out more at reedsy.com

For all of the girls who stayed-when they shouldn't have.
For all of the girls who've stared down their demons and told them to go back to hell.
For all of the "broken girls"- You're more beautiful than you know.
I see you.
And you're not alone.

Contents

Acknowledgments

It's so hard to say thank you to everyone who helped make this book possible. Your endless hours of support and work on this project were more than I could have hoped for. I don't have all the words for thank you, but I am going to try.

First off, thank you to my amazing readers for taking the time to give this book a shot. I hope you enjoy journeying through Valeria.

A big shout-out to my friends, Nádia and Anna, who supported this project, let me bounce ideas off them, beta-read, proofread, shared my content, and overall hyped me up. You all are the best.

To my beta, arc readers, and street team members—thank you for all your help and hard work. You guys are amazing!

Thank you also to Uncle Mickey and my Nana for believing in me and my ability to succeed. Your love means everything to me.

Thank you to my cover designer, JMBeth Covers, for giving me an incredible cover that screamed: THIS IS MY BOOK.

Thank you to my doggies for enduring countless hours of snuggles while I banged out words on the keyboard, fueled by caffeine and your cuddles alone. Yes, I know they can't read.

Steven, thanks for the books to help me research, for listening to my crazy ideas, and helping to fund my wildest dreams. Thank you for being supportive. You helped make this possible! Thank you for telling me over and over that I was awesome and to f*** my feelings when I got down on myself.

Mom, thanks for believing in me, adding commas, and proofreading even when you were insanely busy. Thanks for giving my book a shot, even though fantasy is not exactly your thing. Thank you for instilling a love of reading and cultivating a creative mind in me. This book came from that. Thank you for being the picture of strength... I think Remmy got her survival skills from you!

Thank you to Jesus for giving me a creative mind and the support I needed to reach my goals.

To my Papa—for being the hero in my story. I hope you're proud of me.

And lastly, but certainly not least, thank you to my husband for being my muse, my sounding board, my best friend, and my biggest fan. Your belief in me made this possible. I couldn't have done it without you. I love you forever and a day.

I'm not crying; you're crying!

Seriously though, I couldn't be more grateful for you all.

Author's Note

This book has scenes depicting violence, mentions of abuse, both verbal and physical, attempted sexual assault, death, and animal death.

Please be mindful of other potential triggers.

Author's Note on AI

No generative artificial intelligence (AI) was used in the writing and creation of this book. The author expressly forbids any entity from using this publication in the training or programming of any AI technologies. The author reserves all rights to license the use of this work for any generative AI development or training.

Map

The continent of Amengor

Prologue

The Kingdom of Elysia
Year 526 AV

```
The Battle of Five Hundred Years
```

The battleground stretched out before me, empty of all but a few elite warriors. Blood pooled in puddles beneath my feet, and countless Fae bodies littered the field. We'd lost this battle. I could only hope that we would win the war.

Tears formed in my eyes as I stepped over the body of my Lieutenant, but I would not allow them to fall. I would mourn my men when this was over, if I survived. Rhye was a good man of the phalynx clan. He left behind a wife and a daughter of only four years.

I pushed aside the unwelcome thought of all the families left behind from this fruitless war. It was for this reason I'd never married. I had been born to war, and war was all there was for me. The cold Elysian wind ripped at my armor as I spotted the Vantan commander across the field.

I was the last known of my kind, and that saddened me. If I died today, my clan would be eradicated, for I bore no offspring in my short time on earth. I could only hope and pray to Afrontis that my sacrifice would not be in vain.

The Valerians were coming to our aid, as they tore through the Vanta in their own country. Word had come through the ranks that they had sent ten thousand soldiers and ripped a hole in the Vantan army. The thought made me smile. For too long, we had been slaves to them. Too long, we lived in subjection.

The creature's eyes glowed gold as he spotted me making my way toward him.

Cut off the head, and the body will flail.

The reminder sounded in my head over and over again as the commander took on the form of a great golden dragon. I should have known he would fight dirty. Half the Fae on this field had been ripped to shreds by one beast or another. The commander was the strongest of his kind, able to take on any form and control all magical elements. The mighty dragon stalked toward me, Fae bodies crunching under his massive feet.

In retrospect, if I had stayed in Fae form and found a way to get under him with my sword and pierce his heart, I might have lived. But I chanced shifting instead and took flight.

The golden dragon plowed into mine, hurling me backward. My dragon was half the size of his.

A roar ripped from my throat as pain lanced through me. I recovered an instant before he charged me again. With one swipe of his massive claw, he shredded my left wing. Agony blinded me as I tried to pivot, swinging my torn wing away from him, desperate to gain an advantage.

I dove low, ramming my head into his belly. A snarl of rage thundered from his throat as I shot out from beneath him.

I realized too late that I didn't stand a chance.

He rammed me again, jaws clamping on my neck. I heard the snap before I felt it.

My dragon plummeted toward earth, shifting mid-air. My broken Fae body slammed to the ground, my head twisted at an unnatural angle.

As my life force drained from me, my blood stained the stones, my death heralding the end of the era of the dragon.

I

Part One

One

Shred of Hope

* * *

Remmy
Year 1026 PV

My heart heavy, I stood in the doorway of my childhood home, running my fingers over the grooves in the door frame. Each nuance in the grains of wood held a memory that told a story. I soaked in the smell of freshly baked bread. The sound of children's laughter echoing off the dusty walls. My sister's soft, yet scolding voice. The creaking of my father's chair as he rocked beside the warm hearth.

The tiny shack, nothing more than a three-room cabin with a chamber pot, had been home for all twenty-five years of my life, and now I didn't know when I would see it again—if I would see it again.

I sighed heavily and kissed my young brother and sister on their cheeks, holding them tightly against me. Echo and Eridian were too young to grasp the full weight of the situation, but they knew I was leaving—and no one could tell them when, or if, I would return.

Their tears stained my thin cotton dress as they clung forlornly to my side. Emerie stepped forward and took their little hands in hers, pulling them gently away. The twins buried their faces in her dress, not wishing to watch my departure. I pulled my sister into a fierce embrace; her slender body shaking with quiet sobs. She held our younger siblings, resting her chin on my shoulder as silent tears rolled down her sun-kissed cheeks.

I hated the thought of burdening her with this responsibility. She was but a child herself, only seventeen years old, but Father was… incapable, and our mother had abandoned us shortly after the twins were born.

They were only a few days old, and Emerie, eleven. So, as the eldest at nineteen, I was left with the responsibility of raising my three young siblings.

Following my mother's abandonment, Father took to drinking, which resulted in the loss of part of his leg at the job where he mined quilldust for the royal family. I was never told the full story of his accident, as he refused to talk about it. I only know what the other miners told me.

He was drunk, fell off a ladder into a cavern in the mine, and lost his leg from the knee down. After that, he gave himself completely to the alcohol, and nothing I could ever do brought him back from it.

He spent all of the family savings, leaving us steeped in debt and forcing me to find ways to provide for our family.

I'd taught myself to sew clothes for the children and how to grow fruits and vegetables in the garden. As it turned out, I was rather skilled with plants. I'd even learned how to hunt in the woods behind the village with a bow.

I wasn't exceptional at it, but we did have meat at least once per week, and the earnings from the produce I sold at the market allowed me to keep buying tips for my arrows every time I lost one. I had yet to teach myself how to make them.

That had been our entire existence for the last six years, but now a new opportunity had arisen. A glimmering shred of hope for a better future, and I was determined to seize it.

I cupped Emerie's face in both of my hands and looked her steadily in her tear-rimmed eyes. "I will return to you, my strong, brave girl. And when I do, our lives will be better. They will be so much better. You will see."

She blinked back tears from her honey-colored eyes and nodded her head firmly. "I love you, my sister. Be safe, and may Lunaire shine down on your journey."

"I love you too, and may Skotos keep watch over you in the darkest of times," I whispered softly, the words echoing in the stillness of the dawn.

With one last glance at Echo and Eri, I turned and headed down the long gravel path that led to our shack on the edge of town. Clutching the parchment against my chest, I adjusted the pack on my back and set out down the dusty road.

* * *

Remmy

As I entered the valerian-lined roads of Merda, the villagers called out, wishing me well.

I doubted anyone expected me to return, yet they wished me well all the same. I had not wanted to make it known that I was attempting this feat, but word spreads like wildfire in a village as small as Merda.

Mt. Malus was known to be the most dangerous place in all of Valeria. Home to the Darkhelm Forest and all the creatures of nightmares. It's rumored that there even lies a cave with a portal to the Netherworld in the mountain, from whence all manner of demons may emerge. I seemed to be the only woman from Merda brave enough to try.

Or desperate enough. I thought wryly.

As far as I knew, two other women had attempted the journey, only to be killed before making it halfway up the mountain. I glanced down at the brochure in my hands, reading it again with growing resolve.

At the edge of town, I stopped at the bakery to buy a loaf of bread to take with me. Along with the hard cheese and the dried meat in my pack, it wasn't much, but it would have to do. I was hoping to fish, hunt, and forage along the way.

I swung the door open and stepped inside. I heard Alice call out from the back, "Be with you in a moment!"

I waited patiently, eyeing the sweet treats lining the counter.

If only I had an extra coin.

Sweets were a rarity that I could not often afford. Sometimes, when I made extra coin from selling produce at the market, I would bring one home. Other times, Emerie would bake something for us to share. Usually, it was only on holidays or special occasions, such as Yule Fest.

My mouth salivated as I peeked at the numerous treats. Powdered pastries. Nut-filled scones. Biscuits with jam. I licked my lips.

Alice emerged from the back of the bakery and smiled widely at me. "Remmy! I'm delighted you stopped in. I have something for you."

She reached under the counter and took out a brown paper package, pushing it into my hands. "I know you're setting off for Mt. Malus. I wish you wouldn't… but… I understand why you need to. I hope this makes the journey a bit more enjoyable."

The older woman came out from behind the counter and pulled me into a snug embrace. Alice was the only villager to offer help after Father's accident; the rest of the town chose to ignore our plight.

She frequently brought leftover bread from the bakery after closing, teaching Emerie to bake and letting her spend time there after school to learn.

"Please be safe… this town… it wouldn't be the same without you." She sighed dramatically and let me go.

"Thank you, Alice, but what is it?" I asked, sneaking a peek inside the paper bag she handed me.

"Just a little something to make you smile, dear. Don't open it until you leave."

I smiled and handed her the coin I had set aside for bread, but she shook her head.

"No, you keep it. This is a gift. I want you to have everything you need."

I started to stutter a protest, but she narrowed her eyes at me. "No argument from you, girl. Now, get out of here before I cry."

I grinned at her, shoving the bag into my pack. "Thank you! I'll see you again soon!" I called out as I exited the store.

Behind me, I heard her muttering about tears and goodbyes as the bakery door swung closed.

With a last glance, I left the town of my birth behind and took off down the narrow dirt road.

* * *

Remmy

Hours later, my feet ached, and my skin was red and sore from being under the burning sun for so long.

I surveyed the road, thinking about the task ahead of me, still clutching the parchment securely in one hand.

Dusk was fast approaching, and no shelter was in sight. I'd have to find somewhere to set up camp soon. It wasn't safe to travel alone at night here, but the dirt road stretched on for miles ahead of me, seemingly endless.

With no other choice, I plodded faithfully forward.

According to my map, Mt. Malus was a three-day walk from Merda. Inwardly, I groaned at the thought of two more days of walking. Taking the map from the side pocket of my pack, I unrolled it carefully. Relief flooded me. By tomorrow, I'd leave the desert, and the terrain would improve significantly until reaching the Highland Pass at the base of the mountain. Sadly, though, I would not make it there before nightfall.

Putting the map back into my pack, I surveyed the road ahead again. The last light of dusk was beginning to fade, as hues of deep plum and orange streaked the horizon, like fire cutting across the desert sky.

I've got to find somewhere to stop before it gets dark.

With an edge of panic, I peered around for some semblance of shelter.

Up ahead, I spotted an oversized shrub. It wasn't much, but it would have to do.

I'd never spent a single day traveling on my own, but all of Amengor knew the tales of the beasts that roam the night in the Therion Region.

The country of Valeria was split into two regions. The Therion Region, which encompassed Merda and all the surrounding villages to the south, the Sankot Desert where I was now, and all the land leading to Mt. Malus. It was known as the region of beasts.

Beyond Mt. Malus was the Stardust District, home to Lunestair, the capital city, the royal palace, and everything that stretched north of the city.

The Stardust District was known as the region of light. The legend states that it was once the home of the goddess Lunaire, although I was not sure how accurate that was. I had never visited Lunestair or even been inside the Stardust District. Having never anticipated leaving Merda, I had not often ventured beyond the surrounding villages. I'd been to the neighboring village of Feydore a few times to sell vegetables, and only once been to Crenya, the village half a day's walk to the south.

When Father had his accident, I had been sent there to fetch their village healer. Abigor Hermstat was the best healer in the Therion Region.

Slowly, I shuffled to the brush ahead of me and set my pack on the ground beside it. It was only slightly larger than me, but it would provide a small amount of coverage for the night, hopefully enough to keep me out of some beasts' claws.

Snatching a stick off the ground, I banged it into the shrub, hoping to scare off any potential snakes or mice that might have taken up residence inside. Nothing vacated it, so I quickly set to work building a fire for the night. I hoped to get a large enough one going that it would burn well into the night and ward off any animals or creatures that may come prowling, giving me the chance to get a few hours of much-needed sleep.

Unfortunately, there was not much kindling around, and I was afraid this fire would not last long enough. Exhaustion was settling deep into my bones, but I prayed to the gods that I would awaken should the fire go out.

Back home, everyone knew not to go out at night unless they wanted to encounter something of nightmares; as a result, I spent little time outside after dusk. Rarely did I see the stars light the night sky. The beasts didn't enter the villages, except on rare occasions, but it was safer to stay indoors after dark. This was how life operated in the Therion Region.

Once the fire was roaring at a safe distance from my bush, I dug my thin wool blanket out of my supplies and shoved some of the fresh bread into my mouth. It was not a lot, but I was too tired to eat anything else.

Shifting the rest of the bread to the side, I spotted what Alice had gifted me. My mouth watered as I beheld the sweet pastry at the bottom of the package, sprinkled with sugar and spices. I would be having a fresh tart with apples, cinnamon, and slivered almonds for breakfast. A tired smile tugged at the corners of my mouth as I pulled my cloak around me tightly.

Wrapped in my thin blanket, I burrowed deep under the low-hanging branches of the scratchy bush. It was thin and not decidedly warm, but it would keep me from freezing to death in the cold of the desert night.

"Skotos protect me from your creatures of darkness," I murmured as sleep overtook my aching body and I drifted off, with dreams of apple cinnamon pastries dancing in my mind.

A few hours later, I woke with a fearful start at the sound of low growling close by. Motionlessly, I glanced toward my fire to find it was nothing but smoldering embers.

"No, no, no!" I hissed frantically.

I refuse to die on my first night!

I was exhausted enough that I had slept through the fire burning out, leaving myself exposed to whatever was out here.

Moving slowly, I slid my hunting knife out of the sheath on my hip and clutched it tightly in my right hand.

Maybe if I make no noise, the beast will go its way and leave me be, I thought hopefully, while listening again for the sound. Hearing nothing, I chanced a glance in the direction the sound had originated from and was met with a pair of glowing green eyes.

Two

Monster Killer

* * *

Remmy

Oh gods, oh gods, oh gods. A Lemian. And the thing is watching me.

A snarl ripped from its lips, and I bolted upright from my makeshift bed, knife grasped securely in my hand.

The creature stood on two legs, its yellowed, canine-like fangs dripping with tendrils of drool. This was a small one, only about a foot taller than me. Lemians could reach heights of ten feet, so I guessed I was lucky to be facing off with a six-foot one. Its gray fur shimmered in the moonlight as it crouched on all fours and sped toward me with lightning speed.

Quickly weighing my options, I charged at the demon, screaming wildly as I leaped onto its back. My heart pounded in pure terror as I grabbed its scruff, hauling myself on top. I landed facing the opposite way as the creature skidded to an abrupt halt, trying to shake me off its haunches.

It howled, terrifying and wild, as I clung to its fur, struggling to recall what little I knew about Lemians and where to strike.

Desperate, I drove my dagger into its hindquarters, stabbing chaotically.

My mind blank, I continued my frantic attack until a massive gray paw struck my left arm, sending me sprawling into the dirt. I screamed, clutching my left arm, as pain sent fiery white spots into my vision. I landed a few solid stabs on the Lemian before it threw me off, but it wasn't enough—only serving to slow it down slightly.

Throat!

My answer came to me all at once.

Kill a Lycan by the heart; kill a Lemian by the throat.

If only I had my bow, I lamented, as I crashed to the ground in a pile. I scrambled to my feet rapidly, still desperately clinging to my bleeding arm. The claws had cut deep into the tissue, and blood leaked at an alarming speed from the gaping wound.

Panicking, I searched around me for the knife I had dropped. If I didn't find it soon, I wouldn't survive this night.

There!

A flash of silver glinted in the moonlight about three paces away.

Meanwhile, the creature's paws thumped harshly against the dry ground as it charged toward me, undeterred. The Lemian and I reached the bloodied knife at the same time, colliding in a ball of fur, claws, and limbs.

I shrieked in frustration and agony as the knife was knocked a foot away, the beast's claws raking into my thigh. Our tumble came to a stop, with me atop the beast. I smashed a fist as hard as I could into its face, hearing bone crack. From the pain radiating through my hand and wrist, I wasn't sure if it was his bone or mine, but I didn't pause to find out.

Throwing myself off the beast, I snatched the knife from the ground and raced back to it. The creature was still on the ground, yowling in pain from the blow to its face.

I prepared to make the killing thrust, raising the knife high into the air above the Lemian, but the punch to its snout hadn't been enough to keep it down for long, and it leaped forward, pulling me to the ground and pinning me beneath it.

The creature hovered on all fours above me, as if savoring the kill, its fangs dripping thick ropes of saliva onto my face.

Oh gods, oh gods.

Tearfully, I tried to free my knife hand from under its ridiculously strong leg. With as much force as I could muster, I brought my knee up, ramming it into the undercarriage of the canine. It let out a yelp and shifted enough for me to wrench my arm free from its grasp.

Without hesitation, I plunged the knife deep into its meaty throat. It let out a harrowing screech and toppled onto the ground beside me, writhing in pain. I jumped onto its chest and sank the knife deep into its neck again and again.

I must be sure it is dead.

I manically stabbed it over and over, a sob escaping my throat. When the light had finally faded from the beast's otherworldly green eyes, I collapsed in a heap on the earth beside its body, blood oozing from my wounded arm and leg.

I lay there beside the dead animal for several minutes, attempting to catch my breath, staring up at the stars dotting the night sky.

I must get up. If I lie here, I'll surely bleed out alongside him... it... whatever. Do demon creatures have genders? Not important. Focus, Remmy. Must get up. Patch wounds. Start fire. Or become dinner for some other demon. It's a few hours yet til dawn.

That startling thought threw me into motion, and I pulled myself upright with an agonized moan.

Limping painfully back to the brush where my supplies were, I rifled through my pack, grabbing the jar of willowroot I had packed. Magical plants were a bit more scarce in the villages, including willowroot, making the potency not as strong as morsious salve and other magical healing remedies. This one was intended more for burns from the sun, rashes, that type of thing, but it was all I had, therefore, it would have to suffice. The healing would be a little slow, but quicker than if I had none.

Grabbing my cloak, I cut two small strips from the bottom of it. I hated to cut it—it had been a gift from my mother—but since she had left her children to this fate, perhaps I shouldn't have any attachment to it. It was also the only cloak I had, but there was nothing else to use for bandages except my blanket, and I needed that more.

Grimacing woefully, I slathered the willowroot onto the large gashes in my thigh and arm, wrapping the pieces from my cloak snugly around them. The cuts were deep, but the skin was not hanging. Hopefully, it would heal properly.

The pain was almost unbearable as I hobbled back over to the dead beast.

Using my knife, I began to hack away at its throat, attempting to sever the head. With my strength waning and the smallness of the knife, it was quite an ordeal. It's dark blue blood splattered my dress as I chopped away.

Great. Exactly what I need. A mixture of blood on the only dress I have.

My thoughts took another turn as I finally managed to release the head from the body.

I wonder if I can eat Lemian meat?

I dragged it over to the fire and threw it into the smoking ashes. The flames sputtered to life as I threw a few more sticks in.

Heading back to the body, I grabbed one of its front legs and slowly dragged it a few feet closer to the now lively fire.

This is going to be revolting, I thought, as I lay down and curled my body into the dead beast's. The carcass would serve to keep me warm and safe throughout the rest of the night, allowing for peaceful rest, while the fire would ward off any more potential creatures lurking in the night.

My injuries throbbed as I adjusted myself to comfort, shifting painfully to one side.

Finally, with a ragged but peaceful sigh, I succumbed to sleep once more.

* * *

Remmy

I cracked open my eyes slowly, dragging my tongue over my parched lips. The sun was high in the sky above me. With a jolt, I realized it must be close to midday.

Groaning, I drew myself up from beside the Lemian's body and looked around me. Not many people passed through the Sankot Desert; only those on their way to trade in Lunestair. I hadn't passed a single soul on my way here. With this in mind, I decided I would make full use of the body. It was unlikely anyone would pass by and witness the gruesome task I was about to perform.

My wounds ached as I staggered over to my pack and pulled out the pastry Alice had given me, along with my canteen of water. Knowing I had to conserve it until I left the desert, I drank only when necessary yesterday.

I took a small swig of the water before setting the canteen onto the ground. After I left the desert, it would not be long before I came to another water source, but I would need some for cleaning the Lemian's fur after I skinned it.

Greedily, I shoved a few bites of the apple pastry into my mouth, savoring the mixture of sweet and spicy. I tasted cardamom, nutmeg, cinnamon, and something else I couldn't quite place.

Saffron, maybe?

Whatever it was, it tasted of the nectar of the gods to my starving taste buds.

Dolefully, I replaced the rest of my pastry and shoved it into my pack, committing to save the rest for tomorrow. Who knew when I'd get to have another sweet treat?

Grabbing my knife, I trudged back over to the Lemian and began the appalling task of skinning the gnarly thing. It was grisly work and certainly not something I enjoyed, but the fur would make a warm blanket once I got into the colder climate of Mt. Malus.

If I got to Mt. Malus.

I shuddered. There was always a chance I wouldn't make it. In the back of my mind, I knew that. If there had been any question, last night had proven it, but I distinctly refused to entertain that idea for long.

I have to make it. Emerie needs me. Echo and Eri need me. Father needs me too. I can't fail. I just can't.

One bloodied hour later, I had the skin stripped from the meat of the Lemian and had gotten it as clean as I could. It wasn't great, but it was good enough that I could stand to put it in my pack now.

Folding it as small as possible, I shoved the skin inside my bag. I glanced back at the revolting carcass sitting on the ground and contemplated the best way to save as much meat as possible. It honestly didn't matter how it tasted. I had to get nourishment, and I could not waste all the free food sitting in front of me.

Regrettably, there was no way I would be able to save all of it. The Lemian was too big, and I would be unable to carry it.

I decided the best course of action was to eat my fill now and chop as much as I could into small pieces to fit into my bag. I cut off as big a chunk as I could imagine eating and carried it over to the fire.

With the steak cooking, I set to work chopping and cutting the rest into small pieces and placing them on the fire to cook. I tried gauging how much would fit into the remaining space in my pack, but it didn't seem as though it would hold much.

Glancing over to the shrub, an idea suddenly sparked in my mind. Sitting down to eat the large slab of meat I had cooked, I debated how my idea might work.

The meat was not horrible. A little tough and not tremendously flavorful, but it was filling, and I appreciated that. Feeling as though I could eat more, I took another chunk off the fire and gulped it down.

Finally sated, I removed the remainder of the charred meat and laid it about to cool, while I started breaking limbs and leaves from the shrub.

Fashioning the basket was a little more time-consuming and tedious than I had anticipated. I had some old string in my bag that worked perfectly to secure the leaves to the limbs, creating a completely adequate small basket with a carrying handle.

Swiftly placing the cooled meat into the basket, I covered it with the lid of leaves I'd made from the shrub. The poor plant was nearly bare now. I asked a quick blessing on it from the gods and packed the remainder of my supplies into my pack before setting out down the road.

Considering the particularly late start I had gotten to the day, I knew I would need to travel quickly to make up the time I had lost. The wound in my left leg made that task nearly impossible, but I pressed on at the fastest pace I could manage.

A gasp of relief left me when I spotted grass and trees up ahead. I was leaving the Sankot Desert!

Thank the merciful gods.

I hobbled forward excitedly, careful not to put too much weight on my injured leg.

The river can't be far, and what I wouldn't give for some relief from this sun.

My pace quickened as I neared the edge of the desert, relief crashing over me as I stepped under the canopy of trees.

I never knew shade could feel this good.

Vibrant purple valerian dotted the gradually sloping hillside in front of me. Valeria's namesake. The herbal plant grew in abundance in Valeria, flecking every field, every mountainside, and lining every roadway in the country. It was harvested for its many medicinal properties, including treatments for sleep, anxiety, and, in larger doses, as a sleeping draught for healings. I slumped against the closest tree and let loose a savage laugh.

I made it. I actually made it through the desert—alone. I killed a Lemian and survived the night in the Sankot Desert.

If only Mother could see me now.

The thought was wry as I sank to the ground beneath the large Elm. She'd always believed I was too soft. I could hear her voice in my head now. *'You need to toughen up, Remmy. Life doesn't cater to weaklings.'*

Well, guess what, Mother Dearest? I'm a monster killer now.

Another laugh ripped from my throat at the thought. I felt a little unhinged laughing about it, but this entire endeavor was crazy. I thought about the flyer in my bag. It stated that any woman able to defeat the beasts of the mountain and rescue Crown Prince Sterling from his prison would be married to him, and the king would abdicate, passing the kingdom over to his son.

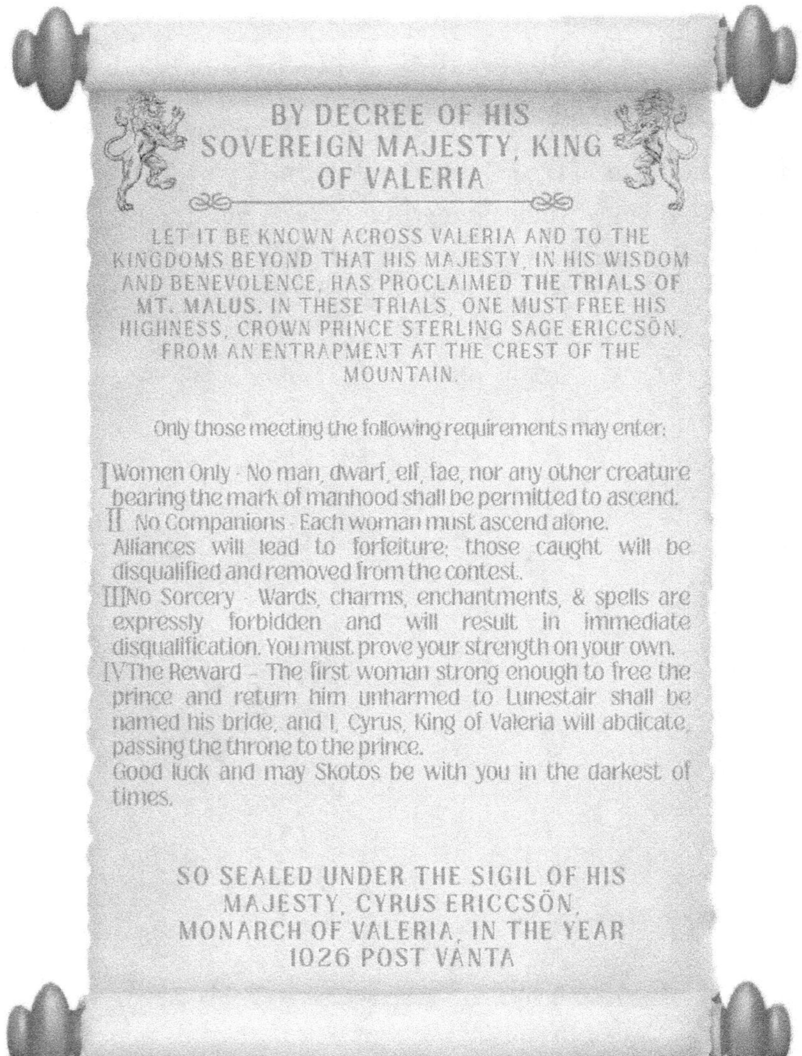

BY DECREE OF HIS SOVEREIGN MAJESTY, KING OF VALERIA

LET IT BE KNOWN ACROSS VALERIA AND TO THE KINGDOMS BEYOND THAT HIS MAJESTY, IN HIS WISDOM AND BENEVOLENCE, HAS PROCLAIMED THE TRIALS OF MT. MALUS. IN THESE TRIALS, ONE MUST FREE HIS HIGHNESS, CROWN PRINCE STERLING SAGE ERICCSÖN, FROM AN ENTRAPMENT AT THE CREST OF THE MOUNTAIN.

Only those meeting the following requirements may enter:

I Women Only - No man, dwarf, elf, fae, nor any other creature bearing the mark of manhood shall be permitted to ascend.
II No Companions - Each woman must ascend alone. Alliances will lead to forfeiture; those caught will be disqualified and removed from the contest.
III No Sorcery - Wards, charms, enchantments, & spells are expressly forbidden and will result in immediate disqualification. You must prove your strength on your own.
IV The Reward - The first woman strong enough to free the prince and return him unharmed to Lunestair shall be named his bride, and I, Cyrus, King of Valeria will abdicate, passing the throne to the prince.
Good luck and may Skotos be with you in the darkest of times.

SO SEALED UNDER THE SIGIL OF HIS MAJESTY, CYRUS ERICCSÖN, MONARCH OF VALERIA, IN THE YEAR 1026 POST VANTA

The whole of Valeria knew the King of Lions to be a cruel ruler, but to entrap his own son, heir to the throne, and auction him off like a piece of meat? That gave new meaning to the word. I held no love for royals, but I did pity the prince for the life he must live. I knew the only reason King Cyrus put on this charade was because he believed no woman would be able to survive the mountain alone. Which was a likely assumption, considering all that awaited there. It was a sick taunt to the people under his subjection and the prince himself, but I had to make it. The decree was sealed with the royal seal; Cyrus had to honor it, and this was my only shot. I had to rescue that blasted prince. I refused to entertain any other alternatives.

If I died, Emerie would... I let the thought trail off. I couldn't let myself go there. I had to make it; that's all there was to it. And *when* I rescued Prince Sterling, I would marry him and move my family to the Royal City to live a life we could only have ever dreamed of.

I had never anticipated marrying for love, anyway. It was always going to be a necessity, not that there were many men in my village jumping at the chance to marry me. I held no status or title whatsoever, and my family was the poorest in Merda. The prospect didn't appeal to many men. I wasn't unpleasant to look at, leading to my fair share of male callers searching for other things, but I never had time for that, nor did I have a desire to debase myself in such a way. Which left me with overwhelmingly few marital prospects.

So off I set to rescue a prince.

Sobering, I determined that I couldn't be too far from the river. That was where I would camp for the night. I pulled some dried cheese and meat from my pack and gulped it down like a starving animal.

After a few minutes of rest, I dragged myself to my feet and surveyed the sky. The sun was starting to dip, and I surmised I had maybe two hours until sunset. That would be plenty of time to get to the Cushing River—if I hurried.

Grabbing my supplies, I shoved them back into the pack and basket and started toward the river at a steady limp. If I could make it soon enough, I might even have time to wash the animal fur in my pack and bathe in the river. That sounded incredible. I was covered in dust and blood from my wounds and those I had inflicted on the Lemian. My skin ached from the harsh sun, and my gashes oozed frequently.

An hour later, I heard the sound of a babbling brook in the near distance and hurried my stride. I followed it until the noise of a rushing river invaded my ears.

It was still an hour until sunset, leaving me barely enough time to do what I needed to do.

Setting my supplies down on the bank where I could keep watch on them, I stepped into the river fully clothed. I had no soap, and my clothes needed washing desperately.

Staying close to the shore where the current was calmer, I waded in until my hips were fully covered and sank into the water. The cool liquid washed over my sunburned skin and injuries, alleviating some of the pain and calming my frayed nerves.

I lifted my legs and floated up onto my back. I didn't want to go too far from the shore because I was not confident in my swimming skills, nor was I sure what was in this water.

In Merda, I did not go in the water often, only visiting once or twice per week to bathe with the children. I knew how to swim, but I wouldn't trust my skills in such a strong current.

My thoughts drifted to my siblings as I floated on the water, staring up at the cloudless sky. I'd only been gone two days. I had tried to hunt and store enough meat for a while, but I couldn't help worrying. I could only provide what I could find, and I had spent several days sitting in the woods hunting. Emerie could bake bread and care for the twins, but she didn't know how to hunt, and her skills in the garden were lacking. The blight on the plants made it much more difficult to find food to harvest, but I had tried to teach her, should anything recover; she just didn't have much interest in it.

My mind wandered to Echo and Eridian. I had never left them this long, save when Father had injured his leg, but they were only a few months old when that had occurred. My arms suddenly ached from the emptiness of their absence. They were my siblings, but I had raised them since they were only days old. I loved them as though I had birthed them myself.

A scream wrenched from my throat as I was suddenly dragged underwater, a cold hand wrapping around my ankle. I thrashed about, kicking wildly with my free leg at the creature that was pulling me deeper and deeper beneath the surface.

Pain shot up to my thigh as I kicked hard at the hand gripping me. It let loose, and my eyes darted up in a panic. I was deep enough that I could barely see the light reflecting from the surface, and I was quickly running out of air. I frantically tried to swim upwards toward the surface when a hand clenched my wrist, and I looked down to meet the eyes of the horrible creature dragging me back down.

A Selkie.

It flashed its sharp, pointed teeth at me in an evil smile as it overpowered me, dragging me farther beneath the murky surface.

I'm not strong enough to defeat a Selkie underwater... especially when I can't breathe. I'm injured too... what do I do?!

Panic clouded my mind as I fought against the slimy hand grasping my wrist. Not knowing what else to do, I dug a fingernail deep into the creature's skin. Black blood floated in the murky water as my nail punctured the back of the Selkie's hand. It let out a muffled screech as it released my arm, and I shot toward the surface as quickly as I could swim.

I broke the water with a gasp, inhaling as much air as I could with a water-logged cough, and began to swim for the shore.

I didn't make it.

I barely had time to release another shaky cry before I was being dragged below again.

My energy spent, my wounds sending fiery bursts of pain through my body, and my lungs straining, the Selkie overpowered me with ease.

The last thing I saw before darkness crept into my vision was something large slamming down onto the head of the creature, and it fell fast away from me.

Three

A Daring Rescue

* * *

Remmy

I awoke with a splutter, light peeking painfully through my lids. I hacked and coughed, gasping for breath, glancing frantically about. My wounds from the battle with the Lemian screamed at me.

A tall boy was on his knees beside me, smacking my back in a vigorous attempt to help rid my lungs of water.

"There, there. Get it all out." He soothed. "You're safe now."

I put a hand out to stop his smacking, and he subsided, squinting at me with worry in his big brown eyes.

"Who… are you?" I rasped, my throat gravelly from all the water I inhaled. "What happened?"

"Name's Teigan." The boy replied nonchalantly. "I was passing by on the road when I heard your scream. I dove into the water after you, but it was dark, and the current was so strong, it took me a while to find you. I was afraid I hadn't made it in time."

"You saved me?" I questioned, looking over the boy. He couldn't have been much older than Emerie.

The boy merely shrugged, uncomfortable with the scrutiny. "Sure. Yeah, I guess so… who are you?"

"My name is Remmy. Thanks for saving me, Teigan. I would probably have died without you. What are you doing out here, anyway?"

A flicker of pain flashed across the boy's face briefly before he replied. "I'm heading to Lunestair to rescue my parents. They were taken from our home by the Blood Guard for a debt owed the king." He stared off into the distance as though he could see Lunestair. "I've been… working…" He stumbled over the words, "to gather enough coin to pay the debt and buy them back."

Sympathy coursed through me at his words. I couldn't imagine what he had to do to acquire that coin, but I wouldn't judge him. I would do the same to save my brother and sisters.

"I'm heading to Mt. Malus. You may join me as far as there, if you wish."

Teigan's eyes grew wide. "You're going to Mt. Malus?!" Realization suddenly darkened his eyes, and he narrowed them at me. "You're going for that contest, aren't you? To rescue the prince?"

I nodded my confirmation.

"You can't!" He exploded.

My surprise must have shown on my face, because the boy hurried on. "I didn't risk my life dragging you away from that Selkie, only for you to die on some idiotic quest for riches! Or do you just want to be queen?" He grounded out, his jaw tense, teeth gritted.

Taken slightly aback by the boy's outburst, I studied his expression carefully before responding.

He hates them because the king took his parents. I don't blame him. He thinks I'm only doing this for the crown.

"Teigan," I said slowly. "You'd do anything to save your family, wouldn't you?"

He nodded a bit sullenly.

"So would I," I stated emphatically. "Now it's getting dark, and I need to set up camp. Are you going to join me or not?"

He stared at me for a moment as if trying to see into my soul, then nodded once. I stood cautiously, my thigh still aching from the giant tear in it. I ran my fingers through my long, sopping-wet hair.

We need to get a fire going in order to dry before the cold sets in. There's already a chill in the air.

I turned back to Teigan. "Can you gather wood?"

"Sure." His reply was quiet, but he set about gathering sticks into a pile. I grabbed my canteen and slowly made my way back to the river.

I had no desire to go near it, but I had no choice. I had only a swallow of water remaining, and the fur in my pack still needed cleaning. I crept to the edge of the water and warily stuck my canteen in, scanning for black eyes and sharp teeth.

The sun was sinking low on the horizon, making it harder to see. I snatched my hand back once the canteen was filled and hobbled quickly back to where Teigan had finished gathering sticks and twigs into a pile.

I grabbed my flint and steel and hurried as fast as my wounds would allow to get the fire going. We sat down close to the warmth, attempting to dry out our wet clothes.

I'll wash the fur in the morning. With the sunlight fading, I won't be able to see adequately, and only the gods know what else the water may conceal.

Sensing eyes on me, I peeked over at Teigan to find him staring at me. "Whatever it is you want to ask, go ahead."

"You're not entering the contest for the wealth or to be the queen." He declared quietly.

"No, I am not," I shook my head. "I told you I would do *anything* to save my family. In Merda, I have three young siblings awaiting my return. My father is disabled and can no longer work. Our mother… well, she's gone. Emerie, Echo, and Eridian rely on me to provide for them. Our father squandered the savings on alcohol, and this year the garden was ravaged by a blight. I could barely harvest enough for us to eat, let alone sell. This is the only hope we have. I could not care less for riches, and I have no desire to be queen… of anything; but along with those riches and that title comes everything my family needs to survive. *That* is why I am going to Mt. Malus."

Teigan gazed at me sadly and nodded his head. "I understand. I'm sorry I judged you too harshly. It's just…" He trailed off, swallowing nervously. "My friend Koretta… we grew up together. We were best friends… she… she didn't come back."

I placed my hand lightly on his arm in what I hoped was a comforting gesture. "I'm so sorry. I can't imagine losing a friend in such a way." I'd never had a close friend, but I could understand what the pain must be like.

"As soon as she saw the flyer posted on the city board, she got it into her head that she would do it and that we would never be poor again. Her parents refused to allow her to go, so she snuck out in the dead of night. She left a note for me on our cabin door." He shook his head sadly. "I didn't even get to say goodbye. She left me alone. Barely turned eighteen, and she was just…gone. It's not even been a week since the courier arrived in Castillo with the news. When I realized you were going… I… I… my mind went to Koretta. Her desire for riches took her life. I didn't want to see you become another victim to that greed."

Castillo was a larger town about three days south of Merda. The courier had passed through Merda on his way, and the news had spread of a young girl's death in the contest. She'd been the second to die, the first being an older girl from a town up North. The city of Outis, if I remembered correctly. I gazed at Teigan's face sorrowfully, as tears glistened in the corners of his eyes.

"I'm sorry, Teigan," I murmured again.

"Just don't die." His voice was a little lighter now, a slight smile pulling up the corner of his lips. "Because I think I'm going to enjoy having you as a friend."

I grinned widely at him, pleased to see his mood shifting in a more positive direction. "I'll do my best, I assure you."

Teigan gathered more wood and helped me construct a small shelter against one of the large trees, close to the fire. Once it was done and our clothes were finally dry, we crawled under the shelter with our packs and my basket of food, lying beside each other, foot to head.

"Remmy?" Teigan whispered my name tentatively.

"Yes?"

"I ran out of food yesterday."

Reaching into my basket, I took out a piece of the dried Lemian meat and handed it down to him. He took it from me, muttering his gratitude, and began chewing it slowly.

"What is this? It tastes odd." He asked after a few moments.

"It's sustenance, Teigan. Just eat it."

"Thanks, Remmy. Goodnight."

"Goodnight," I mumbled in response, closing my eyes and praying that the pain would not keep me awake.

* * *

Remmy

The morning of the third day, I woke to the sound of clanking. Jolting from my slumber, I realized I was alone under the shelter. Peeking out, I saw Teigan bent over the fire, stirring a small pot.

Last night, he said he was out of food! What could he have to cook? I thought irritably. *Why would he lie to me about food?*

I hauled myself out of the shelter and limped over to the fire deliberately.

"I hope I didn't wake you," Teigan exclaimed cheerfully, his golden locks falling into his face, as he stirred whatever was in the pot. "I took the liberty of catching some fish for breakfast. I hope you don't mind. I thought I'd repay you for the meat you gave me last night."

I relaxed at his explanation and smiled at him sleepily, rubbing my tired eyes. "Not at all. I'm relieved not to have to cook this morning. How did you learn to fish?"

"My father taught me. Fishing is a big part of life in Castillo. It's how my father made his living." Castillo was a coastal town; it made sense that fishing was a significant industry there.

"When I was eleven, my father started taking me out in the boat to teach me the trade. By the time I was twelve, I was going with him every day. The extra income made a great difference for us." He smiled proudly, handing me a small bowl filled with fish stew.

I took the bowl he held out, thanking him.

Gazing up at the sky, I took in the sight of dawn beginning to break on the horizon. The glowing tones of pink and gold streaked across the sky, illuminating the towering mountains in the near distance. A cool breeze whispered through the jade and olive leaves of the trees surrounding our campsite. Autumn would arrive soon, turning the leaves brilliant shades of gold, crimson, and copper, putting an end to the harsh summer weather I had traversed through in the desert of Sankot. This time of year was my favorite in Merda. The vibrant hues of the flora and the crisp, cool air had always served to lighten my heart. Unfortunately, it gave way to the most relentless time of year. Winter had always proven to be a chaotic struggle for survival in the Therion Region of Valeria. I'd heard the Stardust District had a milder climate, year-round. I hoped it was true.

I turned toward Teigan as he spooned stew into a small stone mug. I had not thought to bring any dishes with me, as my food supply consisted of dried meat, cheese, and bread. He had given me his bowl and used his mug for stew to accommodate my lack of planning. Remembering the pastry in my bag, I took it out and broke off a small piece, handing it to him.

The grin he gave me lit up his entire face. "Holy gods! I haven't had a sweet in full ages!" He blurted excitedly. He beamed at me as he inhaled his piece and then peeked over at me sheepishly. "Sorry, I should have thanked you. I don't get sweets very often."

I chuckled. "Neither do I, but I'm glad to share it with you. We should be making the mountain pass by evening. We can camp at the edge of the pass and then part ways in the morning."

Teigan's face darkened at my words before he turned slightly forlorn eyes back on me. I couldn't quite blame him. I didn't relish making the rest of my journey alone either. The companionship, while brief, had been a welcome relief from the foreboding silence of traveling alone, and we had bonded, he and I.

"Have you seen them?" He asked tentatively. "The Fae?"

Valeria was ruled by a race of Fae that shifted into various clans, including lions, bears, wolves, phoenixes, sphinxes, the dreaded phalynx, a large cat-like beast with translucent wings, and various other creatures.

Each clan was blessed with the ability to harness some type of magical element. Several clans had gone extinct in the last millennium, including the dragons and wyverns. The ruling Fae of Valeria was a family of lion shifters, hence the name The King of Lions. It was rumored that Prince Sterling had never been able to shift, therefore, incurring the ire of the ruthless king. The king was a self-proclaimed "Clanist," viewing all others, and those lacking the ability to shape-shift as lessers, including those of us who were human and other races such as the Dwarves, the Elves, and the Merpeople.

"I don't think so," I admitted. "I've rarely left Merda, traveling only to a few of the surrounding villages. It's mostly a human village; the Fae don't care to bother with it much."

"Neither have I, at least I don't think I have." He confessed, shifting somewhat nervously. "Castillo is a town that brings in a lot of people, for tourism and trade. And the Fae... they look like humans when they're not in clan form, right? So, how would I know if I had seen one? I've never had anyone tell me they were Fae, though." Teigan chuckled dryly.

I could tell he was somewhat afraid of encountering the dreaded creatures, but Lunestair was the capital city. It was the city of the Fae. He must prepare himself. He was on his way to the palace after all.

"Not all Fae are as the king. There is nothing to be fearful of. You dove into the Cushing River and battled a Selkie to save the life of a woman you didn't even know. You are brave, selfless, and strong. You're more than ready to make your case to the king." I encouraged him.

A blush painted Teigan's cheeks at my praise, but I smiled at him. "Now let's get this fire out. I need to change my bandages, clean the Lemian fur in my pack, and we need to get on the road."

"Clean your what?!" Teigan blustered loudly. "You have a Lemian fur?! How??"

I grinned knowingly at him. "Well, I killed it, of course."

"Holy gods! That's amazing!" He shouted excitedly. "Can I see it?"

I laughed and tugged the fur out of my bag. "I was unable to wash it well in the Sankot due to limited water, so it's a little gross." I handed the fur to him and watched as he unfolded it, marveling all the while at the grotesque thing.

He smiled a bit mischievously. "I don't know why I was worried about you on Mt. Malus. If you can cut down a Lemian, I suppose you can handle Mt. Malus pretty easily."

I huffed at him. "I don't know about that. I almost died at least twice attempting to kill that beast."

"How did you do it?"

I rolled my eyes and snatched the fur from his hands. Grabbing the stew bowl, I shuffled painfully off toward the river.

"That's a story for another day," I called over my shoulder.

Meaning that we both must live another day to tell it.

Given both of our directions, I wasn't sure there was hope for either of us, but I forced myself to maintain positive thoughts. I couldn't let my fear show to Teigan. He was already worried enough.

I'd only known him for a short time, but I was already developing a brotherly connection with him. He had saved my life, therefore I guessed that was a normal reaction to have. The thought of him going to the royal court pained me. The king was known for being heartless and ruthless, especially in his treatment of humans. I breathed a silent prayer to Lunaire for his protection. She would guide him. I knew she would.

Wouldn't she?

In the wake of my mother's abandonment and my father's crippling, my faith in the gods had waned to a degree.

However, I did believe Skotos had protected me from the Lemian in the desert.

I think...

I approached the bank of the river cautiously. The Cushing roared before me, the current wild and untamed. I stared into the dark waters from the sandy shore for a few moments, filled with dread. Visions of pointed teeth and depthless black eyes haunted my mind. Involuntarily, I reached to my wrist, bruised from where the Selkie's strong hand had grabbed me, rubbing it unconsciously.

Steeling myself, I knelt beside the water and filled Teigan's bowl. Using another strip of cloth from my poor, tattered cloak, I dipped it into the water and applied it in sections to the back of the fur, removing the now-dried blue blood and gore from the underside of it.

Once finished, I removed the dressings from my wounds and scrutinized them closely. Having only been a day and a half since the attack, they were still raw and inflamed, aching with every motion. Immersing the strips into the river, I endeavored to wash out the crimson blood staining the fabric, eyeing the waters around me as I worked, keeping an eye out for beasts lurking beneath the murky surface.

My task complete, I began to wrap the strips of cloth back around my lacerations. When I made it back to my pack, I would dig out the willowroot to slather on it, and then redo the bandages.

Before I had time to gather my things back up, a tremendous roar resounded from the woods to my left.

My head snapped up, and I scanned the area for Teigan. My eyes landed on his panic-stricken face, confirming he had heard the noise. He was cramming things into both of our packs, swiftly motioning for me to hurry.

Seizing hold of the fur and bowl, I raced as fast as my injured thigh would allow, back up the slight incline to our campsite and deposited them into my pack. I would return Teigan's bowl later.

Right now, we needed to get out of here before whatever animal or creature that was brave enough to be about in daylight spotted us camping here, exposed and waiting.

"What was it?" I breathed uneasily.

"Sounded like a bear. Whether it was a shifter or a wild animal, I don't care to find out."

"Agreed," I said as we threw our packs onto our backs and departed hurriedly down the gravel path, veering off in the direction of the mountains.

Four

Quirky Companion

* * *

Remmy

The rest of the morning passed uneventfully, and we stopped around midday for lunch. The sun was high in the sky, but the canopy of towering trees above us provided blissful shade as a cool breeze rustled through the branches, whispering promises of autumn.

I munched dried Lemian meat and cheese, while Teigan gnawed on the last remnants of the fish from breakfast. I hadn't even seen him pack it, but we had been in such a frenzied state that it wasn't surprising.

It's a wonder he had the presence of mind to snatch it off the embers.

The terrifying strength of that roar had left me frantic.

My musings were interrupted by the clacking sound of wheels on the dirt road behind us. I looked at Teigan quizzically, but he merely shrugged his shoulders. In my three days of traveling, Teigan had been the only other person I had met out here.

"Hi-yo!" A male voice bellowed loudly from the trail. Turning toward the voice, I saw a Dwarven man with a scruffy, unkempt beard and wild red hair riding a merchant cart, heading our direction. His horse slowly clomped along the gravel, as though he hadn't a care in Amengor.

I waved a hand in acknowledgment, and the man reined his horse to a stop. "Where ya headed?" He asked boisterously.

I glanced toward Teigan, and he shrugged once again like nothing mattered to him.

I guess I should get used to making decisions alone again, as this is my last night with him, anyway.

"I am heading to the Highland Mountain Pass, and Teigan here is on his way to Lunestair."

The gruff man nodded his head like that was precisely what he had expected us to say.

"Hop on! I'm on me way to Lunestair to do some tradin'. I'll drop ya off at the pass and take this 'ne 'ere all the way to Lunestair with me."

I studied Teigan once again to see his reaction.

If he shrugs at me again, I am going to wallop him.

This would change my camping plans for the night, but it would speed up our trips and also take some pressure off my aching legs and feet.

"Yes, sir, that would be mighty gracious of you," Teigan answered for us.

Well, okay then. At least he didn't shrug again.

The boy took my hand and helped me climb up into the rickety cart, my injured leg making it difficult, before jumping up and settling in beside me, setting our packs and the basket in front of us.

The merchant guffawed noisily, for no reason whatsoever, and then said, "Name's Rogard Blithinton, from Feydore. How 'bout yers?"

I chuckled at his introduction. "My name is Remmy Alina Silva, from Merda."

The Dwarf looked at Teigan in an unspoken prompt.

"Teigan Andor Berger, from Castillo," Teigan said shortly as he inspected his fingernails.

What is with him right now? I suppose he could just be apprehensive about this journey, but he could be a bit more accommodating, especially since he is the one who accepted the invitation.

The man nodded firmly, then turned back to his horse, ushering it forward once again. "Nice to meet ya, Remmy and Teigan."

I returned my gaze to Teigan, whose head was tilted down toward his lap.

Placing my hand lightly on his shoulder, I implored, "What is it, Teigan?"

Teigan raised his eyes to meet mine, fear reflecting in their warm ocher depths. "What if it's not enough? What if I can't get them back?" His shoulders slumped.

Uncertain of what else I could do to console him, I wrapped my arms tenderly around his slumped shoulders.

Rogard whistled and hummed in front of us, seemingly unaware of the tension in the back of his cart.

"The gods will be with you," I whispered gently to him. I did not want to give him false hope because the reality was that they may already be dead. It was well known that the king's favorite form of punishment was execution. Telling him the gods were with him was all I could offer him in good conscience.

Teigan buried his face in my hair for a moment, similar to how Eridian used to, and I felt the sharp pang of missing my siblings seep into my bones. In the short time I had known him, Teigan had become like a little brother to me, but I still missed my family more than words could express. I patted him on the back softly, and he sat up, looking at me sheepishly.

"Thanks, Remmy." He smiled shyly. "You're a great friend."

I gave him a quick smile in return, and we settled into our ride, listening while Rogard chatted amiably about nothing and everything.

* * *

Remmy

Three hours into our ride to the Highland Pass, we had learned Rogard's entire life story. The Dwarf barely took a breath from his chatter for more than a minute. I found it amusing but didn't mind, as it gave me an excuse not to talk.

Occasionally, he would ask a question in that quirky accent of his, and I would answer, only for him to keep chatting about something else or start into a different story of his wildly eventful life.

Teigan nodded off a few times, jerking to attention whenever Rogard loudly pronounced his name. I snickered, and Teigan shot me a glare, only to crack up a little himself before nodding off again, while Rogard droned on.

Rogard was a well-traveled merchant of fine linens. He explained how his wife, Ramilda, weaved them on their farm in Feydore. Every few months, Rogard would take his linens to some bustling hubbub to trade, then return home to gather more. He'd even been on several trade runs in Tangeer and Rothton, the kingdoms to the east and west of us.

Upon seeing my tattered and worn cloak, he lifted the burlap covering his baskets and produced a deep emerald frock, presenting it to me with a flourish.

"An emerald cloak to match the color of yer lovely emerald eyes." He blustered proudly as he pushed it into my hands.

"Oh, Rogard! This is gorgeous, but I couldn't possibly take it."

"As are you, me, dear. Put 'er on, put 'er on." He urged excitedly.

I sneaked a peek over at Teigan to see him grinning stupidly at me as I took the cloak from Rogard's hands to slide it on. I shrugged out of my old cloak, laying it on my pack beside me.

Wrestling into the new one in the back of the moving cart without falling out was a bit of an effort, but I finally managed, and Rogard turned in his seat ahead of us to look back. His amber eyes shone with satisfaction, and my gaze swiveled to Teigan. He stared at me with a bit of awe.

"Wow, Remmy. You look sensational."

A flush of pink spread across my chest and rose into my cheeks at their admiration. "Thank you, Rogard. I don't even know what to say."

"Never ye mind, girl. I'm glad to show off me wife's handiwork. I've got one with yer name on it too, boy," he stated and began rifling around in his baskets, the horse trotting faithfully forward without any direction. He finally snagged a tan cloak from the depths of a basket and tossed it in Teigan's direction. He nodded once with a gleam of pride on his rugged face as Teigan pulled it on.

"Looks right good on ya, it does."

Teigan looked over at me and grinned cheekily. "Not nearly as good as Remmy's does on her!"

He sniggered.

I laughed and ruffled his golden locks playfully as he slapped lightly at my hands. Rogard regarded us thoughtfully. "Now, how do ya two 'ins know each other?"

Slinging my arm over Teigan's shoulder, I exclaimed exuberantly, "Teigan's my hero! We met yesterday when he dove into the raging Cushing River to save me from a Selkie that was trying to drown me."

Teigan's face turned crimson at my account of his heroics, and I smirked triumphantly at him. "In all seriousness, though, Teigan did save my life, and because of that, I've adopted him as my little brother. Apparently, I am the older sister he always secretly wanted."

Teigan laughed out loud as Rogard guffawed from the front seat good-naturedly.

"Ya seem quite close for two youngins that only just met," Rogard remarked lightly.

"I guess when someone risks their life and fights off a monster for you, it's easy to form a connection. We're kind of... trauma-bonded, I suppose." I replied thoughtfully.

Rogard nodded his head as though he understood exactly what I meant and began anew his attempts to regale us with tales of his glorious travels.

As Rogard chattered on, I tore new strips of cloth from my old cloak and smeared more willowroot onto my throbbing injuries.

"Now, where did ya go gettin' those nasty gashes from?" Rogard boomed from in front of me.

"Remmy killed a Lemian!" Teigan exclaimed with admiration before I could respond.

"Did ya now?" Rogard asked me. "How did such a small thing like yerself manage that?"

Teigan looked at me expectantly. I had denied him the story earlier this morning, and we only had a few hours left together, so I guessed I owed it to him now.

Without another thought, I launched into a narrative of the grisly attack, explaining how I had charged forward to meet the beast, jumping onto its back in one swift, desperate motion. Their eyes widened to the size of saucers as I recounted my tale with an extra dose of exuberance for Teigan's benefit.

"Ya jumped yerself on a Lemian's back?!" Rogard practically shouted.

"What did it feel like being on him?! Do their eyes actually glow? How did you stay on?" Teigan and Rogard peppered me with questions, and I shook my head at their zeal. They both were enamored with the idea of slaying such a tremendous beast.

My stature only served to make it that much more of a novel concept. I stood barely over five feet, coming only to Teigan's shoulders. I answered their questions as best as I could, until they both relaxed in satisfaction, their eyes gleaming with wonder. I explained how I'd been forced to learn to hunt in the woods behind our home in Merda after my father's money had evaporated to pay for his drinking habit. Something akin to respect flashed in Rogard's amber eyes as I talked, and I wasn't sure why. I had only done what I had to for my family.

Overhead, dark clouds began to roll across the azure sky, and a low mist enshrouded us, signaling that we were nearing the mountain pass. The wind picked up, gusting down from the towering mountains now ahead. Something thick and heavy hung in the air like an ominous hug, encircling us.

I glanced at Teigan to see if he sensed it too, and the tightness of his jaw confirmed he did. We had been so engrossed in our stories of travel, creatures, and battles that we had not realized we were approaching the pass.

Our time together is almost at an end. But I will see you again, Teigan, my friend. When we both walk away from our trials unscathed, we will meet again.

Sadness and fear began creeping in at the thought of being alone again.

"We're approachin' the 'ighland Pass!" Rogard called out, pulling on his horse's reins to slow him.

Turning to me, he spoke quietly, for the first time in our hours of travel together. "I know yer goin' to do the contest. To rescue that there prince. I don't know why yer feelin' the need to do such a 'xtraordinary thing, but I know if anyone can make it up that ther mountain, it's ya. Ya've got steel flowin' through yer veins. I seen it the moment ya got in me cart. And I'm 'xpectin' to see ya when ya get off that mountain, girl. Ya've got a warrior's heart. Don't ya be forgettin' that."

Rogard's words reached into the depths of my soul and tugged lightly on my heartstrings. I realized with a bit of a start that I would miss the quirky old Dwarf. I smiled slowly at him, my eyes glistening with unshed tears. Reaching toward the seat in front of us, I threw my arms around him, giving him a tight hug. He chuckled deeply and patted my back. "Stay safe, girl. May the gods keep ya."

I jumped down from the back of the cart with a wince, and Teigan handed me my basket and pack before hopping down beside me. We stood silently for a moment, staring at each other before he said slowly, "I don't know why I feel such a tether to you, Remmy, but I am going to miss you."

"I'll miss you too, little brother," I said, before reaching up to lightly ruffle his blond hair.

He bent down to hug me tightly, and I whispered in his ear, "When you find your parents, we will see each other again. Of this, I am sure. Good luck, and may the gods keep you."

Teigan nodded tightly before giving me one last glance and hopping into the back of Rogard's cart. The Dwarf urged the horse forward, and I waved mournfully at them both.

I turned my back away from the cart, facing the mountain pass, before I was forced to watch the cart fade from sight. An ache settled deep in my chest at being alone once more.

I will miss you, Teigan. And you too, Rogard. My mind whispered the words sadly, the sense of loneliness closing in.

Looking into the mountain pass, I steeled myself for the journey ahead. My will forged as iron, I took one step forward—the magic of the pass enshrouding me.

Five

The Black Lake

* * *

Teigan

I slumped back into the cart, watching Remmy fade into the mist. Rogard was unusually quiet, as if sensing my distress at leaving her to traverse the mountain pass alone. I watched as she paused and then proceeded to take one step, as if convincing herself to go into the Highland Pass.

Guilt gnawed at my chest. It wasn't my responsibility to protect her, but I felt like it was all the same. I had been drawn to her the moment I had seen her lifeless form sinking into the dark depths of the river. I shook my head. I couldn't let myself think about it.

She will be fine. She can do this. I have to get my parents back. That... that is my responsibility.

They were no doubt suffering in some treacherous dungeon

somewhere, far beneath the royal palace, at the mercy of some brutal guard. I'd heard the rumors. I knew how the King of Lions treated his prisoners. Especially non-Fae.

All of this because of some stupid land debt.

Until the Blood Guard had beaten down our door, snatching my parents in the night, I had believed we owned our land. But it wasn't paid for. King Cyrus owned it, and Father had missed his payments. I can still hear my mother's hysterical sobs echoing through the night, as the guards dragged them both away and threw them into the prison cart.

I'd run after the cart on foot, tears streaming down my face, my parents' fingers reaching through the bars toward me.

"Be brave, my boy." My father had admonished, his fingers wrapping around mine, before a guard had batted my hands away with a wooden club. I heard my mother cry out at the hit. It had shattered two of my fingers, forcing me to seek out Abigor Hermstat, the healer in Crenya. The healers in Castillo had claimed they couldn't be saved, but Abigor had not only saved my fingers, he ensured I had use of them.

Koretta had come, and she had stayed with me all through the night, smoothing my hair as I cried in her lap, holding my broken fingers. That had been many months ago.

Since that night, I had done more than a few unsavory things to acquire the money needed to pay my parents' debt and barter their release. That was what I couldn't tell Remmy. I couldn't bear the judgment in her deep green eyes at the things I had done. I wasn't proud of it, but fishing would never have been enough. It would have taken me years to earn enough money to pay that debt off. My parents would probably be dead by then.

I'd spent my days fishing and trading, and my evenings were spent rotating between working in the tavern in Castillo and pilfering the carriages that came through town.

Castillo was a coastal city with a moderate climate, compared to the villages north of us—Merda, Feydore, and Crenya. The stunning beaches and pleasant weather brought in wealthy travelers with plenty of coin to throw around.

One evening, I thieved an entire bag full of money through the window of a carriage, right off of the seat from beside the pompous ass who sat inside. Now that I think about it, I suspect that he was Fae. I hadn't thought about it at the time, having no experience with them, but most humans around Valeria don't possess that type of frivolous carriage and money. Sure, there were plenty of wealthy humans, but none were as well off as the Fae nobility. Most of the victims of my thievery had probably been Fae.

I hated being a thief; it went against my moral code, but that particular heist did amuse me. The bag with all its contents now resided in my pack, along with all the rest of the money I had "earned" since my parents had been taken. I could only hope it would be enough. I had to pay the debt *and* the fee for their release.

About an hour after we dropped Remmy off, the sun began to set in the western sky, painting vibrant colors of magenta, gold, and violet across the horizon.

The farther north we got into the mountains, the lower the temperature around us became, the cool breeze and ethereal fog, a constant reminder that autumn was drawing near.

I knew that Lunestair was situated in a valley to the west of the Highland Pass, but I wasn't sure how long it would take us to get there from our current location. My answer soon came in the form of Rogard's chattering.

"We'll make the city tomorrow 'round noon, but fer tonight we'll set us up camp right over yonder." He pointed to a clearing to the right of the path, overlooking a mist-enshrouded body of water. I'd been thoroughly engrossed in my thoughts and hadn't even noticed it.

I nodded my agreement, and Rogard directed the horse into the clearing. Something heavy swelled in the air around the lake, leaving me with a distinctive sense of apprehension. I stepped closer to the water while Rogard tied the horse to a tree, observing the obsidian waters.

I suddenly had the jarring realization that we were at The Black Lake. The magical lake was home to many evils, including the fearsome Baga, a creature of myth and legend. It was alleged to be a worm-like aquatic creature with tentacles, sporting four giant heads and an affinity for human flesh, should any be dumb enough to wade into its waters. The creature had dull square teeth in each mouth and used a toxin sprayed from a gland in its throat to soften its prey so it could rip it apart before devouring the flesh. With that terrifying thought in mind, I stumbled quickly away from the dark waters, glancing back at Rogard, who had begun lighting a fire.

"Is it safe to camp here, Rogard?" I called out. "We're at The Black Lake."

I understood the Baga was a water-breathing creature, but was it able to come out of the water?

"The Baga don't be leavin' the lake, and the other creatures that dwell in it, well, they don't come out 'less provoked. I've camped 'ere many a time." He patted my arm reassuringly. "We should sleep in the wagon, though," he added with a shrug, reaching into his cart to get some food.

Great. I'm going to get eaten before I can rescue my parents. Some hero I am.

Begrudgingly, I opened my pack, desperately searching for any scrap of leftover food.

Nothing.

My original plan was to fish, but I couldn't fish the Black Lake. Who knew what demons I might catch?

Reaching for my canteen instead, I took a big gulp of water, letting it wash down the back of my throat.

That's dinner, I guess.

I let out a despondent sigh.

Rogard eyed me knowingly and tossed me a loaf of bread and a block of dried cheese.

"Oh—I—I—" I stammered helplessly.

The Dwarf grunted at me, cutting me off. "I know ya ain't got no food in that bag of yers. And me wife would never forgive me if I let ya starve. Just eat, kid."

I thanked him sheepishly and broke off a piece of the bread, stuffing it into my mouth hungrily.

"How old are ya, anyway?" He asked.

"Eighteen." I munched greedily on the cheese he had gifted me.

He nodded at me. "Bout what I thought yer were. Ya 'mind me of me boy, Jasper. Sixteen he is, but a sturdy boy. I got twelve of them, ya know?"

I raised my brows.

"Kids, that is. Twelve kids. Freya is me eldest. She's twenty. Bjorn nineteen, Jasper sixteen, Nida, she's fifteen, Eva and Elsa are twins, and they be thirteen. Alma is eleven…Erik, ten. Orrm and Orson are twins too, and they be about six. Asger is four, me thinks, and me youngest, Henrique, just turned two."

He beamed at me proudly as he recited the names and ages of his children. All I could do was stare. I'd heard that dwarves tended to have large families, but as a single child, the idea of so many siblings was something I couldn't quite fathom.

The Dwarf winked at me mischievously. "The wife can't keep 'er 'ands off me, she can't."

Rogard roared with laughter at my awkward expression, and I smiled at his mirth. He was certainly jovial. The most somber he had been in the hours we had spent together was when he had told Remmy goodbye.

My gaze swept over to the horizon, where the last remnants of the sinking sun colored the sky with deep hues of purple. With the fading of the sun, the swell of magic in the air around the lake seemed to increase, pressing in on us from all sides.

Rogard's amber eyes followed mine to the horizon and voiced my thoughts. "Best to settle in fer the night. Be dark 'ere shortly and don't wanna be 'anging 'bout when the lake 'wakens."

He grunted as he pushed himself up from the ground, throwing more sticks onto the fire, before moving in the direction of the cart.

Following suit, I grabbed my pack and hurried over to the cart, wondering what he meant by the 'lake awakening'.

I climbed up into the back of it and settled into my spot, wrapping my cloak around me snugly. I pulled my thin linen blanket over it and positioned my pack under my head, using it as a pillow as I had done every night since leaving our home in Castillo.

Rogard hopped into the cart after me, pulled a burlap cloth over the back of the entire cart, and laid down in Remmy's spot, with his feet near my head.

"Scent of the burlap deters the creatures and adds some warmth to yer sleep." He explained as he settled in.

As I closed my eyes against the cool night, I prayed to the gods he was right.

* * *

Teigan

Sleep did not find me as thoughts of my parents, Remmy, and the Black Lake bombarded me like a barrage of arrows, shooting continuously through my tumultuous mind.

I rolled to my side, hoping a new position would quiet my mind, only to be met with Rogard's foul-smelling feet. I sighed impatiently and turned the other way, facing the side of the wagon.

The Dwarf's snoring echoed through the clearing, and I wondered how the reverberating sound didn't lure the beasts to our cart.

Here lies Teigan. Killed by a Dwarf's snoring, I thought humorlessly.

A splash resounded from the lake, followed by an odd clicking noise, and fear charged through me swift as a lightning bolt.

Holy gods, isn't that the noise the Baga makes?

A roar rang out, followed by another splash. Rogard shifted and woke at the sound, rummaging through one of his baskets in the cart. With the burlap over us, there was not enough light for me to know for sure, but I thought I saw something gleaming in the moonlight, and I prayed it was some kind of weapon.

"Never ye mind." He said, quieter than I'd ever heard him. "The creatures 're battlin' but they won't bother us none."

Then why did you grab a weapon?

Saying nothing, I reached into my pack and took out a short skinning knife I used for fishing. It wasn't much of a weapon, but it was sharp, and at present, it was all I had.

Clutching the knife securely to my side, I listened to the two animals clash. I guessed it was two. I couldn't be sure, but I only heard two noises.

A loud shriek rang out, followed quickly by the sound of tearing flesh. I cringed at the sound. I could only assume the Baga had won the fight and was currently ripping into its victim.

After several lengthy moments, the lake quieted again, and Rogard's snoring resumed.

I tried to will myself to sleep, still firmly grasping my knife in my hand and praying for daylight to come quickly.

* * *

Remmy

I'd been traversing the pass for approximately an hour when the sun began to set, and I decided to stop for the evening.

The night was eerily quiet; the wind creaking through the canyon, the only sound to be heard. It spoke of a bad omen, and I found myself vigilant as I gathered sticks to make a fire at the base of Mt. Malus.

The canopy of trees had come to an end when I entered the pass, leaving less wood available, but there were plenty of shrubs and various vegetation around to gather from.

I went about quickly snapping off twigs and branches to light my fire. I did not want to be caught in the pass after dark without a fire, especially not at the base of the mountain.

Tomorrow, I would start my ascent, passing first through the Darkhelm Forest. I had set up camp within sight of the edge of the forest, but far enough away to feel safe. I didn't relish waking whatever lurked within the trees. There were plenty of dangers already in the pass.

Peering toward the forest, I observed the dark mist-cloaked trees uneasily. A shiver ran up my spine when a low howl went up from within the forest.

Whatever it is, I hope it stays in there.

My wounds from the Lemian attack were not even healed yet; I didn't need any more additions. Glancing toward the gash in my thigh, I cringed at the pain that still cut through it and my arm. I had unwrapped them earlier, deciding to air out the wounds a little bit.

Sighing heavily, I rubbed more willowroot into both slashes and re-wrapped them tightly. Hopefully by tomorrow, the magical properties of the willowroot would be taking effect, making my journey a little easier.

Lying down close to the fire, wrapped in my cloak and blanket, I nibbled on some dried meat and cheese. I was grateful for the Lemian meat in my basket. It provided some peace of mind, knowing I didn't need to worry about sustenance for a while, but tomorrow I would need to find somewhere to fill my canteen. I was running dangerously low on water… again.

Shifting in my blanket, I turned to face the forest. With my back to the fire, I drifted off into a fitful sleep, the faces of my family and Teigan haunting my dreams relentlessly.

Six

I'm Not Crazy

* * *

Remmy

Groaning audibly, I peeked through my cracked eyelids to see the sun starting to crest the horizon, splashing the sky with brilliant, vivid colors. My eyes were so dry they had crusted over as I slept. I rubbed them slowly, trying to muster the motivation to crawl from the warmth of my blankets.

Snatching my map from my bag, I unrolled it and studied it carefully. After a few moments of observation, I found what appeared to be a small stream or creek an hour's walk into the Darkhelm. I just had to make it there, and I could fill my canteen and rehydrate.

Remembering the dangers ahead, I pulled out my willowroot and rubbed it liberally into my Lemian wounds. I needed to be as strong as possible to face Mt. Malus and the dangers looming there. The cuts were beginning to heal, but I still needed to keep them clean and medicated. Infection could be a death sentence on Mt. Malus.

Sighing, I climbed out of my blanket into the crisp air and began stamping out what was left of the burning embers of my fire from the night before.

I quickly choked down some Lemian meat and now dried-out bread, and gathered my things together.

Throwing on my pack, I looked toward the gray forest ahead of me with trepidation. A thick, eerie fog enveloped the towering trees with a stillness that caused a chill to skitter up my spine.

Startled, I noticed a man sitting at a table at the entrance of the forest.

When did he get there? How did I not see that before? I must pay more attention to my surroundings!

Being clueless and unaware was dangerous in a place like this.

He had to have set it up this morning. He definitely was not there last night.

I marched over to the table with purpose, and the guard glanced at me with boredom all over his weathered face.

"Name and hometown," he demanded, passing me the quill.

"What is this for?" I questioned him.

The man eyed me resentfully. I supposed, for having the audacity to question him.

"To notify your family when you inevitably die." His gravelly voice was laced with amusement.

Bile rose and burned the back of my throat. Gulping it down, I took the outstretched quill from his hand. Dipping it in the ink, I wrote my name and town of birth:

Remmy Alina Silva. Hometown: Merda, Valeria

I didn't know why I had written Valeria. I highly doubted anyone from neighboring countries was desperate enough to endure Mt. Malus to marry the Valerian prince. I handed the pen back to the snickering guard, and he waved his hand, gesturing to the opening of the path leading inside the Darkhelm Forest.

"Good luck." His menacing laugh followed me as I approached the forest.

Hardening my resolve, I stepped under the canopy of sinister trees, leaving the Highland Pass and the haughty guard behind me.

I'd been walking for under half an hour when I began to hear what resembled whispers around me. Stopping in my path, I spun warily in a circle searching for the source of the noise.

Nothing.

Silence. I could see nothing but trees.

Shaking my head, I resumed walking, quickening my pace ever so slightly.

I must be delirious from dehydration. Beasts don't whisper anyway; they growl.

Something rustled in the bushes to my left, and I held my breath anxiously, my hand going to the knife holstered on my hip. A deer sprang from the brush and bounded down the path in front of me.

A raspy chuckle left my chest as the tension in my body eased.

Blast! I should have tried to kill it. I'll need to replenish my food supply shortly.

I trudged ahead again.

I had been so relieved it wasn't a beast that thoughts of food had never entered my mind.

There! There it is again!

The whispering.

I'm not crazy!

Frantically, my eyes darted all around, landing on a tree not far ahead of me, as the whispers grew increasingly louder.

The bark! It's moving!

My body frozen in terror, I racked my brain trying to remember everything I had learned about this forest. I could think of nothing mentioning trees that came alive. There was so little known about the Darkhelm that I couldn't come up with much information about it at all. I knew that most who enter never come out, and the few who do, spout all kinds of horrid tales of their survival.

A noise resembling a squeak left me when I glanced around to see more trees moving. With a strange yowl, something flew off the closest tree in a blur of motion and collided forcefully with my face.

Screaming, I grabbed at the tiny demon, trying to pry it from my face. Its claws were digging into my cheek, while it yelled something resembling words at me.

Can the bloody thing talk?

Panic-stricken, I heard stirring in the trees around me. There were more of them. Grasping firmly at the creature latched onto my face, I wrenched its claws free and threw it aggressively into a tree.

A crunch sounded, and it fell to the ground with a pitiful moan. I barely had time to glance at it before more yowling rang out around me, and tiny blue creatures began to surround me.

The creatures were no bigger than my hand, blue-ish brown in color, with skin resembling tree bark. They had flaming red eyes, pointed teeth, and horns protruding from their tiny heads, which were wrapped in leaves and vines. The little demons were chanting something that sounded like, "Protect forest from invader," while they closed in, forming a circle around me.

Running through everything I knew about beastology, I tried to determine what creature fit the description.

Suddenly, it clicked.

Forest Imps. I am surrounded by Forest Imps.

I knew little about Forest Imps; few did, but they were supposedly protectors of the forest. Apparently, they took that job very seriously.

Taking a somewhat naïve chance, I spoke, "I am not here to hurt the forest. I am just passing through on my way to the top of the mountain. Please, let me pass, and I will leave the forest as quickly as I can."

A low snarl erupted from a slightly larger Imp near the front. It pointed a twig-like claw at me. "Invader! Protect forest from invader. Attack!"

Cries of "Invader!" rang out all around me as the Imps charged me.

Spinning, I aimed for the back of the circle and leaped.

Landing nimbly on the other side of the line of Imps, I took off at a fast sprint through the forest, pain lancing up my injured leg.

Shrieking in anger, the group charged after me.

Dodging tree branches and roots, I ran as quickly as I could, desperately trying not to fall on my face.

Craning my neck behind me, I saw the Imps gaining on me.

How?!

They were impossibly fast for being so small.

A sharp pain raked through the back of my thigh as one of the creatures shot through the air and latched onto me. A piercing scream that I barely recognized as my own assaulted my ears.

Another pang hit my right shoulder as a second small demon sank its claws into me. Fear coursed through me as the pain in my leg caused me to stumble.

I cursed.

Withdrawing my knife speedily, I whacked relentlessly at the Imp on my shoulder. Landing a brutal stab, the Imp let out a strangled gurgle as my blade pierced its body. I shook the thing from the end of my dagger, preparing for the next attack, but it was no use. The blood loss from my leg and shoulder was already making me weak. The demon had torn my leg to ribbons. I glanced behind me to see a flap of skin hanging down the back of my leg. Nausea overwhelmed me, as the world began to darken.

Something isn't right. It's not just blood loss.

My thoughts were fuzzy and confused.

I've only been on this mountain for an hour, and I am already going to die. I'm sorry, Emerie.

The Imps converged on me, slashing and tearing at my skin. Spots clouded my failing vision, and I sank to the hard earth, the world going black around me.

Seven

A Sick Ploy

* * *

Teigan

The increase in traffic indicated that we were nearing the Royal City of Lunestair. We encountered horses and carriages of every kind, filled with humans and Fae alike. I could not tell the difference, and that concerned me. How would I know I was talking to a Fae if they appear exactly as humans? The thought had never bothered me before, but now, being in the capital city, the worry was plaguing my mind.

Though I think their eyes are a little brighter... aren't they?

Remmy had said not to worry, that not all Fae were alike, but the rumors of the king echoed through the back of my head, causing me to worry anyway.

I thought back to the guards who had taken my parents. Had they been Fae or human? I had not thought about it until now. They had appeared perfectly human, but they must have been Fae. They were huge. They had to have been Blood Guard, and only Fae are a part of the king's Royal Guard.

My thoughts shifted as I realized we were entering the Capital. I stared in awe and wonderment, my mouth gaping open like a child.

All around me, ornate towers stretched nearly to the sky. People swarmed the streets selling and trading at vendor stands filled with freshly baked bread and pastries, vegetables and fruits, furnishings, rugs, fine silks, clothing, and various other delights.

Luscious gardens with fountains dotted the city, lit up by fiery lanterns. Dancers and entertainers performed throughout the streets, and music sounded on every corner. The air smelled of cloying spices, baking bread, and sweat.

It was utterly intoxicating. I laughed out loud, causing Rogard to glance back at me and chuckle.

I didn't care. This was the most incredible place I had ever seen. It made Castillo appear to be a small and lifeless village. Okay, that wasn't completely fair. Castillo was beautiful in its own right, with its white sand beaches and palms swaying in the ever-present ocean breeze, but it was nothing compared to Lunestair. The gardens alone spoke to the incredible beauty of this strange and alluring city.

My breath hitched as the Castle of Stars came into view, the home of the Ericcsön line—the royal family. I'd never envisioned anything like it. It was the grandest building I had ever seen, stretching a full city block with countless spires towering into the clouds above. Maybe that's why it's called the Castle of Stars? Because it touched them? It was constructed of black granite, and somehow lit… without fire?

How is that possible?

Another bit of information I had yet to learn about the Royal City. At the entrance to the castle was a staircase, lit on either side by the fireless lanterns. It rose gradually to a black stone bridge, crossing an enormous waterfall that cascaded into a turquoise pool far below. The pool was alight with lanterns that floated gracefully across the water. White moon lilies surrounded the pond in a luscious circle. I heard the stunning flowers glowed translucent under the moonlight, hence the name: moon lilies, but I had never seen them before, so I couldn't say how accurate that was.

Tucked away in the left-hand corner of the pool of water, I noticed another staircase leading down below the castle.

No doubt to a bloody dungeon.

Sobering at the thought, I was reminded why I had come to this grand city.

Are my parents at the bottom of that staircase?

"I'll drop ya off right near the palace gates." Rogard's voice echoed back to me. I nodded my consent even though he couldn't see me and watched as he directed the horse to a spot a few paces away from the castle guards.

We were far enough away to say goodbye in private, but close enough that it was an easy walk to the gate. I went numb at the thought of parting with Rogard.

Remmy and Rogard had become good friends, and when I told him goodbye, I would truly be alone. Shame filled me that I had entertained the idea of stealing his coin when we had first encountered him.

Rogard stopped the horse and stepped down from his place at the front of the cart. Coming around to the back, he said, "Now ya take care of yerself, 'ear me?"

He pulled me into a tight hug, his head only coming halfway up my chest. I chuckled and returned his embrace.

"If ya need me, I'll be on Market Street sellin' and tradin' me wares. Ask anybody 'round 'ere, they'll know where to find me."

"Thanks for everything. I appreciate all you've done for me."

"'Ere, take this. Ya gon' need it." He shoved a small bag of coins into my hands.

"Oh no, Rogard, I can't take your money!"

"Hush now and take it. It ain't no bother. Be safe, and 'member what I said. Ya can always come find me, should ya find yerself needin' anythin' at all."

Then he turned from me, climbed back into his wagon, and set off toward Market Street.

Nausea roiled through me at the thought that I had ever intended to steal from this kindly Dwarf.

Slowly, I made my way toward the palace gates, my trepidation growing with every step.

"Papers!" The guard bellowed, barely sparing me a glance.

My mind raced.

Papers? What papers? No one told me I need any papers.

The burly guard stared at me expectantly, hand outstretched. "I—uhhh—what papers… do I need?"

"All citizens are required to have approval papers, with a scheduled appointment from the tax collector's office, for entry into court. No papers, no entry." He sneered at me, his voice booming out for everyone in the vicinity to hear. Several people stopped what they were doing to watch the commotion at the palace gates.

"Umm, where do I find the tax collector's office?" I asked timidly.

"Do I look like I am here to give you directions?" The sentry snapped indignantly.

Shaking my head at the bitter man, I stumbled quickly away from the gate, thoughts closing in on me as a rushing wave.

How would I find the tax collector's office? How long would it take to get approval? What if I didn't get approved at all? Why hadn't Rogard told me about this? Perhaps he didn't know. He didn't seem the type to go to court often. I couldn't imagine there were many Dwarf courtiers, given the king's dislike of them.

Calming my thoughts, I surveyed my surroundings. Spotting a pub-style inn called The Starlight Oasis, I decided to rent a room for the night. Perhaps someone at the inn could point me to the tax collector's office.

Making my way inside, I approached the tall lady at the bar. The pub on the first floor of the inn was loud and smoke-filled, but it would have to do.

Shrill laughter rang out from my left, and I glanced over to see a scantily clad blonde woman sitting on the lap of a man who resembled a grizzly bear. The hairy man leaned forward and whispered something in the woman's ear, and she cackled a high-pitched laugh in response. I averted my eyes quickly, having no desire to know what would follow.

Returning my gaze to the woman behind the bar, whom I was not remotely certain was a woman at all, I said, "I'm in need of a room for the night."

The large woman had red hair the color of a tomato, more hair on her upper lip than I did, and a snaggle-tooth protruding from her top lip.

She eyed me uncertainly. "That be all for you, dear?" She asked, her deep voice cutting through the din of the pub.

"Is there any chance you could tell me how to get to the tax collector's office?"

"You're close. Just two streets that direction." She pointed outside, to the right. "You'll be looking for Arner Road. Tax collector's office is a small gray building right next to the bakery."

Thanking the woman, I gave her one of the coins Rogard had given me, and she pointed me up the stairs. "Sixth door on the left."

I took the key she held out and cautiously made my way up the narrow staircase. The dingy hall reeked of sweat, urine, and mirthwood. I had never tried mirthwood due to the rank smell of the plant, but it was supposed to have highly hallucinogenic properties. I supposed people derived pleasure from smoking the nasty plant.

Inserting the key into the lock of the sixth door, I turned the handle and stepped inside, closing the door firmly behind me. I was met with a small, dank room sporting a single bed, a tiny table, a dilapidated desk, and a small wooden chair leaning against a streaked and dirty window. All of the furniture had a layer of dust coating it like a blanket.

Sighing, I threw my bag onto the small bed and sat down beside it. A cloud of dust floated up around me, and I coughed.

Waving a hand in the air, I tried to clear it, groaning aloud. When the dust had settled, I reached into my bag and grabbed some of the coin Rogard had given me. After stashing the bag under the bed, I returned to the door, intent on getting something to eat and locating the tax collector's office. It was nearly dinnertime, and I surmised the office would close soon. I did not want to wait until tomorrow.

When I opened the door, I was met by a petite girl no older than fourteen holding a plate of steaming hot food. She smiled shyly and held it out to me. "Your dinner, sir."

"Oh! I—uhhh—how?"

"Maggie sent it. She said you would need to eat before heading to the tax collector's office. It will close in one hour."

"Oh, thank you..?"

"Deidre, my name is Deidre."

"Thank you, Deidre. I appreciate the food... and the information!" Deidre smiled and turned back down the hall.

"Wait! Don't I owe you for the food?" I called after her.

The girl paused her stride and glanced back at me. "Maggie has put it on your tab."

"Oh, of course. Thanks again!" I said, closing the door. Maggie must be the red-haired woman I spoke to earlier.

Turning toward the desk, I scarfed down the scalding beef and potato stew and prepared to make my way to the tax collector's office.

* * *

Teigan

The gray building was easy enough to find, located right where Maggie had said it would be. The sweet smell of pastries and bread from the bakery wafted lightly on the breeze. I thought about the coin I had left and wondered if it was enough for a small treat.

No, I'll have to pay my room tab at The Starlight Oasis.

Shoving all thoughts of sweets aside, I approached the tax collector's building and opened the door. In the middle of the room was a large desk, surrounded by scroll and book-lined walls. The books were shelved almost up to the ceiling of the small building, with a small ladder sitting off to the side.

At the desk sat a gray-haired man with spectacles perched on the end of his bird-like nose. At my entrance, he lifted his head and smiled wanly at me.

"May I help you?"

"I was told I needed to get approval papers here to enter the Royal

Court?"

"Ah, yes!" He exclaimed as though this was the most exciting part of his job, and began to rifle through the drawers in his desk.

I briefly scanned the office while the elderly man searched for whatever he was looking for. The desk was decorated with piles of paper, quills, and ink, askew in every direction. I wasn't sure how he could find anything in this mess.

To my left, I heard a skittering sound and glanced down in time to see a small rat run across the top of my boot. I shivered involuntarily.

I hate rats.

Silently, I willed the old man to hurry up. This dingy old building unsettled me.

After what felt like an eternity, the man let out an "Aha!" and waved a stack of papers over his head. His glasses perched precariously on his face as he smiled at me triumphantly.

"Here you go." He handed me the stack of papers. "Fill these out and bring them back tomorrow before closing."

Thanking the old gentleman, I took the papers and started heading back to The Oasis.

All these just to get into Court? There's like ten papers here.

Exhaling in frustration as I entered my room, a thought suddenly occurred to me.

I have no ink pen.

* * *

Remmy

Light peeked through the corners of my heavy eyelids as I opened them slowly. Raising my head, I tried to look around me, but gasped as pain wrenched through my body.

How am I even alive? The last thing I remember was... the Forest Imps chasing me. They were on top of me and then... I must have blacked out. Why did they leave me alive?

As I struggled to see the damage to my body, I realized that they must not have intended to. There were lacerations everywhere. My arms, legs, chest, stomach… I even felt them burning my face. Tears stung my eyes.

Silly, I knew, but I didn't want my face to be scarred. It's bad enough that I would have them all over my body.

I should be grateful that I am alive. It's a miracle I didn't bleed out.

Lifting my left arm where I could see it, I understood why. The cuts were superficial. Still, they were all over my body, and the numerous amount should have led to quite a bit of blood loss. I remembered the cuts on the back of my thigh.

Or slices, I should say.

They were so deep that my flesh was hanging loosely.

Grimacing, I worked my hand down the back of my thigh, feeling for the injury, forcing back a shriek as my hand made contact. Tears coursed down my cheeks as I tried to think.

I could barely move, I was lying on the forest floor, and the last light of day was fading. It would be nightfall soon, and I needed to come up with a plan or I would die, lying here in a bundle of leaves.

My frantic thoughts paused when I heard it.

Voices.

Who in the worlds would be trudging through the Darkhelm this close to nightfall? No one good, that's who.

Instinct took over, and I forced myself onto my side before rolling onto my stomach. The pain was almost unbearable, and I barely kept from screaming in agony.

Steeling myself, I lifted onto my elbows and began to drag my body forward. A short distance from me was a small patch of dense shrubbery. Pulling myself through the bushes, I was pleased to find a ditch there.

Shaking from the pain and exertion, I crawled into the ditch behind the shrubs and began to cover my body with fallen leaves and sticks.

Silent sobs wracked my body as I breathed a prayer to Lunaire and all the gods, past and present, that I wouldn't be discovered. The voices were coming closer and closer. I strained to hear their words, my breath catching in my throat.

"... thought this would be a quick job..."

"... can't find... girl..."

"... not paid enough..."

They were close enough now that I could discern about five male voices.

A slapping noise sounded as one voice came closer. "Come on, men! It's just a girl, alone in the forest... with darkness approaching. The guard mentioned only one girl signed up, and she can't have made it far with those Imps around. The crazy demons have killed off plenty of people. They've probably made our job easier. Not to mention the Banshees and the other beasts in this gods-forbidden wood."

I sucked in a ragged gasp.

These men are trying to kill me? Why? Who would want me dead? I barely even know anyone outside of my village...

My frantic questions were answered by another voice.

"I thought working for the king would be more fun than this." Another voice grumbled as they meandered toward my hiding place.

"All we do is kill stupid girls on this stupid mountain. I got cut by one of those stupid Imps!"

Panic seized me. The king was killing off the contestants! That's why he claimed he would give up the throne to the prince.

He knew there would never be a winner.

This is all just a ploy to torture his son and wield his control over the kingdom.

What kind of sick mind would do this to his own child? Is this some kind of warped way of preventing the prince from marrying, so he can't be king?

It was law in Valeria that a king could not ascend the throne unwed.

"Quit complaining, Leland. This is the best job we have had in years, and I don't want you idiots screwing it up, so shut your bloody traps and find that blasted girl!"

The man who must be Leland mumbled some curses under his breath while the other men chuckled at the tongue-lashing.

"Oh, Reee-mmy! Come out, come out, wherever you are. This won't hurt, little birdie. I promise you won't feel a thing." The voice chanted. Several of the men laughed threateningly.

I put a trembling hand to my mouth to stifle a sob at the sound of my name, tears of terror streaming down my face. They must have gotten it off the form I signed at the forest entrance.

If they find me here, I'm dead. They've already killed the other two girls; they won't hesitate with me. Come on, Remmy, you've been in worse situations than this. You battled a Lemian... and won!

One Lemian or five to six hired killers? It's not a comparison, especially considering the Lemian wasn't even full-sized. The odds were not in my favor.

The men walked past my hiding place, and I heard the leader muttering, "The king will have our heads if we let someone win this bloody contest."

A pair of boots stopped directly in front of me, and I held my breath, my shaking hands covering my face, praying the trail of blood wouldn't be noticed.

This is it. This is the part where I am discovered. This is where I die. I'm going to be murdered in the woods, and Emerie will be left to care for our family.

For a moment, nothing happened. Then I heard it. The belt buckle clanked, and his pants came undone.

Oh gods. He doesn't even know I'm here. He's going to relieve himself, right in front of my hiding spot.

I gagged silently, plugging my nose to block the sour smell. The splashing sound stopped, and someone shouted from up ahead.

"I'm coming! I had to take a leak." The man shouted back, then he re-buckled his pants and took off to rejoin his comrades.

I released a slow, shaky breath and closed my eyes as the sounds of the men faded into the distance.

Will they keep hunting me? Or give up and claim a beast got me?

I had planned on encountering beasts on this excursion, but men… men were not something I had planned for.

Sitting up at a glacial pace, I reached for my pack, which somehow had stayed on my back during the Imp attack. My basket with my leftover Lemian meat was not so fortunate. I hadn't had time to search for it before I heard the men coming, but I guessed the Imps took off with it.

Pulling out my willowroot, I surveyed the small canister. Between the Lemian wounds and the multiple lacerations from the Imps, there was not going to be enough of it to cover all my injuries.

Starting with the back of my thigh, I chose the most severe cuts and slathered them with willowroot. Then, I began to pack the gashes with dirt. It was all I could do at this point. I prayed it was enough.

Taking a small sip from my canteen, I let the water soothe my cracked and dry throat. I needed to conserve what little was left of it. Tomorrow, I would have to drag myself to find water, but for tonight, I was staying right here in these bushes.

Knowing I needed sustenance to heal, I munched on some of the bread from my bag. There was not much of that left either.

Blast. Blast it all. This is not good.

My stomach turned violently as I lay back down, once again covering myself with leaves and sticks. Better to stay hidden in case anything else came calling during the night. Within seconds, sleep overtook my exhausted, broken body.

* * *

Remmy

The throbbing pain is what woke me the next day. I slit my impossibly dry eyelids open and glanced up into the sky. The sun was high, and I realized I'd slept well into mid-morning.

Shifting with a slight moan, I brushed off the branches and leaves and began to crawl out of the shrubs. I sat down on the ground in front of the bushes and unrolled my map from my pack. A raspy chuckle left my throat when I saw how close I was to the stream.

Of course, that would be my luck. I lie here dying, mere minutes from water.

Bracing myself, I stood to my feet and began to slowly trudge in the direction of the water, pulling my leg behind me awkwardly. I let out a relieved sigh at the sight of the creek ahead, but my steps halted abruptly, fear encroaching on my thoughts. I rubbed my injured arm absently.

What if there are creatures in the water? I'm in no shape to fight right now. I can barely take on magical creatures when I am not injured.

I was not the best of fighters. Skimming over my dirt-caked injuries and empty canteen, I knew I had no choice. Approaching the water cautiously, I bent down on shaky legs to fill my canteen. I'd barely been on them for a few minutes, but the pain was already making me unstable.

With my canteen full, I collapsed on the riverbank. Bringing the water to my lips, I took a small sip. I choked on a sob as the water cooled my burning throat. Anxious and greedy for more, I gulped it down, unable to stop the tears that now poured from beneath my eyelids. I was surprised I could even produce tears, but somehow they were there, flowing freely down my smudged and bloody cheeks.

When I had emptied the canteen, I shifted toward the water again and refilled it. When nothing reached out of the water to pull me under, I stumbled into the large stream and began washing the dirt, blood, and stink off of my body. As close as it was to autumn, I was sure the water was cold, but it felt wonderful to me. My body was raging with fever, and I had felt like I was on fire since I woke.

I think there was toxin in the Imp's nails. I shouldn't be this feverish and weak.

Finally clean, I curled up on the riverbank with my pack and rested. I lay there for some time, my head supported on my bag. I knew I couldn't fall asleep, but I was too weak to travel. Mulling over what to do, I ultimately decided to try for some fish. I hadn't eaten, and I needed nourishment to recover my strength.

Praying to Skotos that this was a normal stream, I gathered some hemp twine from my pack and began to weave it into a simple but sturdy fishing net. I was no expert fisherwoman, but my options for food were limited, and I was not strong enough to hunt. I had to do something.

A selfish part of me wished that Teigan were still with me. I knew I shouldn't because he was hopefully being happily reunited with his parents right now, but he would be much better at this than I.

Wading out into the shallow water, I cast the net I had made and slowly dragged it. Pulling the net out of the water, I observed two small fish caught in its snares. I smiled at my success, but a wave of dizziness slammed into me, the net slid from my hands, and the ensnared fish fell back into the clear water.

Blast, this cursed poison!

With a sigh of frustration, I steadied myself and recast my net, tugging it through the water. My legs were numb from the cold, and I was not sure how much longer I could hold myself upright.

Panic clawed its way into my mind as I repeatedly cast and pulled in nothing.

What was I going to do? I could barely stand on my own.

On the verge of hysteria, I raised my dragnet one final time, thanking Skotos when I saw three small fish stuck in its twine. The addition of an extra fish made me slightly grateful for my faint spell, as I would need all the sustenance I could gather. I hauled the net to the shore and collapsed once again on the bank, laying the net with its fish beside me on the hard ground. A wave of dizziness once again hit me, and I lay there for a moment until the spinning subsided.

I needed to start a fire and cook the fish before the dark of night alerted the mercenaries to my location, but I was completely exhausted. My wounds were aching, and my head felt as if someone had cleaved it open with an axe.

Sighing heavily, I wrapped my woolen blanket around myself and stared out over the water.

Where are the Forest Imps? Did they just... assume their job was done and move on? Maybe they are preoccupied with the mercenaries?

I could only hope. I had to stay alert for other creatures, but the fever was making me weak and fatigued.

Standing slowly, I began to gather the necessities to start a fire. Once the blaze was roaring, I threw the fish on and sat back while they cooked, attempting to stay awake and observe my surroundings.

I chewed on one of the cooked fish and stowed the others in my bag. The nourishment gave me enough strength to stamp out the fire, gather my belongings, and make for the nearest line of shrubbery, but the fever was causing the beginning stages of delirium.

I stared around in a state of confusion, trying to remember what I was doing for several moments before my mind cleared and I gathered my wits about me once again.

Some sense of rationale told me I needed to cover myself, lest the mercenaries find me, but I was having a hard time discerning what was real. The world began to warp around me, growing smaller and then larger than real life. The woods were hazy and then suddenly clear, shifting in and out of focus.

Fearfully, I crawled beneath the brambles, not caring when my hair caught on a thorn, and pulled the leaves and sticks over top of me and my bag.

I wasn't sure, but I thought I felt a warm tear glide down my cheek, as the fever overtook me and I succumbed to the darkness once more.

Eight

Fever Dreams and Delirium

* * *

Remmy

I awoke in the darkness, thrashing under the bushes, my mind a muddled mess of confusion. A feverish sheen of sweat coated my skin. I was chilled to the bone, but my skin was hot to the touch.

Where am I?

The panicked thought reverberated through my fuddled brain.

Emerie?

I collapsed again into the stabbing shrubbery, falling into unconsciousness once more. My fever dreams were filled with visions of

Emerie and the twins frolicking in the grass, as though our life was happiness and peace; our family not impoverished and broken.

In my dreams, I watched them dance and chase each other through the greenest of grasses, Eridian trying to catch Echo's hair as it glistened in the sunlight. Her hair was the same color as our mother's, golden with the lightest streaks of red throughout. It was such a lovely color, one I'd always been jealous of.

Emerie's laughter floated through the field; the sound of it magical as she scooped Eri's little body into her arms, and Echo tackled them, the three of them going down for a romp in the grass. Squeals rang out as Emerie tickled the twins relentlessly, their laughter resounding through the dream world my mind had created.

"Remmy, darling, won't you come join us?" A strangely familiar voice called out. My head turned with astonishment toward a lovely stone cottage—not our own—as both of my parents stepped through the threshold to join my siblings.

Mother.

Her golden auburn hair flowed to her waist, and she appeared vibrant and healthy. In this dream, my mother loved us, and our father was whole.

They walked hand in hand toward my siblings, then stood gazing at me, smiling brightly, as though a portrait of a perfect family had been painted. Vibrant yellow sun illuminated them, shining down through towering Elm trees.

My beautiful mother stretched her hand toward me. "Remmy, my love. Come. Come to me."

* * *

Remmy

I drifted in and out of consciousness for what seemed like days.

Time didn't make sense.

I tried to open my eyes, but my lids felt made of stone. The world around me was a blur of shapes and shadows.

There was hazy light and deep darkness.

I was cold, then I was hot, my body burning up from the inside.

There were dreams, and then there was blackness.

My body was heavy, sinking into the cold, hard earth.

I can't say how long I lay beneath the bushes this way. Only that I was glad when it finally ended.

* * *

Remmy

I startled awake with a strangled sob. Memories of my fever dreams flashed before me before I realized I was staring up at… *bushes? What? Where am I?*

The sun was high enough in the sky to indicate mid-morning. I sat up with a groan as sharp stings of pain shot throughout my body. Licking my parched and dried lips, I remembered what had happened. I'd been attacked by Forest Imps, pursued by mercenaries, and infected with a fever-inducing poison.

I'm in the Darkhelm Forest.

I struggled to free myself from the branches—my hair was caught in them—and slowly stood, testing my strength. I glanced down at my body, surveying the damage from the Imps and Lemian. My Lemian wounds were nearly healed, and the cuts from the Forest Imps were scabbed over. I moved my hand down the back of my thigh, where the slices had cut deeply, leaving my skin hanging. The pain was more present there, but those too had begun to heal.

I must have been unconscious for days. How am I not dead?

I wiggled my leg, testing it to see how difficult it would be to walk. It wasn't comfortable, but I needed to get moving. My stomach rumbled with hunger.

I was certain I had lost plenty of time. I reached under the brush and snatched my pack. Grabbing my canteen of water and a small piece of fish to munch on, I started walking.

I stopped abruptly when I realized that I had no idea where I was. I'd been in quite a delirious state after the fever took my mind, and I couldn't remember which direction I was supposed to be heading.

Unrolling my map from my pack, I determined I was a mere hour's walk from the edge of the forest. I cringed inwardly at the thought of what came next.

The Cave of Beithir. It was the origin of all the beasts that roamed the Therion Region, containing a portal to the Netherworld—the realm of the God of Death. I would need to petition Skotos and Lunaire before entering. I must pass through the Cave of Beithir to get to the Emerald Lake. There was no other way. I shuddered. This would be a greater test than all the others. I hoped I had enough strength to endure.

* * *

Teigan

At first light of dawn, I dressed quickly and gathered my paperwork, setting off for the tax collector's office.

Upon approaching the slate building, I noticed a line forming outside the door. Groaning, I realized the lack of people yesterday must have been due to the lateness of the hour.

With an exasperated breath, I stepped into line behind a light-haired woman with a small girl clinging to her skirt. I cleared my throat loudly, and the woman angled in my direction. "Excuse me, ma'am, sorry to bother you. Is this line solely for the tax collector's office?"

The lady's smile was sympathetic. "Yes, there are usually quite a few people in the morning attempting to handle business before the start of the day. The other office is clear across town, on the westside."

Briefly, I wondered if it would be better to go to the office on the western side, but not knowing how far it was or how I would get there, I thanked the kindly woman and stepped back into place behind her.

My thoughts were getting carried away with themselves until I noticed the little girl peeking up at me from behind her mother's skirts. I didn't have any siblings, but I had always hoped one day I would. I smiled brightly at the girl, and she grinned shyly.

Her umber eyes shone brightly as she held out her little cloth doll to me. The doll was ragged and worn and had one button sewn on for an eye. I squatted down in front of the girl, and she whispered conspiratorially as though sharing a secret, "My dolly's name is Sigrid."

"Sigrid! What a lovely name that is. And your name must be just as lovely?" I exclaimed enthusiastically.

The little girl giggled with delight. "Of course it is. My mother picked it!"

"Well, what might it be, I wonder? Is it… Grunhild?"

The girl shook her head vigorously. The girl's mother was now watching the interaction and smiling with amusement at her young daughter.

"What about… Oh, I know! It must be Hilda!"

The girl burst into fits of laughter. "But Hilda isn't a pretty name!"

Her mother clucked her tongue at her. "We mustn't make fun of people's names, daughter. It isn't kind."

The girl peeked contritely at her mother. "Sorry, Mama. I didn't mean to." The mother stroked her daughter's hair as she turned back to me.

"My name is Gretchen!" She pronounced proudly. "Gretchen Thronfeld."

"You were quite right, Gretchen; that is indeed a lovely name. Mine is Teigan. Do you think it's lovely as well?"

Gretchen laughed again, and I wished that I had a little sister.

Perhaps I'll marry and have a daughter someday.

The thought came from nowhere and startled me. I hadn't entertained the idea of marriage since Koretta had died. I'd always assumed we would marry and settle down in Castillo. We weren't in love, per se, but I had loved her, and I believed I could have grown to love her in that way. It had always been the practical assumption. To build a life with her. If only she had not been so foolish. The thoughts of my closest friend pained me as Gretchen's voice pulled me from my reverie.

"Men don't have lovely names! They have… ummm…" She looked to her mother for the word.

"Handsome." Her mother supplied.

"They have handsome names! And Teigan is quite a handsome name, I should think."

She sounded wise for her age, and I smiled at her. I spent the time waiting in line conversing with Gretchen and her mother, whose name I learned was Xula. She was here to pay property taxes on her husband's plot of land. They were collected on a yearly basis in all of Valeria. I was keenly familiar with what happened if land debts were not paid.

When Xula questioned me about my visit to the tax collector, I hesitated before sharing. I wasn't sure I wanted to detail the entire story, so I explained briefly that I was requesting admittance to the Royal Court to see my parents and changed the subject quickly. Xula's eyes widened slightly, but she didn't press me for information, for which I was grateful. The time passed more swiftly than I expected, and before I knew it, Xula was next in line.

I waited with anticipation for my turn, bouncing on the balls of my feet while she spoke quietly with the clerk. I heard coins jingle as she dug them out to pay her family's taxes, and then she and Gretchen were waving goodbye.

Gretchen left her mother's skirt and ran back to me, throwing her little arms around my legs. The action took me off guard, but I bent down and let her encircle my neck.

She whispered in my ear, "I don't know why you want to go to Court, but I hear my mother and father talk. I know the King of Lions is a mean and bad man. I am going to pray to the gods to protect you. Lunaire will guide you."

With that, she was gone. Her words shook me.

How could one so young be so wise?

The clerk was impatiently calling for me to step forward now, so I put Gretchen and her words from my mind and advanced to the cluttered desk.

Smiling politely, I handed my bundle of paperwork to the flustered clerk.

"I'm requesting approval to enter the Royal Court."

"I can see that, boy. Give me a minute to sort through your papers."

The bespectacled man flipped through my papers languidly, reading every line. Then he began searching through the drawers in his desk, stopping when he found a packet of several scrolls bound together with twine.

He looked up at me through the eyeglasses balancing on the end of his nose. "The earliest I can grant you entrance is a fortnight from today."

"A fortnight! Why, that's… that's… fourteen full days?! What am I to do in the meantime? Why can I not go sooner?" The questions tumbled out of me, an edge of panic creeping into my voice.

The birdlike man waited for my outburst to end and regarded me carefully, as though I might explode at any moment.

"Young man, there's a process for petitioning the king, and appointments have to be made. Unfortunately, there are no openings for a fortnight. I suggest you go home and find something to keep you busy in the meantime."

"Okay," I mumbled under my breath, feeling as though I had received a reprimand from my father.

The old man nodded his head and stamped APPROVED in big bold letters on my papers, writing the date, a fortnight from now, beside the approval stamp. He handed the packet back to me, and I thanked him, exiting the dusty office as quickly as I could.

What am I going to do?

Including the coin Rogard had given me, I did not have enough to pay for two weeks' stay at The Starlight Oasis.

Maggie seems friendly enough. Maybe she will allow me to work for room and board.

The thought set my mind at ease, while I made my way back to the inn.

At The Oasis, I found Deidre working behind the counter, serving up drinks and food to demanding customers.

Do these people have no life? It's barely mid-morn and they're already getting drunk in the pub.

"Hi, Deidre. Is Maggie around anywhere?"

"She's working in the back. Let me get this drink, and I'll tell her you're asking for her. What's your name again?"

"It's Teigan Berger. From room six." I added.

The young girl nodded her head with barely a glance in my direction, and after she finished pouring an ale, she stepped into a dark room behind the bar. I had assumed it was a storage closet, but it clearly served as an office and combined store-room.

The door was only open for a moment before Deidre shut it behind her, but I spotted a small bed in the corner.

Does Maggie... live in there?

The door swung open, and Maggie stepped out, followed closely by Deidre, who promptly went back to work, making plates of food and handing out mugs of mead and ale.

"Let me guess," Maggie's deep voice boomed out. "There's a wait before you can get into Court, and you don't know how you'll pay your room tab?"

I swallowed the lump that formed in my throat at her foreknowledge and solemnly nodded my head. I opened my mouth to speak, but she cut me off.

"No matter. Teigan, is it? I had a sense about you when you came in. Got any experience bar-keeping?"

"Yes, ma'am, I worked for a good six months at The Salty Olive in Castillo."

"Good, good. Deidre here needs some help. This pub is the busiest in town due to being in Market Square. How long have ya got before your appointment?"

"Fourteen days, ma'am."

"Right, okay." She sighed. "Get started helping Deidre with that rowdy table in the corner. Mr. Borg, there is a bear shifter, and their clan's a heap o' hooligans."

"Thank you, ma'am." I nodded my consent and glanced over at the indicated table to see the grizzly of a man I had seen my first night here, surrounded by five or six equally large and woolly men.

Well, that makes sense now. They actually are bears.

I took a deep breath and went over to help Deidre take the orders they were enthusiastically yelling at her.

If a fourteen-year-old girl can do it, so can I.

A random thought crossed my mind, and I turned back to the fiery-haired woman.

"Maggie?"

She looked at me expectantly.

"The Castle of Stars… it's alight without fire. How?"

Judging by the expression on her face, the question had surprised her, but she responded in turn.

"Quilldust and magic. The king has it mined all over the country. It's transported to the palace, and with the use of Fae magic, it creates light. But… best not to be asking those types of questions around the city, ya hear?"

The warning disturbed me, but I nodded, and my thoughts reeling with magic and whatever quilldust was, I sauntered toward the bear shifter's table and began taking their dinner requests.

Nine

The Faceless One and The Dance of Death

* * *

Remmy

I had been walking for just shy of half an hour when I heard the sound of rustling through the trees ahead. Fear rooted me in place, and I watched warily for whatever it was that was shifting through the trees.

My injuries were mere scabs now, thanks to the limited magic in my salve, but I was weak from days without food or water, and uncertain I was up to battling another beast… or man. The mercenaries had barely crossed my mind since I had awakened from my feverish stupor, but I doubted they had given up. It sounded as if the king paid well for murdering women in the woods.

Perhaps a bear had eaten them? Or the Forest Imps?

Or whatever else lurked within these sinister woods. Not many people survived the Darkhelm and lived to tell about it, so what animals and beasts lived therein was not well known. The obscure, mist-enshrouded wood was famous throughout the entire continent of Amengor for its deadly nature.

The sound of voices intruded on my musings, and I was disappointed to find out that a bear had not eaten the mercenaries. Spurred into action by the noise, I looked around wildly for a hiding place.

Finding nothing, I decided my only option was to attempt to outrun them. Probably not the best plan, but it was the only one I had.

Sprinting forward, I veered away from the mercenaries toward the cave and out of the Darkhelm Forest. I could not afford to get lost in this wood and lose any more time than I already had. Who knew what condition the prince would be in after being stranded on this mountain?

A shout rang out as the mercenaries spotted me darting through the trees.

"There she is!" I recognized the voice of the leader yelling. Branches crashed, and heavy footfalls resounded as the men pursued me, shouting orders to stop.

Not going to happen. Dumb brutes.

Chancing a glance behind me, I saw only four of the five men I remembered from before.

Well, perhaps one of them did get eaten.

I chuckled and turned back around, just in time to slam headfirst into a low-hanging branch. I crashed to the ground, pain reverberating through my forehead and back.

It only took a moment for me to scramble back to my feet, but it was a moment too long. Strong hands wrapped around my throat as I found my footing, squeezing off my breathing and yanking me tight against a firm, foul-smelling body.

Blood trickled down from the scratch on my forehead as my captor wrenched me around to face his approaching companions and held me pressed against his chest. I fought with all my strength, kicking backwards and doing my best to elbow him in the gut, though my arms were pinned. He grunted a bit but held firm, unbothered by my pathetic blows.

"Look, men. I caught a little birdie." The voice of Leland, the complainer, sneered.

I stopped fighting when I noticed the expression on the other men's faces.

Fear.

"What are you bloody lot staring—" His question was cut off as he was violently yanked away from me, and I found myself suddenly free.

Screams rang out. I turned to see what had happened, and pure terror surged through me. I stood frozen, my limbs heavy as granite.

Leland's body lay sprawled and broken thirty paces away, a mess of tangled and bloodied limbs. He didn't even moan.

Dead. He's definitely dead.

I don't know how I mustered the courage to raise my eyes, but somehow I did, and found myself face to face with a creature of nightmarish beauty.

It was larger than I had imagined, towering at least twelve feet tall. Its translucent wings were tipped in blue and stretched out from either side of its lithe body, as though preparing to take flight at any moment. The black feline creature had ridges up its spine, piercing blue eyes, and a blue sigil resembling the shape of its wings, in the center of its forehead. Its mouth hung open in a snarl, Leland's blood dripping from its sharp canines.

A phalynx. Can shifted Fae control their clan's nature? Why do I know so little about Fae?

I snorted in frustration.

The remaining mercenaries behind me yelled as they found their senses and attempted to flee.

With no time to even reach for my dagger, I stood trembling, but resolute, staring down the massive demon. I held my breath as it bent over, hovering inches above my head, and smelled me. A thick drop of drool rolled off its mouth and drenched my hair.

Well, that's disgusting. But I'm not dead yet, sooo... that's interesting.

The creature snorted, blowing my hair around me in tangles, leaned back on its haunches, and rose into the air in pursuit of the screaming mercenaries.

"Lunaire's hair!" I muttered, staring dumbfounded at the beast's back as it chased its prey.

I'm alive. It just smelled me and... and... left me. Why? And who was it?

Not wanting to question fate too much, I thanked Skotos and resumed my journey to the cave. I wasn't sure how far I had run when the men were chasing me, but it was only minutes before they caught me. I was still at least twenty or thirty minutes from the edge of the forest. I decided I would find my way out before stopping for lunch, then take a long break to gather my strength before entering the Cave of Beithir. I would need it.

I stopped when I approached Leland's body. He hadn't made a sound.

He has to be dead, right?

Even though I knew he planned to kill me, I didn't want to leave a man there to die slowly, if there was a chance he was still alive. I could at least end his misery quickly. I squatted down beside him and felt for signs of life.

Nothing.

There were deep gashes ripped across his chest, and his left shoulder was hanging loosely, barely attached to his body. His legs were tangled together, twisted and gnarled. My stomach wretched at the gruesome sight, and I turned away.

I wiped my mouth and turned back to the body. Unbuckling his sword belt, I strapped it around my waist. There was no telling when a sword might come in handy. Especially in these woods. The belt was cumbersome on my small body, sitting loosely around my hips over top of my dagger holster. I tightened it as much as it would go.

"It will have to do," I murmured.

Bending back over his body, I searched his pockets and bags for anything that might be of use. A small leather pouch contained some coins and dried meat. Unhooking it from his side, I dropped it in my shoulder pack and stood up.

"You should have picked a better career, Leland," I muttered somberly. Then I turned and walked away.

* * *

Mt. Malus

Nestled somewhere deep within a forest, high atop a bitterly cold mountain, a dark-haired man took a ragged breath and succumbed to the darkness. His body was frail and tired; his ribs poked through his tattered, blood-soaked clothes; and his mouth was crusted over from days without water.

His last thought before the hunger weakened his body to unconsciousness was of his younger brother. A memory played on repeat in the man's mind. One of him and Soren splashing in the garden pond. Their father had come. The man, as a young boy, had clenched his fist firmly at his side, holding back his sharp words. His brother had pouted and demanded, "Why do you always get to go with Father? It's never me."

"Be thankful you get to stay and play, Soren," was the only response he had given as he followed their father back inside, ignoring the sounds of his little brother's grumbling.

How he wished he could save Soren from this pain. Soren, who still laughs. Soren, with his blond hair and piercing blue eyes. Soren—the perfect replica of their father.

With his death, the tides would change.

* * *

Remmy

I exhaled with relief when I saw sunlight breaking through the dense overhanging trees. I was leaving the forest! I had survived the Darkhelm and only encountered two evil creatures... and some evil men. Leland's sword clanked at my side as a reminder.

My thoughts drifted to the phalynx. If that was a phalynx, how in the world did the lion clan rule? That creature was far more terrifying and fierce than I could imagine any lion being, though I'd never seen one in person.

Trying to think back to what I knew of history, I remembered learning that the Ericcsön family had come into power about a thousand years ago, after the Battle of Five Hundred Years.

Our realm had been invaded a few millennia prior by a species called the Vanta. Little was known about them today. The quilldust my father mined before his accident was a leftover remnant from the days of the Vanta.

They had taken over Amengor and bred with the humans, creating the first Fae shifters. After thousands of years of servitude and subjection, the Fae had risen up and vanquished the Vanta to regain control of our world. The battle that ensued spanned five hundred years and multiple continents.

Cyrus Ericcsön's great-grandfather had led the charge in Amengor and, with their victory, became ruler of Valeria. The family had been ruling ever since. The other kingdoms of Amengor were split between generals in Cyrus's grandfather's army.

Elysia to the north, Tangeer to the east, and Rothton to the west, which had been given to another member of the Ericcsön family, and today was ruled by Cyrus's brother. The former ruler had no heir and therefore passed the kingdom to Cyrus's younger brother, Tyran.

Cyrus had been king for almost two hundred years, but had no heir himself until shortly before I was born, though he had doubtless taken plenty of women to bed prior.

No one knew what became of the queen. She'd disappeared one day when I was about five and was never heard from again, that I knew of, anyway. There was always speculation that Cyrus had murdered his father to seize the throne, but no one would stand against him. Maybe he had also killed his wife? It seemed likely enough.

The sunshine beat steadily against my face as I said goodbye to the Darkhelm Forest and planted myself on a large boulder, treating myself to lunch. I took out the meat from the pouch I pulled off Leland and chewed it slowly, savoring the taste.

Dried lamb.

I knew it would be my last taste of food for a while. I wasn't sure how long it would take me to get through the Cave of Beithir, but I didn't expect to be stopping on the way. Who knew if time even worked the same way in there?

My back was aching from my fall, I had a giant bump forming on my forehead from where I had collided with that branch, and my ribs were already starting to become more prominent. I must have slept for five or six days when I was out with the infection. Reaching deep into my pack, I took out the last bite of now stale bread and swallowed it down with a sip of water.

Briefly, I debated making camp and waiting until tomorrow morning to proceed to the cave, but I knew that I could not afford to squander any more time. It must have been at least a week since I came through the Highland Pass. Prince Sterling needed me, and I sure as the stars needed him.

Resolutely, I repacked my supplies, glancing at the container of willowroot. There was barely any left. Perhaps after I got through the cave, I would be able to find ingredients to make some more. Gods knew, in all likelihood, I would need it.

It wasn't long before I was approaching the cave. The atmosphere around me changed. The air felt heavy and dense. Thick with magic and... darkness. It was barely mid-afternoon, but the sun had retreated behind the clouds, and a slight fog began to roll in, creeping across the ground like a ghostly blanket. A cool breeze hung in the air.

It whispered of ill fortune, but I pressed forward anyway, knowing I had no other choice. The cave came into view, and I sucked in a gasp. The sight that greeted me was not what I anticipated. There were rumors of a guardian, but I had believed them to be conjecture. Tall tales from the few men who had survived this mountain.

The Faceless One.

That's what they had called him. I understood why now. He stood at the mouth of the cave, cloaked in a black robe, a hood concealing his gray head. Depthless obsidian eyes peered out from under it, and a sword hung at his side.

He spoke straight into my mind, for he had no nose or mouth to speak from.

"Only those brave enough to battle may enter the Cave of Beithir."

His ethereal voice in my head startled me, striking fear into my soul. Not something a person was used to encountering every day. He unsheathed his sword and raised it, asking the unspoken question.

Was I brave enough to fight him? I had limited training with a sword. My father taught me a little before his accident. In a fight with an average man, I might be able to best him, but a ten-thousand-something-year-old creature from the Netherworld?

No, I could not win that fight. He didn't specify that I had to win, though. He only said I had to be brave enough to fight. Five lives depended on me making it up this mountain and back. Four of those, I would do anything for. So yes, I was brave enough. I only hoped I was not bravely stepping forward to my death.

I unsheathed my sword in answer and walked forward to greet The Faceless One.

"I accept your challenge." My hands trembled as I raised my sword.

With lightning-fast movements, he swung. I dodged right, away from the strike, but not fast enough. The tip of his sword grazed my shoulder, and I cried out in pain.

Regaining my footing, I had barely a second to parry the next thrust left. The blows came in quick succession. Hard and fast, leaving barely any time to block, let alone land a counterstrike. I knew I had no chance, but still I fought on, trying to land a strike whenever I could. Parrying left, then parrying right. Dancing the dance of death.

My death, of course, not his.

I was on the ground in no more than five minutes, the faceless creature looming over me. Without preamble, he stabbed his sword into the ground beside me and spoke into my mind again.

"You, Remmy Alina Silva," *How does this creature know my name?* "Have passed the test. You are brave of heart and worthy of entry to the cave of Skotos."

The cave of...? Skotos? What? Is Skotos truly in there? I thought it was just a portal? Isn't he restricted to the Netherworld?

I had no desire to dance with the gods today. This ancient Being was as close to a god as I ever wanted to come. I only wanted to pass through the cave and make it to the top of the mountain.

"Rise!" He commanded, "and enter."

It had not sounded like he intended to kill me, but still, I was relieved when he sheathed his sword and resumed his post.

I stared at the cave in trepidation.

What awaited me there? Hopefully not Skotos himself.

Sure, I prayed sometimes, but that did not mean I wanted to meet him face to face. And if Skotos was in that cave, that would mean he was no longer restricted to the Netherworld. And that would be incredibly bad.

Bending, I retrieved my sword from where it had fallen. Sheathing it, I surveyed the cave before me. I knew it was thousands of years old, but seeing the cracked and weathered stone awed me. The mouth of the cave loomed before me, stretching high enough for a Lemian or Lycan to enter without bending.

Trembling slightly, I stuffed down my fears as deeply as I could and stepped into the ancient stone opening.

Ten

Good Advice

* * *

Mt. Malus

"My prince!" A familiar voice pierced the darkness, but I was too weak to raise my head or open my eyes.

My body was numb.

Everything—distant.

Light seeped in and then dissipated slowly through an obscure fog.

"My prince!" Again, the voice. "Please wake!" This time, a hand touched my face.

I tried to reach for the voice through the haze of blackness. Again, the urgent voice, tinged with panic.

But I couldn't reach it.

Something cool and wet touched my lips.

He was too far away. Who was he?

And then once again, there was nothing. The remnants of light and voice faded away.

* * *

Teigan

It had been a week since I started working at the Starlight Oasis. Maggie had been good to me, and I had befriended Deidre fairly easily. I was even paid a small wage. It was paltry compared to what I would be paid if I were not living at the inn, but since I did not expect to receive any compensation at all, I was grateful for the extra bit of coin.

I found out that it was not Maggie, but Deidre who lived in the storeroom. Maggie adopted her when her father had been killed in one of the king's pointless wars with Tangeer. Deidre's mother had died in childbirth, and so the girl had wandered the streets until

Maggie caught her digging through the refuse bin behind the tavern and had given her work and a warm bed six years ago. The tall, gruff woman loved Deidre as though she were her own.

Rogard had even come into the tavern twice in the last week. We chatted and shared stories. He apologized for not knowing I needed an appointment to enter the King's Court. He was leaving the next day to head back to Feydore and pick up more goods from his wife. His next trip was to my hometown of Castillo. I was sad to know I would not be seeing the Dwarf again. He planned to stop at The Oasis tonight to say goodbye and, knowing Rogard, drink a pint of ale. The Dwarf could drink his weight in it.

I spent my free time sitting in the courtyard across from the Castle of Stars, observing the comings and goings of all the people at the castle. I was positive there was a dungeon on the other side of the pond, beneath the castle. At precisely half past the hour after sunset, two guards went down the stairs, and ten minutes later, two different guards came back up and disappeared across the great stone bridge into the castle. A nightly guard change. I filed this information away, hoping I would never need it. Surely the king would release my parents once I paid their fine.

He had to.

I knew I couldn't take on two guards and escape unnoticed should I try to break out my parents. I didn't even know what the layout of the dungeon was. There could be more guards below.

But it doesn't matter; the king will release them. I am sure of it.

There was no reason for him not to.

I have his bloody money.

Still, I watched and waited.

* * *

Teigan

Later that evening, I was filling drinks when I heard a familiar voice.

"Hey boy, gimme an ale!" Rogard shouted from the far end of the bar. I chuckled and filled a mug, taking it over to him.

"What time are you heading out in the morning?" I asked him casually, thudding the ale down on the bar.

"Oh, I'll be outta 'ere 'fore the first light o' dawn." He exclaimed between chugs. Rogard loved his ale, and with twelve kids at home, I reckoned he deserved it.

"Another!" He demanded, enthusiastically slamming the glass down, the last sip splashing out into the air.

Laughing, I refilled his glass and watched as he gulped it down, same as the first.

"Now, boy, I'm gonna tell ya the secret to life 'n few easy steps. Ya ready? Travel! See Amengor! Gods, get off this 'ere continent! This ain't all there is ta life. Find ya a good woman while yer out 'n' about. Keep 'er happy and settle down. Then, step three! And this is the most important, ya hear? Are ya listenin' ta me? Make... A LOT OF BABIES!" He roared with raucous laughter, as did the gentleman next to him, who had apparently been listening in.

My cheeks heated with the comment, which brought more exuberant laughter to Rogard and his newfound friend. Soon, the noise had others joining in, and Rogard had befriended the entire bar.

Some hours and many pints of ale later, Rogard was ready to head to his abode for the night. He had mentioned he stayed with a cousin who lived in the city when he did his trade runs to Lunestair. I questioned if he was sober enough to make it there, but he laughed me off, muttering something about how dwarves could handle their ale.

It was late, and traffic was slowing down at the tavern, so I asked Deidre to cover for me and walked Rogard out. When we reached the door, the fiery Dwarf sobered for a minute and looked at me through wise eyes.

"Believe we'll all be reunited 'gain someday, ya hear? Me, ya, and Remmy. The three unlikely travelers. If anyone can survive that mountain, it's that girl. I said it 'fore and I'll say it again. She got steel runnin' through 'er veins, that one. Now I got to git. If yer ever in Feydore, find me wife and kids, boy. Ramilda Blithinton. She'll take good care of ya."

I nodded. "Thank you for everything you've done for me, Rogard." I smiled and pulled the old Dwarf in for a hug. I hated to see him go. Rogard had been a friend to me these last weeks, and I would miss him fiercely. He gave me one final pat on the arm and then disappeared into the night. I stepped back into the tavern feeling somehow older than I had been when I stepped out.

Eleven

The God of Death

* * *

Remmy

I was not sure what to expect as I entered, but the temperature became cooler as I walked, and there was a foreboding hum of magic in the air. I thought I'd be walking blind as I had no torch, but the cave was bathed in an eerie blueish-green glow. I surmised it must be due to the portal to the Netherworld that lay inside. I was grateful for the light it emitted, but wary with each step forward, anticipating something jumping from the shadows to consume me whole.

I clutched my dagger tightly in hand as I walked, my other hand resting on the sword once again strapped to my hip. The deeper I went, the more the temperature plummeted. When my teeth began to chatter, I moved close to the cave wall and took off my pack. Setting it gently on the stone floor, I dug around inside until I found the green cloak Rogard had given me. Shrugging it on and pulling up my hood, I reclaimed my pack and continued walking deeper into the abyss. Magic swarmed in the air around me, tugging at my hair and making me lightheaded. I had never sensed magic that powerful.

A wave of dizziness washed over me as I neared the glowing portal, and I gripped the cave wall to steady myself, my fingers digging into the rock. It was cold and moist against my already freezing fingers.

My vision began to warp in and out, and I gasped in fear, desperately clinging to the wall. I was barely able to stay upright, leaving me in an extremely compromising position. I made an easy target for anything lurking within the darkness of this cave.

My mind screamed. Horror gripped me as I fought to discern reality from whatever was happening to my head.

What is going on?

Without warning, the glowing portal began to emanate a strange whirring noise and flared to life. What happened next left me questioning my sanity. A man stepped from the portal. Well, not a man… exactly. A god.

I knew without a doubt that Skotos had entered the mortal realm. I should be afraid. I should be trembling and groveling at his feet.

Yet, I was doing none of those things. Instead, I stared. In wonder. In awe. In confusion. Power emanated from him. The Being in front of me was unlike any I had ever seen.

When I pictured the god of death, this was not what I envisioned. I thought he would be some creepy skeletal figure with glowing eyes and a scythe. Or something.

The god in front of me was resplendent. Tall, with eerily pale skin, dark eyes, and flowing white hair cascading down his back. It wrapped around his waist in feathery ribbons. He stood shirtless, a black robe belted around his waist with a gleaming silver buckle. He strode toward me with bare feet, walking on flames of blue that followed him with every step. When he stood a few paces from me, he stretched out his hand.

"Remmy." My name sounded like the sweetest of honey rolling off his perfect lips. "Come with me, sweet love."

The god of the Netherworld wants me? To take me with him? Will I be queen of the Netherworld?

Mindlessly, I put my hand in his and let him draw me forward. His grip was firm as he led me to the portal. I stared up at him lovingly, my mind ensnared by his ethereal beauty and magic.

I am going to the Netherworld. Skotos desires me. He called me his love. We will be happy together. I belong in the Netherworld. I shouldn't be in Valeria.

Reality slammed into me as my mind fought against his magic. My gaze snapped from him to the portal as we drew closer and closer.

HE shouldn't be in Valeria, not me! What am I doing?!

I tried to jerk my hand free from his, but he held me with an iron grip.

"Let me go!"

But Skotos did not budge. I struggled violently against him. If he pulled me through the portal, I would never see my family again. What had I been thinking, giving him my hand?

What did he do to my mind? I cannot abandon my family!

Using my right leg, I kicked him with as much strength as I could summon. The god barely grunted, but his grip became more demanding, bruising, around my wrist.

"Stop fighting." He commanded, his voice no longer sweet and entrancing. "Your family will be better off without you. They will find happiness and move on from the burden you have placed on their lives."

"What burden?" I screeched. I had not seen myself as a burden to my family. I was their protector, their provider. I had stepped up when my mother abandoned us and my father took to drinking.

But what if I am a burden? Just another mouth to feed?

My thoughts took on a mind of their own, intruding on the reality I knew. I shook my head, trying to clear away the thoughts that were clearly not my own. He must be using some strange magic to lure me and alter my mind.

He sneered and pulled my wrist harder, nearly jerking my arm from the socket. With one quick shove, I was flying through the portal. The scream that left my throat hardly sounded like me as I plummeted through a haze of blue and green.

My vision warped again. Then all at once, the scene changed.

Home.

Looking around me, dumbfounded, I tried to remember how I had gotten here. I was in the Cave of Beithir, and Skotos threw me through the portal. And now I was… home?

A flash of movement caught my eye, and I saw Emerie move past the window of our cottage. Except it was not Emerie. It was older Emerie… and thinner… really thin. Her face was sickly and pale as death.

Panicking, I ran to the cottage door. Reaching for the handle, I stepped inside and called out to her. But she did not hear me. None of them did. No head turned my direction. No one noticed my arrival.

My father was nowhere in sight, and Eridian and Echo lay on the floor beside the cold fireplace—their small forms emaciated to skin and bones. No fire burned in the hearth. Tears burned my eyes at the sight. This could not be. I had failed my family, and now they were dying. The twins were dying. Emerie was dying. A strangled sob left my throat as Emerie sat on the floor beside the twins and whispered to them.

"It's okay. Let go. It will all be better soon."

I stood frozen in place, sobs wracking my body, as Eridian took his last ragged breath, his eyes staring unblinking at the ceiling above.

Silent tears rolled down Emerie's cheeks, but she did not falter as she turned to Echo and grasped her wan hand tightly.

"Your brother is in Lumess with the goddess now, Echo. He will dine with Lunaire and eat until his belly is filled. You must follow him. There is nothing left here for you. Remmy did not return. She is dead. Father is dead. And now, Eri too, is dead. I cannot feed you any longer. Let go, little one. Let go."

A tortured scream left me, but neither girl reacted. Because I was not really there. I was wrenched from the scene, my vision once again distorting, and the atmosphere swirling and buzzing around me like lightning.

When the world stopped spinning, I was in a strange room I had never seen before. Glancing around, I tried to discern where the cave had spit me out.

I started when my eyes found a man lying on the floor, not ten paces from me. His clothes were the finest I'd ever seen, and his black cotton shirt had a silver crest embroidered on it. I inched closer, straining to see the design, afraid of what might happen if I got too close.

The Ericcsön crest! Oh no, the prince...

I fell to the floor on my knees beside him, shaking him hard.

"Prince Sterling!" I cried out. His head only lolled to the side lifelessly. Dried blood stained the wooden floor beneath him. He was dead. He had been dead for several days.

Oh no, oh no! The prince is dead. I'm too late! Everything is ruined. The twins are going to starve to death. Oh gods! I'm so sorry, Emerie.

I lay down beside the body of the prince of Valeria and wept in earnest until I fell asleep from exhaustion and emotional turmoil.

* * *

Remmy

Groggily, I opened my eyes, expecting to be lying in a strange room beside a dead prince. I was not. I was on a cold stone floor. I sat up quickly enough to make myself dizzy. The air hummed thickly with magic. I was back in the Cave of Beithir. How had I gotten here?

What happened to me?

I lived out my worst nightmares, and then the cave just dropped me back on my behind.

Is my family okay? Is the prince really dead? Where in the name of the gods is Skotos? He cannot truly be in this realm... surely?

Thoughts crashed into each other like tidal waves, my mind whirling in tangled confusion.

Slowly, I stood, glancing warily around for the dark god. I saw nothing. Even the portal's glow appeared dimmer than before.

Was this another strange test?

Taking a deep breath, I rallied enough courage to move forward.

Cautiously, I approached the portal and rounded to the other side of it. Seeing nothing, I advanced, my thoughts in turmoil and my alertness heightened, as a sense of foreboding lingered.

"This bloody cave must be trying to turn me crazy," I mumbled. The air in the cave was frigid, leaving me chilled to the bone, even with my thick woolen cloak draped about my shoulders. I pulled my hood over my head to shield my ears from the draft and continued walking.

Searing-hot pain slashed across my back, and I tumbled forward, a scream tearing from my lungs, but I did not allow myself to fall.

If I fell, I was dead. I tripped over my own feet as white spots blurred my vision.

A fierce snarl echoed off the cave walls behind me as I wrestled to regain my footing.

Painfully swinging myself around, I was met with two glowing red eyes and a snout with gaping jaws, saliva dripping from its enlarged canines. A hulking, clawed hand, stained with my blood, swiped at me.

With excruciating effort, I dodged the razor-sharp nails and flung myself over a boulder, backing away from the slowly approaching Lycan. It looked at me as though it were not concerned in the slightest that I might escape. Intelligence flashed in its glowing eyes. It knew it had caught me off guard, and I was critically injured. The chances of outrunning it were dubious.

It dawned on me that I now had a sword. In the chaos of Skotos' tricks, I'd nearly forgotten it hanging at my side.

Unsheathing it in one quick motion, I swung blindly, slicing through the creature's arm. I aimed to disable it enough that I could plunge my sword through its heart without too much resistance. It let out a terrible bellow, and a thudding sound rolled through the cave as its arm, severed at the joint, fell to the floor.

Blood squirted into the air as it thrashed at me with its intact arm, growling ferociously.

I jumped, veering away from the slashing arm, but I was not quite fast enough, and its claws tipped my arm.

The wound was not deep, and I barely noticed it as I ducked to avoid another lunging blow from the creature. The movements raked at the pain in my back.

Those gashes were deep and leaking blood with every lunge and dodge.

Lifting my sword, I maneuvered it again, aiming for the Lycan's other arm. I missed, and it clattered as it bounded off the cave walls, the force of it almost pulling me over.

Panic-stricken, I strained to lift the sword as the beast reached for me again, the jarring impact rattling my arms and shoulders.

Tears filled my eyes from the pain in my back with each motion, but I did not falter as I raised my sword and aimed again for the charging creature's arm. I had to disable it. It was my only chance. My sword came down, slicing clean through the creature's wrist.

Close enough.

The Lycan shrieked with rage, trying hopelessly to smack me with its dismembered arm. Something resembling surprise flashed across the beast's face as I plunged my sword through its chest, piercing its fleshy heart.

Neither one of us had expected me to win this fight. The glow went out of the creature's scarlet eyes, and it slumped forward. I yanked my sword from the gaping cavity in its sternum, and the beast fell face-first onto the ground directly in front of me.

Convulsive gasps shook my entire body as I slid against the cold rock wall to the ground. I tried to steady my breathing and think of what I needed to do next, but my mind was foggy from the agony in my back.

After the Imp attack, I had passed out, but I could not risk passing out again. I fought to stay alert and in control of my body.

Shaking my head to clear my vision, I glanced around the cave again. The attack from the Lycan had shredded the strap of my pack, and it lay on the ground near the wall.

Dragging myself toward it, I reached inside and slipped out the strips of cloth I used for my previous injuries, and what was left of my willowroot.

Bracing myself, I used the cloth to blot what I could reach of my back. Unfortunately, I couldn't reach it all, and I could only pray that I didn't pass out from blood loss.

After soaking up what I could of the blood, I opened the container of willowroot and scooped a little bit out onto my fingers. There was hardly any left, and certainly not enough to cover all my wounds.

Grimacing, I gingerly spread some on the ones I could reach. Replacing the container, I tied together my shredded straps and leaned back against the cold cave wall, careful not to put any pressure on my back. The salve began to work immediately, soothing some of the ache.

Resting my head against the cool stone, I sighed with mild relief and let the tears flow freely down my face.

Why did I think I could do this?

I'd been injured repeatedly, fought beasts and ancient beings, and spent days unconscious with fever and infection.

I don't think I'll survive another infection. I need to get out of here and find some fresh water to clean these wounds.

I was so exhausted and dazed that I just sat there staring into the bluish glow illuminating the cave.

A low rumbling, deep within the cave, had me on my feet again faster than I should have been able to move.

Nope. Absolutely not. I cannot handle another thing in this cursed cave.

I set off as fast as my feet could carry me, heading toward the other side of the cave. A short time later, I was stumbling into the cold night air.

It seemed autumn came faster this high up on a mountain. I collapsed in relief against a large tree about twenty paces from the mouth of the cave, tears flowing anew, staring up at the deep night sky. The stars look like crystalline diamonds thrown onto a blanket of luscious black silk.

Are there this many stars in Merda? It seems like there's somehow more here. Millions... there are millions more.

Nestling myself as comfortably as I could with the pain of my wounds against the gnarled tree roots, I pulled my wool blanket tightly over me and prepared for sleep.

Tomorrow, I would find water and clean my wounds.

Hopefully, nothing tries to eat me while I sleep.

Twelve

Monsters & Venom

* * *

Remmy

Mercifully, I slept through the night, unbothered by animal or beast. I supposed Skotos was giving me a break from his torments. My mind flitted back to the god, unbidden. I thought of the way he had mesmerized me, as though I were in a trance and he was the only thing that existed.

It was common for men in Merda to work shirtless in the brutal heat of summer, but I had never seen muscles like *that.* My cheeks burned at the forbidden thought. Hopefully, Skotos could not peer into our minds.

Shaking my head vigorously to clear it of the ridiculous thoughts, I sat up from the tree root I was burrowed in and scrutinized my surroundings. I was under one of the few trees within sight. The trail, as far as I could see, was seemingly bereft of them, with only grass, shrubbery, and little purple valerian buds.

I wondered how far I was from the Emerald Lake. I needed water, both to drink and to clean these wounds. I risked infection. The willowroot had helped last night, but I was out of it now, and the cuts needed to be thoroughly cleaned.

Rifling through my pack, I pulled out the last of the dried fish and started stuffing it into my mouth. I was utterly famished, having not eaten last night.

Obviously, I need to find food as well.

Without even a glance at my map, I repacked my tattered pack and set out up the trail. It didn't matter at this point. I would get to the water whenever I got to it. I could only hope it would be soon.

I'd been dragging myself up the inclining mountain path for about an hour when something red and small in the grass caught my eye. I dropped to my scratched knees, pawing frenziedly at the grass. Clutching my treasure in my hand, I stared at the small berries in unadulterated astonishment.

Wild strawberries!

I was holding wild strawberries in my hand.

How?

I could not believe my good luck. Strawberries only grew in the autumn, and they certainly never grew in Merda. The climate was too torrid and harsh for the temperamental berries. I had never even seen one before, but I had viewed drawings in my mother's old books and recognized the luscious, tiny fruits immediately. In my garden back home, I was only able to grow very hardy vegetables and fruits—things that were able to withstand the heat and limited water supply. It rained in Merda, but it was not an overly common occurrence in the summer and autumn.

Typically speaking, we had to slog to the river or pond to collect water for washing, drinking, and growing. Those of us in the village who had gardens tried to accumulate water with rain collection bins, but it was never enough.

Winter was frigid and often brought rain, but the cold temperatures prevented most plants from surviving. Spring was our only relief.

I popped one of the ruby-red berries into my mouth, its saccharine juices exploding onto my tongue. I sighed headily, relishing the sweetness, both quenching my thirst and satisfying my rumbling stomach.

Ecstatically, I raised my eyes, scanning the area around me for more red spots scattered in the green grass. Seeing several, I scrambled to them, snatching up every berry I could find, laughing out loud as I tasted each one. This was a miracle. It had to be a gift from Lunaire. Certainly, Skotos would not allow such succulent berries to grow on Mt. Malus.

I can't wait to tell Emerie about this!

The thought crashed into me like a boulder, sobering me instantaneously.

Emerie.

My sweet little sister, no doubt wondering if I was alive and how she would care for Echo and Eridian alone. I couldn't leave her with that burden.

I wonder if the meat I stored up has run out? The produce? The blight... the garden was not producing nearly enough when I left...

Swallowing down my fearful doubts, I picked up my pace a little, all the while knowing it would not make a difference, but it still made me feel better to move with more urgency.

The slight tone of trickling water reached my ears, and I realized I was approaching a small stream.

This must mean I am close to the lake.

The creek was small—too small for my drag net. I doubted there would be many fish in it anyway, but it was enough to fill my canteen, wash my cloth strips, and cleanse my wounds. I would have to wait until I got to the lake to clean my clothes and try to fish.

My cuts from the Lemian were almost healed now, as were the scratches from the Forest Imps. The scabs peeled and fell loose as I scrubbed my skin, leaving behind tiny white scars across my face, arms, torso, and legs.

The more severe cuts on the back of my thigh had not yet healed and were only beginning to scab over. I flushed them tenderly with the icy water and then proceeded to gently clean the Lycan wounds on my shoulder and back. I bit my lip at the pain lancing up my spine like a bolt of lightning at the contact.

Tears gathered in my eyes, but I refused to let them descend. I had never wept so much in my entire life as I had the last week... two weeks... how long had it even been? The days all blurred together with the constant pain and the relentless fight to survive.

The air was crisp and cold as I lumbered out of the water and slid my shift and flimsy cotton dress back over my shoulders. I couldn't risk getting it wet until I could build a fire to dry it. In this cold, I would certainly become ill wandering up the mountain in drenched clothing.

I didn't want to waste the time doing that, considering that it was not even lunchtime yet, but my clothes were now torn and coated in not only my own blood but the thick ichor of the dead Lycan. I'd have to clean up and make a fire to dry as soon as I reached the lake.

Hopefully, I would be there by noon and be able to catch some fish to sate my hunger. The strawberries had staved it off for a time, but they would not last long. I needed something more substantial.

Donning my snug green capote, I resumed my hike toward the lake, pulling the hood up over my head.

As I suspected, I arrived at the lake fairly quickly. Taking it in, I realized how it had gotten its name. Emerald. The water was as green as my eyes.

Leaning over it, I could see my reflection staring back at me from the surface of the crystal emerald waters. I grimaced at the scars now marring my once clear skin.

Sliding off my cloak and leather boots, I crashed into the water. It was bitterly cold, but relief washed over me when I submerged my aching back.

Working as quickly as possible, I combed my hands through my tangled hair and scrubbed over my dress as best I could.

Without soap, there was only so much I could do. I needed to find some laour leaves to lather, but I had not been too worried about cleanliness on this hazardous journey. I hadn't even looked for any before rushing into the lake. The plant usually grew near water sources in Valeria. It was a sturdy plant that could thrive in most any climate as long as it was near water.

Checking the shoreline, I saw a bush of it about fifty paces from me. I hurried over, tugged off some leaves, and waded back into the water.

Sinking deep, I rubbed the leaves over my hair and body, lathering it up satisfactorily, before rinsing it.

Once finished, I climbed out of the water and shrugged out of the sopping wet dress, followed by my shift.

Flopping them both over a nearby shrub, I removed the Lemian fur from my pack, wrapped it around my naked body, and sat to work building a fire.

I shivered as a chill went through me and shuffled closer when the flames began to lick higher, my body craving the warmth. The fur kept me warm, but my hair still needed to dry, or I would risk getting sick. The higher I climbed on this mountain, the colder the climate became.

When my hair finally began to dry, I decided to try to catch some lunch.

Shrugging off the fur, I slid my cloak on instead and waded back into the water with my fishing net. Again and again, I dragged it through the jade waters only to come up empty every time.

I cast it back out and once more came up with nothing in my net.

Panic was worming its way through my skull as I began to wonder if there were any fish in this lake at all. What was I going to eat? I dragged my net through the water several more times, still not snaring a single thing.

Stumbling out of the water, yet again on the verge of tears, my eyes explored the grass and plant life around me.

I wonder if there are any edible plants around here? If only I could find more strawberries.

I had to be careful of poisonous plants, but I stood in that water for half an hour and didn't catch anything. Not even lake kelp had graced my net.

Walking over to the shrub where I had hung my dress, I ran my hands over it to see if it was beginning to dry.

Discovering it was not, I added my now-wet cloak beside it and returned to the fire to grab my fur, wrapping it around myself once more.

Searching through my pack, I took out Teigan's bowl, and a pang of loneliness went through me. I had forgotten to give it back to him before we parted ways.

I wonder if I'll ever see him again?

We promised each other we would meet again, but I was never

sure at any given moment if I'd make it off this blasted mountain.

Clutching the fur tightly around my shoulders, I scrounged through the plant life and shrubs nearby and found several I knew to be edible, picking them off and placing them into the clay bowl.

When the bowl was filled to the brim, I returned to my still-blazing fire and began to shove the plants into my mouth, grumbling to myself about being forced to eat leaves. One in particular had a rather pungent taste. I gagged as I choked the ripe leaves down.

Clamorous splashing sounded behind me, and I jumped to my feet, spinning toward the lake. Something colossal and scaly rose from the water, staring at me with beady eyes and sharp, pointed teeth.

My legs were wobbly beneath me as I stood on the shore, wrapped only in a fur. The massive creature had spiked ridges jutting out from its head as far down its elongated body as I could see. It surged upward with alarming speed, emerging from the water on four legs. I froze.

What in the Netherworld is this? I never read about anything like this thing in beastology!! What do I do? Holy gods, I am going to die—naked. Skotos! Help me! I'm going to die naked!

I cried out to the god of beasts, but I knew my plea fell upon deaf ears when the monstrous creature rumbled toward me.

I was not sure how fast this unknown creature could run, but given its size, I came to the conclusion that I would not be able to outrun it. I snatched up my sword, holding it in front of me unsteadily. I was not thinking any rational thoughts at all when the monster charged with a fearsome roar.

Why does everything on this bloody mountain want to kill me?

My brain screamed the thought, aiming it at Skotos.

Curse that guy; he clearly couldn't care less about humans.

I swore I heard a laugh echo through my mind and I jolted, glancing around for the dark god. Could he hear my thoughts? I shuddered.

I surely hope not.

Returning my focus to the monster ahead, I tried to study it. I'd lived in the Therion Region my entire life, and beasts had always roamed the night, but I had never seen anything more terrifying. The waters in Merda didn't even have Selkies, although one or two had been spotted in the far-off Potamilv River. I had never encountered one until this journey.

"Aaahhh!" I cursed and dodged out of the path of the creature, my fur falling from my shoulders. I was too disoriented to even swing my sword at it. My mind was reeling as I tried to steady myself and regain my balance.

The beast whipped around and doubled back at me, and I realized its size might actually prove to be a disadvantage for it.

Bringing my sword over my right shoulder, I brought it down with all the force my torn back would allow, slicing into the tail of the thing. The creature bellowed in fury—its blood sprayed into the air, coating my body.

I can't believe I'm fighting a giant water demon, naked. Naked! At least this'll be easier than cleaning my dress again. That thing is practically torn to bits.

I barely had time to process the thought before the creature had turned itself around and was chomping its yellowed fangs at me. A wild thought occurred to me, and I remembered my fight with the Lemian.

In one smooth motion, I scaled the beast's side, grasping onto one of its spikes and pulling myself into a crouched position on its back. The furious animal tried to lash at me with its clubbed tail, but I was faster, pulling myself along its back using the spikes.

The beast shook its great body powerfully, and I lost my grip, falling from its back and landing on mine.

White pinpricks flared in my eyes, shooting across the blue-ish gray sky. I rolled onto my stomach in time to barely avoid being crushed under the monster's foot. I drew myself onto my knees, gasping from the pain of the action.

Reaching for the sword which had fallen from my hand when I was thrown, I stuck it into the ground in front of me and used it to pull myself shakily to my feet. I lifted it and pointed it at the massive animal, my hands trembling.

"I will not be the one to die today, demon!" I shouted the words and barreled toward the creature at full speed. The beast lunged, its long neck striking down, jaws gaping wide to snap me in half—but I moved faster. With a desperate cry, I drove my sword upward, plunging it deep into the back of the creature's throat. Its shriek tore through the air as blood sprayed hot against my naked skin.

It gurgled and groaned as I withdrew my sword and stabbed again, this time driving it through the creature's eye. Its jaw fell slack, and it collapsed with great force, shaking the ground beneath us, the rumbling sound echoing across the mountain.

Driving my sword into the earth beside the beast, I stumbled back to the water. I hesitated only a moment, knowing that anything else that could be in that frigid water couldn't possibly be worse than the monster I had just killed.

Submerging myself, I quickly washed the animal's blood from my body and staggered back to my clothes, draped across the bush.

I tried to wipe off as much of the water as possible with my hand before sliding my shift and dress over my head and shrugging my cloak on top of it. I was freezing. My teeth chattered in my skull aggressively.

I had no idea how much time had passed, but the sun was setting earlier now. I glanced up. Wisps of rose-tinted clouds stretched across the endless sky, as if painted by an artist's brush.

My stomach rumbled loudly, reminding me that I had battled for my life through dinner, and had only eaten some plants for lunch hours before. I glanced back at the dead beast.

I guess I am eating you for dinner. Please don't be poisonous.

How was I going to go about skinning that thing? The hide was so tough that it had taken all my strength to pierce its tail with my sword. Skinning it with a dagger would be a nightmare.

A rustling in the bushes startled me, and I jumped back, preparing to flee. I was already on the verge of collapsing; I couldn't handle anything else.

A small rabbit leaped from the bushes and stood stock still in front of me for only a brief moment, but I had learned my lesson with the deer, and a moment was all I needed. I pounced on it, snatching it up. It squirmed and writhed in my arms, trying to get free and squealing at me, but I held it firmly.

"I'm sorry, little guy, but I have got to eat."

Carrying the animal over to the fire, I brought my dagger down on its neck remorsefully, asking Lunaire to bless the poor creature's soul as it transitioned to the afterlife.

After skinning the rabbit, I fed some more tinder into the smoldering fire and tossed the rabbit on, as the ashes blazed back to life.

After eating some of the meat, I packed the remainder of the dried rabbit into my pack and began to set up camp for the evening.

Irritation clawed at me over the setback. That giant water beast had cost me almost half a day.

The night air was biting, piercing me through to the bone, and I wrapped up inside my blanket and fur. Staring up into the onyx sky, I marveled at the vast array of stars littered across it.

I've never seen stars like this before.

Of course, we have stars in Merda, but there seemed to be immeasurably more here.

A thought occurred to me: *I must have crossed regions. This must be why it's named the Stardust District. There are millions more stars here than in the Therion Region. It doesn't even seem real. I hope I get to see stars like these... when I'm not fighting for my life, every minute of every day.*

The ache in my back kept me awake for several hours, as I rolled uncomfortably in my blankets, listening to the noises of the mountain. I had rarely been awake after dark since starting my trek up Mt. Malus, and it was disconcerting. It left me with a gnawing feeling of unease.

When I finally fell asleep, it did not last long before I was awake again, the need to relieve myself pressing on my bladder.

Peevishly, I crept from the warmth of my covers, the night air raising goosebumps on my skin, and plodded over to the bushes where I had draped my wet clothing earlier today.

Before I could finish, a hissing sound came from within the bushes, and I stumbled back, attempting to replace my clothing and withdrawing my dagger from where it was strapped around my waist.

A writhing snake fell from a branch and slithered across the ground toward me, intent on making me its next victim, but I had other plans. The tan and yellow stripes indicated it was a Tangeerian Vesper viper. I was surprised to see it above ground during a colder month; the snakes usually preferred warmer climates, being native to the torrid country of Tangeer, on our eastern border.

The venom from this viper could be very useful in the future. It was particularly potent, paralyzing its victim for hours. I had no idea what I could use the venom for, but I also had no indication of what was left for me on this journey, or what awaited me in Lunestair, should I survive it.

Angling myself behind the serpent, I reached out swiftly, grasping it by the back of the head.

Carrying it over to my campsite, I hunted through my bag with one hand, searching for the cloth strips I used for wounds and the empty willowroot container.

Finding them, I stuffed the cloth into the snake's face and watched in fascination as it bit down on the cloth, its jaundiced fangs releasing venom into the material.

Growing up in the southern, warm region of Valeria, we had many snakes, but I still found the slithering demons to be interesting.

When the snake released the cloth, I asked a blessing on it and tossed the writhing demon into the fire, the flames hissing and popping at the new addition.

Returning my attention to the venom-soaked cloth, I squeezed it into the empty container, then replaced the container in my pack before gathering the cloth strips. I hurried down to the water and rinsed my hands and the cloth thoroughly.

The last thing I needed was to forget and try to wrap that around an injury. I headed back to the makeshift bed and settled into it.

This time, I drifted easily into sleep.

Thirteen

Brutal Lessons

* * *

Vincent

Frantically, I patted the boy's face, my thoughts a chaotic torrent. I shuddered to think what would happen if Cyrus discovered I had been coming up here. He'd kill me, and Sterling would be left with no one. Or worse, he would kill Sterling and be done with the boy altogether.

Three days prior, I had visited to find that Sterling had been rendered unconscious. The king tried to keep a guard on me—whom I was usually able to shake—but at one point I thought there was someone following me up the mountain.

I couldn't risk smuggling out too much food or being gone for very long. Cyrus would find out. It seemed that what I had managed to bring up the mountain had not been enough.

The boy, while used to abuse and rigorous training from the king's cruel tactics, was not used to starvation. He was kept alive by magic alone.

I blamed myself for not figuring out a better plan. For not being able to smuggle out more food. For not being able to save him from this horrific fate.

I tried again to rouse him, but the prince only moaned in response.

In the three days since I had last been able to come, it seemed that Cyrus had sent another guard to torment Sterling.

He's already been through enough! Can that monster not just leave him be?

Since stashing his son away on this beastly mountain, the king had periodically sent guards who were loyal to him to fly to the top of the mountain and "teach that ungrateful maggot a lesson." The wounds from this most recent "lesson" festered and oozed now. I set to work trying to clean them with what little supplies were available.

Where is that blasted girl?

Unless I could formulate an escape plan for Thalia, that girl was the only chance Sterling had to make it out of here alive. I had done my best to protect Sterling since his birth, but I had no doubt the king planned to kill his heir as slowly and as brutally as possible.

If I released him, Thalia would be endangered, and I wouldn't do that to her. My daughter had been only a year old when Sterling came into the world. She and her mother had been my entire world when I started working at the Castle of Stars.

Choosing between my daughter and my prince was one of the hardest decisions I had to make since Sterling's conception twenty-six years ago.

The last time I had checked on the contestant, she had been injured and trying to outrun the king's mercenaries in the Darkhelm. I had not seen her since that time, but she seemed tenacious enough, and I had to pray to whatever gods still existed that she survived and was nearing the prince's prison. I needed her to be. Sterling needed her to be.

The prince groaned and writhed unconsciously as I rubbed the salve into his lashes. It was a risk to use the salve, but I couldn't allow myself to leave him this way. I didn't even have any water to wash the wounds.

Fearful of infection, I placed my hand on his forehead.

I cursed. His skin was burning up. I cursed again.

I have to get some better medicine up here... a healer... at least some water...

Resolving to check in on the girl, I ruefully left the prince to fly back to Lunestair with a heavy heart.

* * *

Vincent

I landed in front of the girl with a loud thud, and a scream erupted loud enough to wake anything that still slept.

Oops.

It was barely past dawn, and the sun was lightly tinting the violet sky with shades of pink and gold. The girl was already awake and bustling about, disassembling her campsite. I had merely meant to check on her progress, forgetting that she may be unaccustomed to Fae clan forms.

I couldn't chance revealing my Fae form, so I tucked my translucent wings in tight at my back and lowered my head in an effort to seem less intimidating.

The girl paused, though she still kept her sword raised in front of her.

Brave one.

The smell of blood floated to me on the breeze. She must be injured. Who knew what kind of horrors she'd encountered on this deadly mountain?

Gently, I placed my nose against the flat side of the blade and nudged it away. She obliged, though hesitant, keeping a wary eye on me.

I dropped the bag from my mouth, containing the salve I had used for Sterling, and pushed it in her direction with my paw, begging her to take it.

Never taking her eyes off me, she bent to retrieve it. They widened when she opened it, and her gaze shot up to me questioningly.

Her mouth hung open. "You're giving me…" She sniffed the container and her head jerked up.

"Morsious!" She gasped. "Who are you?"

I nodded my large head once in her direction and raised into the air, racing back to the palace before the court was due to awaken.

* * *

Remmy

I stared in bewilderment as the great phalynx took flight, its blue-tipped, pearlescent wings reflecting the soft sunlight with each beat.

What in the worlds just happened? That thing just gave me... morsious salve.

This was the second time I had seen the phalynx, and both times it had helped me.

But why? Why would this Fae randomly bring me healing salve? And who is it? Why does it want to help me?

The thoughts plagued me as I stripped out of my dress and rubbed the salve onto my wounds. The relief was immediate, sweeping through me and pulling a sigh from my lips. My shoulders sagged, as for the first time since that night in the Sankot desert, I felt limited pain.

The Dol plant, from whence the morsious salve is made, had very potent magical healing properties. It was not a common remedy in the villages, but I had seen it when my father's leg had been injured.

I was amazed at how quickly it worked. I rotated my back, testing the wounds and feeling only a slight twinge. I smiled elatedly. I could not believe my good fortune.

I placed the rest of the morsious into my pack and unrolled my map. I should be nearing the crest of the mountain soon.

Examining the map, I realized with excitement that I would make the summit by nightfall if I made good time today.

I would be camping with the Prince of Valeria tonight!

The map revealed no other great hurdles or landmarks after the

Emerald Lake. It was also surprisingly sparse for water sources. It seemed as though there might be a small stream near the crest, but I couldn't be sure based on the map. I would fill my canteen here before leaving.

Packing my map back into the bag, I hurried to the water and filled my flask. Rejuvenated from the healing salve and finally ready to leave, I headed back to the path and set off up the mountain.

After spending the morning traversing gradually sloping treeless fields, the trail became much steeper and narrower.

On a few occasions, I could even look off the side of the mountain, over a steeply dropping cliff.

Surveying the path ahead of me, I concluded that it was going to get much worse before it got any better, so I decided to break for a few minutes and have some food.

It was too early for lunch, but I was not sure how the conditions would be farther up the mountain, and my shoulders were already aching from carrying this heavy pack.

Truthfully, the journey up until this point had been too chaotic and wrought with terror for me to even note the weight of the pack.

Sliding it off, I saw the straps I had tied together were beginning to come undone. I re-tied the straps and laid it on the ground, positioning myself on a mildly uncomfortable boulder.

I stuffed a few pieces of dried rabbit into my mouth and marveled that I had yet to see any animals thus far today.

Hopefully, once I made it past the next treacherous part of the mountain, the path would even out a little once more and be hospitable to wildlife. The map did show some dense patches of trees farther up the mountain.

Rolling my aching shoulders, I decided to use a small amount of the morsious salve on them before setting out again.

Trudging up the sharp incline was perilous. At several points, I was not sure I was going to make it. There was no place to stop and rest, and I was breathing so heavily that I was heaving every time I tried to take a breath.

For every step forward, I slid two steps back. The soles of my boots were wearing out, and I had very little traction, slipping on the rocky incline.

My heavy pack was pulling me down, and I had to grasp onto rocks to pull myself upward.

Forlornly, I thought I might not make it to the peak this evening after all.

Reaching above me for a stone to grab, my hand slipped, and I lost my footing, careening toward the side of the cliff-face.

I screamed in terror, my hands flailing out to latch on to anything close by and snagging on the tough root of a large shrub sticking out from the path. I grabbed at it frantically with my free hand, hoisting myself back onto the path with my feet still hanging over the side of the mountain.

I stayed there, rooted to the spot, my breath coming in short, jagged sobs. I've fought numerous animals and beasts, survived harsh climates and conditions, and been faced with starvation, but I have never been more frightened than just now, as I was seconds away from plummeting to my death.

I clung to the root, breathing raggedly, as I waited for my heart rate to decelerate and my breathing to come more easily.

Gradually, it slowed and evened out, and I began to make my way up the formidable path again.

What seemed like an eternity later, I noticed the steep, craggy route beginning to level and widen back out. Relief coursed through me as I pulled myself up to where it tapered off. I sat there on the ground, catching my breath for several minutes before moving.

I glanced up at the sun, noting the position. It was long past lunchtime now, and I was unsure if I could make it to the summit before dark. I was also not sure what I would find there, and I needed to be prepared.

I settled on the idea of stopping for an early dinner and establishing camp for the night. It would allow me to be well-rested for whatever lay at the top of this mountain.

A few small trees dotted the path ahead of me, and I decided I would set up closer to them, hoping to find enough branches and sticks to build a fire and a shelter of sorts.

* * *

Remmy

I rose before dawn the next morning, revitalized and ready to make my ascent. I packed my things while the sun rose, stamped out the fire, and set out through the elevation stumped trees.

The air was cold and biting this high up; the wind whipping at my chapped cheeks. It felt like winter had arrived at the top of Mt. Malus, skipping autumn altogether.

Based on my calculations, I expected to reach the summit by lunchtime.

What will I find there?

No longer fighting to survive every moment left me anticipating meeting the prince, but what if this had all been for naught? Some cruel joke to play on the stupid villagers? What if the prince was locked in a cage and I had no way to release him? What if he were dead… or had never been there at all?

My thoughts spiraled wildly out of control from one outlandish thing to the next, my nerves getting the better of me.

I plodded on until I came to a small stream with a variety of plants and herbs growing around the shore. The essence of magic increased in the air as I neared the creek.

I wonder why I haven't sensed it before?

The entire mountain was magic, but it certainly buzzed more in some locations. Stopping by the water, I filled my flask, drinking deeply.

I glanced around at the plant life.

Pulling out Teigan's bowl, I began to fill it with herbs and roots that I found growing around the stream. Following the water farther, I even found a bush filled with small ebony berries.

I was unfamiliar with the berries. I prayed they weren't poisonous as I popped one into my mouth. I decided to wait in the area for half an hour, and if the berry caused no reaction, I would fill up on them.

I slipped the roots and herbs I gathered into my bag for later and sat down to wait. After some time, when nothing happened, I went back to the bush and began to pluck as many of the berries as I could and stuff them into my mouth.

Thorns dug into my fingers, and the wild berries were slightly tart, but they were not terrible, and I needed something to eat. I still had yet to see any more animals.

Maybe the animals don't come this high up? All the vegetation is stunted and grows oddly up here.

I had also not seen any beasts or creatures from the Netherworld since the Emerald Lake. I would not complain about that, but it was curious.

Once I had picked the bush clean, I resumed walking.

I probably shouldn't have eaten so many of those berries. But if animals don't come up here, who knows when I will get to eat again. I should be there soon. Hope the prince isn't expecting some noble to come to his rescue.

I chuckled dryly. He would be sorely disappointed when the destitute village girl showed up.

While amusing myself with silly thoughts of noble women attempting to survive this contest, I had failed to observe my surroundings. I came to a standstill when I saw it.

An old, dilapidated shack. An overgrown garden that had been unattended for ages. What appeared to be an ancient dried-up well.

Is this it? Should I... go in?

The large oak door seemed as though it might fall off its hinges at any moment.

What if the prince is inside and I am just standing here like an imbecile?

I inched up to the old cabin and slowly swung open the creaking wooden door, my other hand on the hilt of the sword at my waist.

There.

At the back of the cabin was a man. His head hung low, chin resting on his chest, restrained to the wall with... serpents?

No. Not serpents. Vines.

Living vines, writhing and squirming while they held him pressed tightly against the wall, his arms pinned to his side.

Gasping, I rushed across the cabin and swung my sword, chopping at the vines holding him. They were created with strong magic, and it took several attempts to cut them. I brandished my sword steadily, chopping over and over at the vines.

When I finally cut through them, I hurriedly fought to untangle them as the man tipped forward.

He was completely unconscious. He slumped into me; his hot breath on my neck reassuring me that he was still alive.

I laid his body as gently as I could manage onto the cabin floor and knelt beside him. He was handsome. Unbearably so. I'd never seen anyone more... *beautiful.*

Dark tussled hair fell over his eyes, and a week's worth of growth covered his strong, square jaw. He reeked of urine, and his skin was drawn and pale.

My heart clenched at the sight of him. I didn't care much for nobility, but this man was a prince, reduced to skin and bones; his clothes soaked in his own bodily fluids.

I can't understand how a father can do this to his son! And get away with it! Why has no one ever stood up to this ruthless... worthless sack of a king? I ranted.

What power did the king hold over his son that the prince was unable to fight back?

"Prince Sterling?" His name came out as a croak as I gently rubbed his hand, trying to wake him. It was unnaturally warm for how cold the cabin was.

Oh no.

I leaned forward and timidly put a hand on his forehead. His skin was scalding.

Fever.

"I'm sorry for this," I whispered, as I began to disrobe him. I stared in horror at the white scars cutting across his chest and abdomen.

"Who did this to you?" I gasped at the unconscious prince.

Once the prince was stripped to only his underclothing, I gathered up the filthy clothes, snatched up an old pitcher that had been thrown carelessly onto the cabin floor, and headed toward the stream I had passed on the way up.

I made the trip as quickly as possible, doing my best to rinse the clothing using some laour leaves I found growing along the bank.

Then, I filled the pitcher and hiked back up to the shack. I draped the clothes on a post outside and returned to kneel at Prince Sterling's side. Dipping one of my cloth strips into the water, I placed it on his forehead to try to cool him and began to slowly cleanse his body with the other.

In most circumstances, this would be a violation of some kind, but the prince was going to die if I did not get his temperature down. I gently tugged his arm up to try to roll him onto his side so I could wash his back as well.

I inhaled sharply when I saw the freshly healed slashes and red puckered scars covering his back. They couldn't be more than a day or two old.

The king... had his son tortured... while he was imprisoned.

I felt sick as I cautiously rolled Sterling back onto his back and stared at his face for a few minutes. I did not want to pity someone who was born to royalty, but I couldn't help imagining what he had endured.

I dipped the cloth back into the water and placed it across his chest, using the fur from my bag to prop up his head.

Taking out my canteen, I dribbled a little water onto his cracked lips, parting them gently with the nozzle so the water would slide down his throat.

After situating him as best I could, I went back outside and gathered as many sticks and branches as I could carry and came back in to light a fire in the dusty old hearth.

I sat on the floor beside him, munching on the roots and herbs I had gathered earlier.

Tomorrow, I would scrounge through that tangled garden and see if anything was left in there.

Before curling up to sleep, I rubbed some of the morsious on his back. I didn't know if it would help or not, but it certainly couldn't hurt.

It was only dusk, but this was the first time I had been inside a shelter in a long time, and I was thoroughly exhausted.

I settled a few paces away from the handsome prince, resolving to check on him throughout the night, and passed out beneath my woolen blanket.

END PART ONE

II

Part Two

Fourteen

Large Shoes To Fill

* * *

PART TWO
Emerie

Father sat in his usual chair, staring blankly into the fire I'd managed to stoke in the hearth. When the mead money had run out, he had disconnected completely, barely uttering a word.

The twins had learned to stop asking him questions because he never deigned to respond. He only stared at them without emotion. The light had gone out of his eyes when Mother had left. They slowly started to accept that the man they knew as "Father" was no longer there.

They were children, though, and they were resilient. For me, it still hurt. I could remember how he was before he became this shell of a man, though the memories were faint. It was Remmy who had raised and cared for all of us since Mother left.

In the beginning, Father went to work at the quilldust mines. He would come home after, eat the dinner Remmy prepared, and then drown in his alcohol.

After his accident, the man he had been slowly started to slip away until there was nothing left but alcohol. Gin, mead, ale, whiskey. Whatever he could get a hold of, he'd drink it.

Now there was no money for it, and without the alcohol, the shell of a sad, broken man had replaced the father we once knew.

My thoughts drifted to Remmy as I surveyed the store of goods she had left behind. The food she had stocked up was running dangerously low. I surmised we had about six days left—if we rationed it. I tried to give as much of my portion as I could to the twins to make sure they stayed healthy. They needed it more than I did.

I smiled as I listened to Eridian's laughter drifting on the wind outside. No doubt, he was chasing Echo with some type of bug or creature he had plucked from the ground or pond. His favorite pastime was chasing his sister with the wildlife.

Sighing heavily, I returned my gaze to our remaining stores. The wood Remmy had cut and piled for the fire had run out several days ago, and I had to force myself to swing the axe in order to cut more wood. I did it daily in the chill of the morning, leaving myself some time to recover before the rest of the family woke. I hated my slight body. Remmy was stronger, more accustomed to manual work.

I wish I were stronger.

All I had ever done was the household chores and cooking. Remmy would hunt, garden, or fish, and I would prepare. Remmy chopped the wood, and I lit the fire. Remmy bathed the children, and I read them stories. That was the way it had always been. My body was unaccustomed to physical labor.

In hindsight, I wished I had not placed so much on Remmy. We, her siblings, were the burden she had to bear. Now, as I stood here having to fill her shoes, without the slightest idea how, I regretted not learning more from her. Not letting her teach me to be stronger. Because if Remmy were gone… if she didn't come back, it would be up to me to raise the twins, and provide for the Silva family. And I didn't know how to do that.

She has to come back. And not only because I don't know how to do this. I don't… I don't know how I will live with the loss of her.

She was not just our sister. She was a mother and a friend. Our rock.

My gaze turned from the measly stack of potatoes and meat to the mountains in the distance, searching as though I could see her there. Remmy was the toughest person I had ever known. Circumstances had shaped her, and she was tenacious. She was a fighter. She was alive out there. It had to be true.

I'd know it in my heart if she were gone.

* * *

Teigan

In the short time I had been working at the Starlight Oasis, I had learned much about the Fae and life in Lunestair. Including hushed conversations that alluded to a resistance. It seemed not all Fae were loyal to the brutal King of Lions.

The idea sparked a fire in my bones, but I knew my parents would be heartbroken if I pursued such a thing.

The truth was, I was destined to follow in my father's footsteps and become a fisherman in Castillo as soon as I freed them and we returned home.

Though I couldn't deny the romantic allure of joining a resistance and helping to overthrow the evil king of Valeria, so I had asked around a bit.

Apparently, there was talk among the rebel leaders to install the king's heir, Prince Sterling, as king.

Prince Sterling.

The man tormented by his father and trapped somewhere to the east of here on a mountain of beasts, waiting to be rescued by my friend, whom I prayed to the gods was still alive.

The rumor was that the prince had never shifted into a clan. A clanless Fae was as bad as the lesser species in the eyes of the clanist king, and he lorded that power over his son. I was not sure that he was the best choice for king, but I knew little about the prince and couldn't judge his character.

I didn't have any other suggestions for king, anyway. If he wasn't already dead, I hoped to find out more about him soon. It had been a fortnight already since I had parted ways with Remmy. If she made it to the top of the mountain, she would be heading back to Lunestair with the prince by now.

I listened unnoticed, while I served beer and ale, to every subtle murmur of the resistance. Maggie shut down all mention of it and forbade me from asking, as it would no doubt trigger unwanted attention for the pub and bring down the wrath of the Blood Guard upon our heads. She told me this with a face as red as her tomato colored hair. I had not listened, though, asking as covertly as possible of anyone who mentioned it. That was my truest skill—convincing people to talk to me. It helped when they were drunk, as most of our patrons were.

The Blood Guard was an army of ruthless Fae, composed of elite clans, mostly handpicked by the king or his Captain of the Guard, loyal to the throne at any cost. I was convinced that Maggie was Fae, although I'd yet to figure out her clan, but the Blood Guard had no concern if you were Fae, human, Dwarf, Elf, or any other species. If there was a whisper of a transgression, you'd either be slaughtered in the streets or carted away to the dungeons beneath the palace.

Still, I wanted to know more. The passion to do something greater than thievery and fishing burned deep inside me like smoldering embers. So I listened. And I befriended everyone who came into The Oasis, begging for a trickle of information.

If I can only learn the name of the resistance, then maybe I can...

I let the thought trail off. I can what? I couldn't stand the idea of going back to Castillo and fishing my life away. I was good at fishing, and I was proud of that skill. It had served me well enough on my trip here. But I wanted more.

I can't rescue my parents only to abandon them.

These thoughts were foolish. I pushed them out of my head and returned to work, hoping that my resolve would hold, but knowing in my heart that it was unlikely.

* * *

* * *

Remmy

I woke to him towering over me, peering at me through the most beautiful silver eyes I had ever seen.

Wow, that morsious salve works fast! Fae must heal much quicker than humans.

Granted, he was still gaunt and pale, but he was also *standing* over me. Last night, he had been completely unconscious.

"Oh, good. You're awake." He rumbled, as though he had not just been standing there waiting for me to wake. His voice was smooth and deep, abyssal like a dark pool. "Where. Are. My. Clothes?"

He practically growled the words at me. I rolled my eyes, trying to keep them on his face and not his bare chest.

Grateful much?

"Nice to meet you, too, *Prince* Sterling. Your clothing is outside on a post—hopefully dry by now."

He grunted at me and began to make his way slowly to the door of the dilapidated shack. He may be walking on his own, but he was obviously still weak.

Real charmer, that one. I have to marry this absolute beast? He literally grunted at me. Grunted. Like an animal. A gorgeous animal. But still. An animal. This is going to be a nightmare.

As long as it fed my family, I would endure it.

Endure him. I shall call him 'Your Grouchiness.'

The thought almost had me giggling out loud, but I chastised myself for my insensitivity.

"I can get those for you if you'll hold on a moment," I called after him. I didn't know why I was offering to help this brute of a man, but I didn't need him passing out; that much was certain.

"I'm fine." He muttered as he pulled the door open, a loud groan echoing throughout the tiny cabin.

Okay fine, you can get them yourself... you... you... broody Fae... highness. What?

I released a sigh of frustration and rolled out of my blanket to follow the prince out the door into the cold morning air.

"Sterling." I said his name without his title, and he turned steely-gray eyes on me, his rage-filled gaze affixed on my face. I didn't care. I was not inclined to spend the rest of my life cowering to him and calling him some absurd title, in private quarters.

He didn't speak, but steam practically roiled off his body.

"Look, I don't mean this to come off offensively, but you... you're still... umm... weak. I don't know how long you have been up here, but when I found you, it was quite evident that you had been a while without food or water. You need to rest and recover before we start the journey down the mountain." As much as I hated the idea of waiting, His Broody Fae Highness was in no shape to travel.

"Why was I unclothed when I awakened?" He demanded indignantly.

Good goddess in Lumess. Sorry, I rescued you from being starved to death by magical vines and cleansed you of your own urine.

"As I said before, you were in rough shape when I arrived. Your clothes were covered in blood from the wounds on your back, and... well... you... smelled awful!" I forced out the words, cringing a little as the prince's handsome face colored. Of course, he was embarrassed. Who wouldn't be?

"So you took it upon yourself to strip me... and what?"

Exhaling with all the patience I could muster, I tried to remind myself that the prince had been through a horrid ordeal. He was no doubt feeling very vulnerable right now, and in front of a village girl, no less.

"I washed your clothes and your wounds. I rubbed healing salve on your injuries, and I tried my best to force some water down your throat. You had a raging fever, and I am baffled to see you up and about right now."

The prince's face softened the smallest amount. "I'm still a little feverish. And hungry." He admitted begrudgingly. "Where did you get the salve?"

I hesitated, unsure how to explain. "It's a long story. Now, if you don't mind returning inside, I will restart the fire and attempt to sort through this… mess of a garden and find something to eat."

He only nodded slightly and returned inside, now fully clothed in his torn regal attire. I wanted to ask what had caused that, but based on his temperament, decided against it.

I put a hand wearily to my head and stood outside for a moment to regather my thoughts. This was going to be a nightmare.

Stepping back into the cabin, I found Sterling standing awkwardly in the middle of the floor, his huge frame nearly filling the space, looking around as though he was unsure what to do.

Last night, I had been too exhausted to even glance around the musty shack. There was an old, dirty mattress in the corner, a hearth, and a small table with two rickety chairs. That was it. No wonder he was awkward. Had he been chained to the wall with vines the entire time he had been here? Gesturing to the bed and the fur still lying in a pile on the floor, I said, "Why don't you get some rest while I gather some wood?"

He seemed as though he were about to fall over at any moment.

"I'll just…" he glanced around aimlessly, "sit here." He motioned to the chair.

I shrugged and shook my head as the stubborn man attempted to fold himself into the unstable wooden chair. It was almost too small for his towering frame.

Hopefully, when he passes out, he doesn't hit the floor too hard.

Gathering wood was easier than I had anticipated, considering the stunted growth of the flora here.

After I get a fire started, I'll go out to that garden and see what survived this frost. I can't imagine it's much, but our options are limited.

Autumn was in full swing on the crest of the mountain, the temperatures dropping lower than those near the base.

Returning inside with the wood I had managed to procure, I found the prince slumped over the table. I cursed under my breath and dropped the wood by the door, hurrying over to him.

He was awake, but barely. "Sterling!"

The prince mumbled incoherently. "Is okay… not tired… be fine… "

"Come on." I motioned for him to put his arm around my shoulder and lean on me. He did so, his weight almost more than I could withstand, and we stumbled over to the rumpled, dirty bed in the corner. I had hoped to be able to clean it up a little before he needed it, but nothing could be done about it now.

He flopped unceremoniously onto the old mattress, muttering something about mortification and not being proper.

Shrugging him off, I lifted his legs into the bed and proceeded to unlace the black leather boots he had just put on, not half an hour before.

"Hush your grumbling, and rest. Your body is weak, and you are not going anywhere until you regain some strength."

His feeble protests died off as exhaustion won out. He was asleep in seconds, his mouth gaping open, curled onto his side like a child. Chuckling, I picked up the fur from the floor and covered him with it.

Outside, I passed through the gate into the overgrown garden, and with delight, I discovered something I had been unable to see before. In the far right-hand corner stood a fruit-laden apple tree. It was early in the season for apples, but I supposed the cool mountain air accelerated the apple development, and I was not one to question a gift from the goddess.

Blissfully, I fought my way through the other overgrown plants, to the corner and began to pluck the apples from the tree, using my cloak to hold as many as I could.

Smiling like it was Yule Fest, I carried them back to the cabin, peeking at Sterling when I set them onto the dusty counter. The prince was snoring lightly, and the sound left my insides feeling like flame moths. I shook my head.

Nope, still can't stand him.

I returned to the garden and proceeded to discover ginger root, carrots, potatoes, rosemary, and a variety of other herbs. Satisfied with my findings, I gathered my small pitcher and flask and made my way back to the stream.

Fifteen

Your Highness

* * *

Prince Sterling Ericcsön

The smell of something laden with spices cut through the haze, assaulting my nose with a pleasant aroma.

I must be dreaming.

But no, I distinctly remembered a girl. A girl, whose name I had never learned, before shamefully passing out again.

It didn't matter. If she thought my father would abide by his proclamation, she was in for heartbreak.

Nor would I, for that matter. I had no desire to be wed to some random girl who was no doubt only pursuing the crown.

The world shimmered and faded for a moment, light filtering in and out through the obscurity. I blinked to clear it away, and my gaze focused on the source of the mouth-watering smell. The woman leaned over an open fire in the hearth, stirring a large pot filled with steaming stew.

I shifted in the uncomfortable bed and licked my cracked lips. She glanced up at the motion and smiled softly at me.

She was uncharacteristically beautiful for a low-born village girl. More often than not, they led difficult lives, leaving them hardened and weathered, though I had not honestly spent much time around anyone from the villages. The humans in Lunestair tended to blend in to the city.

Her long dark hair flowed freely down her back and clung to her forehead as tiny rivulets of sweat trickled down her face. Eyes the color of an emerald, locked onto mine, as if searching for something hidden deep within me.

She straightened and made her way slowly to the bed where I lay. As she drew closer, I noticed her tanned skin was marred with tiny white scars, lining her face and exposed arms. Shock rippled through me.

What could have caused that?

She stopped and stood looming over me.

"How are you feeling?" She asked it like she genuinely cared, but I knew better.

None of them care. They only want the crown and the title that it comes with. This girl is just another Magette Vaneer. No one has ever truly cared except... I stopped the thought before it could finish.

Glaring up at the girl, I said, "I'm famished. Not that it's any of your concern."

She sighed heavily and rolled her eyes, reaching for my forehead with one delicate, small hand. I flinched away from her, and she laughed outright, serving only to deepen my glower.

"Well, I am not going to smack you, *Your Highness*," She said the word 'highness' with acid on her tongue. "I'm only checking your fever."

I nodded once, giving her permission, and she placed her cool hand gently on my head and mumbled, "Good, your fever must have broken during your sleep. Your skin feels normal. I'll get you some stew."

She spoke lightly, but it was clear from her shuffling about and tinted cheeks that my behavior had flustered her. She shifted away from the bed, rummaging around in the cabinets and withdrawing a small clay bowl. She blew the dust out of it and wiped it with her jade frock. It did not escape my notice that the color was an exact match to her startling eyes.

How does a village girl procure such a cloak?

When she turned her back to me, I saw her long hair concealing some jagged rips in the back of the material.

Oh, I guess it's not quite so extravagant. Although the vibrant color is rare for villagers.

Fine colored cloth such as this was expensive, and few humans could afford it. They tended to wear only subtly colored cloaks in varying shades of brown, black, and gray. I sat up in the bed, leaning against the wall while she ladled the stew into the bowl.

"Why are you here?" I demanded of her.

"Wow, you haven't even asked me my name yet!" She responded somewhat indignantly.

"That is because your name is irrelevant to me." She blanched as the words left my mouth, but I wouldn't take them back. It was true.

As soon as we got off this mountain, I would never see her again. She would go back to whatever village she hailed from, and I would return to receive whatever punishment my father would dole out to me for having the audacity to survive.

"You've spoken a total of perhaps five sentences to me, and I can already tell your life in the seat of luxury has helped you to master the art of condescension." The girl snapped back at me.

I almost laughed out loud at the words 'seat of luxury'. Yes, I lived in a palace, but this woman had no idea the horrors of my life. I could hardly expect her to, though. My father kept his treatment of me hushed—wouldn't want the entire kingdom to know he tormented his heir.

Didn't she see the scars?

The thought blackened my mood even more.

"Why are you here?" I asked it again, this time slower, as if she lacked intelligence. She stood near the fire holding my bowl of food in one hand, the other perched on her hip like a reprimanding mother.

"Saving your ass, I suppose." She sneered at me.

"My… ass…" I grimaced, "…does not need saving."

"The vines strangling you to death would have indicated otherwise." The smirk on her face grated on me as I snatched the bowl of savory stew she held out to me. The first bite scalded my tongue, and I flinched slightly, trying not to let her see.

I must be ravenous because this swill tastes delicious.

I began to shovel the food into my mouth, hardly pausing to savor it.

"Careful, Your Highness, or you'll be throwing it back up in a few moments."

I scowled at the interruption, but did as she suggested. She might be annoying and demanding, but she was correct.

"It's Remmy, by the way. The name you refused to ask. Remmy Alina Silva. I think if we are going to be… spending so much time together, you should at least call me by my name."

She clearly hadn't known how to say what she intended, believing my father would honor his word.

She thinks we will be spending forever together, as king and queen. What a lovely, naïve, ridiculous thought. I will not wed. And Father will never allow me to be king, whether I marry or not. He'd rather chop off his front paw, I'm sure.

I said nothing to the girl, and she huffed in frustration.

"We are going to be stuck here for at least another day, while you recover from your… ordeal," she hesitated, "so I am going to go gather more supplies."

Without waiting for me to reply, she stormed out the door of the tiny shack. A sigh of relief escaped me, and I sank back down into the mattress and closed my eyes. It smelled musty and old, but I didn't care.

I really am so tired.

* * *

Remmy

"What a dolt," I grumbled in irritation. "What a frustrating… pigheaded dolt."

I knew a noble was more than likely not going to be the most accommodating to a lower class, but regardless, I hiked all the way up this bloody demon mountain, freed him from the magical vines that were strangling the life from him, and cared for him throughout the night and morning.

The least he can do is ask my name.

I had decided this morning to try to be as amiable as possible to him, understanding that he had been through things I couldn't begin to fathom, but my patience was waning with his scowling and snapping. He had said my name was irrelevant, like I was some piece of refuse he planned to throw out with the garbage.

"What a dolt," I said again, as though that would ease some of my frustration.

I told him I was going to gather supplies merely as a means of getting away from him and out of that dingy shack. It was suffocating, and I craved the fresh air.

I spent most of the day outside when I was home in Merda. Here, the air was cool and crisp, buzzing with magic, the sweet scent of autumn floating on the chilly breeze.

I pulled my hood up over my head and decided to chop wood for the fire. Grabbing the rusted axe from the ground by the door, I set off down the trail in search of some better trees.

The chopping part was easy, but getting the wood back up to the cabin was a difficult venture. I had no wagon to carry it—I was using my cloak—so I was forced to make several arduous trips.

It was nearing dinner now, so I stacked the wood by the door and fought my way back into the overgrown garden. My stomach rumbled noisily as I gathered what herbs and vegetables I could find in the mass of tangled leaves and vines.

I'd give anything for some venison right now... or even fish.

I was grateful for this garden's existence, but I desperately desired some meat.

My thoughts drifted to Emerie and the twins as I plucked root vegetables from the earth.

I hope the food I stocked up on has not run out. I don't know what Emerie will do if it has.

I had tried to teach her how to tend the garden, but little had survived the blight, and I had never been able to teach her to hunt. If the meat I had managed to stock up ran out, they would be left with only whatever she could salvage from the blight.

Maybe one of the townspeople will help?

I snorted as soon as the thought entered my mind. Alice was the only one who had ever cared about us. No one else in that town had much to do with us. We were poverty-stricken, and my father was the town drunk. But maybe Alice would take them some bread if the food stock ran low. She had a kind heart, always giving us bread and pastries and taking care of the other destitute families in Merda. She had even taught Emerie to bake.

Though Emerie might not even mention it to her if the food was diminishing. I love my sister dearly, but she was a prideful girl. She never wanted the villagers to see our struggle. Our social status had always embarrassed her. Emerie wanted to make friends and to have a good standing with the townspeople. She never understood how hopeless that was. She remained blissfully optimistic after that Beck girl had befriended her.

Lunaire bless her. I hope she always stays innocent and kind.

I found Sterling asleep on his cot when I returned with the vegetables. Throwing them onto the counter I had fretfully cleaned this morning, I crept over to his side and reached for his forehead. Silver eyes popped open, and his hand shot out swift as an arrow, gripping my wrist tightly in a defensive maneuver.

Gods, why is he so stubborn when I am only trying to help him?! What does he think I am going to do?

This close to his face, I found myself staring into his bright Fae eyes.

I've never seen eyes so... breathtaking and... unique.

My brain fumbled, and I inhaled deeply, trying to regain my composure. My nostrils were permeated with the scent of *mahogany and mint and... something smoky?*

It was intoxicating. I jerked back quickly and yanked my wrist out of his grasp, my mind whirling with emotions I couldn't understand.

"I'm only monitoring your temperature… to ensure your fever has not come back," I murmured breathlessly.

His sharp eyes narrowed, but he said nothing.

Taking that as an invitation, I reached forward. This time, I hurriedly felt his forehead, then turned away.

"The good news is, Fae apparently heal much quicker than humans. Your fever has stayed away for several hours. So you should be able to travel soon."

Without giving him the opportunity to reply, I hurried to where I had dropped the vegetables and began to prepare the soup for the evening meal.

It certainly wasn't the most alluring food, but I had managed to find enough variety of herbs outside to make it taste slightly different from this morning's porridge.

We ate it in silence, Sterling brooding like a petulant child from his bed in the corner.

Finally, having had enough, I dropped my spoon into my bowl. It clattered loudly, disturbing the strained quiet.

"What is wrong with you? You obviously don't care much for me, and I'm not sure I understand why. Is it because I am just a *lowly village girl,* or is it merely your natural disposition to be broody and demanding?"

The prince let out a deep breath, his steely gaze washing over me.

"Remmy, is it?"

I nodded my head once in confirmation.

Surprised he even remembered my name. I figured his head was too filled with his dark, broody prince thoughts. I chuckled inwardly, not allowing my thoughts to show on my face.

"I'm sorry to inform you, but as soon as we are off this mountain, we will be going our separate ways. There is no need for me to get to know you, or converse with you, as we will not be getting married and living happily ever after, or whatever you thought was going to happen with this little trip."

My blood turned to ice, and my heart sank in my chest like weighted lead.

He can't be serious. No. No! I can't accept that. I won't accept that! He's just saying that because he's angry.

I knew he wouldn't want to marry me, but it was a royal decree!

I stared dumbly at him for a moment before responding. "What—what do you mean?"

"How much do you know about my father? The so-called King of Lions?" He continued, without allowing me time to answer. "Well, it doesn't matter. The harsh truth is that my father never intended to act upon his outlandish proclamation. And he never intended for you or any other woman to survive Mt. Malus. Frankly, I am not sure how you did it, but I applaud you. I know my father hired killers to murder every contestant who entered. I'm unsure how you survived; it's commendable. But anyway—do you see my point? My father never intended for anyone to win. He never intended for me to live. He sent me here to die, and as soon as he knows I've escaped, he will send the Blood Guard. And they will kill me. And they will kill you if you are with me. You need to go back to your village and return to your life as you knew it. There will be nothing for you in Lunestair."

I could barely concentrate—my thoughts spun wildly out of control.

I do not accept this. The king issued a proclamation to the entire country. Word of it even spread to Tangeer and Rothton. Maybe even Elysia. It has to be honored! Doesn't it? If he takes it back, he will appear weak to the rest of Amengor. I can't—I climbed—I—all the way up this mountain—I almost died a dozen times! No, I will make the king listen. I will—I will—make a scene—I'll get the entire court there and then he will have to listen. He'll have to honor his promise. Won't he? Sterling may hate me for it, but I can live with that.

Despondently, I sank onto the edge of the cot, and surprisingly enough, Sterling did not grunt at me or demand I move. He merely watched me through cold silver eyes.

"I can see this upsets you, and for that I am sorry."

"I—I—no—that—well, it can't be… it just can't… "

"I'm afraid it is."

Suddenly realizing I was sitting on his bed, I jumped up as though I were on hot coals and rushed from the cabin into the cold mountain air.

* * *

Sterling

The girl had taken the news more difficultly than I had anticipated. She had looked utterly devastated. I tried not to let it bother me, but to a small extent, it did. I wasn't completely heartless.

She needs to stop being so bloody naïve. What did she believe was going to happen? We were going to ride off into the sunset together? Even if I thought Father would honor his declaration, I do not want to marry her, and I would protest the matter before the entire court.

No matter how mesmerizingly green her blasted eyes were. I would not be forced to marry. Not after what happened before. There was nothing left for me, and I would submit myself to my father's wrath as soon as I returned to Lunestair.

The problem was Vincent. He would attempt to intervene.

Perhaps I can send the old man away somewhere? I can forge a need for some... supplies or something from... Castillo... or... or even from Eirikstad. That's it! I can demand he be an emissary for me to my Uncle in Rothton. I'll say something about the trade route agreements... blah blah blah... and how I must send someone to fill in at the council so that I may... arrange marriage preparations to... what's that girl's name? That will work. I have sent him before. He won't suspect, and having the marriage as an excuse will be perfectly viable.

I sighed audibly with relief about having a plan to keep Vincent safe. My manservant cares too much for me. He had always been more of a father to me than Cyrus ever had.

No one expects the king to not fulfill his word. No one but me, that is.

I shifted on the stale bed, groaning from the stiffness in my limbs. I needed to get up. I'd been lying in this blasted bed all day. I rose from the bed glacially, testing my strength, and moved slowly to the cabin door. I hesitated when I remembered Remmy.

Should I go out there? What if she's just sitting there... crying... or something?

Shrugging off the thoughts, I opened the door and stepped out into the early evening air. Remmy was nowhere in sight.

I had no interest in marrying her, but it was almost dark, and I didn't want to see her harmed. The setting sun streaked the horizon in pale violet and soft shades of gold. A flock of blackbirds dotted the sky as I glared toward the path down the mountain.

Where could she be? I know she is upset, but traipsing around on Mt. Malus after dark is plain idiocy.

Feeling the need to stretch my legs, I wandered over to a patch of bushes on the far side of the cabin, behind the overgrown garden.

I wonder what old crone my father evicted from this place to use it as my prison, I thought idly, while I surveyed the jungle of plants.

This must be where Remmy collected vegetables to make the soup.

Spotting something on the ground amidst the brush, I bent over to pick it up. It was a tarnished brass canteen. It looked like something was engraved on it. Using my hand, I rubbed the dirt away to read the words:

Malrick Cornwin

Isn't that the name of the old earth Fae that Father had arrested last year?

I looked around at the overgrown plants surrounding the cottage.

That would explain how the garden here remained fruitful in such a harsh climate.

He'd been given notice time and time again to move, as no residence was allowed on Mt. Malus, and refused.

Stowing the canteen in the pocket of my tunic, I returned to the front side of the cabin. Sitting down on the steps to wait, I kept my eyes trained on the trail. Silvery moonlight painted the dark mountainside in a swath of light as the last of the setting sun faded away. My anxiety rose at Remmy's continued absence.

What if she has injured herself or been attacked by something? Why do I care so much? She is just an impetuous, deluded woman on a quest for riches.

I scrubbed my hands down my face in frustration at my conflicting thoughts.

I let out a breath I hadn't realized I was holding as a silhouette emerged from the stunted dark trees. I stood as she approached.

"Where did you go? Don't you know how dangerous it is out there?"

Her eyes shuttered, and she eased herself down onto the step I had just been sitting on. "I realize far more than you know, Your Highness." The way she said my title was cold and reserved, not as she had been with me thus far.

"You seem different," I muttered the words beneath my breath as I collapsed onto the step beside her. It was loud enough for her to hear, though.

"Isn't that what you wanted? To alienate me? To drive me away so that I don't follow you to Lunestair? To scare me into not fighting for what I was promised? For what I am owed?"

"I don't care how you feel about me. Nor do I care what you think is owed to you. I only wish for you to be realistic about the situation we are in. Whatever you hoped to gain by completing this quest is not to be. My father will not keep his word, and I have no desire to be married to you. It is as simple as that."

She turned toward me, steel in her emerald eyes, the cool autumnal breeze whipping her dark chestnut hair over her left shoulder.

"You have no idea what I hoped to gain on this quest. You know nothing about me. I do not wish to marry you either. Goodnight, *Prince* Sterling." Her eyes flashed angrily as she rose and disappeared into the dank shack, leaving me alone with my thoughts.

If she doesn't want to marry me, then why is she here?

Sixteen

Fig Scones and Crushed Dreams

* * *

Emerie

"Eeemerieee!" My name echoed off the walls of our tiny cabin as my best friend let herself inside.

Inara's dark brown curls bounced as she bounded in and tossed her arms around me, pinning my flour-covered hands to my side.

Her eyes shone mischievously as she released me from her hold. "I brought something for you and the twins."

Inara had been my best friend since childhood. She had that kind of persona that lit up a room, vibrant and full of life. Her father was one of the few wealthy merchants in Merda and looked upon our friendship with hostility, but Inara would not be swayed. Mr. Beck resented the association of his only daughter with someone of such a low class.

Inara had seen me sitting alone in our first year of school and decided to befriend me.

We had been friends ever since. It didn't matter to her that I was not allowed at her home, or that I was poor, or that my father was the town drunk, and my mother had run off. She had wanted to be my friend, so we were friends. I loved her for it. She had been there for me when my mother left. She had been there for me when Father had lost his leg. And she was here for me now that Remmy was gone.

"Oh no, Inara, what have you done? You know how your father gets when you spend his money on me!" I exclaimed anxiously.

Once, Mr. Beck had made it a personal mission to disparage my father to the entire village when Inara had taken it upon herself to buy me a new baking stone.

Inara just shrugged her shoulders indifferently. "He will never even know."

She turned and disappeared out the door, reappearing a moment later with a brown sack in her hands. Her smile was all teeth as she shoved the bag at me.

I wiped my hands on my apron and took the bag from her, tentatively peering inside.

"Jam! You've brought me jam!" I squealed the words loud enough for my father to hear from his spot by the hearth. He twisted in his chair, eyes vacant.

Also inside the bag were three fig scones—sprinkled with almonds and drizzled with honey.

"Holy gods." The words were an awe-filled whisper. Sweets were rare in our home. Occasionally, I was able to make something for Yule Fest, depending on the produce available, but more often than not, we had nothing.

My head snapped up from the bag, and I scowled at Inara suspiciously. "Why did you bring us these now?"

She sighed and rolled her eyes. "Remmy's gone, Em. Who knows when, or if she'll even be back?" She hesitated when I shook my head vigorously. Her eyes filled with sadness, but she pressed on, uttering the truth I did not wish to hear. "I know the food is running low. You need help."

She was right, as I was currently using up the last of the wheat to make a loaf of bread when she arrived.

Still, I shook my head and insisted, "We are fine. Remmy will be home soon. You don't have to take care of us, and your father will be furious if he finds out you're spending his money on us. Here." I held out the bag to her. "Take this back before he hears of it, and we all pay the price."

Inara shook her head stubbornly at me. "I'll do no such—" Her words were cut off as Echo and Eridian came screeching into the house, asking about dinner while simultaneously demanding to know what was in the bag. Eridian charged me and snatched the bag from my hand with a bout of playful laughter.

"Eri!" I demanded, reaching for his arm. "Give me—" His squeals rent the air, as he saw what was inside the bag.

"A pastry! Echo, there's pastries in here!" He tried to snatch one, but I stopped him, pulling the bag neatly from his hands.

"Enough of that! You may only have a pastry once dinner is finished and you complete your chores."

I had been forced to resort to giving the children simple chores around the house and garden in order to keep up with everything. I had no idea how Remmy managed all of this, especially with a blight on most of our crops. "And thank Inara for bringing you such a delicacy."

"Thank you, Inara, for bringing us such a dec-al-cy." Echo botched the word, trying to mimic what I said, her blue eyes wide at the idea of the rare dessert.

Inara hid a laugh behind her hand and put an arm around my little sister. I stared pointedly at Eri, but he just stuck his tongue out at Inara and tried to dart into the bedroom. He was not quick enough, and I stopped him with a single, swift motion, tugging on his ear. He yowled dramatically as I firmly pulled him over to Inara, who was now barely containing her laughter.

"Say you're sorry and thank you for the pastry."

"Sorry. Thanks for the pastry." He muttered while rubbing at his ear, which was only slightly red.

"You're welcome, Eri." She ruffled his strawberry-blonde hair lightly. Eridian grunted and shot from the room at full speed.

"Eri, wait—" The front door slammed closed as he exited. I sighed heavily and closed my eyes, shaking my head at the boy's antics.

As soon as the door shut, Inara's velvety laughter rang out through the house.

"That child is something else, Em. I don't know how you do it." She laughed and pulled Echo closer to her in a hug. The girl was laughing now, too.

"Eri thinks Inara is soooo pretty," she said in a sing-song voice.

Inara laughed harder now, tears streaming down her face, her umber eyes dancing. "Sadly, my heart belongs to another."

I started at the words.

What does she mean, her heart belongs to another? She never mentioned—

"Who?" Echo squealed, waiting with bated breath for Inara to reveal her secret lover.

"Why... you, of course!" She stuck her fingers in Echo's side, tickling her relentlessly. I shook my head at the pair of them, thoughts churning in my mind.

She was joking, right? She doesn't have a suitor. Surely, she would have told me. Wouldn't she?

Inara was my only friend. If she married and could no longer visit... I let my thoughts trail off. Worrying about it would do no good. If Inara had something to tell me, she would tell me when the time was right.

Turning to me, she smiled jovially. "Now you must keep the scones and jam. You couldn't possibly give them back now that the children have seen them."

Echo's eyes widened and quickly began to well with tears. "We can't have our pastries?"

Glaring at Inara, I gently reassured the now weeping child that she could have her sweet after dinner. My friend shrugged her shoulders innocently at me behind Echo, an impish smile playing at her lips.

Her breathing restored, I sent Echo outside to do her chores with Eridian before dinner.

"I should go now, before Father figures out where I am and sends the entire household in search of me." Inara had a slew of servants who often kept tabs on her and reported her whereabouts to her overbearing father. Being the youngest, she was the only one still at home. Her two elder brothers had married and now resided in Lunestair. She never heard from them.

I wrapped my arms around my friend tightly, giving her a brief hug before she left, then leaned heavily against the counter, sighing with relief that the house was finally quiet.

I had less than an hour before the children finished their chores and would be back inside, clamoring for dinner. I admired Remmy more and more every day.

* * *

Teigan

I checked my appearance in the dull looking-glass of my room and nervously straightened my tan tunic.

I had purchased a new one from a vendor on Market Street with some of my earnings, so I would look my best for my appointment with the King's Court. I did not look like Fae nobility, but I supposed I looked passing enough for a human peasant.

The streets of Lunestair were already bustling with merchants and vendors, milling about selling their goods to anyone who would stop. The air smelled of succulent spices and baking bread.

As the day wore on, street performers and dancers would be added to the mix of people crowding the beautiful roadways of the bustling city. Lunestair was pure magic. That is, until the Blood Guard marched through, striking fear into the hearts of its denizens.

In my time here, I had taken note of the warrior's routines. They marched through the streets in formation once per day, at high noon, as a show of force, to remind the people of the totalitarian control of our king. They trained behind the castle gates with the dawn and rotated watches over the palace gates and the dungeon entrance.

Their presence hushed the streets until they finished their daily march and resumed their postings. Then life would carry on, the city buzzing as though it had never happened.

It was odd the first time I witnessed it, but I had been warned by Maggie, my second day here, to keep quiet during the march and to mind my business. The power show seemed ludicrous, but residents of Lunestair say it has been going on for one hundred and fifty years, since King Cyrus formed his Royal Guard, fifty years into his reign.

Passing by the valerian-lined garden in the center square, I approached the nearest guard at the castle gate.

I bowed respectfully and handed over my packet of papers. "I have an appointment to see the king today."

The guard scanned my papers, nodded, and then handed them back to me.

"Gunther!" He called to someone behind the gate while pushing a lever to raise the giant iron portcullis.

A Dwarf, dressed in the king's royal colors of sapphire and silver, emerged from a small door nearly hidden within the castle wall. "I need you to escort this young man to the throne room. He has an appointment with the king."

"Yes, sir." Gunther motioned for me to follow, and I hurried to catch up. The portcullis lowered behind me, clanging loudly.

He led me up the stairs lit with quilldust lanterns and across the great stone bridge. The waterfall below roared in my ears, and my steps were heavy and leaden. I was moments away from entering the Castle of Stars and facing the most brutal king in Valerian history since the time of the Vantan rule.

A bead of sweat trickled down my forehead, despite the cool autumn temperature.

Come on, Teigan! I scolded myself.

Pull yourself together. The king isn't going to give an audience to a blithering idiot with nervous sweating soaking his shirt.

I wiped the sweat apprehensively from my brow as the big oak doors swung open in front of me, revealing a long corridor lit by the same type of flameless lanterns that lined the outside of the castle.

From the arched ceilings hung iron candelabra, dimly lighting the gray stone walls around me. Our footsteps echoed off the cold flagstones. There was a frigid and ancient atmosphere in the castle. I shuddered as we walked down the faintly lit hall.

Did the Vanta rule from this castle, or did the Ericcsöns build it?

I had never paid much attention in school.

"This way," Gunther said as we rounded a corner. The walls here were lined with paintings of the royal family, spanning back centuries. I noticed all the paintings of the queen had been removed, and only one remained of the Crown Prince.

Every few paces, there were small silver tables, draped in blue velvet, sporting various plants and golden trinkets. I almost knocked a vase with gold filigree off one of the small tables, and Gunther glared at me in reprimand.

I hurried to move away from the hall tables, catching up to his short frame quickly. He stopped before two grandiose wooden doors and knocked twice before pushing them open. Before me sprawled a huge throne room crowded with Fae in both forms, humans, and Dwarves from all around Amengor.

I stood dazed by the spectacle. High cathedral windows, with stained glass depicting lions in various forms of battle, were on either side of a massive midnight blue velvet dais with silver embroidery.

Hanging above the throne was a shield, presumably made from tilian steel, with a great lion etched on the front and two steel swords crossing behind it.

Huge brown bears stood on either side of the dais, serving as royal guards. King Cyrus sat upon the throne, surveying the people, boredom on his cold face. A crown of silver inlaid with stones of sapphire sat regally upon his blond hair, icy blue eyes peering out from beneath it.

"Take a seat at the back here. When your name is called from the roster, approach the dais and wait for the king to allow you to speak." Gunther's voice startled me from my awed observations. He motioned to a place along the wall nearest us, where many other people sat in chairs, waiting for their turn to petition the king of

Valeria.

I swallowed nervously and nodded my thanks to the Dwarf. Something akin to pity flashed briefly across his face.

"Good luck."

He exited the throne room, the great oak doors closing behind him with a resounding thud.

I found an empty chair and took a seat beside a man with a long beard and a scar cutting across his face.

The throne room was clamorous with members of the royal court and nobility mingling, but no one in the chairs along the wall said a word as we waited anxiously for our turn to plead our cases.

I'd been observing for only a few moments when the sound of an oliphant horn rang out, and a man standing in front of the throne called the court to order. The members of the royal court and visitors filed out to both sides of the room, with a large split down the middle. A large man in regal armor, whom I assumed to be the Captain of the Guard, took up a place standing near the base of the dais.

The announcer with the horn called out the first name, and a man to the left of me slowly walked toward the newly created walkway and approached the throne. He bowed briefly before Cyrus motioned for him to rise and make his appeal.

The king heard each plea, showing no emotion, oftentimes cutting off the person's request before they could finish speaking.

Some left in tears, but Cyrus remained utterly unfazed.

Once again, I was not surprised that there was a budding revolution. This king had no concern for his citizens.

As I awaited my turn, my anxiety continued to heighten. I was almost nauseated by the time my name was called by the herald. I snapped out of my musings and approached the dais, weak-kneed and full of trepidation.

I bowed slowly before the king and waited for him to speak.

"What is it you approach my court for, Teigan Berger?" His voice rang out with authority into the stillness of the room.

Inhaling with a shaky breath, I spit out the words I had practiced in front of the looking-glass a thousand times. "I've come to request the release of my parents from the dungeon, Your Grace. I've brought the money for the debt they owed, as well as money for their freedom." I held up the large bag of coin I had been saving.

The king gazed at me curiously. "And who, pray tell, are your parents?"

Cyrus's voice held a note of something I couldn't place—irritation or annoyance, as though I were a bothersome fly near his dinner.

"Ronan and Freya Berger, Your Majesty."

The king motioned for the Captain of the Guard to approach and whispered something to him. They conferred for a moment before the king straightened and looked at me without a semblance of sympathy on his stony face. "Your parents were executed. You may go."

He waved his hand in dismissal as my world came crashing down, like meteors falling from an angry sky.

A cry of anguish left my throat as darkness swarmed my vision. I could no longer feel my feet, and spots of black dotted the room around me. I stood motionless, unable to move, unable to think.

No. They can't—I can't—It's not... It's not possible.

I fell to my knees in a heap, tears cascading down my face like rivers of sorrow. I barely heard the king's voice as he called for the guards to remove me.

I didn't fight when rough hands grasped my elbows and hauled me to my feet. I didn't respond as they dragged me from the hall and down the long corridors, back to the castle gate. I didn't even feel my feet moving forward, as I was pushed through the raised portcullis.

I heaved my breakfast onto the ground beside the palace walls, as deep, wrenching sobs wracked my body. I sank to the cold, hard earth, still clutching the bag of coins.

He murdered them. Cyrus murdered my parents.

Seventeen

Tonics and Vows

* * *

Remmy

Loud cries woke me from my slumber, and I rose quickly from my bed on the floor. The chill in the cabin caused my breath to catch; the fire in the hearth long extinguished.

Hurrying to Sterling's side, fearing the fever had come back, I found him thrashing and calling out in his sleep—his words unintelligible.

"Sterling!" I grasped his forearm and shook lightly, trying to wake him without startling him. He moaned and swatted at me, muttering something that resembled a name.

I ducked out of his way, narrowly avoiding getting hit by his wild motions. Sweat beaded on his brow, and his eyelids fluttered as though he were in some deep trance.

"Sterling!" This time, I said it louder, shaking him with more urgency, and his startling silver eyes flew open.

His gaze took me in for only a moment before his eyes shuttered, and his panicked gasping slowly evened out.

"What?" His voice was low and rough with sleep, causing my toes to curl unconsciously.

"You were yelling in your sleep and… and thrashing about. It… it must have been… a bad dream?" I asked a little hesitantly, pulling back from the bed now that he was awake.

He gave me one slow nod. "I'm fine, Remmy. Leave me."

I stared at him resolutely as he refused to meet my gaze. His shirt was soaked in sweat, and his dark hair clung to his head and the back of his neck.

"No. No, you're not. If you're not sleeping, then it won't be safe to travel. Your body will be too exhausted to heal, and you will fall ill again. I'll be right back."

"Wait! Where are you—" His words cut off as I stepped out into the cold evening air. I hadn't bothered with my cloak, and as the mountain wind blew across my bare skin, I quickly began to regret it.

The shimmering moonlight illuminated the darkened tree line as I searched for what I needed. The sound of the door creaking on its hinges brought my eyes back to the shack.

Sterling stepped outside, and the moon bathed his golden skin in a luminescent glow. Something I couldn't understand stirred in me at the sight of him standing there, under a sky full of stars, pale eyes scanning the area for me.

When they met mine, I found my voice. "Go back inside. I will be there in just a moment!"

Ignoring my instructions, he stood in the doorway, looking at me with thinly veiled concern.

After only a few days of eating my vegetable stews, his body was already starting to fill back out. As long as we survived the trek down the mountain, he would be looking healthy and nourished in no time. Even with his ribs protruding slightly and his face thinned, it was easy to see how muscular the prince was. It was obvious he spent a good deal of time training.

I wonder if he trains with the Blood Guard warriors?

"It's not safe out here at night. What are you doing?" He demanded, frustration lacing his deep voice.

I didn't respond, bending over to pluck several blossoms from the purple flower I had been looking for.

His Highness huffed impatiently from the doorframe as I worked, waiting for me to acknowledge his aggrievance.

The moon provided barely enough light for me to see what I needed as I located some cloves and chamomile. Unfortunately, there was nothing to mask the taste of the tonic I was going to make. Luckily, chamomile petals had a mild sweetness to them, so hopefully it wouldn't be too bitter.

It'll serve him right if it is, though.

"If you get yourself killed by an animal or beast out here, I won't have to worry about getting you back to your hometown." He smirked arrogantly.

I smiled sweetly at him, showing my teeth, as I pushed past him and headed to the counter, where I'd been keeping my bowl.

"What are you doing?" The prince growled at me, seemingly annoyed by my lack of response.

Sighing patiently, I dumped the ingredients onto the counter and used my dagger to chop them into small pieces.

Regrettably, I did not have a pestle, so this would have to do. "I am making you a sleeping tonic, Sterling. You need to rest, and this valerian root will help you sleep—dreamlessly."

The prince didn't respond; he just stood watching me.

Scooping the chopped ingredients into my bowl, I used the hilt of my dagger to mash them a bit more and poured some water from the pitcher on top of the mixture. I stirred it around, then handed the bowl to him.

"Drink," I ordered.

He eyed me warily as he took the bowl from my hands. Lifting it gingerly to his nose, he wrinkled it at the scent of the tonic.

"This smells like garbage." He grumbled pettishly.

I rolled my eyes at the petulant prince. "It won't taste good either. Drink it anyway."

He sneered at me and downed the pungent-smelling liquid in one large gulp, slamming the bowl down on the decrepit counter.

I started to head over to my pallet on the floor, but Sterling swept past me. "I'll take the floor. You should sleep in the bed."

Now he decides to be chivalrous?!

"But I—" I didn't manage to finish the sentence before he settled himself on my pallet, without even bothering to glance up at me. Pulling the blanket over his shoulder, he rolled to face away from me.

Shrugging in resignation, I climbed into the old bed and pulled the fur up over me. It smelled of the arrogant prince. Mahogany and mint. With a hint of something smoky.

Well, at least it's an improvement over how he smelled that first day.

I chuckled and then chided myself for my insensitivity. The way I had found him had been... unjust. Cruel.

* * *

Sterling

I couldn't stand seeing the pity in those jade green eyes of hers. The way she looked at me, like I was a broken thing that needed fixing. I didn't need her sympathy. I sighed.

I resented her for it. I resented her for the fact that she'd found me starved, beaten, and soaked in my own urine.

My face heated at the thought alone. It was mortifying.

Urine. I'd been soaked in urine.

I'd never been more humiliated. The vines had restrained me for days. So many, I had lost count of them. I rolled over on the pallet, shifting uncomfortably.

Yet here she was, taking care of me like a mother would a sick child, seemingly not at all repulsed by me.

And she'd seen the scars.

I'd snapped at her and pushed her away, and made her feel inferior, and what did she do?

She makes me a bloody sleeping potion. What is she playing at? Does she think this... this nurturing is going to change my mind? Ugh.

The embarrassment grated on me like a blade against stone. No one but Vincent had ever seen me this way. No one else had ever been allowed to. I'd even kept Soren away after my father's beatings, but I couldn't always hide them from him.

Thoughts slammed into me like a tidal wave. All of the times I'd taken a beating from my father or his men, and Vincent had stayed by my side, giving me healing potions and cursing my father for his brutality.

This was my father's favorite form of punishment, for whatever sin he contrived that I had committed. Imprisonment. Although this was the first time he had ever imprisoned me outside of the Castle of Stars.

Usually, it only lasted a few days. Just long enough to weaken me. Just long enough to let me know the power he wielded over me. Without a clan, I was practically defenseless against his massive lion. He could easily overpower me, and he had an army of guards at his disposal at any time. It was pointless to fight back, though I tried.

It had only resulted in the scars now painting my body. The only reason I had not taken off for Tangeer, or some world far from here, was because of Soren. If I disappeared, Cyrus would turn his ire on my younger brother, and I could not allow that. Soren's clan form was much weaker than Cyrus's.

Soren still had hope in his life. I would not let that be taken from him.

A memory played in my drugged mind. One of Soren and me as children.

We were chasing flame moths in the gardens in front of the castle. I had become so caught up in chasing one particularly bright moth that I hadn't noticed Soren was no longer with me. I began to call his name, searching around the fountains and in the aster bushes. When I found him, he was on the ground digging in the dirt manically. I had thought nothing of it at the time. He'd been only four years old, doing what four-year-olds do.

"What are you doing?" I had asked him.

He looked up at me with a strange glint in his eyes. "I found you something."

He stood up and shoved a small rock into my hand. It was abnormally cold for having been dug up from the earth.

"It will keep you safe." The words were so serious, and then he turned to chase a flame moth, like nothing had happened.

I remember nodding and shoving it into my pocket, appreciating that my little brother wanted to protect me. I'd carried it in the pocket of every outfit I wore for years. Somehow, I'd lost it when my father had forced me up this mountain.

Before I could fall much farther into the dark recesses of my mind, Remmy's sleeping tonic began to take effect on me, and I drifted off into a dreamless slumber.

* * *

Sterling

I woke up groggily at the first light of dawn, from the first full night of sleep I had gotten in years, and rubbed my dry eyes.

That potion the girl had given me allowed me to sleep the rest of the night through, without the constant nightmares that usually plagued my sleep.

The cabin was cold, since Remmy had not relit the fire last night when we woke, and my tongue stuck to the roof of my mouth from the dry autumn air.

I pulled my silver-trimmed black surcoat over my torn tunic and glanced around for Remmy.

She's probably collecting food or getting water or something.

I stood up cautiously, stretching out my legs that were stiff from disuse. I'd gotten no exercise in the days I'd been confined to this paltry shack.

I opened the front door, intending to go outside and freshen my mouth, but spotted Remmy plucking vegetables in the garden.

I wonder if there is any mint growing in there?

How she had gotten that garden under control so quickly, I couldn't fathom. The thing was a tangled mass of weeds and dying twigs when my father had sequestered me here.

She looked like a goddess of flora—serene, radiant, and at one with nature. She was truly exquisite. The girl evidently had an affinity for plants, but there was also magic in the mountain left over from the homeowner. Perhaps it helped accelerate the plant growth.

At the sound of the door, she glanced up from her gardening and smiled tentatively, giving me a small wave.

How can she smile at me after how I've treated her?

Was she really not as miserable as I?

"I am just getting the vegetables and herbs for breakfast, and then we will get ready to go." She called brightly.

Why did she have to be so... so... bloody happy?

Grunting, I nodded at her and rounded to the back of the expansive garden, searching unsuccessfully for mint. Not knowing what I was looking for, I found nothing. I was not very familiar with many plants.

I was not sure what Remmy had planned, but I doubted she was going to let this contest go without a fight. I was certain she would attempt to follow me back to Lunestair, and I could not... *would not* allow that to happen.

Giving up on my search, I reentered the tiny cabin, where Remmy was attempting to start a fire. She carefully placed the food into the large pot over the fire and poured a small amount of water over the top.

Turning to me, she questioned, "I am not sure what the topography is like on the Lunestair side of Mt. Malus, as I came up from Merda. Is there a water source close by where we can refill my canteen?"

"Yes. There's a large river that is roughly an hour from here, if I remember correctly. I haven't been there, but I've studied the maps of the entire country extensively."

I thought I saw her eyes roll, but curiosity laced her voice when she asked, "Do you enjoy cartography?"

I nod. "It's an interest of mine. It's also helpful to know your kingdom."

"Right. That makes sense. A prince who doesn't know his own lands would make a poor ruler indeed."

I did not correct her—did not tell her I would never rule Valeria. I just nodded and plopped into one of the shaky chairs to await breakfast.

"Are you quite sure you are well enough to travel today? The trek down the mountain will be treacherous."

"I appreciate your concern, but I assure you, I am in good health," I respond stiffly, bristling slightly at the insinuation in her words.

The truth was, I was not certain I had regained my strength yet, but I did not want to be cooped up in this cabin any longer with her, and I was only delaying the inevitable the longer we stayed here.

She asked me no more questions after that, hovering by the warm hearth, stirring her pot of stew.

* * *

Teigan

A soft rap sounded on the door, and I debated not answering. My face was wet with tears, and I had no desire to ever leave this bed again.

Realizing that Maggie or Deidre might need me, I rose, the bed creaking beneath me, and cracked the door.

Deidre stood there, holding a plate of steaming roasted meat with herbed carrots and potatoes. The tantalizing scent filled my nose, and my stomach rumbled loudly. I had not eaten or left my room since returning yesterday.

Maggie had been kind enough to leave me to my grief, but I suppose they had determined I wouldn't eat if they didn't feed me. They were correct. Maggie was a bit gruff around the edges, but she had taken to mothering me the same way she did Deidre—like a hen with her chicks.

Deidre's brown eyes bore into my tear-filled ones.

"May I come in?" she implored, her voice trembling slightly.

Over the last two weeks, Deirdre and I had started to form a sort of friendship of circumstance, working together and running errands throughout the city for Maggie.

Two days ago, we had celebrated her fifteenth birthday, and Maggie had bought her a ginger honey cake from the baker on Market Street, who always has fresh bread available.

We had not spent much time together outside of working, because I was usually staking out the castle dungeon and trying to mingle on the streets, listening for word of the brewing rebellion.

I knew she would ask about *them*, but I nodded solemnly and, swinging the door open wider, I motioned for her to enter.

She set the plate of food down on the small table and then proceeded to perch awkwardly on the edge of my bed, as though it would bite her if she sat all the way down.

I plopped on the bed beside her, waiting for her to ask the question I knew was coming—the one I wasn't ready to answer yet. But she said nothing. She merely sat there in silence, letting me speak when I needed to.

Unable to stand the quiet any longer, I blurted it out. "They're dead. My parents are dead. The king murdered them. They weren't even honored with the death rite in their execution."

This was the first time I had said the words out loud. Hearing them spoken shook me to my core, the grief exploding in my chest, taking my breath away. Tears welled in my eyes again, and Deidre placed her hand softly on my forearm.

"I know." She whispered, her voice low and soft. "I am so sorry."

"I want to kill him." Violence infused my words. "I want to kill him, like he killed my parents."

Deidre's eyes widened fearfully. "Teigan!" She hissed. "You can't say things like that. If someone were to hear you—"

"Let them hear!" I raged. "What can he do to me now, Deidre? I have no one left." My voice had lowered to a hoarse whisper. "I have no one left."

"You have me." She hurried on, her face flushing a soft pink. "And Maggie. We care about you, Teigan. I am sorry about your parents. I truly am. I know what it is like to lose your family. But we will be your family now, okay? Just… don't do anything drastic."

"Will their souls even pass to Lumess without the sacred rite being performed?"

"I think that the goddess probably sees a lot of unjust deaths. I don't believe she would turn a soul away that deserved to be there."

I nodded my head at her, grateful for this budding friendship, and assured her that I would do nothing dangerous, but my mind was filled with thoughts of the rebellion. With nothing now to hold me back, I vowed to get my revenge on the King of Lions. Tomorrow I would seek out the information I needed. I would join the rebellion.

Eighteen

The Water Is Delightful

* * *

Sterling

It was mid-morning by the time we left the tiny shack that had been my prison. Remmy hummed quietly to herself, the cheerful sound setting me on edge.

What is it with this woman? We are about to spend days hiking through the most dangerous terrain in all of Valeria, and here she is, singing a bloody tune. What in the worlds is there to be so happy about?

I would be impressed if I weren't annoyed. Why did it grate on my nerves so badly, anyway? Remmy was not a wealthy villager; she had traversed an incredibly treacherous mountain only to find out it was for naught, and she had faced demons and been left with the scars to prove it, but somehow, here she was, happily humming like all was right in Amengor.

I glowered at her, trying not to admire her, as we made our way down the path toward the river. As if sensing my look, she suddenly glanced over, catching me staring.

A pale pink flush started at her collarbone and graced its way up to her forehead. I smiled unintentionally.

"What? What is it?" She asked self-consciously, reaching up to tuck a loose strand of hair under her dark green cowl.

"Nothing—I—never-mind. We should be coming to the river before too long." I fumbled my words, searching for something to say and feeling flustered.

Her smile was coy, as though she knew I was scrambling to cover my thoughts.

Holy gods, Sterling. Get a hold of yourself, man.

Clearing my throat intentionally, I surged ahead of her, calling back that it was safer for me to lead. "After the river, the terrain will become more difficult. We will need to be fully prepared. I think we should break for a while at the river. Get some water and rest."

"That's fine. I'd enjoy washing up a bit."

My head swiveled back to her in alarm. "You're going to bathe?" I asked incredulously.

"No! Of course not. I just want to wash up with a cloth. And frankly, you should do the same, *Your Highness*. You stink." Remmy wrinkled her nose and smirked.

"I do not stink!" I replied indignantly, my face heating.

"Have you smelled yourself recently?"

"I—" Okay, I probably did stink, but I was not about to dignify her taunting with a response.

Snapping my mouth closed, I turned back to the trail, scouting for signs of the approaching river.

I heard Remmy let out a spirited laugh behind me; the sound of it was melodic and enchanting.

How does she do that?

I've never been more irritated by anyone in my life, but the sound of her laughter—it was like music.

Sighing, I pushed down my thoughts of annoyance and turned them back to the approaching river.

* * *

Remmy

I smiled at having flustered Sterling so. The prince had disquieted me often enough in our previous interactions. It was childish to be glad about that, but this man was driving me crazy.

Any time he has even spoken to me, it's been to act like he is better than me, or to attempt to educate me on something. I am beginning to lose my sympathy for him.

I chided myself for the heartless thought, but he was trying my patience. He was so hateful and snide to me, and any time he had done something kind, it seemed as though it was more out of duty than anything else.

For instance, his taking the bed last night. That had been peculiar and didn't fit with how he had been dismissing me the last few days.

The stiff blankets he'd slept in had smelled good, and yet, I had just told him that he reeked. I didn't understand why his essence was so strong to me. Any time he was near, the scent permeated my nostrils and clouded my thoughts.

Rushing water filled my ears, and excitement coursed through me at the idea of washing.

Sterling had been mortified when I mentioned it, assuming that I was going to strip down in front of him to bathe.

Is that really what he thinks of commoners? That we have no propriety at all? He must think we are all daft.

His deep voice pierced through the haze of my thoughts. "We've made it to the river! I am going ahead to fill my jug!"

What jug?

He hadn't had a jug when I arrived at the cabin. It must have been something he had found and brought with him. At least he had some preparedness, but I doubted he knew how to fish or hunt.

It didn't seem like nobles would need to learn those kinds of survival skills. I watched as Sterling's lithe body jaunted out of view and through the trees, picking up my pace to join him.

I cut through the stunted evergreens at the same place he did and made my way to the bank. He was leaning over the clear waters, filling some sort of cloudy canister. I kneeled beside him and filled my canteen to the brim, taking a swig and refilling it again. Turning back, I saw Sterling had planted himself on a large boulder on the shore. "What are we going to do for lunch?" He questioned.

Funny how he is such a grouch until he needs something from me.

“I will try to catch some fish after I clean up a little.” I tried to make my response sound as cheerful as possible, but I was still frustrated with his coldness and snide condescension toward me.

Approaching the stone he sat on, I dropped my pack to the earth and dug out my cloth strips.

“You know how to—Hey! What are you doing?!” The prince jumped up as I began to shrug my dress off over my head, stripping down to my shift.

“I am going to clean up a bit. Aren’t you coming, Your Highness?” I threw over my shoulder as I strutted to the water, clad only in my thin shift.

I picked some laour leaves from the bank before stopping when I got to the water, peering into the depths searching for black eyes and sharp teeth.

Sterling would save me. Wouldn’t he? Or maybe he wouldn’t. Maybe a Selkie drowning me would be the solution he needed to the problem that is me.

Grunting aloud, I stuck one foot into the water. It was bitterly cold. The time that had passed since I left Merda had brought autumn in full swing, and the mountain waters were bone-chilling.

Holding my breath, I walked into the water up to my knees and began to rub the cloth with the laour leaves.

On the shore, I could hear Sterling muttering to himself about modesty and decency and how this was just not proper. He had been mumbling something similar when I put him to bed after he collapsed in the cabin.

I chuckled at his ravings. Perhaps he was right about commoners. We lacked some propriety compared to nobility.

I am sure he would keel over if I stripped off my shift. But then, I might keel over as well.

Not a soul had ever seen me naked, and I was not about to let the first be this haughty prince. My body was too covered in scars now, anyway. I'm sure he would find me abhorrent. We had to marry, but that didn't mean we had to do anything else. I heard rustling and glanced up to see Sterling peeling off his surcoat, followed by his shirt.

I sucked in a too-loud gasp at the sight of his muscled chest, covered in scars. His head flew up at the sound, and I turned quickly away, hoping he had not seen me staring.

"The water is delightful. Are you coming in or not?" I threw the taunt at him casually, pretending I hadn't just marveled at the scars gracing his body. "You really should wash up."

The prince did not bother to answer; he just splashed into the water several paces from me, stopping suddenly with an exaggerated gasp. "I thought you said it was delightful?!"

I howled with laughter as Sterling's face became more and more red. His head whipped toward me in outrage. "This water is freezing!"

"Well, Your Highness, what did you expect? It is autumn in Valeria."

"But you said, for word, 'The water is delightful!'" He waved his hands about wildly, indicating the water we were currently standing in, his face flushed, whether from cold or vexation, I wasn't sure. I giggled at his exaggerated motions.

"Perhaps I find freezing water to be delightful. Like a nice cozy ice bath." I responded flippantly.

Sterling huffed indignantly and began splashing the freezing water on his skin, chill bumps forming on his hard chest.

I averted my eyes quickly, lest I be caught staring, and held out a laour leaf in his direction, refraining from making contact with his piercing, angry eyes. He snatched the leaf from my hands without so much as a thank you and began lathering it against his body.

I observed him for a moment discreetly, taking in the hard lines of his body and the scars marring his chest. He was truly striking. It had only been a few days since I had found him starved and injured in that cabin, but he was already starting to fill back out, and the muscles in his chest were once again becoming more defined. He had a very muscular physique and was incredibly handsome. It practically hurt to look at him.

How can such a prick be so... ugh!

I did not want to think about him in that way. Sterling was a brute, and no level of physical attraction would change that.

It's a good thing you don't need to like someone to be married to them.

And we would be married. Or I would die trying to fulfill my promise to Emerie.

I saw the water ripple out of the corner of my eye a few paces from the alluring prince, and swiveled my head in that direction, trying to see what had caused the disturbance.

"Ster—" I opened my mouth to issue a warning, but was cut off before I could finish.

The prince let out a startled yell as he was suddenly dragged into the river. The water was not deep enough where we stood to completely submerge him, and I watched in horror as he clawed at the riverbed frantically, before disappearing beneath the murky depths.

Nineteen

Embarrassing Rescue

* * *

Remmy

O*h! Oh gods, oh gods! What do I do? What do I do? Skotos, help me, please!*

Panicked, I fell to my knees in the frigid water, searching for a weapon of some kind on the riverbed. My hands came up with a large stone, and I crashed through the water in the direction I had watched Sterling disappear.

Lunaire, please let him still be alive.

Black eyes, pale gray skin, and razor-sharp teeth swam through my mind, and I almost froze, crippled by fear.

Move Remmy! Sterling will die!

I urged myself forward, but my near-drowning experience with the Selkie plagued my thoughts. I was not a good swimmer, but hopefully, Sterling would still be conscious and could get himself to the shore.

I don't know how I will swim with him if he isn't.

I whispered another prayer to the gods as I dove deeper into the cavernous water, searching desperately for any sign of the handsome prince.

* * *

Sterling

The glacial water engulfed me, causing my skin to tingle as I struggled and kicked against the demon holding my leg. My lungs burned with the clawing need for air.

Thanks to my father's varying punishments, I could hold my breath for a long while, but that did not mean it was pleasant.

I whirled my body around, struggling to see what was dragging me, and was met with the face of lore.

Black hair, gray skin, depthless onyx eyes. The creatures only inhabited the waters of the Therion Region. Selkies didn't exist in the Stardust District. I would not even know what it was if not for books or stories from travelers. My travels were strictly regulated to matters of court with neighboring countries. I'd spent no time unsupervised in this beast-filled region of my own country.

The creature pulled me downward, holding tightly to my leg. I tried in vain to maneuver my way to it, but the Selkie swam so fast that the momentum pulled my upper body away from it, making it impossible to reach.

Using my other leg, I kicked as hard as I could at the hand wrapped around my lower leg. The Selkie glared up at me, but did not release its grip or slow.

I decided to try another tactic and pulled my free leg as far as I could and then swung it straight into the side of the Selkie's head. I was not even sure how I had reached it, but the surprised creature released my leg and grasped its head angrily, as grayish sludge leaked from the gash my boot had caused.

Needing no further encouragement, I swam frantically for the surface but encountered a silhouetted shape swimming through the water. Thinking it was another Selkie, I started to lash out before realizing the shape belonged to a woman.

Remmy? She came after me?

Shaking off my surprise, I snagged her wrist and hauled her toward the sunlight. We surfaced, and I coughed violently as air filled my burning lungs.

"Come on! We need to get out of the water!" An edge of hysteria filled Remmy's voice as she urged me to continue. I followed behind her as she made a beeline for the shore, with uneven, weak strokes.

The moment we hauled ourselves up onto the hard ground, Remmy spurred into action, gathering sticks and wood to build a fire.

"Take off your pants." She ordered as she began to pull out the fur and her thin woolen blanket. I didn't move as I watched her begin to slip her shift over her head.

"Remmy, I'm flattered, but I don't know if you noticed... I almost died." I coughed and spat up more water.

She rolled her eyes. "Sterling, this isn't a joke!"

"Fine."

I knew why she told me to do it, but the idea was appalling. Crawling naked into the blankets beside her was not appealing, but as my limbs became heavy and lethargic, I knew I had no choice. Hypothermia would soon set in, and I'd rather share a blanket naked with this maddening woman than freeze to death.

The air was cold on Mt. Malus during autumn, but the water was frigid. These rivers froze several feet deep in the winter.

Sliding off my waterlogged pants, I stumbled to where Remmy was climbing beneath the fur, trying to keep my eyes off her body but unable to not notice the scars lining her back. They were the same as the ones I had seen before, lining her arms and face. Tiny and white—they painted her back like lines on a canvas.

I forced my eyes away from her silken skin before they had the chance to wander any farther, as she hurriedly covered herself with the blanket and turned away from me, facing the fire.

I fell onto the blanket beside her, resting on my back with my side against her. Her body trembled slightly at my touch, but she did not shy away; rather, she pushed lightly into me. I sucked in a ragged breath, my brain freezing at the contact.

Body heat, I reminded myself.

Sleep began to close in quickly as the shaking in my limbs subsided.

My mind reverted back to Remmy's scars. She was exasperating and annoying, but she was also good and kind.

She dove into freezing waters to try to save me from a monster.

I had no idea what had given her those scars, but something about them drew me to her, no matter how badly I resented it.

It felt… unfaithful to be drawn to anyone else in such a way.

* * *

Remmy

I listened as Sterling's erratic breathing leveled out and he slowly fell asleep, then I shifted closer to him. I was numb from cold, but I didn't want to move any closer while he was awake. The warmth radiating from his body was inviting.

This situation is embarrassing enough.

I had felt his eyes on me when I took off my shift. My face heated with the memory, but there was nothing else I could do.

The autumnal waters were too cold to be fully submerged for so long. We were both at risk, and Sterling began to show signs of hypothermia almost immediately. He was under for long enough that I don't know how he managed to hold his breath.

How did he escape? And did a Selkie take him or something else? I guess I'll ask when he wakes up. I assume he'll sleep through the night. It's already almost dinner time, anyway.

My stomach rumbled slightly, but I ignored it. I couldn't bear to leave the warmth, and Sterling still needed me. Food wasn't as important right now. I rolled over, facing him, and curled against the side of his body.

There was a light scent of mint mixed with smoke and wood, and I inhaled it deeply, sighing with relief that he was alive. Seeing him ripped beneath the water that way… it was something out of nightmares. An image that would be burned into my mind for eternity. The fear had almost paralyzed me. I had hardly believed it when I found him swimming away.

I wasn't sure why the thought of losing him had terrified me so.

If he hadn't saved himself...

I looked over as the colors of the sunset painted Sterling's face in golden hues, his chest rising and falling in time, and something I couldn't quite put my finger on bothered me about the situation.

How did he get away? Without a clan, it would be nearly impossible to overpower any of the creatures in the Therion Region, especially after being caught so unaware.

Twenty

The Drunken Dragon

* * *

Teigan

I followed the Dwarf down a dark alley through the seediest part of town. The westside was the underbelly of Lunestair. The place where you bought crathe, Vesper venom, weapons, and the place where the resistance met.

I had met Rufus shortly after learning of my parents' execution, and not so subtly inquired about the rebellion I'd heard rumors of. He'd let something slip after a night of too much ale, and I had been relentless in my pursuit of information. He had denied knowing anything about the resistance the first several times I inquired, but Dwarves love their ale, and after a few pints, he had finally admitted to knowing someone on the third night of questioning.

He was suspicious at first, but quickly learned I had nothing left to live for. The best fighters are the ones with a death wish, he had said.

Now, I trailed behind him through the crathe-infested, unsavory part of the city. The drug was an epidemic here, and I had never even seen it at all in Castillo. This was not the Lunestair I was used to.

Every black corner, every garbage-filled ditch, every dingy pub, was overrun with prostitutes or other low-born citizens under the influence of the dangerous drug.

"It kills the hunger," Rufus said. "The poor flock to it in droves to dull the starvation-inflicted stomach pains. You'll see it everywhere here."

I swallowed down the rising nausea as we approached a building with a lopsided wooden sign reading: The Drunken Dragon.

The pub was dimly lit and filled with smoke. The air reeked of urine and other unmentionable things. The perfect place for a rebellion to meet. No one would suspect.

Rufus took a seat at a corner table, and I gasped when I saw who was seated there. Surprise flickered across her face as well when she recognized me. She quickly stood and took my hand, urging me to sit.

"Teigan! When Rufus said we had a recruit… I had no idea! How are you? Is everything okay? Did you find your parents?" Xula held my hand tightly as we sat, while a man seated at the table looked on questioningly. I had not anticipated seeing her again. I couldn't believe she was part of the rebellion. The idea seemed odd, as the woman reminded me of my mother. Not in appearance, just her nature. I stared at her for a few moments before recovering my thoughts and speaking.

"Cyrus murdered my parents," I whispered, the words burning my tongue like acid. Her yellowish-green eyes filled with understanding and sorrow. She knew why I was here.

"I am sorry for the circumstances that brought you here, but I am glad you have found us. We will avenge your parents," Xula said gently, her hand still gripping mine tightly. "This is my husband, Ivor."

She turned to the dark man in the booth, her ash hair flipping slightly over her shoulder.

Ivor's skin crinkled at the eyes as he smiled politely. "I am sorry for your loss, Teigan. Most of us have lost someone to that flea-bitten lion. I am happy to meet you, though. I am not often able to meet the new recruits."

I started to ask why when Rufus began speaking, "Ivor is the leader of The Dragon's Fire, and our numbers are growing every day. He's usually too busy to come to these meetings." I stiffened at Rufus's words.

I'm meeting the rebel leader on my first day?! And he is Xula's husband...

"We appreciate you making it to this one, sir," Rufus continued. "I met Teigan at the Starlight Oasis a few nights ago. He was... very persistent, but the Magpie vouched for him." The Dwarf chuckled and thumped me on the shoulder.

Who the heck is the Magpie, and why did they vouch for me? I thought Rufus trusted me?

Xula released my hand and placed it over Ivor's. He turned his dark eyes to his wife as she spoke, the admiration there clear.

"The Dragon's Fire was formed over a year ago when the Blood Guard took Ivor's sister. She and her husband spoke out against the atrocities of the king, holding protests and trying to rally the citizens. First, they..." She cleared her throat, sadness reflecting on her face. "They took Ivanna; they did gods only know what to her, and then they took Boris."

Ivor's eyes darkened as Xula talked, a deep-seated rage lurking beneath the surface. "They dragged their bodies through the square, tied to the back of a prison cart, and labeled them as traitors. People spat and threw stones at them. They urinated on their corpses and dumped mead and ale on them." Tears trickled from beneath her light eyes at the still-fresh memory. "That was the day The Dragon's Fire was born. We were forged from the ashes of the original rebellion."

My brows raised as she spoke.

"My grandfather fought in the Battle of Five Hundred Years, and the Dragon's Fire you see today is a remnant of those old ideas and values that led the Fae to rise against the Vanta. Our numbers have grown exponentially since our formation, but there have been no more rallies or protests."

Rufus spoke up. "My mother married a royal guard. My father died when I was a young boy, and Mother fell in love again about five years ago. The man, Horis, was a sphinx shifter who helped Mother after her horse's shoe broke. A fellow Blood Guard reported their relationship, and they came in the night and slaughtered them in their home. I found them in the morn, when I brought my children to visit their grandparents. There's no law against interracial marriages, but Horis, he was Blood Guard… and my mother, a Dwarf."

"As you see, Teigan, we all have a great loss, fueling our desires for revenge. Tell me a little more about yourself. What skills do you have to offer the Fire?" Ivor's voice was soft, but filled with authority.

The man was intimidating in a way only someone born to lead could be. I gulped nervously as I answered. "Well, I am… I'm good at… stealing." I whispered the word conspiratorially and rushed on. "I'm also a fast learner. I don't have any training, but I am good with a knife, and I know I could learn to use a sword pretty easily. And, uuumm—my father was a fisherman and he taught me everything he knew. I work in a pub, so I overhear things, and I am good at convincing people to talk to me." I finished lamely.

My resume sounds pathetic. Why would they want me? It's just a bunch of random, useless skills that aren't even related.

"The truth is, sir, I've got nothing left to live for. Revenge… it's all I have. My best friend was killed in the king's idiotic quest to save the Crown Prince, and my parents were executed by him. They were everything to me." My shoulders slumped as a weight lifted with the admission. It was the truth. Everyone I loved was dead, and I had no idea if Remmy was ever coming back.

She's probably dead too, her body being eaten by crows and monsters on Mt. Malus. Lunaire's hair, Teigan! Stop being morbid!

"Well, that's certainly an interesting skill set you have. When you say you are good at stealing… what do you mean by that?" Ivor pressed.

It occurred to me that I still had the money I had acquired to barter my parents' release. Perhaps it can be of use to the Dragon's Fire. I glanced at Xula, who had stayed silent for the last few moments. Her friendly smile encouraged me to go on.

"When my parents were taken, I needed a quick way to make enough money to pay off their debt and secure their release. I became quite good at… acquiring it from wealthy tourists in Castillo."

"So you're good at stealing money. What about things? Have you ever tried to steal something bigger than coin?"

"No, but I imagine it would be much the same. I think I could pull it off just as easily. What things were you thinking of specifically?"

"Weapons to start, but a skill like that could come in handy for many reasons."

He turned to Rufus. "Add Teigan to the training roster for the new recruits so he can get some experience sword fighting. Make sure he is in hand-to-hand combat as well."

Ivor looked back at me. "We train with the dawn. Rufus will get you all the information. Welcome to the rebellion, Teigan."

Twenty-One

Screaming Squalls

* * *

Sterling

Remmy stirred against me, her soft body pressing into mine, as rays of sunlight shot across the morning sky. I feared moving would wake her, so I had stayed rooted to my spot beneath the thick fur. Being this close to her raised emotions in me that I had longed to forget for years.

Ever since that fateful day.

Isolde.

My chest constricted at the mere memory of her name—I tried not to think it often, for the pain still felt fresh.

Just then, Remmy's big green eyes popped open, and she stared at me in abject horror.

"Oh! Oh, gods!" She exclaimed. "Shut your eyes! I need to find my dress." I did as she bade. The cold bit against my skin as she shifted quickly away and rolled out of the blankets. Footsteps—as she scrambled, and then a relieved sigh.

"Can I open my eyes now?" I growled, though I didn't know why I was so irritated. Something about the girl rumpled me. She'd looked like an angel while she was sleeping, but the moment she was awake, the resentment festered. It wasn't her fault, but I couldn't help my reaction.

Remmy mumbled her agreement, and I crawled out from under the blankets, the frigid air whipping at my naked body. Autumn on Mt. Malus was nearly as cold as winter in Lunestair. The city was known for its mild climate, while Mt. Malus and the Highland Mountains were known for harsh winters. The wind cut at my skin, chilling me to the bone, while I hurried to gather my clothes from where they had been scattered about.

I don't even have a cloak. This surcoat isn't made for these temperatures.

I glanced up to where Remmy was lighting the fire, her green cloak already pulled up over her head.

At least she has a cloak.

The thought was slightly bitter as I pulled on my surcoat, teeth chattering.

"It's not much, but I have my old cloak in my pack if you want to borrow it. It's torn, but it would provide a little warmth until we get farther down the mountain."

I knew she intended to be kind, but her words grated on me. I didn't need her help, and I didn't like that she had noticed I was cold.

"I'm fine." I snapped. "What are we having for breakfast?"

Remmy exhaled heavily before answering. "I brought some apples and cherries from the cabin."

"That's it? Apples and cherries?"

We might starve to death before we make it to the warmer climate.

"Yes, *Your Highness,* that is it. If we eat anything else, we won't have food for the rest of the day." She responded airily.

She always used my title as though it were a derogatory term.

Your Highness. She practically sneers it.

I couldn't figure her out. Sometimes she was diving into half-frozen waters, intent on saving my life, and other times she acted as though *I* were beneath *her* for being royalty. I put my hand to my head and dragged it over my eyes, frustration seeping from every pore. She had been awake for merely ten minutes, and I already had a headache.

Her voice softened a little as she added, "Why don't you sit by the fire for a few minutes while I get breakfast out? It's cold and you have no cloak."

There she goes again, acting like she doesn't despise me as much as I do her. This is going to be a long trip.

Saying nothing, I sat on the cold ground beside the fire and held my hands in front of it in an attempt to warm the chill from my bones, listening to Remmy rummage around behind me.

This girl is going to be the death of me. One minute she is cold and sharp, the next she's sweet as a scone.

I huffed in irritation.

Why can't I get her out of my head?

I hated myself for it.

* * *

Remmy

The Prince of Valeria was driving me insane. I had barely opened my eyes when he started snapping and snarling. He smelled so good and felt so warm when I woke that I had almost forgotten who he was.

In a mental haze, I'd envisioned myself waking with a lover. Someone who adored me and gave me forehead kisses. But that was not to be. Sterling could hardly bring himself to travel with a commoner such as myself, and I knew the idea of being rescued by me infuriated him.

How dare I save his life?

I wasn't sure if it was because I was a woman, a peasant, or because I was human. Regardless, he hated me. And he refused to marry me. It didn't matter, though, because he would marry me. The king had made the decree, and no matter what Sterling said, I would do whatever it took to enforce it.

Surely, before the entire court and representatives from our neighbors, the Valerian king won't go back on his word? A man who can't fulfill his promises will appear weak. That will tarnish his reputation with Tangeer and Rothton, and the yearly trade council is coming up. Relations with Tangeer are shaky as it is, especially after the last war.

As far as I knew, we no longer had any alliances with Elysia. Father said we used to, but the country suddenly cut ties with Valeria and disappeared into the mountains when I was a young child. They refused to send an emissary to the council for the trade meetings, and Valerians were turned away at the border. We were not welcome in the northern mountainous country.

I munched on fruit as we walked, the path beginning to narrow as it had on the other side of Mt. Malus. I had no map of this side of the mountain, and I was uncertain what we would face. Sterling was more familiar with this route than I, so I allowed him to lead the way, and he seemed more than happy to do so.

My curiosity had piqued when he said he was interested in cartography. It was the first real thing he had shared about himself, and I found it fascinating, but he shut down, refusing to talk more about it. I'd always loved to study my father's old maps, but they were outdated and not very detailed. There had been no maps at all of what lay beyond Amengor—if anything—and no detailed maps of our neighbors. I would have loved to chat with him about cartography, but he was too reserved and bitter. He only spoke to me when he needed to.

Although this morning, when I had woken, snuggled against him and undressed, his silver eyes had looked softly at me for a moment. A shield had gone up as soon as I had spoken, though, effectively shutting me out again.

I didn't understand what it was about him. Despite his rudeness and seeming haughtiness, something warm lurked beneath that cold exterior. Something I wanted to know.

Someone I wanted to know.

I'll get him to open up to me. This is going to be a long journey, so we may as well talk to one another.

I studied his back as he walked ahead of me. Lean muscles rippled beneath his tattered tunic.

What must he look like dressed in his finery?

That would be a sight to see, as handsome as this man was. There were decent-looking men in Merda, but none such as he. He was stunning.

Can a man be stunning? Is that weird? I feel like that is a weird thing to think.

Occasionally, when I looked at him, I would forget what I had been trying to say, and my mouth would just hang open like an imbecile.

But then he opens his mouth, and I don't feel so bad for staring. I don't understand why he hates me so. Other than embarrassment. I can't imagine what it's like to be a prince who has to be rescued by a poor, common woman. But it seems as though it is more than that. Maybe if I ask him about the path... he will talk to me? Ugh, why do I want him to talk to me, anyway?

Still, I opened my mouth, and the words came falling out. "Sterling? Since I have no map of this side, can you tell me what the terrain is like?"

The trail was so narrow now that we were forced to walk single file, so he raised his voice to call back to me in response.

"This side of Mt. Malus is not what you are used to coming up from the villages. The terrain is more rugged, and the mountain is more of a cliff-face once we leave the peak. It will be steep and treacherous like this for quite some time, with few water sources until we get a little over halfway down."

"What is halfway down?"

Sterling stopped walking and turned back to face me, blocking the path so I couldn't continue forward. His face was tight as he wrestled with whatever he was trying to say. I searched his face as he opened his mouth, then stopped with a frown.

"What?" I asked cautiously. "What is it?"

He reached forward like he was going to touch me, then withdrew his hand as he struggled to find the words. My trepidation was mounting as I waited for him to answer.

Finally, he did. "The Temple of Deliritas."

Well, that sounds ominous, but not what I was expecting him to say.

Maybe a magical lake we could bathe in or something.

"I have never heard of that temple."

"You wouldn't have. My father keeps it a secret. No one in the kingdom knows it's here, except my family and the priestesses stationed there."

"But why? Why so secretive? And who is it a temple to?"

Sterling let out a deep sigh, something unreadable reflecting in his moonlight eyes. "It's a temple to Skotos, the god of The Netherworld. There are a lot of secrets in this country, Remmy. Most of them come from the Ericcsön family. The things that happen there… it's a dangerous place—that's all. We will be required to spend a night in the temple on our way down, and when we do, my father will know we have survived—if he doesn't already. Be cautious of the priestesses and do not tell them anything about your family, okay? Or anything that they could use against you. Promise me!" He reached forward urgently and placed a hand on both of my shoulders. "Promise me."

"But—I don't understand! What goes on there? Why do we have to stay the night?" The gravity in his voice shook me.

What is he talking about? There are temples to Skotos everywhere.

"I cannot tell you what goes on there. Just that you must be wary and on your guard at all times. Like the Cave of Beithir, no one is permitted to pass down or up the mountain until spending an evening in the temple. It is decreed by Skotos himself."

If no one may pass without staying in the temple, and no one outside the royal family knows of the temple... that must mean—I swallowed in realization. No one survives the temple.

The prince dropped his hands to his side and looked off into the dark gathering clouds, lost deep in his thoughts.

"Okay," I whispered.

I was expecting him to tell me about some large caves, or forests, or something. Not a creepy temple to the god of the dead where bad things happen. Things that he can't tell me. Why can't he tell me? Does he even know? I wanted to get him talking, and this is what he tells me.

After a few moments, he spoke again, the urgency in his voice replaced with something else.

Yearning maybe?

"It looks as though it may storm. Perhaps we can fill our canteens with rainwater. The storms up here can get out of control, though. We need to try to find shelter." He glanced around the narrow path.

On one side, the mountain rose steeply above us, and on the other, it dropped off sharply over the cliff.

He looked back at me and pursed his lips in thought. "Let's go ahead and continue for a little while and see if we can find a cave or something to ride out the storm in." I nodded my assent and followed behind him, thoughtful.

Something had changed in him at the mention of the Temple of Deliritas. His mood had shifted.

Was it sadness? The look in his eyes... he seemed... heartbroken... and terrified. What waits for us at this temple?

The shift in him frightened me. He'd been cold, hard, haughty, or condescending ever since we met. But never sincere. Never afraid.

* * *

Sterling

I'd refused to think about the temple since we left the hovel at the top of the mountain. I hadn't wanted to relive the memories. I could still hear the screams in my mind. The gut-wrenching sobs coming from my own throat. Still feel Soren and Vincent holding me back.

I shook my head, trying to clear away the thoughts, and surveyed the path ahead of us, searching for somewhere to take refuge from the impending storm and finding nothing. I could only pray to the gods that it didn't blow us over the cliff before I found something. The storms on Mt. Malus were not to be taken lightly.

The sky around us grew dark, appearing as dusk, but it was barely noon. Visibility reduced greatly, and the path became even more treacherous by the time the rain started.

I motioned for Remmy to get in front of me. I would not be able to protect her otherwise. The path was growing narrower, and she pressed against me to get past. Her foot slipped on a wet rock, and she cried out, throwing her hands to the side in an attempt to balance herself. I reached for her elbow just as she started to fall.

Yanking her back, I yelled above the din of the squall, "Stay close! The storm will only grow worse."

The woman nodded, her dark hair already drenched and sticking to her forehead in little ringlets. A measure of fear was reflected on her face, but her gemstone eyes were resolute.

They probably do not have storms like this in the villages.

The climate was not the same off the mountain.

"What are we going to do?! Surely, we can't continue in this?" She shouted above the roar, her hand latched onto my forearm. It tugged at me, seeing this woman, who had been nothing but strong and relentless, now quaking with fear. I wanted to protect her for some unknown reason, and I hated that. I hated how it made me feel as though I was betraying *her* to have any positive thoughts toward Remmy. I hated that I wanted to despise Remmy, but admired her instead.

Why? Why can't I despise her? She pushes me to the brink of utter insanity.

I took her hand from my forearm and used it to spin her around again, placing my hands on her waist and prodding her forward. I leaned over her shoulder, speaking directly into her ear.

"We have to keep going! There's no place to take shelter. This tempest is sure to build, and it will blow us straight off the mountain! Go slow. I'm right behind you."

* * *

Remmy

One wrong move and I'm... I glanced at the edge of the looming cliffside, not letting myself complete the thought.

I was not frightened of heights, but I had never seen a storm like this. The rain was torrential; the wind roared so loudly it sounded as though a great beast were hunting us. It beat down upon our bodies almost painfully, as we slowly made our way down the trail that I could now barely see.

Sterling kept one hand on my waist, steadying me as we trudged forward. The feel of his hand on my body muddled my mind. Something in him had changed when he mentioned the temple. It was *almost* like he no longer hated me. I wanted to ask him more about the Temple of Deliritas, but the tempest had cut off all non-essential communication. Our only goal now was to survive.

I had encountered no storms like this on the way up, but the climate and terrain changed on this side of the mountain. Magic still hung heavy in the air like a sinister curtain, but the weather seemed to match it now.

The rock rose beside us on the left, and I tried to keep my eyes peeled, looking for a cave or a large cutout in the stone that we could take shelter in.

Nothing.

The hands at my waist receded, and I turned back to see Sterling stumbling, his ankle twisting on a protruding root, unseen, no doubt due to the raging storm around us. He started to go down, but flung his hand out, clawing at the rock wall to keep from slipping over the side. He went down hard on his knee, but kept steady.

I moved to help him, but he held up a hand and shook his head, shouting above the din. "Don't! I'm fine."

I watched anxiously as he pulled himself up and made his way back to me.

"Are you okay?"

"I'm fine." He repeated. "Keep moving!"

He was limping. He'd likely injured his knee when he fell on it, but was stubbornly determined to keep going.

"Your knee!" I yelled, pointing at the offending limb.

He shook his head. "We can't stop!"

There wasn't anywhere to stop, anyway.

I turned and resumed the slow progress down the treacherous trail. The path was all rocks and roots now, with hardly any place to put our feet.

Every wind gust threatened to send us careening over the side of the cliff to our deaths, and my skin was beginning to ache from the pelting buckets of rain assaulting us. My teeth chattered from the cold, so I knew Sterling was more than likely frozen to the bone. The temperature was low to start with, and now we were soaked through.

I wish he had taken my cloak. Why does he have to be so stubborn? Well... now that I think about it, maybe it's good he didn't. Maybe it will stay dry inside my pack.

My pack was the only expensive thing I owned, besides the cloak that Rogard had given me, which now had slashes in it due to the Lycan attack. It was made of bearskin and burlap and worked well to keep the water out.

Although this heavy rain will certainly test its waterproofing abilities.

My father had given it to me as a gift years ago. Long before Mother had left and he had lost his job. I'd never been as grateful for it as I was now. I prayed to whatever gods were listening that it was keeping our blankets and supplies dry. The rain was stinging now. Every drop burned as though I were being stung by a bee.

What is going on?

I turned back to Sterling. "Why does the rain hurt?!"

"It's frozen! The rain is frozen…" He trailed off, and I knew why. This was becoming more dangerous by the moment. Ice was falling from the sky; we were drenched, and there was nowhere to stop. He looked at me, and I could see it there on his face. His lips were drawn into a thin line; his jaw clenched.

We were not going to make it down this mountain alive. It would take an act of Lunaire to stop this weather, and that was our only hope for survival. I swallowed down the rising bile in my throat and tried to turn around.

I was so cold now that I couldn't feel my extremities, and each movement felt wooden, my body numb.

The wind galed fiercely causing me to stumble. I tried to right myself, but my boot caught on something in the path and I lost my footing.

Sterling reached for me, but it was too late.

"No!" He shouted, but suddenly I was flying. The wind carried me straight over the side, a scream ripping from my lungs, as I was suddenly plummeting thousands of feet to my death. The last thing I saw was Sterling's panicked face as I hurtled over.

The sound of a roar unlike anything I've ever heard rent the sky, as my eyes closed and I knew nothing, blackness swallowing me whole.

Twenty-Two

How Long Have I Been Dead?

* * *

Remmy

Something warm moved against me. A fire crackled somewhere in the near distance. A smoky scent permeated my nostrils. Surely the Netherworld is not this warm and cozy.

Am I in Lumess?

I inhaled deeply before trying to pry my eyes open. They adjusted very slowly as the world came into focus, through a dim fire-lit glow.

The source of the warmth against me appeared to be a muscular body turned away from me, black tattoos winding up his back in swirling motions. Stars and moons weaved between worlds and clouds in a mural of the heavens. It was the most beautiful painting

I had ever seen on skin.

Who is he?!

My senses suddenly recovered, I jerked back, pushing against the man's back with both hands. I stumbled from the makeshift bed, holding the blanket to shield myself.

"Who are you?!" I screeched at the stranger, scanning around frantically for my sword or dagger—anything I could use to defend myself.

Sterling rolled over quickly and sat up, holding his hands out in surrender.

"Sterling?!" I gasped. "When did you get tattoos? You don't have tattoos! How long have I been dead?! Holy gods! What happened to me? Where are we?" I practically screamed the questions at him rapid-fire, panic clawing its way into my warped thoughts.

Sterling does not have tattoos. I have seen his back. He does not have tattoos. I am dead! I'm... supposed to be... dead. I fell over the cliff. The wind... it blew... I tripped..! Lunaire's hair! Did he die too? Did we die together? What in the Netherworld is happening?

Sterling rose from the floor and approached me, his hands still outstretched cautiously. "Remmy, it's okay."

And then his arms were around me. I hadn't even realized I was crying until I buried my face in his chest, my hysterical breathing dying down into low sobs. He held me tightly, saying nothing, while his fingers traced soothing circles on my lower back.

It was ironic, this man who'd been so cold, being the one to comfort me in a time of such unexplained shock.

"What happened?" Finally starting to calm, I leaned against his chest, having no desire to move away from the solace of him.

"You were in shock and on the verge of hypothermia. I found this cave shortly after and..." He shrugged and pulled away, peering down at me, arms still pressed against my back.

His eyes were different. Still silver, yes, but a brighter, piercing silver. Like tilian steel.

How is he so different? How long have I been out?

Only then did I become aware that we were both unclothed. Again.

Wow, this hypothermia, naked cuddling thing is turning into a habit for us.

I cleared my throat awkwardly, and he released me, handing me the blanket I had dropped in my hysteria. I wrapped it around myself quickly, trying not to look as he resumed his place within the fur.

I can't have been unconscious too long if we are both just waking from the 'hypothermia cuddle'.

"Why am I not dead, Sterling?"

His lips tightened and pursed to the side. He ran a hand over his eyes—something I noticed he did when he was frustrated—and released a weighted sigh.

"I'm not entirely sure what happened. All I know is I saw you go over, and I reached for your hand and pulled you up. You must have blacked out. Your clothes, sword, and pack are over there." He gestured to the fire that was lighting the cave we were in. "But your dagger slipped from its sheath when you went over. Sorry."

Unconsciously, I reached for where my dagger should have been, and my shoulders sagged when I realized he was right. My sheath contained nothing. At least my sword and pack survived. But I still didn't understand how he had caught my hand. He had been too far away when I went over.

"I don't—"

"Remmy, I—"

"Go ahead," I said, motioning for him to speak first.

"Nothing. I just—well—" He sighed. "I'm glad you're okay." He finished lamely, with another heavy sigh.

"Thank you. For saving me."

The prince smiled a bit sadly and nodded his head.

How is it possible that he has gotten more handsome in such a short time?

"I heard a noise… when I went over? It sounded like a giant ogre or something… roaring..? Did you hear it?"

Something dark flashed across his face, but he merely shrugged. "It was probably just the storm. Get dressed. We may be stranded here for a while."

"What? Why?"

"The storms can last for days up here."

Oh no. We don't have enough food or water to last for days.

I grabbed my dress from where Sterling had placed it near the fire, blushing at the thought of him undressing me.

Did he look?

I glanced over to where he lay.

Can I trust him to be honorable?

Disappointment filled me when I realized my dress was still slightly wet. The dampness in the cave would make it difficult for things to dry. I reached for my shift, knowing the thin cotton would likely dry faster. I was relieved to find it completely dry.

I slipped it over my head and reached for the prince's clothes. They were still damp as well, and a button was missing from his trousers.

"Your clothes are still wet." I turned back to him, dressed only in my thin shift. At least it wasn't too sheer. "What happened to the button? It wasn't missing before, was it?"

"Uhhh—it probably popped off when I stripped." A mischievous smile lit up his face as he reclined back in the fur, crossing his arms behind his head and staring up at the ceiling of the cave. "I have no problem being naked. You're the one who is awkward about it."

I laughed outright, the sound bouncing off the walls and echoing back, causing Sterling's smile to widen even more.

Have I ever seen him smile before?

My heart fluttered at the sight.

What is happening to me? And who is this? Sterling does not make jokes. NOR lounge naked.

"And you said I lack propriety?" I huffed with mock indignation, but smiled as I sat down across from him on the cold stone floor.

"We are stuck in a cave, Rem. During one of Mt. Malus's famous storms. What difference does propriety make? We could be in here for a week."

Rem. He gave me a nickname?

He was so different. He seemed happy, almost. I realized with a start that I loved hearing my name from his lips. I wanted to listen to it over and over until I was drunk on the sound of it rolling off his tongue.

My breath caught, and my pulse began to race; for a brief moment, I wondered if his lips tasted as good as they looked.

Oh, gods! What am I thinking? He saved me as any good person would do. Just because he doesn't hate me anymore doesn't mean he likes me. I mean, I don't even like him! Do I? Oh, gods. Do I?! He is handsome. He's sooo handsome... and those muscles... Skotos! Stop it, Remmy! This is ridiculous. You're acting like a schoolgirl.

"Are you all right? You seem nervous?"

"What? I—no—nothing. I'm fine!" The words came out squeakily as my voice rose higher.

How did he know that?

I rose quickly and started to sort through the supplies in my pack, ignoring the flush creeping up my neck and the sound of the beautiful prince chuckling behind me.

Where are these thoughts coming from?

We didn't even like each other. I pulled the food from my pack. I had stuffed so much into it that my shoulders ached from carrying it. Six potatoes, four carrots, a few apples, and a handful of cherries.

I returned to the prince, once again sitting cross-legged in front of him. "Well, we don't have much to eat, so let's hope this storm doesn't last."

"Don't worry, I saw some cockroaches scurry into the corner."

I gagged only a little bit dramatically, feeling green at just the idea, and he laughed boisterously. A real belly laugh. I didn't think I'd ever heard that from him before, and I knew instantly it was a sound I wanted to hear again.

The new tattoos on his back wrapped just slightly around to his throat. It was... extremely attractive. "How did you get those tattoos? I was only unconscious for a few hours. I don't understand." I scrutinized him closely, an array of emotions passing over his face in a few brief seconds. Sadness. Fear. Confusion. Defiance.

Then he smirked and answered, "I will tell you if you tell me how you got those scars."

The request caught me off guard. I hadn't expected him to want to know anything about me. Especially after what he said at the cabin about getting to know me.

"When I entered the Darkhelm Forest, I was attacked by Forest Imps and left for dead. I was also attacked by a Lemian in the Sankot Desert and a Lycan in the Cave of Beithir. Then I battled some giant lake dragon thing. I have scars from each attack." I brushed them off as though they were an everyday occurrence, and lately they had been. I did not wish to elaborate on my trip up Mt. Malus, and I hoped Sterling would not push the issue.

"Lake dragon? The Thalkor?" His eyes looked ready to pop out of his skull. "How did you survive?!" He cried, his jaw slack.

"That wasn't part of the deal. Tell me about the tattoos."

Sterling huffed and said, "I woke up with them."

That's it? He woke up with them? Why is he lying?

"What do you mean? You just woke up a few minutes ago, with tattoos all over your body, and you didn't think to question it?"

"It's just some Fae thing. My father and Soren have tattoos as well. It's not a big deal." Though the look on his face indicated otherwise. The tightened jaw. The thin lips. The bead of sweat on his handsome brow. The hand rubbing the back of his neck.

What is he hiding? And why? It's almost as if—

The thought trailed off as a shiver passed through me. I was still dressed in only my shift, and the dank cave was cold. Instinctively, I scooted closer to the fire.

Fire. How was there —

I glanced down...

There were no logs. Only fire and the cave floor. How? What kind of magic was this?

"Sterling. The fire... it has no wood..?"

"I can't do it again." He muttered, voice low.

"You did this?"

"I—I don't know how. And... I can't do it again."

"But if you have your magic, that must mean—"

"I said I can't do it again!" He bellowed, his face red, as his voice reverberated off the cave walls.

I recoiled, staring at him in surprise. His mouth was tight as his lips twitched to the side, another tick I had noticed during our time together.

"I'm sorry." He heaved a frustrated sigh and laid down in the blankets, rolling over so his back was to me.

What in Amengor was that about?

* * *

Sterling

I had tried to do it again. Multiple times since rescuing her. I couldn't. When I had seen her fall… something had altered in me. My heart had almost broken, and I couldn't watch her die.

And then it had just… happened. I'd barely salvaged my clothing after ripping it off as hastily as I had. I wasn't surprised a button was missing.

I didn't know how I had done it, and I was not ready to tell her that I couldn't do it again. Some part of me had just known that if I took my clothes off, I would transform into something. I hadn't anticipated what. I didn't want to see her disappointment when she realized how weak I was.

This changes things, and I'm not ready for them to change. I can't do this!

I knew what Vincent would say. He would tell me that it was okay to trust someone again, but I didn't want to trust Remmy. It was too painful. I wasn't sure I was ready to let go of Isolde. It felt like a betrayal to her memory.

I closed my eyes, and I could feel her gentle hand on my chest that last night we had shared together. She had whispered softly, *'We could run away together! Let's leave this place behind and never look back'.*

I had laughed and said, *'We cannot. There is no place I can go that my father will not find me. He would hunt us to the end of the worlds.'*

There had been so much excitement in her voice. If only I had listened.

If only. If only. If only nothing! Nothing would have changed what happened! Cyrus still would have found us, and she would still be dead. And dead is exactly what Remmy will be if I let myself care for her. I can't do that to her. I have to send her back.

To her village. To safety. I had seen the hurt on her face when I had yelled at her. She thought things were changing. She will hate me again tomorrow. And that is how it has to be. I could not fail her like I had Isolde.

* * *

Remmy

I waited until the sound of Sterling's breath was deep and even to slide into the blankets beside him. The idea of sleeping this close to him terrified me, but there was no other choice. We would freeze to death otherwise. The temperature was dangerously low, and the fire could only do so much to warm the space.

I had slipped on my dress and cloak when they dried, but Sterling had not moved after his outburst, falling asleep not long after.

Meaning he was… *Yep... okay, Remmy! Stop right there. Not okay.*

He was hiding something from me, but before that… *before that, he was different.*

Before that, he had laughed.

And lounged... naked.

Though he had remained under the fur from the waist down.

Maybe he was showing off his mysterious new tattoos.

I scooted as close as I could to Sterling without touching him, the warmth of his body heat drawing me in. The storm was still raging outside, frozen water falling from the sky, and I wondered how long we would be hemmed in here.

Hopefully, I would be able to convince the prince to tell me what was going on. He had said it was 'just some Fae thing,' but that didn't make sense. To go to sleep and then wake up with changed eyes and ornate tattoos covering your back, only a few hours later.

I don't know much about the Fae, but it sounds as though he has gotten his clan form. Why is he upset about that? Isn't being clanless why his father hates him?

I would swear he was the most confusing man I had ever met, but to be honest, I had not met many men.

Maybe this behavior is normal for men? To be so contradictory... and confusing?

That didn't really make sense either.

Twenty-Three

Welcome To The Resistance

* * *

Teigan

It was four hours from dawn when I followed the darkened path leading to The Drunken Dragon. I had finished my shift at The Oasis, bathed, and left immediately.

Exhaustion was seeping into my bones, but the adrenaline pumping through my veins kept me going.

Tonight was the night. I would be going on my first mission. A weapons supply train from Rothton was due to pass through Lunestair in two hours.

I was not yet finished with my training, but this was the rebellion's first real strike against Cyrus' tyranny, and Ivor said my skill set would be required.

A rat scurried behind me as a steel refuse can rattled. A tingle ran up my spine as I stopped and glanced back.

A shadow loomed on the wall of a building, growing larger as it made its way toward me. Dread filled me as I picked up my pace, hurrying to the pub where I was to meet Rufus and Xula. I was still half a block away, and no good lurked in the shadows at this hour.

The alley was eerily quiet, adding to my sense of dread. My heart raced as the shadow seemed to follow me through every turn.

Then I heard it. A small cough.

No, it can't be.

I darted quickly behind a large stack of crates laden with supplies and waited.

Finally, the shadow took form, passing in front of the crates where I lay in wait.

"Aha!" I yelled as I jumped from behind the wooden crates, grabbing the arm of the figure.

She screeched loud enough to wake the entire westside, attempting to jerk her arm free and swing at me with her small fists. I grabbed her by the shoulders and shook her roughly.

"Deidre! What are you doing here?" The demand was more gruff than I intended, and tears welled in her deep brown eyes when she realized it was me.

"Teigan." She whispered my name as the tears slid from her eyes, rolling down her flushed cheeks. I pulled her close to me and held her tightly.

"I'm sorry, but you shouldn't be here. This place is dangerous. What if someone had seen you?"

Her resolve visibly hardened, her face turning steely as she pushed away from me, both of her tiny hands shoving at my chest. "I followed you. I know you have been sneaking out at night, and I want to know what you're up to. You promised me you wouldn't do anything dangerous!" Deidre's voice rose as she talked, and I hurried to shush her.

"Quiet! You're going to get us both killed! Come on." I grabbed her upper arm and led her down the oddly still street toward the pub. Not even a prostitute in sight.

"What are we doing? Where are you taking me?!"

Ignoring her incessant questions, I tried to figure my way out of this situation.

Rufus is going to be furious. But I don't have time to take her back! Maybe Dante can keep her in a room in the back of the Dragon while we do this? Ohhh, why did she have to show up here? I have to keep her safe, but I can't let her get involved with this. Rufus won't allow it without interviewing her, anyway. I think? Ugh.

My only option was to take her with me and hope there was somewhere safe that Dante could keep her while we were gone.

I huffed in frustration and turned toward her. "Why did you follow me, Deidre? You have no idea how hard you've made this for me."

She chewed her lip nervously, pressing her thumb against the bottom one. "I was worried about you."

I sighed again and rolled my eyes toward the starry night sky. After moving here, I finally understood why it was called the Stardust District. The stars outshone the lights of the city, sitting up there in their blackened velvet blanket. I had never seen this many before coming to Lunestair.

I looked back down and found Deidre watching me solemnly, her eyes wide and sad. In the short month or so that I had known her, our budding friendship was growing into something more for the girl, and I didn't know how to stop it. I would have to talk to her after this. I cared about her, but as a friend only. I smiled softly and nudged her forward again.

"It's okay. Come on, we are almost there."

"I didn't mean to complicate things for you."

"I know."

I stepped into the Drunken Dragon, pulling Deidre inside and closing the door quickly behind me. When I turned to face the group gathered at the tables, all eyes were on me and the young girl I had dragged in behind me.

I had some explaining to do. I cleared my throat and looked to Xula for help, but she merely raised her brow at me like a disapproving mother.

Exhaling slowly, I tried to explain without letting Deidre know what was going on. "This is Deidre, everybody. I work with her at the Starlight Oasis. She's a friend. She just needs a place to lie low until morning." I glanced at Dante, who nodded knowingly and stepped forward, introducing himself to the nervous girl and steering her toward the storage rooms at the back of the pub.

"But wait!" She cried anxiously. "Teigan! I want to stay with you!"

I placed my hand on her shoulder and gave her a reassuring smile. "It's all right. You'll be safe with Dante. I'll come get you in a few hours, okay?"

She remained hesitant but nodded and turned to follow the Dwarf, who was waiting with an arm outstretched. Before they disappeared into the back, I heard him telling her amiably that his daughter was 'about her age.' His daughter was nineteen, but I knew it was only a measure to help calm the girl.

I turned back to the group and found Ivor and Rufus looking at me expectantly.

Blast. I'm in so much trouble.

I smiled sheepishly, but before I could explain, Ivor spoke, his voice filled with authority. I hadn't known he would be here, but it made sense. This was the Dragon Fire's first real mission.

"Teigan, why did you bring her here?"

I took a deep breath and dove into the tale of how I knew Deidre, and how she followed me here. "I think she—uummm—likes me… romantically. I—I—ummm didn't know what else to do with her." I finished with a visible cringe.

"You shouldn't have brought her here!" Rufus thundered. "You should have sent her back immediately!"

Xula tsked. "Nonsense, Rufus, she's merely a child! He could not very well send her back on her own. The westside is dangerous. She could have been lured by crathe dealers, or worse, taken by traffickers. He did the only thing he could."

I nodded my thanks for her support, and she smiled understandingly, throwing me a wink.

Since losing my own, Xula had become like a mother to me. She'd been checking in with me regularly since I had joined the Dragon's Fire. I appreciated her more than words could say. She had vouched for me to Ivor, assuring him that I was ready for this operation.

Ivor, who had remained silent since his original inquiry, his brow furrowed in thought, finally questioned, "How old is she?"

Alarm filled me at the expression on his face. I knew why he was asking.

No. No, I won't allow it. I won't.

I swallowed my angry retort and tried a softer approach. "Ivor, sir, she is—too young. She's too— ." He held up a hand, stopping me before I could complete the sentence.

Innocent.

"How old?" We needed all the help we could acquire for the resistance. The Blood Guard was strong, and so were the king's supporters, but I couldn't justify dragging children into it.

"She's barely fifteen."

Ivor slowly dragged a hand over his mouth, his fingers coming together at the chin, apparently approving of the response. "Is she trustworthy?"

"I would trust her with my life."

Rufus finally spoke again, imploring Ivor not to make the decision we all knew he was already making. "The Magpie will be furious, sir."

Ivor fixed stormy eyes on the Dwarf. "The Magpie has no say in who I recruit."

"But, sir—" Rufus quieted when the rebel leader held up his hand.

My heart sank like lead in my chest, my protests tumbling out before I could stop them. "Sir! She is only a child! She is far too young to be involved in this!"

Ivor slapped one hand down on the table, demanding silence, and I jumped back. Xula placed a calming hand on her husband's forearm.

"She is only a girl, my love. Surely, we cannot allow this."

Ivor studied his wife quietly for a moment. "She is barely younger than Ivanna was, Xula. She is old enough."

He looked to Dante, who had entered the room mid-conversation. "Let the girl decide for herself. Bring her out."

Dante glanced at Xula, clearly not approving of the decision either, but he nodded and retreated to the back room to fetch Deidre.

The girl ran to me, looking questioningly around the room, and my chest tightened as I took her hand in mine.

Say no. Please say no. But what do they do when someone says no?! Surely they won't harm her to maintain the secrecy of the organization?

"Deidre, has Teigan told you what we are doing here?" She shook her head and peered up at me, confusion written all over her pretty face.

I smiled as best I could, and Ivor continued, launching into a spiel about The Dragon's Fire, our mission, and the operation we were soon to undertake. I watched as she listened intently to every word Ivor uttered, apprehension creeping over me.

"So my question for you, Deidre, is this: would you like to join the resistance?"

She hesitated but a moment before answering with a fire in her voice I had never heard before. "I'd like nothing better."

Ivor smiled at the passion she exuded, then glanced at me, his voice firm, leaving no room for objection. "Then it is settled. Welcome to the resistance, girl."

Deidre threw her arms around me enthusiastically and whispered in my ear, "You didn't think I was going to let you do this alone, did you?"

Twenty-Four

The Cave of Carrots

* * *

Sterling

The morning brought more freezing rain and awkward discomfort between Remmy and me. She evacuated the blankets upon realizing I was awake and promptly began to munch on a raw carrot from our food supply.

Rising from the fur, I snatched my clothing from where I'd hung it to dry yesterday, and quickly dressed.

I approached Remmy, taking care that my face remained blank, and sat down on the cold ground beside her.

Staring into the still-burning flame I had somehow created, I requested, "May I have a carrot, please?"

Without a word, she reached back into her pack and withdrew a carrot, handing it to me with a flick of her wrist.

I'm having a carrot for breakfast. A carrot. My father may not have to kill us after all. We are going to die of starvation before we can leave this blasted cave.

She then proceeded to dump a handful of cherries into my lap, taking none for herself.

"Don't you want some too?" She gave a little shake of her head and continued to nibble her carrot like a horse, as though she were savoring the taste, unsure when she would eat again. For that, I couldn't blame her. Who knew how long the tempest would rage? Storms on Mt. Malus had been known to last a fortnight or more. Some believed they were the rage of Skotos at being trapped in the Netherworld.

Lunaire, the goddess of light, along with Afrontis, the god of earth, Ammadon, the god of the sea, and many other gods of old, had imprisoned him in his domain long before the Vantan invasion, leaving him unable to walk the earth. The lore says he was imprisoned for wreaking havoc in this realm, slaughtering innocents in order to take this realm and rule it along with the Netherworld. His power grew too great, and the other celestial beings, fearful of his greed, tricked him, making him a prisoner in his own realm. Only his beasts may enter and leave. The raging storms are his wrath about being trapped for many millennia.

"You need it more than I do."

"Of course I don't! Eat a cherry." I tossed a few at her, and she snatched them up, giving in to my demands.

Finally, she turned her pretty head in my direction, a bit of cherry juice dripping down her chin. She wiped it with the back of her hand and spoke firmly. "I know something is going on, and if it is something that could help us, you should tell me. We both know the path ahead is fraught with danger. I went over the side of the mountain yesterday, for Skoto's sake! I would be dead if you had not somehow saved me. I am still not sure how you did it."

I puffed out a breath of agitation. The tension in the room was palpable. I was not ready to have this discussion. This woman had already seen me in my most vulnerable state. I couldn't bear the idea of appearing so weak over and over again, though I knew she was not going to give up.

What am I going to do?

I scrubbed my hands down my face.

"Remmy," I lamented. "I do not wish to talk about this."

"When are you going to talk about it? I have a right to know what's going on."

I felt the flush of anger taint my cheeks. "You do not need to know everything! Can you not just let it go? For the love of the gods!"

"Fine." She stood, her cheeks flushed and her lips pressed into a thin line, and made her way to the entrance of the cave. She leaned against the wall, watching the storm blustering and blowing outside, her shoulders stiff and rigid.

I ran my hands through my hair, tugging at the ends of it. It was longer than it had ever been before, curling down in a wave over my forehead and covering my ears. I stared at the back of Remmy's green cloak, noticing not for the first time, the slashes in the back of it. A weird desire to buy her a new frock overcame me. I grunted aloud, and Remmy turned to face me.

"Did you say something?"

"No. I am going to train."

"Train?" She questioned, looking at me as though I had lost my mind.

"Yes, train. There is not much else to do in here." I shed my shirt, the cold in the cave forcing goosebumps to pebble on my skin.

I raised my head when I felt Remmy's eyes on me. A pink tint rose to her cheeks, and I couldn't help but stare for a moment. She was achingly beautiful. The tiny white scars decorating her body only made her appear more breathtaking, exemplifying the strength she possessed.

I am losing my mind.

"Care to join me?"

She shook her head and picked up her sword, advancing and blocking against an imaginary foe.

I suppose that is necessary training as well.

I watched her for a moment before dropping to the earth to do a series of push-ups.

Fae were naturally stronger and healed quicker than humans, but after my days of isolation and starvation, I expected to be in a much weakened state. I was not. I pushed myself up one-hundred and twenty times before sweat even began to bead on my brow.

It must be my clan form.

I was doing more than I had at my healthiest before my clan had emerged when I saved Remmy. I went all the way to two hundred before stopping, hopping up to my feet with an amazed laugh, adrenaline coursing through me.

When I glanced at Remmy, she was staring at me, slack-jawed. She closed it, and it tightened. "Let me guess? Just another Fae thing?"

I shrugged and smiled at her sweetly. She huffed and turned her back to me, resuming her sword practice. I wanted to test the limits of my newfound abilities, but that was difficult to do, trapped in a tiny cave. My mind drifted to my clan form.

How do I shift again? I don't know how to get it to reemerge.

There was no one I could ask, either. I would have to do this on my own. I glanced over at Remmy, who was still swinging her sword through the air, my thoughts tumultuous. Her movements were untrained, but she had obviously used a weapon before.

Maybe there is hope.

If only I could figure out how to shift again, maybe we would survive this. All I had to do was get a clan to emerge that had been extinct for thousands of years.

* * *

Remmy

The next two days were spent in strained, hungry silence, the freezing storm raging outside our cave. Sterling's fire burned unattended, fueled no doubt by his rage alone.

The prince spent his time exercising and training for whatever lay ahead, while I stared out the mouth of the cave at the rain pouring down, or tried to cultivate my sword-fighting tactics. With no opponent, all I could do was practice my advances and footwork. I wasn't the best at it, but there was no other way for me to improve.

On the third day, the taciturnity was broken when Sterling came over and volunteered to teach me a superior way to parry and counter-attack, using the momentum of the attack to thrust the melee weapon away, leaving an opening for me to attack from above.

"Use your left foot to step forward, bouncing on your toes, after you block my attack, and swing from over your right shoulder." He thrust his carrot at me in a fictitious advance.

I did as he directed, swinging my sword down as though I were going to slash his throat, while laughing at his carrot-sword. I was surprised he had offered to help me after spending the last two days brooding.

"Remmy, this is important. Be serious."

"Well, I am trying, but you are swinging a carrot at me." My laughter bounced off the cave walls, echoing back to us.

"Do you want to learn or not?"

"Of course I do!"

"Then pay attention and do it again."

My smirk widened even more at his second advance with our last carrot, but I repeated the motions he indicated, stepping forward to swing from above, my sword inches from his shoulder.

"Again!" He demanded.

Since when does he care about me so much? It's like he genuinely wants me to learn. Or maybe I'm just curing his boredom.

I snickered and repeated the movement, this time performing the motion fluidly.

The corner of Sterling's mouth inched upward slightly as though he were suppressing a smile, seeming mildly impressed. "You're a fast learner."

"I'm not completely unfamiliar with a sword. What else have you to teach me, oh great Master?" I batted my eyes at him in mock adoration, and he actually grinned, breaking the carrot in half and handing me part of it.

He shook his head at my antics and ambled over to sit on our bed. We had burrowed into the blankets each night to keep from freezing to death, while staying as far away from each other as we could, but

I had still woken this morning with his arm slung over my waist.

All at once, noticing the stillness, I quickly rushed to the cave entrance.

"Sterling! The rain has stopped!" I cried with excitement.

He joined me at the opening, peering excitedly at the sodden trail.

"By the hair of Lunaire! It has!"

We looked at each other in understanding and hurriedly moved to pack up what was left of our supplies. It was barely midday, leaving time to travel before dark, and we both desired nothing more than to leave this abomination of a cave.

Twenty-Five

Wings With Warning

* * *

Vincent

It had been days since I had been able to sneak away from the palace to check on the prince and that contestant girl.

I had prayed to every god, known and unknown, that Sterling would recover from his lashings with the help of the morsious salve I put on him. He was a strong boy, but the lack of proper nutrition would weaken any Fae.

I circled the tiny cabin from the air and landed with a resounding thump by the front door. It was slightly ajar, and a mixture of panic and hope filled me as I shifted back to my Fae form and hastened inside.

The vines that had restrained Sterling were cut through and brown. The furniture was askew, and the moldy bed had an indentation as though someone large had slept on it for several days. This could only mean the girl had made it and freed the prince from this prison.

They must be on their way back down. I wonder where they are now?

I had not seen them on my way up, but I had not been searching the woods for anyone. Hurrying back outside to the pack I carried with my clothing, and the meat I had brought for them, I snatched it off the ground and made my way into the garden, filling it with as much food as was left on the vines and plants growing there.

With my bag full of dried meats and produce, I set off into the air, searching the ground below me for my beloved prince and his savior.

* * *

Remmy

After leaving our cave behind, the path had remained treacherous and steep for but a short time before tapering off into the woods. The ground was thoroughly saturated, and the chill of the air was full of magic.

Even after leaving the highest altitude, we still had seen no wildlife and were growing weak from hunger. I decided to scour the forest for greens, coming up with very little—at best, a handful of leaves for us to split.

I silently prayed Skotos would end this torture, but I feared I was on his bad side for slaughtering so many of his demons. Perhaps Lunaire would be more forgiving.

A strange sound filled my ears, silencing the thoughts in my head. It almost sounded like… *wings?* I whipped my head up to the sky, searching for the source of the noise, ready to call out to Sterling, when he dragged me up against a tree, pressing a strong hand across my mouth.

His voice was low and deep in my ear, sending shivers up my spine. "Keep quiet. Something is circling us from above."

I nodded, pushing his hand away, but allowing his other hand to maintain its hold on me. We held our breath as the sound of tree branches crashing rang out and a large beast slammed to the ground, mere paces from our tree. Sterling pushed me behind him protectively, reaching behind him for the sword at my waist and unsheathing it before I could protest.

"Hey!" I grumbled, but the prince did not acknowledge me, instead holding the sword out in a defensive stance and aiming it at the beast that had landed. I jumped when he let out a strangled cry and dropped my sword, racing toward the beast, which I could now see was a phalynx.

Surely, it's not...?

I observed the forehead, noticing the sigil there. The same sharp blue eyes.

It is! It's the same creature that brought me the morsious salve when I was injured. But who is it?

"Sterling!" The prince did not stop, nor did he look back. The great phalynx began to shift back into its Fae form, and I edged forward hesitantly, wanting to know but cautious in my curiosity. The man was balled up on the ground as Sterling approached. He snatched the man's bag up and withdrew clothes, handing them to him as he pulled himself up.

I shielded my eyes as he stepped into his clothes, and Sterling's voice rang out through the trees.

"Vincent! It's so good to see you!"

The prince pulled the now-dressed man into a hug and called back to me. "Remmy, come here. It's safe!"

Collecting my sword from where he had dropped it, I slowly made my way to the two men. He was several inches shorter than Prince Sterling, with a head full of thick black hair. He smiled kindly as I approached and held out a hand to me.

I shook it, looking at Sterling nervously. He smiled the biggest smile I had ever seen on him. "Remmy, this is my manservant, Vincent Larssön."

"Remmy, I am so glad to see that you made it. I hope the gift I gave you helped."

"It was you! How did you…? Why did you…?" I shook my head, not understanding.

Vincent smiled softly at me. "I have been Sterling's manservant since the day he was born. What Cyrus has done to him—" He exhaled with a puff, anger flashing in his bright blue eyes. "I couldn't rescue him myself, you see. My daughter… it was not safe."

Sterling looked uncomfortable as he patted the man on the shoulder, and Vincent turned to him apologetically. "I wanted to, Sterling, please believe me. But Thalia… the king—" Sterling held up his hand, cutting off the man's apologies.

"Thalia's life is more important. There is nothing you could have done. No apology is needed. I am only glad to see you now, safe and unharmed. Please tell me, how is Soren?"

"Soren is well, my prince, though he worries for you. He trains with the guard daily."

"And my father?"

"He leaves the boy be for now. I gather he is waiting for something to announce to the kingdom about you before turning his attention to your brother."

Sterling nodded, appearing deep in thought, and Vincent stooped to pick up the bag he had been carrying. "I have brought you both something."

Gingerly, he unpacked his supplies, setting them onto the ground before us.

Food.

My stomach rumbled loudly, and I felt my cheeks heat.

"Please! Enjoy yourselves. The magic is too strong here for the wildlife to frequent the area, so I am sure you must be starved."

I nodded sheepishly, and Sterling and I bent at the same time to retrieve the food, stuffing the remainder in my pack, which he now offered to carry.

Pride almost stopped me, but my shoulders ached from weeks of carrying it, so I allowed him to take it from me. The old man reached into his bag, took out a wrapped package, and handed it to Sterling.

"This is for you as well. It isn't much, but hopefully it will tide you over until you reach the temple. I must be going, my boy, before anyone realizes I'm gone. May Lunaire guide your journey, and Skotos keep his creatures at bay. You will make it through the temple. I have faith that if anyone can, it is you. I will see you soon." Vincent pulled Sterling into a tight hug, and I was surprised by the familiarity he used with the royal heir.

Turning to me, he once again extended a hand, and I took it. "Remmy, I am looking forward to getting to know you better in Lunestair. Do take care of this stubborn prince."

Sterling smiled fondly at the man, and Vincent quickly shed his clothes, transforming into his clan form once more and shooting off into the sky, his bag clutched firmly in his mouth. He stopped once, glancing down before leaving us to our own once again. I turned to Sterling and noticed a frown turning down his full lips.

What is at this temple? Why does no one survive it? And how will we?

Motioning to the package he held, I questioned, "What is that?"

He carefully unwrapped it, and we simultaneously inhaled the scent of dried meats.

Sterling's smile returned with the smell of the meat, and he handed me a slice, greedily shoving another into his mouth and exhaling deeply. "Vincent, Vincent. However will I thank you?"

I savored the taste of the dried lamb in my mouth before biting into one of the apples the manservant had brought. "You are close to your servant?"

"Vincent is more than just my servant. He is my friend, and he has been more of a father to me than mine ever has been."

The prince's tone was borderline defensive, and I hurried to assure him, "I am sorry, I didn't mean to pry. It's only that it is uncommon for someone of your… title to befriend commoners and low-born."

He turned to me, his silver eyes flashing. "Vincent is not a lowborn, and I am not so cruel as you think. I do not merely hate someone for their class. Or clan." He added.

"Then why do you treat me so?!" I exploded, days of pent-up tension boiling over in one charged moment. "Is it not because I am a villager?"

"Enough of this!" Sterling boomed, his face red and nostrils flaring. Turning from me, he stalked off, slinging my pack over his shoulder.

Chasing after him, I subconsciously decided to make matters worse. "We are still stuck together, no matter how much you despise me, and it is a long way to Lunestair!" I shouted the words angrily at his retreating form.

He stopped then, gradually turning back to face me.

"Don't you worry your pretty little head about it, sweetheart." He sneered. "We will probably both be dead tomorrow, anyway!"

Dead tomorrow?

"What are you being dramatic about now?"

He snorted in disgust, turning his back to me.

"You have no idea what kind of danger we are in."

"Then why don't you tell me!"

The prince just shook his head and continued through the forest, apparently finished with the conversation and refusing to divulge information once more.

I sighed heavily and moved to follow him, hating myself for my lack of control. The more Sterling hid, the more frustrated I became, the situation gnawing at my restraint constantly.

Tomorrow, we would arrive at the hidden temple. He had said we would probably die tomorrow.

What does that mean?

What terrors lie in wait at the Temple of Deliritas?

Twenty-Six

The Challenge of the Gods

* * *

Sterling

My mind raced as we neared the location of the temple. Having been here only once before, and under duress, I could not be certain how far we were, only that we were close. Remmy had stayed paces behind me, keeping to herself and stewing since yesterday afternoon when we had fought.

I hadn't meant to be so aggressive with her, but she kept pushing, and I was not ready to deal with any of this.

Least of all, the Temple of Deliritas.

If only I could shift again, I could get us out of here.

The closer we got to the temple, the more my apprehension

heightened, trepidation gnawing at me.

I glanced back at the woman following me.

I don't know how to protect her.

She looked exhausted. The hood of her frock was pulled up, wisps of chestnut hair peeking out from beneath it, fear and worry drawing rings under her beautiful, deep eyes.

I can't let anything happen to her.

I tugged my hands through my thick hair and called out to her.

"Remmy, we are approaching the temple. Please, stay close to me." She raised her head and glared defiantly at me.

"Oh, now you care about me?" She scoffed. "Perhaps if you cared so much, you should have warned me what we are facing. It is not lost on me that you said everyone must pass here, yet no one knows of its existence outside the Ericcsön family. I am walking to my death, and you have not told me why."

I let out a frustrated breath and waited until she reached me before speaking. "I don't know how to do this, Remmy. I don't know what awaits us inside this temple. I have been here but once before, and I do not care to ever relive that experience. Know that whatever is here will test your sanity while simultaneously trying to kill you. I know you have sensed the dark magic in this place. It permeates the ground and saturates the air. It will try to infect your mind and… make you… do things. Things you don't want to do. But we are stronger together." I snatched her elbow, attempting to draw her closer to me, but she yanked spitefully from my grasp. "Which is why I am asking you to stay close to me. When we arrive, we will be met with a guardian who will ask a test of us before a priestess comes to escort us inside the temple."

"Okay… and what is inside the temple? Besides priestesses and dark magic?"

I paused before replying, wishing I could make her understand without knowing how to explain. "That's all there needs to be."

She did not appear satisfied with this answer, but before she could protest, I grabbed her arm, steering her toward the temple and the looming danger.

* * *

Remmy

Well, that was not comforting.

The prince had managed to make it sound even more likely that we would die. He was correct, though. I had sensed the dark magic growing as we approached this place. The air was suffocating, feeling as though lightning buzzed through it.

Before long, two great stone obelisks appeared before us. They were ancient and crumbling in places, with moss wrapping around them in swirling patterns. The stone was etched with runes in a language I had never seen before.

But where is the temple?

I started to ask Sterling when, before my eyes, a figure materialized, cloaked in brown.

The Faceless One!

But no… it couldn't be. The Faceless One guards the entrance to the Cave of Beithir, and this one had a different colored robe.

Could there be two? The faceless two?

"How many Faceless Ones are there?" I whispered, and Sterling looked at me incredulously.

"That is what you are thinking about right now? Why does that even matter?"

I shrugged, and the prince rolled his eyes as the creature spoke, its gravelly voice echoing through the recesses of our minds.

"Remmy Alina Silva, you have been deemed worthy to enter the Temple of Deliritas, having already proven yourself at the Cave of Skotos."

The ancient being turned its hollow black eyes on the prince. "You! Sterling Sage Ericcsön, heir to the throne of Valeria, son of Cyrus the Lion, must prove your worth to the god of the Netherworld. Skotos demands to know your heart. Will you accept my challenge or face the wrath of the gods?"

What is it talking about? There is no temple here! It's just two stone columns with creepy etchings.

Fear gripped me as Sterling accepted the faceless creature's challenge, his deep voice booming out in the stillness of the wood.

As he grabbed the hilt of the sword I held out to him, I placed my hand on his and met his steely eyes, pleading with him. "Be careful. Please."

Then, in a failed attempt to lighten the mood, I shrugged and said, "I still need a prince to marry!"

Sterling rolled his eyes again, prying the sword from my grasp and surging forward to meet the guardian beneath the intimidating stone gate.

I wanted to stop him. I wanted to cry out that something was not right. There was no temple here, but I could do neither of those things.

This was a challenge issued by a servant of Skotos. He must face this, or the consequences would be dire. At the Cave of Beithir, it hadn't been about the battle, but about the bravery to fight. And the Crown Prince of Valeria was brave if he was anything.

Maybe the obelisks form a portal to the temple? Like the portal to the Netherworld in the cave?

The clash of swords rang out through the eerie quiet of the trees, and I held my breath as I watched Sterling's battle.

He moved as a god, swinging and slashing with skills unrivaled. The muscles in his arms strained against his shirt as he aimed with practiced motions. I stood in awe as he met every advance of the ancient creature with a thrust of his own.

They moved so quickly I could barely follow, grunts of effort spilling from Sterling's lips with each steady swing.

Even in his tattered clothes, he looked regal, combating an otherworldly guardian with the grace and skill of a born warrior. Something in my heart clenched at the sight of him, chill bumps forming on my skin. I didn't know why. The strain between us could be cut with a dagger, but the thought of him in danger… it crippled me.

My thoughts were interrupted by a loud *thump* and a cry of pain. The Faceless One had somehow put the prince on his back and now stood over him, his weapon outstretched. A gasp escaped me, and I covered my mouth with my hands.

In a motion swift as lightning, Sterling kicked out his leg, knocking the creature's feet out from under him and sending him crashing to the saturated earth. Sterling leaped up, pointing his sword at the ancient being's throat. My breath caught.

"Yield!" He demanded, his voice firm and authoritative. The guardian gave a shallow nod, and Sterling withdrew his sword, waiting resolutely for his judgment.

The Faceless One rose quickly from the ground. One would think his bones would creak with age, but he was lithe and spritely for being a few millennia.

I moved to stand by Sterling, placing my hand gently on his forearm. He looked down at me, and I gave him a tentative smile, which he returned, and then faced the guardian again.

His shirt had fallen open at the collar, and sweat beaded down to meet the tip of the mysterious tattoos stretching up his neck, creating the illusion that they were growing.

The voice penetrated our minds again, pronouncing judgment on Sterling's fight. "Prince Sterling Sage Ericcsön, you have fought with the heart of a great warrior. You are valiant and noble. A king in truth. You have been found worthy to enter the temple of Skotos."

I let loose an audible breath, and Sterling's shoulders noticeably sagged in relief. The ground began to tremble, and the sound of tearing filled our ears, as the space between the stone obelisks sizzled and popped, ripping back an invisible veil of magic.

I stared in wonder and fear as light began to seep through the rend in space to reveal a young woman clothed in a dark robe. A tattoo of symbols and sigils dotted her forehead, and fiery red hair protruded from under her hood.

Inadvertently, I reached for the prince's hand. He took it, pulling me toward the priestess, whose smile did not meet her crystalline blue eyes.

"Welcome to the Temple of Deliritas, Remmy. My name is Zyphara. Prince Sterling, it is lovely to see you again. Please, follow me."

A strange look passed over Sterling's face, but he bent down, his warm breath brushing my forehead as he whispered, "You bested that creature at the Cave of Beithir?"

"No. He had me on the ground in less than five minutes. But I don't believe the point is to defeat him. I believe it's to prove what your intentions are. How you fight will demonstrate the type of person you are, and it seems as though Skotos doesn't want evil in his temple."

"Well, he let my father in."

I glanced at him questioningly. That didn't make sense, though. If the king was so cruel, what was the point of these tests?

The prince's jaw tensed, and he shook his head. "I'll explain later."

* * *

Sterling

We followed Zyphara up the path lit with blue flame candles, a sinister fog settling in around us like a thick blanket of magic. I still clutched Remmy's hand tightly, and surprisingly, she allowed me to, no doubt as unnerved as I was.

When we entered through the doors of the great stone temple, the priestess led us down a narrow entry to a small dining hall and gestured to the feast spread out on a table in the center of the room.

A pitcher of water was placed in the center of the table, and Remmy released my hand, hurrying over to it and then pausing, turning back to me in question.

Zyphara nodded her head toward the table. "Please. Eat and drink whatever you desire. When you are finished, Lirial will come to escort you to your rooms for the night."

I nodded politely, but Remmy still stared at me. When the priestess had exited the room, she voiced her thoughts.

"Is this safe to drink? Is the food poisoned?"

"The food and water are safe. It's only the dark magic that we must worry about. The priestesses will not harm us."

"I feel lucid so far…?"

"The magic seeps into your mind slowly, infecting you before you realize what's happening." I moved to sit at the long wooden table, and Remmy chose the chair directly across from me. "I am merely hoping that with the foreknowledge of it, we will be able to better shield our minds from the darkness."

Remmy shuddered visibly, exhaling low and slow. "What happens if you try to leave the temple before morning?"

"Skotos drains the life out of you before you make it to the veil." Her eyes widened, and her face paled. "The dark god likes his games."

"We are stuck here until then?"

I nodded solemnly. "From my understanding, we only must stay the night. I'm assuming that with first light, a priestess will escort us back to the veil."

Remmy nodded and began spooning food onto the plates that were laid out for us.

My stomach rumbled as the scent of stewed lamb, roasted carrots, potatoes, braised sausages, honey cakes stuffed with apples and spices, and sheep's cheese wafted through the air.

We chewed our food in silence, the temple air thick with an unsettling dark energy. The dining hall was lit with the same blue flames as the walkway, ghostly shadows clinging to the ancient stone walls, leaving me uneasy. It was as though the very walls were sentient, watching us as we ate, a low hum whirring in the air.

I glanced at Remmy, a flash of irritation shooting through me.

Why is she chewing so loudly? And eating so much? She's going to eat all the food!

I wasn't sure why that bothered me. She was not eating any more than normal or chewing very loudly at all.

Grinding my teeth to keep from saying anything, I hoped the priestess, Lirial, would come soon to release me from my growing discomfort.

Remmy sniffled, leaning forward to grab the pitcher of water to pour herself some more, and I snapped. "What is wrong with you? Are you sick? You're drinking all the water!"

Her eyebrows raised in surprise. "I'm not drinking all the water, Sterling. I just want a glass. I'm thirsty."

"Well, why do you keep bloody sniffing?"

The color drained from Remmy's face as the realization set in.

"It's starting already, isn't it?" She whispered.

Why is she asking me such idiotic questions? Of course, it's starting. Is she not an adult? Can she not figure this out for herself?

I rubbed a hand down the back of my neck, feeling the slightly raised skin of the fresh tattoos, and sighed. "Yeah. I think so. Sorry."

"What should we do?"

"Let's call for the priestess to take us to our rooms. If we can turn in early, perhaps we can ride it out until morning, in the solitude of our own chambers."

I scrubbed my hands through my hair, trying to clear the nagging thoughts of resentment toward her. They made no sense at all.

Remmy rose quickly from the table, jerked open the door to the dining room, and called out for the promised escort.

"Hello? Ummm—Lirial? We'd like to be taken to our rooms now!" Her voice sounded hesitant and uncertain as she called down the hallway to no avail.

The Temple of Deliritas was silent.

Panic clawed its way into my mind.

Did they leave us to fend for ourselves? What are we going to do if we can't find our rooms?

Perhaps the priestesses of Skotos were not so innocent after all. My mind flitted back to the last time I had entered this temple, and I scolded myself for assuming the priestesses had no nefarious intentions. My gaze drifted to the food, and I grabbed my throat.

What if Remmy was right? What if they had poisoned the food? What if they were sacrificing us as they had her?

Paranoia clouded my judgment as I grabbed one of the dinner knives in my hand. We had to get out of here.

I rose from the table just as Remmy turned back to me, face devoid of all color. "I don't think Lirial is coming."

"I don't think so either." I grabbed her hand and jerked her roughly into the hall. "We're on our own. Come on. We need to find somewhere safe to wait it out."

I tugged her along behind me, but within seconds, the candles lining the ancient stone walls all concurrently blew out, a rush of air sweeping down the cold hall, leaving us in utter darkness.

Remmy's intake of breath broke the stillness of the temple, and she pressed herself closer to me, her sweaty grip tightening in my hand.

Whispers echoed around me, as though the stone walls were speaking to me, whispering doubts into the subconscious of my mind. They chipped away at my sanity, invading my thoughts. 'You will never be strong enough. Your father will kill you.' 'There's no hope for survival.' 'You'll never be able to shift again, so you may as well not try.' 'You don't deserve to be blessed with this clan.'

I shook my head, desperately trying to drown them out, but they continued relentlessly, driving me to madness. 'Your father will always be stronger than you, because you are a weak, pathetic boy. That is why you could not save Isolde. It is why you will not be able to save Remmy either.' 'You are a failure.' 'The girl hates you anyway.' 'It's her fault you're not at peace in Lumess.'

My thoughts warped, turning to delusion, polluted by the darkness that would not leave me. Shadows crept through the blackness around me.

Remmy. This is all your fault. We wouldn't be in this situation if you had just left me to die in that bloody cabin. Why did you have to swoop in, like some star-crossed heroine? You've ruined everything. Forcing me to face my father, making me betray Isolde. Making me feel again. I don't want to feel! I hate it.

"And I hate you!" The darkness overtook my mind, and I yelled the words aloud, ripping my hand free from hers. "I'm going to kill you for what you have done!"

My voice was not my own, but I was powerless to stop the fury spilling out of me.

Deep down, I was aware that it didn't make sense, but it was too late; the dark magic had infected me, and I no longer had control of my actions.

"What?! What are you talking about? Sterling?!" I heard her footsteps and the ruffle of her skirt as she shuffled away from me, against the wall. "What have I done?!"

"YOU RUINED EVERYTHING!" I roared, raising the dinner knife from the table and stabbing it blindly into the darkness.

Twenty-Seven

Dark Magic

* * *

Remmy

The knife clanged into the wall beside me, catching on the sleeve of my dress.

"Sterling!"

Screaming in terror, I abandoned the wall and charged down the black hallway, my footsteps echoing loudly off the flagstone.

The dark magic! It's fully infected him. He tried to kill me!

I huffed heavily as I ran.

Where are the priestesses? Don't they care that this happens to people here? Or is that why they disappear? To allow it to happen?

Behind me, I heard the sound of Sterling's boots thumping slowly and methodically in my direction.

I have to find a place to hide.

The idea of dying at his hands seemed worse than being eaten by one of Skotos's demons. I had come to know him well enough in our time together to know that killing someone innocent would leave him wracked with guilt.

Running to the wall, I pulled myself along, feeling frantically for a doorknob or crawlspace to hide in.

Nothing.

I continued, the temple halls stretching much farther than it had seemed from the outside.

Finally, the wall turned a corner and moonlight glinted through a high window at the end of the hall.

Racing forward, I realized the window was in a door leading outside the temple. I reached out and grasped the knob, twisting frantically, knowing that if I left the temple grounds, Skotos would kill me.

I'd rather die by Skotos's hand than Sterling's.

The door was locked. I swung around desperately, my back to the door, the light from the moon illuminating the hall enough for me to see. Several doors lined the corridor on either side.

Sterling's deep voice boomed through the eerie temple, coming closer to the turn in the hall.

Fearfully, I picked a door and ran to it, trying the knob.

Nothing.

Blast!

"Remmy! You think you can run? You cannot outrun me. I will find you! I will make you pay for everything you've taken from me—my sanity, my peace, my hope for escape. You've ruined it all, and you deserve to pay for what you've stolen from me."

Gods. He's completely unhinged. What in the bloody worlds is he talking about? This isn't real!

My heart hammered against my ribs as I raced to another door.

Locked.

This can't be real!

On the verge of hysteria, I crossed the hall and tried a third, yanking on the door handle. It opened with a groan that almost sounded alive.

Thank Lunaire.

I crashed through the door and felt my way along, realizing the floor gave way to steps leading downward. I wavered; the idea of descending a darkened stairwell to the depths of a sinister temple filled with black magic seemed like the worst possible idea, but Sterling was getting closer, and it would only be moments before he found the door.

My fingers brushed the pommel of the sword at my waist, and I shook my head resolutely.

No. I cannot kill him. I will not kill him. He doesn't know what he's doing.

Taking a deep breath, I began heading down the stairs, clinging to the wall for support. It was damp and cold; my fingers slipped off over and over as I tried to claw for purchase. I couldn't see a thing, and I was bound to twist my ankle if I didn't have some support. The stairs went on for what seemed like forever before I heard the door at the top swing open, that awful groan filling the stairwell.

"I know you are down there, Remmy! Don't think I won't find you."

I pressed forward, clinging to the wall for stability, the winding stairs descending into the dank depths of the Temple of Deliritas.

How far down does this go? Surely, I'm well below ground by now! Why is this here?

I stopped for a moment, listening, my breath coming in short, shallow gasps.

I can't hear Sterling...?

I turned, facing up the spiraling steps, straining to hear a sound from him.

A pained groan came from not far above me, and the sound of him slapping the stone wall rang out in the quiet.

My hand flew to my heart, and I whirled, rushing down the stairs once more.

What's happening to him? Will the dark magic ruin his mind? Will Sterling be gone forever? Will I be trapped within these walls with a dead man?

My mind flashed briefly to the vision Skotos had forced upon me in the Cave of Beithir; Sterling dead on the ground. I hadn't known him then.

I hadn't cared for him then.

I knew it was pointless to do so, considering his distaste for me and refusal to marry me.

Why? Why must I care for someone who despises me? Stop torturing yourself, Remmy.

But I couldn't turn off the feelings. Tears flowed freely down my cheeks now, the salty taste clinging to my lips, as they dripped off the end of my nose. I choked back a sob as my feet landed on level ground.

Blast, I wish I could see!

The blackness pressed in around me, as though an ancient evil dwelt within the room. Whispers echoed around the darkened chamber, bouncing off the seemingly conscious walls. A shudder ran up the length of my spine as I listened to the menacing mutterings.

Is someone down here? Or is this temple truly alive?

The thought made me want to move away from the walls, but if I did, I would have no ability to find my way.

A tormented shout came from the steps, just above me, and Sterling's footsteps stumbled. My hand covered my mouth as I tried to muffle the cry that rose in my throat, hurrying to get away from the stairs.

What is happening?! I wish I could help him.

As long as he wanted to kill me, that wasn't an option. I could only pray to the goddess that morning would break before the darkness consumed him completely.

Why have I not been affected?

It didn't make sense that a weak human mind would not be affected, but it was effectively breaking the mind of a royal Fae.

Perhaps the magic is attracted to power? Sterling hasn't transformed into his clan yet, but he is from a powerful family. Maybe the magic isn't interested in me because humans aren't magical beings? We don't offer it any power to consume...

It made as much sense as anything else that had happened in the last few weeks.

I followed the wall around the large chamber, finding no external doors. My heart plummeted in my chest as I realized I was trapped.

Maybe I can sneak past him and slip back up the stairs?

It was risky, but so was staying confined to this room with him.

Taking my chances away from the wall, I crept to the center of the room, hoping to bypass Sterling. I ran into something large and stone, stubbing my toe against it.

A small wheeze of pain slipped past my lips; I realized my mistake instantly, both hands flying up to cover my traitorous mouth. The prince was on me in an instant, one strong arm wrapping around my neck.

"Got you." He whispered, his lips pressed against my ear, warm breath on my skin.

I squirmed, trying to free myself, plunging my nails into his arm, drawing blood.

"Remmy, love, don't struggle. It'll hurt much more if you do." His voice was low and dangerous, the sound of it sending chills through me. My body temperature rose several degrees as adrenaline shot through me.

"Sterling, please! Fight this!" I tried to plead with the rational part of his mind.

His body shifted against me as he moved his other arm, bringing up the dinner knife he'd stolen from the table, and I brought back my elbow as hard as I could, ramming him in the stomach.

"Oooof!" He grunted and doubled over, but his knife strike still found my arm, and I screeched in pain, grasping the wound with my other hand, blood seeping between my fingers.

"Sterling! Stop! This isn't you! The dark magic is affecting your mind; you must fight it!"

"I don't want to fight it." He growled as he recovered from the blow to his stomach. "I want to kill you."

I heard the whoosh of air as he lunged for me again, and my fist shot out before I knew what I was doing, connecting with his nose in a fierce blow.

"Aaahhh! You've broken my nose, you little wench!"

"Good!" I shouted back as I lifted my leg, aiming precisely where I thought his manhood would be, and kicked with every bit of strength I could muster.

It landed hard, and the prince doubled over with a puff of agonized breath, falling to the ground with a thud.

He was quiet for a few moments, and I began to panic, believing I had hurt him more than intended, when he began to shout, writhing about in pain on the cold stone floor.

"Sterling! What is it? What's wrong?!" I rushed to him and started to kneel on the floor beside him.

"Get back, Remmy! Get back!"

He's warning me away. That's a good sign. He can't be completely gone.

I stumbled back, my eyes widening in horror as the room was suddenly swathed in light, the candles in the room flaring to life of their own accord.

In the center of the room was a great stone table stained red with blood, which must have been what I ran into, and on the ground beside it was Sterling, screaming in apparent agony, as he began to change before my eyes. The sound of his bones cracking threatened to bring the contents of my stomach up as large, dark scales began to form along his golden skin.

A horrified scream left my lungs as Sterling's body transformed into a large black dragon, filling the space in the room and forcing me up against the wall.

As the dragon exploded through the room, it crushed the stone table, sending pieces of rock hurtling through the air.

I ducked, pressing myself up against the wall and covering my head with my arms, as debris rained down around me, thanking the gods when none hit me.

When it was over, I stood, staring in terror at the dragon, my body frozen in shock. He heaved from the ordeal of transforming, blowing tiny puffs of smoke from his huge black snout.

Smoke.

It made sense now. Smoke, mixed with the aromas of mint and mahogany.

Is this how he saved me on the cliff? Dragons have been extinct for... well... forever! Holy Lunaire and her hair. Oh, gods! This must be a hallucination of the temple. This can't be real.

The dragon snarled, and fire blasted from his enormous mouth. I dodged to the side, narrowly avoiding my hair being singed off as it flew out behind me.

Nope; not a hallucination. Definitely real.

His head turned toward me, cool silver eyes finding mine. He blinked, and something flashed in his eyes as though he recognized me.

"Sterling?" My voice quaked, the fear evident as I spoke. The great dragon lowered his head in a bow, and I slowly approached, my hand stretched out hesitantly.

Maybe the pain of the transformation warded off the dark magic? He seems to recognize me at least. Or maybe the clan forms are not susceptible to the darkness?

As I drew closer, he lowered himself to the floor, as though he were attempting to appear less intimidating. I cautiously laid my hand on the end of his snout, running it up and down the tough scales. He nuzzled into my hand, and I smiled.

"I am glad you are okay. You had me frightened for a while there."

He paused for a moment and then lifted his head and nudged my body, pushing me towards his stomach. I laughed and did as he directed, sitting down in the dragon's embrace.

"It is a good thing this room is huge, or you would have brought down the whole temple on us." I glanced about the room, noting how the dragon's form filled the entire space. He would be uncomfortable if we were stuck down here for long. Having no windows or doors, I had lost all sense of time and had no idea how long it was until dawn.

"Can't you shift back to your Fae form?"

Sadness filled the dragon's reptilian eyes, and he shook his head. Understanding flooded me.

This is why he didn't want to tell me about his clan form. He can't control it. Oh no. How are we going to get out of here if he can't shift back?

I ran my hand over the scales on his side. "It's okay. We will figure this out."

Now, all we had to do was wait until morning and pray the darkness did not take my mind. I swallowed nervously.

Most who enter never leave.

Twenty-Eight

The Magpie

* * *

Teigan

Maggie's voice boomed out through the living space on the top floor of the pub. "How could you involve her in this? I told you to stop asking around about it! Now look what you have done!"

I winced. "I—"

"It is not his fault, Mama. I wanted to do it! You know what the king did to my father."

Maggie's face softened as she turned toward Deidre. "I know. And I know how badly you want to do something about it, but this is not the way. You are still only a child, Deidre."

"I am fifteen years old! By my age, you were already running The

Oasis!" Deidre took Maggie's large hand in her small ones and wove her fingers through her adoptive mother's. "You cannot protect me forever. This is my chance to make a difference. You must allow me to grow up."

The tall woman placed a hand on Deidre's cheek, holding it there and peering into the girl's dark eyes. I wanted to turn away from the private moment, but there was nowhere else to go in Maggie's chambers.

Finally, she sighed heavily and strode over to where I was awkwardly grazing her bookshelf.

"We are going to speak with Ivor." My eyes widened. How did she…? "Yes, Teigan, I know Ivor. I also know Xula, Rufus, Dante, and the rest of the Dragon's Fire. Come. It's still early. We can get to the Drunken Dragon before I need to open the pub."

Turning to Deidre, she motioned for the girl to follow, and the three of us quickly made our way through the slumbering westside to the rebel headquarters.

It was almost dawn, and my training with Sword Master Ravnik would begin soon in the courtyard behind the pub. I hoped this encounter would not make me late. He hated it when I was late and always made me run more drills than the other recruits. The last time I was late, he forced me to run laps around the courtyard for the first half of training.

Sword Master Aldric Ravnik was one of the hardest men I had ever met. He never smiled, and he barked orders at the recruits without even a shadow of emotion on his face. My classmate, Gwendolyn, had told me that he was Fae, from some city north of Lunestair. We had never seen him shift, and none of the recruits knew what his clan was.

I bet he is a rat or something.

The thought brought a smile to my face as the Dragon came into view and we stepped inside. It was too early for the pub to be open, but the only customers were rebels, anyway. Ivor had warded the place with strong magic to prevent outsiders from wanting to enter. The only way you could get in was if you were part of the Dragon's Fire, or you were invited in by a member.

"Magpie. What brings you in this morning?" Dante asked from behind the counter, a forced smile on his weathered face.

My mouth dropped open.

The Magpie?

Maggie was the Magpie who worked for the resistance?

That can't be right! She tried to force me away from it!

Maggie's face was hard, an unreadable expression on her features. "You know exactly why I am here, Dante. Don't play games with me. Where is Ivor?"

The Dwarf held up his hands in mock surrender. "It was not my idea, Maggie. Don't blame me."

He headed toward the basement door to retrieve Ivor, glancing for a moment in my direction before descending the steps.

The basement housed the rebel leaders' offices, and it was there that Ivor spent the majority of his time when he was not in the courtyard training the recruits.

When Dante returned, Ivor was following behind, his dark face a mask. "Maggie. What is it?"

"How dare you drag my daughter into this! I explicitly said she was not to be involved." Her voice was thunder, a growl emanating from the depths of her throat.

Deidre and I glanced at each other nervously as the tall Fae shouted at the leader of the resistance. "When I recommended Teigan to you, that did not mean to drag Deidre along as well."

"No one dragged Deidre here. She came of her own accord, Maggie, after following Teigan to a meeting. We gave her the choice of joining the recruits or leaving. She made her decision."

The Magpie's voice was steel as she replied, "She never should have been offered the choice. She is fifteen years old. She should not be a part of this. You know that!"

"I'm sorry, my friend, but we need people."

Deidre tugged Maggie's dress, and the tall woman turned to her adoptive daughter. "I told you, I want to be a part of this. I am not such a child as you think, and you recommended Teigan for this! Why am I not the same?"

"Teigan is a full three years older than you! He is an adult. You are a child. The Dragon's Fire is not a bunch of children throwing a tantrum. It's a full-blown rebellion—against the King of Valeria, for Skotos' sake!"

"Please, Mama." The girl pleaded. "Just let it go. I want to do this. I want justice for my father."

Maggie sighed heavily, turning back to Ivor. "No dangerous missions. If anything happens to her, I am holding you responsible." She wagged her finger threateningly at Ivor. "And I will unleash the lion."

The rebel leader did not seem the least bit intimidated.

Unleash the lion? What in Amengor does that even mean?

I looked at Deidre questioningly, tugging her sleeve to get her attention. She rolled her eyes.

"I'll explain later," she whispered, turning her attention back to the events unfolding between The Magpie and the leader of the Dragon's Fire.

Maggie glowered at Ivor, awaiting his response. The man scrubbed his hands through his ebony hair, exhaling loudly. "Fine. No dangerous missions. Now, let us put this behind us. Please, come downstairs. I have your next assignment."

Turning to Deidre and me, he motioned to the courtyard. "Training is beginning."

We took our dismissal and headed for the back door of the pub as Maggie followed Ivor below.

Once in the courtyard, I turned to the small girl beside me. "I am going to need an explanation."

Deidre's reddened cheeks puffed out as she exhaled, and we made our way to our seats, waiting for Sword Master Ravnik to give his rousing speech for the morning.

"Maggie does not like to reveal her clan because of the implications." I waited for her to continue, my confusion evident on my face. "Her clan is the lions. Maggie's family is distantly related to the Ericcsöns. Truthfully, there are not many lions outside of the Ericcsöns."

Understanding dawned on me. That's what she had meant.

"As you can imagine, when people learn she is a lion, there tend to be questions and accusations. People think she must be loyal to Cyrus, based on relation. Which simply isn't true. She hates Cyrus. I've known that she was a part of the Dragon's Fire since its founding, but she forbade me from asking about it. She wouldn't even speak of it and made sure I never met anyone involved. I've known Ivor's name, but never met him until the night I followed you."

"Maggie is a founding member of the Dragon's Fire?"

"Yes, she and Ivor are childhood friends. When the king slaughtered Ivanna and Boris, Ivor and Xula came to her with the idea."

"Wow, I can't believe—"

"Recruits!" Sword Master Ravnik's voice rang out over the courtyard now lit with the rising sun, nearly splitting my eardrums. It's a good thing Ivor's magic was so powerful with the wards, or they would be able to hear Ravnik at the Castle of the Stars. "We are going to be starting this morning's training with timed individual sparing. Mr. Dinkle is going to be announcing your partner. As you are called, please step into the sparring ring. Deidre Olsen, you will not be fighting today. Please see me."

Deidre's nose wrinkled as she rose, and Rufus stepped up to announce the first sparring partners.

"Gwendolyn Nova and Axel Bolten! Select your melee weapon and step into the sparring ring."

I held my breath for Gwen as the fight began. The girl was a good fighter, but Axel was a beast and four years her senior. I hoped our teachers put some thought into our partners. I don't believe Gwen and Axel could be on the same level.

Swords clashed, and the sound of grunts and muttered curses came from the ring. Gwendolyn was a tall and gangly girl, making her slow. What she lacked in speed, she made up for in strength, bringing her sword down on Axel's with surprising force.

Axel was too fast for Gwen, though, and parried her thrust to the right, throwing her off balance, her lanky limbs causing her to teeter precariously as she tried to regain her footing.

She raised her sword, trying to block Axel's counter-attack, but failed miserably.

Rufus called the match, and Gwen and Axel were instructed to see Mr. Ravnik for critiques and tips on their sparring techniques. Poor Gwen. They should have paired her with someone closer to her skill level.

As the next names were called and the match began, my thoughts drifted, somehow finding their way to Remmy. I wonder what she would think of all this? She would probably be down there teaching. I didn't know how good she was with swords, but she was definitely a fighter. Rogard had been so sure she would make it. But where was she now? It had been weeks. If she had survived, wouldn't she be back already?

She is probably gone. She and the prince both. It pained me to admit, but as the days stretched on with no news of her or the Prince of Valeria, the chances of survival were growing weaker. If Remmy were dead, then the prince would probably be dead soon, too. No other women had entered this stupid contest. At least not that I had heard. And if the prince were dead… where did that leave the Dragon's Fire? Who would we install as king? Soren?

I knew very little about the Crown Prince, but I knew even less about his younger brother. The young prince seldom made public appearances and kept to the palace for most festivals and events.

I think he is just a little older than me... isn't he?

"Teigan Berger and Aubern Heil! You're up next." The sound of my name spurred me to attention, and I groaned as my partner was announced.

Aubern Heil should not even be a recruit! She was far too advanced to still be in these classes. Aubern was a thirty-year-old Elf who had joined Dragon's Fire about six months ago, already having superior sword training. She was nearly as tall as I was and always wore her ice-blond hair fitted in a tight braid around her skull.

'Better for fighting,' she had said. Ivor had insisted that she go through the classes the same as every other recruit, but that was utter garbage. She was a better swordsman than Rufus, her only equal being Mr. Ravnik.

Why in Amengor did they pair me with her?

So much for equal partners. I tried to recall who the last few sets of partners were, and suddenly it made sense. In each couple, there was one fighter who was more advanced than the other. They must be pairing us with someone who possesses a certain skill we lack. But then why pair me with Aubern?

As I stepped into the ring and selected my sword, Rufus drew close, issuing instructions for the match. "Teigan, Sword Master Ravnik believes with some additional guidance, you could be one of the best fighters we have ever pushed through this training, next to Aubern, that is."

My jaw went slack at his words. I realized I was advancing quickly, but I did not know that Ravnik deemed me quite that competent. He was always forcing extra exercises on me, yelling at me to run laps.

"He would like you to learn from Aubern's footwork. You are heavy on your right foot, and he believes you will benefit from observing her footwork as she fights. After your hand-to-hand combat class today, we will be graduating you from training to work as a leader in the reconnaissance division."

By the hair of Lunaire! Leader?!

"B-but, sir... why me? I've only been here a few weeks." I stuttered in surprise.

Rufus smiled at me. "Teigan, you're the top of your class. No one has trained harder for this position than you. You deserve it, and I gave my full recommendation to promote you. No one has been as dedicated as you. You relentlessly pursued me until I got you a meeting with Ivor. You're one of the most skilled swordsmen I've seen in the year I've been helping Ravnik train recruits, and you are better at convincing people to talk to you than anyone else I have ever met. Must be those boyish good looks of yours." He chuckled and winked at Aubern.

"He's nineteen, Rufus." The woman responded. I swiveled my head in her direction, expecting to see resentment but seeing only a twinkle of humor in her eyes.

Rufus chuckled again before returning to the task at hand. "Aubern, we are graduating you as well today, and Ivor is turning over a battalion of soldiers to your command. Congratulations."

A battalion?!

The resistance must be growing quicker than I thought, to be able to hand over an entire battalion to a new commander. I didn't even know we had one battalion, let alone multiple.

I realized how little I actually knew about the rebellion, as Aubern nodded in thanks and we moved to the center of the ring.

I decided my best defense was to wait for Aubern to strike first. I watched her feet as she moved forward, barely tapping her right foot against the ground as she thrust, bouncing lightly on both feet. I dodged the attack, attempting to mimic the footwork with my counter-thrust. Aubern recognized my intent immediately and smiled in approval.

"You're a quick learner, Teigan." She said as she parried and thrust again at me.

"Thanks. Congratulations on your promotion to Battalion Leader." I grunted as I swung my sword overhead to block an attack from above. "I—" Our swords clanged, and my arms vibrated from the impact. "Didn't even know we had that many people."

The tall woman let out a low chuckle. "Congratulations to you as well. I didn't know either, but it makes sense they would keep such information from recruits. There is no guarantee we'll pass our training."

She moved with lightning speed, swinging and thrashing, as I exhaled heavily in my attempts to keep up with her, bouncing on the balls of my toes as I had seen her do, and blocking her attacks, with barely any time to parry or counter.

"Somehow, I think—" I lifted my sword to block a thrust aimed at my center. "—That you would have passed either way, Aubern. How did you get so good at sword fighting?"

"My father was a blacksmith. When I was a girl, he would let me visit the forge. When I took an interest in learning the weapons, he began to teach me fencing. I learned from there. I've held a sword since I was eight years of age."

"Wow! They should have you teaching, not training!"

"I don't mind." She heaved from exertion as time was called on our match, sweat dripping down her brow. "There is always room for improvement. And today, you taught me not to underestimate an opponent. Good match, my friend, and good luck with the reconnaissance missions. I doubt we will be seeing much of each other once the fighting begins."

"Do you think they're moving us into leadership positions too quickly?" I asked her hesitantly as we gathered our stuff to exit the ring.

"Stop second-guessing your abilities, Teigan. You've got this, and the resistance needs you." Aubern clapped my shoulder as she walked past.

I smiled to myself as Ravnik dismissed class, and I followed Rufus to hand-to-hand combat. After today, I would be a full-fledged leader of the Dragon's Fire Rebellion.

* * *

Remmy

I woke several hours later, my legs aching from being scrunched into a ball, and my side cold against the stone floor.

Where is Sterling?

When I reached out for the dragon, my hand landed on bare flesh, and I opened my eyes to find a very naked Sterling curled into a ball on the floor beside me, having transformed back into his Fae form during the night.

I gasped and tossed off my pack, sliding out of my cloak and tossing it over his body, shaking his shoulders roughly.

Oh, gods, please be okay. Please be okay!

"Sterling!" He jolted upright, eyes wide in alarm, before looking down at himself and wrapping my cloak tighter around his body, exhaling in relief.

I let out a breath I had been holding at finding him well.

Remorse flashed across his face as he looked me over, taking my face in both of his strong hands and cupping my ears. He moved my head from side to side, peering at my face and neck, and looking intently into my eyes. "Are you okay? Did I hurt you? Are you well? How's your arm?"

I smiled and placed my hands over his as they rested on top of my ears. "I am okay, Sterling. You may release my face."

The prince nodded and let go of me, his hands falling limply into his lap, his head hanging so low his chin almost touched his chest.

"I'm sorry, Remmy. I couldn't stop it. I tried to fight it… I tried so hard… but it was too strong."

I reached out and placed my hand on top of his. "I know. I don't blame you. I am just glad we made it through the night."

A trickle of blood was caked beneath his nose, and I remembered punching him the night before. "Oh gods, Sterling, your nose! I'm so sorry! Does it hurt?"

"Healed already."

I reached for his arm, where my nails had dug into his skin. Also healed. Sighing, I released his arm.

He looked at me intently. "How did you…?"

"I am not sure, but I have a theory that the dark magic is attracted to the essence of power. I am assuming it did not bother with me because humans hold none."

Sterling pursed his lips and nodded slightly. "That makes sense. When we were here before, it was only Fae in our party."

"I would still love to know how your father was deemed 'worthy' to enter, considering his many atrocities."

"I think I have an answer for that, but first we need to get out of this temple." He stood, pulling my cloak tighter around him, and grabbed my hand, ushering me toward the stairs.

I bent and retrieved my pack from where I had tossed it, and we crept up the narrow stairway.

We turned the corner to where I had been last night, making for the exit at the end of the hall as quietly as possible, when a door to our left opened and Zyphara stepped out.

The priestess gasped, covering her mouth with her hand, eyes widening in surprise. No doubt she expected to find our bodies, dead from insanity, somewhere this morning.

My hand rapidly went to my baldric, and I unsheathed my sword, holding the tip to her throat with a menacing growl. She had trapped us in this hellhole, and who knows how many she murdered on that table below.

"Hello, Zyphara! You're looking lovely this morning." Sterling quipped from beside me, a sarcastic grin spreading across his handsome face.

Her eyes flashed between us in question, and she swallowed nervously. "Your Highness! What—uuumm—what is this?"

"The prince requires clothing." I jabbed the tip of the sword harder into her throat, drawing blood, and she cried out fearfully.

"Okay! Please don't hurt me. I'll find you something. Just… just follow me."

"Do not try anything, priestess, or I will slice your head clean off your shoulders."

Sterling chucked before snatching Zyphara's arm. "Lead the way."

I moved my sword to the back of her waist, taking care to dig it in a little, curbing any temptation she may have to run. Sterling's grip on her was strong enough that I probably didn't need to, but she deserved it.

The priestess pulled a set of keys from beneath the folds of her robes and stopped at a door several paces down the hall. She unlocked it, letting us in. "There should be something in here that will work." She pointed to a small chest against the wall of what appeared to be a storage room.

"You first." I prodded her into the room, watching for booby traps. She stepped through the doorway, and when nothing happened, Sterling moved forward to sort through the chest.

I pushed my sword harder into her ribs. "Is this where you keep the clothes of your victims?"

The priestess did not answer me, staring down idly as she fidgeted with her robes.

If she pulls a dagger out of there, I will run her through.

"You would think, since the time of the Vanta, that someone would have created shape-shifting clothing." I snickered, and Sterling turned toward us.

"These should work somewhat decently." He held up a set of clothing and stood waiting.

"If you think I am going back out there in the creepy temple by myself with the priestess of death here, you have lost your mind." I prodded Zyphara again with my sword, and she huffed indignantly at my description of her. "Besides, I've already seen your backside,"

I smirked.

"For the love of the gods, Remmy. At least turn her around!" He jerked his finger at the glowering priestess.

"Come on, Succubus, let's give His Highness some privacy." I pushed Zyphara with my sword, and we both turned to face the door, her face purple with rage.

Sterling laughed out loud. "Should we raid the kitchen before we leave?"

"Unless you plan to unleash your inner dragon again anytime soon, I say we get as far from here as quickly as possible. I'd rather take my chances finding food out there than stay here a moment longer than necessary."

Sterling went quiet behind me as he finished dressing in the stolen clothing.

I guess he is still upset about the clan thing.

"Ready?" He asked from directly behind, startling me and causing me to jump.

Smiling a bit darkly, he extended his hand, presenting me with my cloak once more. I snatched it from him and turned back to the priestess.

"Let's go." I poked Zyphara with my sword, and the three of us exited the storage room.

"You are going to escort us to the gates, ensure the veil opens properly, and then allow us to leave through it. If you so much as utter a word, I'll drive this sword through your rib cage, and your black blood will paint these stones. Understand?"

The priestess nodded emphatically, and we made our way out into the early morning sun.

Sterling eyed me curiously, a wicked grin on his face. I rolled my eyes, ignoring the feeling of flame moths in my belly, and kept my sword trained on the priestess of death.

Why is he looking at me that way?

Zyphara led us to the great stone obelisks that concealed the veil and placed her hand on a rune, just above eye level. The rune glowed blue for a moment before the veil shimmered, rippling with magic and tearing open in a streak of blue lightning.

I looked at Sterling at the same time he looked at me.

"Together?" He asked, stretching out his hand. I shoved the priestess away from us, and grasping his hand, together we plunged through the veil to the other side.

Twenty-Nine

Decisions and Heartache

* * *

Emerie

I closed the door to the empty storeroom, my heart leaden.

What am I going to do now?

Inara stopped by once per week with a package of meat that she concealed from her father, and Alice brought leftover bread from the bakery whenever she could, but that wasn't enough. We were going to starve if I did not figure something out soon.

The letter we received from the king burned a hole in my pocket as I stared mournfully at the children playing hopscotch near the fire, by Father's chair. He rocked aimlessly, an empty look in his eyes.

I'll have to tell them. But I'll let them have one last night of peace.

They're too young for this.

I clapped my hands loudly to get their attention. "Children, go outside and play until I call you for dinner."

Echo groaned, perturbed to have to move from her warm spot, but Eridian leaped to his feet eagerly and dashed for the door.

"Race you to the wood line!" He called to his sister, who giggled and bounced up to join him.

"You'll never beat me, Eri. I'm faster than you any day!"

The ache in my heart grew as I watched their joy. Let them be children for one more night.

Turning to my father, I took a deep breath and kneeled on the floor in front of his rocking chair. His hand rested on his good knee, and I placed mine over it, timidly. He did not make eye contact with me, only continued rocking in his chair as though I were not present.

"Father? There is something I must tell you."

I cleared my throat and summoned strength from deep within me. "It is about Remmy… we received a letter from King Cyrus today."

His chair paused rocking for a moment before he began again, staring off into the fire crackling in the hearth. "She's… dead, Father. She was killed on Mt. Malus." I choked; the words barely a whisper in the room. "Her body… it was not recovered."

The tears left my eyes now and streamed down my face in rivulets of pain. Father's chair stopped rocking, and he looked at me for the first time in months. A tear slipped from the corner of one deep green eye, and he hung his head in silence. This show of emotion from the father who had been lost to me was more than I could handle. I rose quickly.

My sobs echoed off the walls of our tiny cabin as I shut myself inside the empty storeroom once more, sinking to the floor. I had not even had a moment to process the information in the letter until now. I hadn't wanted the children to see me cry.

With Remmy gone, I was all they had left. My throat constricted in anguish as my cries filled the tiny space. I pulled my knees to my chest and folded my arms, resting my head on top of them.

My sister. My darling sister is gone. How can I go on? I can't do this without you, Remmy. I can't do this without you.

My eyes fell on Remmy's bow tucked away in the corner, and all at once, I knew what I had to do. I would save my family.

Thirty

Citrus and Honeysuckle

* * *

Remmy

We walked for hours before finding anything edible on the trail; a couple of wild strawberries and blueberries were tangled in some vines, but we had yet to see any wildlife. The berries were juicy and succulent on my tongue.

Without my dagger, I was not sure how I would hunt. I'd never tried to hunt with a sword. It seemed… difficult and impractical.

Sterling had been quiet since we escaped the Temple of Deliritas, leaving my questions unanswered. Whenever I tried to ask, he shut me down, his mood going even darker than usual.

I glanced sidelong at him now, observing the clothes he had chosen from the chest. The black shirt fit him loosely, the laces hanging open to reveal his muscled chest. Whatever malnourishment he'd suffered in the cabin was far from evident now. His mysterious tattoos peeked out from the collar, winding up the back of his neck, partially covered by waves of his dark hair. I briefly entertained the thought of brushing back his hair to look at them, and then rolled my eyes at the ludicrous idea.

What is wrong with me?

Instead, I asked, "When do we come to water?"

"If I remember correctly, we should be approaching a small stream soon. It was only a few hours' walk from the temple. We'll camp there."

"What? It's barely midday! It's too early to stop."

"I said we'll camp there, Remmy."

"I heard what you said, Sterling. I am neither deaf nor dumb, but I want to know why we would make camp when there are hours left of daylight and we've had but a handful of berries to eat today!"

The prince's face began to redden, and he ran his hands through his hair. "We are going to camp at the stream because shortly thereafter, we will reach the Darkhelm Forest." He said it as though that were decent enough explanation.

"We can camp within the Darkhelm! I stayed there for many nights on my journey up. There is no sense in wasting daylight, when all of Valeria awaits YOUR return!"

"I said no!" He bellowed, his face contorted in fury. "I am too bloody tired to deal with another death trap tonight!"

The stream came into view, and the prince stormed off ahead of me and began gathering sticks for a fire.

I shook my head.

* * *

Sterling

The hurt and frustration on Remmy's face weighed heavily on me, but I couldn't allow her to believe this was anything more than it was.

Without control over my clan form, it was unpredictable and unreliable, leaving me still vulnerable to my father. I couldn't allow Remmy to get pulled into this mess. If keeping her safe meant she hated me, then so be it. Distancing myself was the only way to ensure I didn't go back on my word and allow her to stay in Lunestair.

She must return home. It's the only way to protect her. When Father discovers I'm alive, he's going to try to kill me, and I can't allow her to be a casualty in this war.

I was not sure when I had begun to care for her, only that I had, and it was driving me to the brink of madness.

She was driving me to the brink of madness.

I glanced to where she kneeled, unpacking her remaining supplies, her now tattered cloak pooling in folds of emerald around her feet.

My chest constricted as I turned away, stacking the sticks in a pile near where she worked. I couldn't start the fire without her flint, so I stood there awkwardly arranging the sticks into a triangle, allowing for plenty of airflow to keep the fire blazing.

A sharp stick jabbed me in the hand, prompting a sudden thought.

Remmy lost her dagger, but perhaps she would allow me to borrow her sword. I can sharpen a stick into a makeshift spear.

It would be awkward to use a sword that way, but I was tired of being unarmed and relying on her for a weapon. I stole another glance in Remmy's direction. Her cheeks were still flushed in anger as she spread her fur on the ground, leaving the wool blanket in a pile for me.

The whiteness of her fading scars stuck out against the red in small lines, no wider than a needle. She was so beautiful it hurt to look at her. A dull, twisting ache settled in my chest as I watched. I drew closer to her, placing a hand on the back of my neck. The soft scent of citrus and honeysuckle assailed me, and I realized it was coming from her.

Why have I never noticed that before? Gods.

She smelled like a warm summer breeze. I cleared my throat haltingly, and she looked up from where she perched on the ground.

"May I borrow your sword?"

"Well, that depends, *Your Highness,* on what you intend to do with it and whether or not you are going to tell me what is going on?"

"Aaggghh! You're impossible!" I threw my hands in the air, puffing out a breath.

"Well, if I am impossible, then I am not likely to let you borrow my sword, now, am I?"

"How can you be so stubborn? I simply wish to borrow it for a few moments."

"For what?" She narrowed her eyes at me suspiciously.

"To… sharpen a stick… into a spear." I finished weakly.

She laughed derisively. "That is what you plan to do with my sword? Make a stick spear? You need a dagger for that!"

Gods, she is furious.

She wasn't the type to ridicule. "I'm fully aware, but we don't have a dagger, now do we?" I sneered.

I regretted the words the moment they left my mouth, wishing I could shove them back in. The reference to her fall was too much, and I watched as her eyes shuttered, a grimace of fear marring her lovely features.

"Ugh!" She slammed her hands onto the packed dirt and pushed herself off the ground, sulking off to the water.

"Remmy, wait! I'm sorry."

"Leave me alone, Sterling."

I clasped my hands behind my neck, sighing.

Why am I such an imbecile?

Isolde's face flashed through my mind briefly, and my remorse turned to irritation and then morphed back into sorrow.

What Remmy wanted to know was not something I could share. Why did this woman have such an effect on me? I couldn't even think straight around her.

She has no right to smell so bloody good! Arrghh!

"Lunaire, save me," I muttered. I dragged a hand through my hair again, as I sat on the blanket Remmy had tossed to the side, staring at the pile of sticks I had still been unable to light.

Something thudded onto the ground beside me, and I looked up as Remmy tossed her sword down.

"Do with it what you will." She said tightly before turning to root through her pack.

I'll tell her. I'll tell her everything. Tonight.

I promised myself, as I rose to locate a stick.

Thirty-One

Secrets, Lies, and Revelations

* * *

Remmy

I dropped my net into the water for the fifth time, pulling up empty once again. Fury coursed through me like blood in my veins—at the situation, at my failure to catch anything, at this stupid stream, and at Sterling for his blasted secrets and lies.

I had almost allowed myself to care for him, but that was foolish, and it always had been. He made it clear from the moment we met that he would never feel anything for me. This was a business arrangement, and I needed to remember that.

But that doesn't mean I will allow him to keep things from me, especially if they will affect the rest of this trip. What am I walking into in Lunestair? Are the king and his band of mercenaries going to try to kill me again?

Or the Blood Guard?

Sighing heavily, I jerked my empty net from the water and went to sit on the shore, staring out across the trickling water.

It was still hours until dinner, so I had plenty of time to try again, but I was losing my patience and needed something else to occupy myself with.

Why did Sterling demand we stop this early? It's bloody ridiculous. We could be halfway through the Darkhelm before needing to stop for the night. I don't understand him.

Behind me, I heard him grunt as he struggled to whittle with a sword, an idea taking root in my mind. I hoped the further we got from the dark magic of the Temple of Deliritas, the more we would begin to see wildlife again, making hunting a viable option for food. Without my dagger, hunting would be difficult unless I had another weapon.

Returning to my pack, I fished out the remaining hemp string. There would be just enough for what I needed. I set off toward the trees in search of the perfect branch, without a glance in the prince's direction.

"Where are you going?" He called as I strode away.

Ignoring him, I searched the ground and trees until I found what I was looking for.

This will be perfect.

I picked off a thin branch that was pliable yet sturdy from a nearby tree and returned to where Sterling sat watching me, finally finished with my sword. The prince eyed me warily as I sat on the earth near him.

"What are you going to do with that?"

"You'll see when I am done."

Exhaling with a puff of breath, he rose and snatched my fishing net from the ground.

My head jerked up. "What are you doing?"

"Fishing." He replied stiffly.

I snickered. "The Crown Prince of Valeria is going to wade into a tiny stream and… fish?"

The prince stopped abruptly, turning back to me, anger flashing in his steely eyes. "Well, you didn't have much luck, did you?" He mocked.

I scoffed. "Like you'll do much better! There are no fish in that blasted stream, anyway. It's probably polluted with dark magic." I wagged my finger dramatically at the frustrating steam. My net was too big for such a small stream, adding to the complications of fishing in it.

Sterling rolled his eyes and continued to the stream.

"Good luck!" I called jeeringly, shaking my head as he walked away.

This man is infuriating. Ugh, why does he make me so mean?

My jaw fell open when the prince returned less than half an hour later, holding a small fish. I stared at it. "How did you—? I tossed the net six times!"

Sterling eyed me smugly as I stammered. "I guess I am not completely useless after all. I need the flint."

It was not much, but it would keep us from starving for a little while longer. I would try again before we left this area.

Rummaging through my now sparse pack, I pulled out the flint and steel, tossing them to him. The prince observed the stick and hemp on the ground beside me.

"A bow." It was more of a statement than a question. "What are you going to do with a bow without arrows?"

"I am going to go get more sticks and sharpen the tips like you did to make arrows," I stated as though it were the most obvious thing in the world and trudged off to find more sticks, grumbling to myself about my decision to leave my bow at home.

Home.

My mind went to Emerie, Echo, and Eri, and I realized I hadn't thought about them in a while, the constant fight to survive occupying every crevice of my mind. A sharp pang squeezed my chest as I noted the food supply I had left them would have run out by now.

Hopefully, Emerie can get help from Alice or her friend Inara.

I closed my eyes briefly, uttering a prayer to the goddess for provision for my family. The thought of my siblings struggling left me even more furious with Sterling for delaying our progress. It would still take days after we left the mountain to reach Lunestair, and even longer for someone to reach them in Merda.

"So, what you're saying is… I gave you a good idea." Sterling's voice jarred me out of my thoughts, and I scowled at him, ignoring his remark as I continued my search for sticks.

I had nothing to make a quiver with, so I would have to secure the arrows to the outside of my pack. I mulled over how to solve this problem, while gathering sturdy enough limbs to serve my needs, and then returned to the now roaring fire, seating myself beside the haughty prince with a harrumph.

Sterling gave me an odd look as I sat on the cold earth. "What? What is it now?"

"I'm ready." He responded, a somewhat distant expression on his handsome face.

"Ready for what?" I asked, confused by the sudden change in demeanor.

"To talk."

* * *

Sterling

"What is it you wish to know first? I know you have many questions." Remmy's eyes widened as I spoke.

"Uhhh," She stammered, clearly taken off guard. "Why didn't you tell me you were a dragon?"

I sighed heavily, dragging my hands through my hair. This was frustrating, but I needed to be honest with Remmy to convince her to go back to Merda. She deserved the truth, despite how much it pained me to admit, and keeping it from her had led to nothing but bitterness. "I have no control over it. It will not aid us at all if I cannot use it when I need it."

"You mean you can't transform whenever you want to?"

I shook my head solemnly, waiting for the next blow to my pride.

"So, that's why you couldn't shift back to your Fae form in the temple." Her eyes searched mine for confirmation of her assumption, and I let her find it.

A soft smile lit her face, and she reached forward to grasp my hand. "That's okay! We can work on it. I don't know much about Fae shifting, but I can help you figure it out."

Those green eyes of hers pierced into my soul, and I knew she would do whatever it took to help me, but I didn't want her to. I wanted her to flee. Flee my father's wrath and return to Merda, far from me, and far from Lunestair.

Unwilling to start another argument, I did not voice any of this. I only nodded and asked what she wished to know next.

"The tattoos... they're a sign of your clan's emergence?"

Absent-mindedly, my hand went to the side of my neck where the tattoos on my back wrapped around it in an embrace. I'd felt the tattoos embed in my skin as it happened, but without a looking-glass, I was not sure what they truly looked like.

"Yes, all Fae receive a tattoo of some kind when their clan emerges. Although mine seems to be… uhhh—somewhat… larger than most." I hesitated before asking as casually as possible, "Would you tell me what it looks like?"

Remmy's face blushed a light crimson, and she put a hand to one of her cheeks, but nodded anyway.

Slowly, I slid my shirt over my head and turned my back to her, the cold autumn breeze whipping at my skin. Her fingers graced my back, tracing the lines of my tattoos gently, and a shiver coursed up my spine at the feel of her hands on my skin.

Her voice was soft when she spoke, a touch of awe present, and I could not help but be pleased that I was the cause of it.

"It's beautiful. Like a painting of the galaxies above, stars dot your back, woven between moons and planets I've never seen. So many stars… like… like…"

"The Stardust District." I finished for her.

I'm the heir to the throne... it's marked on me.

She nodded as I turned to face her, slipping my shirt back over my head, already missing the warmth of her touch.

"The region of stars… is painted on your back. It covers your scars." Our eyes locked for a brief moment, and what I saw within her emerald stare shook me to my fragile core. It wasn't pity or rejection I saw there. But admiration and respect.

Forcing a nonchalant grin, I shrugged my shoulders. "At least they serve some purpose. What else would you like to know about me? Tonight, I am an open-ish book!"

I waved my arms through the air with a dramatic flourish, causing the woman sitting across from me to giggle, the sound of her laughter making my heart sing.

Her face turned thoughtful as she spoke. "You said you had been to the Temple of Deliritas before... why were you there the last time?"

Bile rose in my throat at the mention of my first trip to the temple. I had hoped she would forget about it, but I should have known better.

Remmy was like contained sunshine, until something bothered her, and then she was as relentless as The Broken Sea until she got her answers. I swallowed down the guilt and sickness that rose to my throat at the thought of Isolde and pursed my lips to the side.

How to tell her?

"When I was fifteen, I snuck from the castle into Lunestair in search of some trouble to get into. My father allowed me few friends, and being trapped in a castle is the quickest way to drive a boy to madness. In the market, I met an elven girl with silver hair. She was... everything. Everything that I had dreamed of. She was fun. She was beautiful. She was passionate. An orphan from the village of Manya, in Tangeer. I couldn't sneak out to see her often, so my manservant, Vincent, helped me conceal her elven ears and get her a job as a maid in the palace. I saw her whenever I could. Sneaking into broom cupboards or out to the stables to steal a few moments together. I loved her. Gods, did I love her... with the fire of a thousand suns. I swore I would marry her when my clan emerged, and I could fight my father. But my clan never emerged. We concealed our relationship for years, but when I was twenty-one, my father found out about her and, being the elitist that he is, refused to allow us to be together.

I woke one night with a hand over my mouth. He dragged us through the woods and up to the Temple of Deliritas. Five guards for one girl and me. He even forced my brother, Soren, and Vincent to watch. There, on the stone table in the altar room that my dragon destroyed, I watched as my father drained the life from Isolde, sacrificing her to the god of death."

My eyes glazed over at the memory of her screams, my heart almost collapsing in on itself.

"It took two guards, Soren, and dark magic wielded by the priestess Zyphara, to restrain me and carry me back to the palace. Soren stayed with me the entire time, assuring me things would be all right. Father left his guards behind to be consumed by the madness of the temple, and told me if I ever spoke of what happened, Vincent would be the next sacrifice." I turned to Remmy earnestly and took her hands in mine. Her face reflected the horror my story deserved as I spoke my next words cautiously. "This is why you must return to Merda, Remmy. My father… he is brutal. He craves power above all else. There is no love in him, and I cannot defeat him without being able to access my clan form. He never intended for you to make it to me, and if you come with me to Lunestair… he'll kill us both."

Remmy's jaw clenched into a stubborn line, and I glimpsed the storm brewing within her. "I am so sorry. I am so terribly sorry for what you went through. No one should have to endure such things, but I believe in you, Sterling. We will find a way."

"Remmy, please. You don't understand. My father and his guards can transform at will! They will tear you to shreds in an instant. You must return to your father." Shadows flitted across her face at my words, but she did not fire back at me with the argument I expected.

"At least allow me to return with you to Lunestair, long enough to find a horse or carriage. The journey from Lunestair to Merda is long, and I fear I can't make it alone after all of this."

A sigh of relief left me upon her acceptance.

Thank the gods.

"Of course. I will rent you a room at The Starlight Oasis for you to rest a few nights, then I'll procure you a horse to travel. I'll make sure your family has everything they need, Rem. I swear it."

She smiled somewhat timidly, and I released her hands, stretching out my legs in front of me and leaning back, propped up with my arms behind me.

"Was there anything else you wished to ask me?"

"What happened to the queen?" I started at the mention of my mother. I could hardly remember her. She disappeared when I was only a child.

"Well, uhhh—my father claimed she died in a horrible accident while on a journey to visit her family. Though I suspect that is not the truth."

"You believe Cyrus killed her?"

"Truthfully, I have not thought about my mother in quite some time. It's been twenty years since I last saw her, and I can hardly remember her. But yes. I believe my father had her killed. I just wish I knew why." I paused. "Is there anything else you'd like to know?"

"You mentioned having an idea about why Cyrus would have been allowed into the temple?"

"I am uncertain, but what I saw that day led me to believe that he has formed some kind of deal with the dark god. I don't know what for, but it's just another problem I will have to solve when I return to Lunestair."

I let out a deep breath and glanced up at the sky. We must have been talking for quite some time. The sun was beginning to dip on the horizon, coloring the sky with tints of crimson and gold. Wispy clouds caught the light, transforming into a canvas of soft pinks and purples that blended seamlessly into the deepening blue above. "It is getting late. We should try to catch some more fish before the sun sets completely."

Remmy nodded, and we rose from our spot on the hard ground. I noticed as she tugged her capote tighter around her that the cold was not affecting me to the same extent it had been before my dragon emerged.

Probably the fire boiling in my blood right now. If only I could figure out how to use that, too. Then I wouldn't have to ask Remmy for a flint. Perhaps I'll try practicing after dinner.

That seemed easier than trying to get the dragon to resurface. Maybe if I could control it, I could light my father on fire. I chuckled. My father's earth magic was strong, but I wasn't sure if he could put a fire out with it. The visual image of my father dumping dirt on himself to put out a fire on his rear kept me amused for a while after we stepped into the frigid stream.

Thirty-Two

Now Is Our Time

* * *

Teigan

A tear trickled down my face, and I wiped it away angrily with the back of my hand as I made my way through the squalid alleys of the westside.

Remmy.

I had thought it, but hearing it true wrecked me. Sadness, once again, seeped into every part of my existence. The royal courier had announced it in the city square early this afternoon, and news had spread as posters went up all over the kingdom.

'THE CROWN PRINCE IS DEAD! KILLED BY A BEAST ON MT.

MALUS AFTER VOLUNTEERING FOR HIS FATHER'S CONTEST"

Volunteering.

I sneered at the word. The herald had warped the news to fit the king's twisted narrative. Cyrus had put on a charade of a processional to mourn his eldest son. Trumpeters and bards in the street sang Prince Sterling's praises in a mockery of the truth of his death.

I don't know why he even bothers. Everyone knows the truth. He sent his son to die. He thinks we are so naïve. The whole country suffers under his tyranny.

I stormed into the Drunken Dragon, the room already full of rebels, spilling out into the courtyard. I had never seen this many of us together in one place.

Thank Lunaire for the wards.

There was no way a gathering of this size could be kept under wraps without them.

The faces of everyone in the room echoed my own. Hopeless. Our hope was dead—slaughtered without remorse.

Maggie and Deidre were already seated near the front of the room, where Ivor and Xula stood waiting for the last of the rebels to trickle in.

Rufus Dinkle lingered near the door to the courtyard, speaking in hushed tones with Dante Ariti and Sword Master Ravnik.

A rush of air left me as I plopped into the empty seat beside Deidre.

"Where were you?" She whispered, brows furrowed.

I shrugged noncommittally and fidgeted with my fingernails. Without another word, Deidre rested one hand lightly on my forearm. I stared at it for a moment, lost in thought. I had been unable to talk to her, to put a stop to the thoughts that were blossoming in her young mind. I'd been so consumed with completing my training and gathering information for the resistance that I had barely given her obvious affections a second thought.

"Deidre—" I began.

"Thank you all for meeting here tonight on such short notice." Ivor's voice rang out through the pub, amplified to the courtyard by someone's magic. I had yet to understand all the types of magic possessed by the Fae and Elves, but there seemed to be a type for nearly everything.

It was odd that magic had become such a daily part of my life now. In Castillo, it was barely used or mentioned, though most of the permanent residents there were human or Dwarf, with only the occasional Elven or Fae tourist.

Deidre's eyes met mine, and I leaned close to whisper in her ear. "After the meeting, let's talk."

She nodded eagerly, her brown eyes wide. I leaned forward, my elbows resting on my knees, and propped my chin up on my fists as I listened to Ivor speak.

"I know you all must feel the fight is lost after the announcement from the king this morning, but hope is not gone! If we give in now, we will forever be at the mercy of a tyrant. The loss of our prince is a devastating blow, and we must mourn him, but we cannot allow this to derail our mission."

A shout rang out, "But who will be king?"

Another voice raised, as the dissent among the rebels grew. "Yeah! Who will be king? Prince Soren?"

A female voice now, "No! We know nothing about Soren. He could be just as bad as the King of Lions!"

"Yeah! He's a lion too, is he not?"

Ivor moved his hand to hush the disquieted rebels, but Xula stepped forward, her voice silencing the noise as her neon eyes speared the crowd.

"It matters not who is king, only that Cyrus is defeated. The time will come when a leader must be chosen, but that time is not now. Now is the time to fight! We will suffer under tyranny no longer!"

A rebel cry rang out through the building, and the estate grounds shook as her voice raised in defiance of the tyrannical ruler.

"Now is the time to take back Valeria from the reign of a hate-filled monarch. Our children will no longer cower in the corners, fearful of the Blood Guard! Our races will no longer be afraid to mingle! One clan will not rise above the rest! We will not see our families taken from us for debts owed to the Crown or murdered in the streets for a spoken protest." I found myself leaning further forward as her speech rose to a crescendo, a fire stirring in my belly and in those around me.

"Are you willing to sacrifice so that our children may live in peace and prosperity? Are you willing to fight with me!?"

A resounding "Yeah!" echoed through the hall.

"Now is the time of the people! Now is the time of the Dragon's Fire! Through blood and flame! FROM THEIR ASHES—WE WILL RISE!" Xula shouted in triumph, her arm pumping fists into the air.

A battle cry to raise the dead split the night as the rebels rose, hands fisted to the sky in salute.

"Through blood and flame! We will rise!"

* * *

Teigan

Ivor dismissed the rebels, asking the commanders to stay behind to discuss our next steps. I leaned forward intently, a thought taking root in the turbulence of my mind.

Deidre stayed behind as well, as it was unsafe for her to walk home alone.

Taking my arm in both of hers, she leaned forward with me and whispered, "This is so exciting!"

I slipped my arm from her grasp and shushed her as Ivor began to speak once more. A look of hurt flashed across Deidre's face when I pulled away, but I didn't have the energy to deal with it right now.

"The resistance is growing in numbers every day, and I believe with the death of the prince, it will continue to grow. In just over a year, we have grown from ten members to an entire underground network. We now have multiple battalions of soldiers integrated into every part of Valeria, and entire departments dedicated to mission development, intelligence, logistics, recruitment, and reconnaissance. This week, we graduated two new recruits from training as commanders in our army, as well as several soldiers to infantry and logistics. Aubern and Teigan, come up here for a moment."

I balked. After the day I had, I couldn't fathom the idea of standing before a crowd.

Aubern walked up beside me and tapped my shoulder lightly. I rose too quickly from my chair and tripped on the leg of it, catching myself on her arm. Smiling awkwardly at the Elf, I righted myself, ignoring Deidre's snort beside me.

"Thanks," I muttered, as Aubern laughed softly. We made our way to the front of the room. There were about twenty rebel leaders gathered; I guessed not everyone was present.

"Commanders, this is Aubern Heil. She comes to us from the

Highland Mountains, on the border of Elysia. Aubern is one of the best fighters we have seen come through our training. We have assigned the battalion of new recruits to her leadership. This," He tapped on my shoulder, "is Teigan Berger. Teigan is being installed as a commander in our reconnaissance department. Xula and I would like to integrate a system of recognition for our leaders, so we can easily be identified to rebel soldiers."

He pressed a silver coin into each of our hands. The coin was embossed with the emblem of a great dragon, a circle of fire around its body.

Ivor turned to the other leaders gathered in the pub. "These will be your commander medals. We have had one made for each of you. At the end of the meeting, come forward and collect yours."

Aubern and I took our seats as Ivor continued. Deidre leaned forward and asked to see the coin. I handed it to her quietly, and her eyes gleamed as she flipped it over in her hands.

"With the addition of so many new members, we find ourselves in need of more space." Multiple eyes in the room shifted to Maggie, her red hair sticking out from her head in all directions.

Are they insane? Surely they can't think another pub is what we need.

"No." She said firmly. "I told you from the beginning, The Oasis stays out of this. You can drink there. You can eat there. You can fight there. You can even gather information there. But we cannot meet there."

Ivor rolled his eyes at his friend's adamance. "Not The Oasis, Maggie."

The Magpie's eyes widened as Ivor's request dawned on her. "You can't mean—"

"You know exactly what I mean. It is the perfect location, secluded and out of town. It has sat there abandoned for years since your parents passed."

"I came to the city to escape that place," Maggie muttered under her breath. I looked at Deidre to see if she knew what was going on, but she just shrugged her shoulders, clearly as confused as I was.

"Fine." Maggie's answer was reluctant at best.

"Perfect! Our next step then, will be to move some operations out to the old Olsen estate at the edge of town."

Deidre turned to Maggie and huffed. "You have an estate, while I live in a broom closet?"

"Oh, hush, child. Your room is much bigger than a broom closet, and you know that. I will explain when we get home." I listened to their conversation with little interest, as I realized Ivor was wrapping up the meeting.

"Does anyone have anything else?" Ivor asked.

I rose from my seat slowly and cleared my throat.

"Umm, sir?"

"Yes, Teigan, go ahead."

"The contestant who..." I exhaled heavily. "The contestant who died with the prince... she was a good friend of mine." I glanced at Xula, and her eyes softened with my confession. I swallowed and continued with my request. "I'd like to request a horse and a few days' leave to go to her young siblings in Merda. I believe with very little persuasion, her eldest sister would be willing to join our cause and help with recruitment in the villages. They are mostly poor there and suffer greatly at the hand of the king."

Ivor nodded his approval of my request. "I'm sorry for your loss, but I think that to be an excellent idea. While you're there, listen for dissent among the humans. Just be careful in your recruitment tactics. Would you like a soldier to accompany you?"

"No, sir. Remmy's family doesn't know me, and I don't want to bring them any more undue stress by showing up with another unfamiliar face in their time of great loss."

"All right. We will get you a horse, and you can leave at first light."

"Thank you, sir." Ivor dismissed the meeting, and I started to leave, but felt a tug at my sleeve. Deidre's imploring gaze met my remorseful one.

"When were you going to tell me, Teigan?"

Thirty-Three

The Newest Fashion

* * *

Remmy

A haunting silence filled the Darkhelm Forest. Skeletal trees reached toward the sky, looming like dark guardians, their presence blocking the sun from view and darkening the eerie forest. A stifling fog followed our feet as we walked, the effect making it seem like a hazy dawn instead of almost midday. The chill in the air was bone deep, as I kept a vigilant watch for Forest Imps.

Sterling gripped his makeshift spear, and I kept close beside him, my pack on one shoulder and my new bow on the other.

A shrill scream echoed through the forest, turning my blood to ice. The prince stopped abruptly, alarm evident on his paling face.

"What was that?"

"Umm—it was probably just the wind." I tugged on his sleeve, anxious to vacate the area.

"That was not the wind!" He hissed.

The air was eerily still, and the feel of dark magic encased us as my mind raced. The only thing I could think of was a Banshee. Banshees were one of those things we heard whispers of in Merda, but no one knew much about.

Lore dictated they were ghosts that had died horrible deaths and now plagued the Darkhelm, in search of victims to take to the grave with them. I was lucky not to have encountered one on my first visit through the forest. With their abilities, there was no way to outrun them. One must defeat them.

My hair flitted as a whooshing sound circled us, the form too fast for my eyes to see. I glanced wildly at Sterling, his face indicating it was not the same for his Fae eyes. His arm shot out, pulling me against him.

"Back to back! Give me your sword! She's too fast for me to hit with a spear."

"I will do no such thing. You would do well to remember I trekked this mountain alone the first time!"

Sterling snorted, his retort cut off when the whooshing stopped, and she appeared before me—black eyes and stringy white hair, her skin desiccated, mouth dripping black ichor.

A part of me felt bad for her. This woman had died a gruesome death, but there was no saving her now—the horror of it, turning her evil incarnate.

She wailed loudly in my face, latching onto me and then taking off with unnatural, bone-chilling speed, dragging me through the forest by my hair.

My screams tore through the stillness of the forest, Sterling's voice echoing my own as he bellowed my name, charging after us. Sticks and stones cut at my back and legs as she dragged me. I struggled against her hold, but she was too fast for me to gain any momentum, and the pain in my head hindered my success. I was unsure how she had not torn my hair from my scalp.

My hair. Oh no, my beautiful hair.

An idea flashed through my bedraggled mind in an instant, and I lifted my sword that I had fought to keep hold of, my bow and pack lost somewhere along the way. I swung it above my head, slashing at my hair. The chunk of dark hair fell to the earth, releasing me from her hold. I should have slashed the sword at her, but I was not thinking clearly and was too injured to defeat her.

With a pained cry, I shot from the ground and began running before the Banshee even noticed my escape. She would catch me, but at least I had a better chance on my feet. I ran in the direction of Sterling's desperate cries. He caught up to me at the same time the Banshee did.

"Remmy!"

The wail of the Banshee rang shrilly in our ears as she skidded to a stop a few paces from us and smiled creepily, more black gunk oozing from her lips and between her jagged teeth.

"There is no escape, little bird. I will have you." Her voice was a demonic echo. Her use of the term 'little bird' had my mind flashing back to Leland, the king's mercenary, and the original owner of the sword that I now grasped tightly in my hands.

"Not before I send you back to the Netherworld, where you belong!" Sterling shouted, raising his spear.

The Banshee laughed, not even sparing him a glance. "You play with sticks, little prince. You are no threat to me."

"Maybe not. But that doesn't mean I won't try." With a fierce cry, he charged forward like a battle-torn warrior.

"Sterling, no!" I screeched, reaching out my hands as though to drag him back, but the bold move had caught the Banshee by surprise, and his stick plunged straight through the center of her chest.

She slumped forward, but she was not dead yet, as evidenced by the gurgling laughter coming from her twitching form.

"My sisters will come. You will not escape this wood."

Her sisters? That makes it sound as if they have banded together. We have to get out of this forest.

I ran forward, swinging my sword, and severed her head before she could issue more dire warnings. Black blood sprayed out onto my dress and cloak as her body fell to the ground and her head rolled away from us.

I turned to Sterling, who was heaving in exhaustion, and he stretched one arm toward me.

That was all it took.

I collapsed into him, sobs shaking my battered body. He wrapped his arms tightly around me and held me close, stroking the back of my now mutilated hair.

"You're all right." He soothed.

I was exhausted and so irritated with myself for needing saving again.

"I lost my pack with the rest of our supplies, and the bow I just made last night."

"I saw them when I was chasing after you. We will go back and grab them. I think they're fine." He stroked my hair again, finding the butchered section.

"What happened to your hair?"

"I cut it off… to escape. She was dragging me by the hair." I hiccuped.

He put his hands on my shoulders and peered down at my tear-stained face.

Smiling, he shook his head and said, “Don’t worry about it. It’ll be the newest fashion in Lunestair. Everyone will want to look like the woman who fought a Banshee. Long on the sides and short and angled in the middle.” He tugged at the strands of my hair, and I laughed. It was a silly attempt to make me feel better, and it worked. I wiped tears from my dirt-streaked face and hiccuped again with a laugh.

“Let’s go find my pack and bow and get out of this bloody forest before the Imps find us. I need to get some morsious on these cuts.”

“You have morsious?!” He exclaimed, and I nodded thoughtfully. “Well, that would have been nice to know.”

“Why? I used it on you the night I found you. Are you planning to be injured again?”

“No, but you seem to be quite prone to being attacked.” He jested.

I grinned and slugged his arm as we walked back in the direction that I’d lost my supplies.

As we collected our lost things, a noise sounded from a nearby bush.

What if that is one of the sisters?

The thought sent panic coursing through me, turning my blood to ice. But no. A Banshee would be faster and not scurrying around in a bush.

A soft chittering noise came from the bush, and a beautiful young red fox leaped from it. Its fur was reddish-orange like the colors of a dying autumn, except for the chest, which was white, and the legs, which were black.

It sidled up to us slowly, smelling the air.

“Don’t move; I’ll take care of it.” Sterling bent and whispered in my ear.

“What do you mean you’ll take care of it?! Surely you don’t mean to hurt it?” I was aghast at the mere thought of harming the enchanting little creature. He stood at my feet now, sniffing my legs, still chattering amiably.

"Remmy, it's a wild animal. It probably has diseases, and we need food."

I grabbed his forearm and glared at him forcefully. "Don't you dare. He's sweet, and I think he likes me. He's just a baby."

"You don't mean to keep him? It's a wild fox, not a pet!"

"I'll do whatever I like, thank you very much! His name will be Ember." I reached down to pet the little guy, and he nuzzled into my hand. I glowered up at Sterling. "See?"

The prince just rolled his stormy eyes. "Oh, for god's sakes! Fine, whatever."

I smiled with pure elation and held out my arms to the little fox. He scurried into them and nuzzled against me.

"Ha!"

I smirked at Sterling, who rolled his eyes again, muttering about how ridiculous keeping a fox was.

* * *

Sterling

Remmy had stayed close beside me when the Lycan attacked, and I fought it with my spear. She stayed close beside me when the Forest Imps finally converged on us, and I showed her how much they feared fire, lighting my spear to ward them away. And she was close to me now, when the sun began to set and voices echoed through the Darkhelm.

Her arm brushed against mine, and our chests heaved in exertion from battle after battle, the constant fight to survive, taking its toll physically and mentally.

Remmy's fingers dug into my forearm where they had that night at the temple, her eyes wide with fear, as she drew me to a stop. "We must find a place to hide. It's the mercenaries. They're here for us."

"How can you be sure?"

"Because no one just lingers in the Darkhelm Forest. You said it yourself, your father would send someone after us as soon as we left the Temple of Deliritas."

"Come on; this way. We'll try to evade them. They're loud enough that we should be able to hear them coming."

I reached out to tug her arm, but she needed no motivation, moving quickly and quietly through the forest, her little fox on her heels at every turn.

She'd been largely quiet since the Banshee attack, speaking little. I worried this journey was taking its toll on her.

When we returned to Lunestair, I would send word to her family and allow her to stay at The Oasis for as long as she needed to recover. I wished I could provide her with better accommodations. The Oasis, despite its name, was a dingy pub hall that reeked of mirthwood and sweat, though the owner strived to keep out the crathe dealers.

She deserves chambers at the Castle of Stars. She deserves to be queen. Yet, she must remain concealed, and to do that, she needs to stay somewhere less desirable. My father will be looking for us.

I glanced down to where she walked closely beside me. Exhaustion was written all over her lovely face. Dirt was caked in the back of her hacked-off hair. Her wounds from being dragged were healing with the morsious salve, but it worked a little slower on humans, and blood still oozed in spots on the backs of her arms.

Even still, she looked beautiful. She painted a picture of strength and defiance, and I could think of nothing but her. No one but her.

The voices from the mercenaries grew closer, and I recognized one of them, the realization setting in that they were not mercenaries at all, but Blood Guard.

Rathe. Blast it! How many are there?

I listened intently, drawing Remmy behind a tree, my hand resting on her waist. She regarded me with a questioning gaze but remained silent, understanding the gravity of our predicament.

I distinguished four individual voices, my heart sinking. Even with my newfound strength and stamina, taking on four members of my father's elite guard would be near impossible, unless I could shift. We had to get out of here before one of their clan forms detected us. Rathe, a wolf of keen senses, could detect scents from great distances.

I leaned down, bringing my mouth close to Remmy's ear. "Blood Guard."

Her head jerked up, searching my face. This greatly decreased our chances of escape. Lifting one hand, she lightly tapped the tattoo peeking out from my shirt collar on the side of my neck.

I ran my free hand through my hair, a lock of it falling back down and flopping over my forehead in a persistent wave. "I don't think I can."

Her jaw tightened as she looked away, her disappointment evident. This was exactly why I hadn't wanted to tell her; I couldn't bear to see that look—the one that said I had failed her.

She turned her gaze back to me, urgency in her voice. "What are we going to do? They're bound to catch our scent if they haven't already—" A howl went up, echoing through the woods, causing goosebumps to pebble on my skin. Remmy's body went rigid against me.

He knows.

"Come on!"

I jerked Remmy away from the tree and began to run, cutting a path away from the sound. She stayed on my heels as we ran through the darkened forest, the silvery moonlight casting shadows through the wraith-like silhouetted trees, every shadow appearing to morph into our pursuers.

Remmy panted heavily behind me, and I reached back to grab her hand, pulling her along. It had been only a few hours since she had been dragged through this forest by a Banshee, attacked by a feral Lycan, and pursued by Forest Imps. It was exacting a price on her body.

I'll carry her if I have to, but I won't let him have her.

As my father's 'enforcer,' Captain Rathe took particular pleasure in torturing others; the scars on my back and abdomen attested to this.

A menacing growl drew me to an abrupt stop, and Remmy slammed into my back. I put a hand behind me to stop her from moving, as I was met with a pair of glowing yellow eyes and bared canines. Remmy's fox screeched and took off up the nearest tree.

Little bastard.

I couldn't blame him, though. The sight must be terrifying to a creature that small.

The wolf, Captain Rathe, let out another low howl, alerting his companions to our location. My blood heated within my veins.

"Thank Lunaire," I muttered, as I felt it heating up.

Remmy snorted behind me and hissed, "Yes, thank the goddess we are about to get torn to shreds by a wolf shifter!"

Ignoring her, I flexed my fingers, balling them into a fist and then releasing them. Looking up at Rathe, I smiled menacingly.

The wolf drew closer to us, saliva dripping from his gaping maw. I heard a metallic whisper as Remmy slid her sword from the scabbard and poked it around me, pointing it at the wolf. I smiled.

Brave woman.

I shouldn't be surprised; she'd fought many a beast on this journey and was left with the scars to prove it.

The wolf's fur bristled, the evening light catching the sharpness of his features as every muscle in his powerful frame tensed, ready to pounce.

Shouts rang out as Rathe's comrades drew close, still in their Fae forms.

Good. That will make this even easier.

Pushing Remmy behind me once again, I faced Rathe.

"Hey, what are you—" I raised my hand, and a blast of fire sparked from the ground at Rathe's feet, cutting off her words. She gasped as the wolf stumbled backward, trying to escape my flame.

"Say hello to Skotos for me, Rathe." The wolf let out a pitiful yowl as the flames engulfed him, his fur catching easily. I'd never felt greater satisfaction.

The approaching guards, faces I recognized, halted in their tracks at the sight of their captain being consumed by fire. Their expressions shifted to fear, mouths agape in disbelief.

Before I could summon my flames again, two of the Fae transformed into their clan forms, a mountain lion and a bear, and darted toward me.

I struggled to control my flames as I aimed them at the beasts, but they flickered erratically, spurting out of control, missing the intended targets.

Beside me, the clash of swords filled the air as the third guard attacked Remmy.

Suddenly, a flame shot from my hands, singeing the mountain lion's tail. It let out a furious snarl and lunged at me. Closing my eyes, I reached deep within, trying to summon forth my dragon.

Come on! Come on, you stupid creature!

I heard Remmy yell from somewhere close, and the bear roared as its claws raked down my back. I fell to my knees, a cry ripping from my lungs, as the blood ran down my back.

"Sterling!"

My head jerked up at the sound of her desperate scream.

Remmy! I can't let them hurt her!

I struggled to rise from the dirt, but the beasts converged on me, overpowering me.

Bloody dragon, come on!

The large cat prowling behind me used one paw to push me down to the ground, holding me in place, its razor-sharp claws embedded in my back.

I strained to lift my head, the pain shooting through my back like daggers, my eyes searching for Remmy.

My heart plummeted when I found her. The guard had disarmed her and was holding her by the throat; blood dripped from a slash in her forearm as she struggled against the hold on her neck.

Her beautiful green eyes found mine, and tears streamed down her muddied face as she looked at me pleadingly, begging me to transform. Begging me to save us. To save her.

Thirty-Four

Don't Touch Her!

* * *

Sterling

"This one here is a pretty one. Don't think the king would mind too much if we had a little fun. What do you say, boys?" The guard leered at Remmy, jerking her roughly.

My blood boiled at the insinuation and the terror on her face. The two beasts holding me down shifted back into their Fae forms with a grunt and yanked me forcefully to my feet, one on either side of me, as the third guard threw Remmy to the ground violently. She landed in a heap, her face to the earth, silent sobs shaking her shoulders.

"Get your filthy hands off her!" I bellowed, rage clouding my vision.

I will not let them do this to her.

"If you touch her, I will rip your innards out through your throat!"

The Fae on my left sneered, and I felt the cold tip of steel as he pressed a dagger against my ribs.

I need to shift! No wonder dragons went extinct! They have their own bloody minds! Blast it!

"I'd like to see you try, *Prince.* Shut your bloody trap, and maybe we won't make you watch while we take turns with her."

The other two guards laughed derisively, and the one holding Remmy down descended on her, flipping her over and straddling her on the ground, one leg on either side of her. White spots assaulted my vision as he leaned forward and dragged a tongue up her cheek. Remmy, the fighter that she is, spat directly in his face, and the guard snarled, wiping the spittle from his cheek.

He swung back and slapped her face with such force that the sound of it echoed through the otherwise still night.

Angry chittering came from the tree above us as the fox protested, as if yelling would stop the violence of the attack.

I trembled with barely contained fury as blood spurted from her cracked lip. "Let her go, you bastard! It's me Cyrus wants. Get off her!"

One of the men at my side laughed, Bolder, I think his name is, and taunted, "You're right, of course. It is you the king wants. Which is why he won't care what we do with the girl."

"In fact, I'm sure he'd want us to have a little fun, don't you think, Lars?" The other one asked of the man straddling Remmy.

Lars snickered and, unsheathing his dagger, he leaned forward over Remmy, who struggled fiercely against him. "You know, I think you're right, Magnus."

Remmy screamed as his dagger carved nicks across her chest. "That will teach you to spit on your superiors, filthy human whore."

All three of the men laughed as her screams split the night air.

"You have just signed your own death warrant," I growled, the intensity in my voice deadly, my fists clenching and unclenching at my sides.

Lars guffawed loudly as he tossed his rapier belt aside and began to unbuckle his pants. Magnus and Bolder snickered on either side of me as Remmy's sobs grew louder and she hurled her fists at him, attempting to free herself.

My heart shattered as she fought, and the forest around me faded away, consumed by a haze of red-hot rage that clouded my perception.

My vision tunneled, and all I could see was Lars, perched atop Remmy. My Remmy. The strong, brave heart that had battled Mt. Malus and rescued me from my prison.

The blood in my veins became molten lava, and I roared with vengeance as flames exploded from my body, devouring the Fae restraining me, their bodies turning to ash in seconds.

I raised my head very slowly, my eyes meeting Lars' as smoke roiled off my body like avenging wraiths of death.

Remmy's screams silenced, and the blood drained from the guard's face as he looked to the spots where his friends used to stand, now nothing but charred soot.

Remmy seized the distraction and drew her fist back, punching Lars solidly in the side of the head. The man yelled, placing a hand to his head, where Remmy's punch had landed.

I advanced toward him threateningly, a snarl building in my throat. He glanced down at the girl, looked to me as if gauging whether it was worth it, and then leaped off Remmy, running frantically through the woods, one hand struggling to hold up his pants.

Fire ripped from my fingers, and he screamed as it licked at his back, but he did not stop running, and I did not pursue.

Let him run back to my father. Let him tell Cyrus that I incinerated three of his Blood Guard with fire I called from my hands. Let my father wonder and drive himself mad with questions over what power I possess.

I cursed my dragon for failing me as I fell to the earth beside Remmy, scooping her fragile body into my arms. Tears and mud stained her cheeks. Blood dripped from her lips and coated her teeth, and the wounds on her chest oozed, but she smiled at me anyway, causing a hollow ache to bloom in my chest. I swallowed thickly.

"You did it, Sterling. You called your magic."

Then, her head fell back limply as she lost consciousness.

* * *

Vincent

I stood in the council chambers with the other servants, my back pressed firmly against the wall, and sighed with relief.

Sterling is alive.

Very few outside the royal family knew about the Temple of Deliritas, but I had seen the Blood Guards succumb to the dark magic when we entered five years prior. I had felt the tendrils of evil press against the fortresses of my mind, trying to seep its claws in.

I had known it would not be easy for Sterling and his savior to overcome it. It was late in the evening when Lars, a member of the King's Blood Guard, stumbled through the castle gates, screaming for the king and muttering about cursed fire magic. His back was covered in oozing blisters, but the king had not allowed anyone to tend to him, ordering his inner circle into the council rooms immediately.

If Sterling is accessing fire magic, he must have transformed. I wonder what his clan is, though? Could it possibly be the same as hers? It must be powerful if his magic is such a rare form.

Lars mentioned nothing about a clan in his rantings.

"Silence!" Cyrus demanded, hushing everyone gathered in the room. Turning to Lars, he extended a finger. "You! Tell me what happened now!"

Lars stepped forward toward the king, his hands trembling as he wrung them together. "Your M—M—Majesty. The prince… he wields fire magic… he… he incinerated Captain Rathe and the other guards." The man stuttered, barely able to speak through the pain of his burns. "I only just escaped with my life."

"He killed my enforcer?! And the woman? This woman, who survived the dangers of Mt. Malus, my mercenaries, and the Temple of Deliritas… what of her? Have you killed her?"

"N-n-no, Sire. The prince… he burned me before I could… end her life."

"What is my son's clan?" Cyrus bellowed.

The guard looked down at his hands again, a bead of sweat forming on his brow. "I do not know, Sire. He never transformed."

"You are supposed to be the most fearsome warriors in all of Valeria, and you were bested by a simple village girl and a Fae with no clan!" The king shouted in anger, his face turning red, and his eyes bulging from his too-large head.

Prince Soren fought to hide a smirk as his father raged at the guard, bringing a hand to his face to conceal his mouth. The boy had been… different since Sterling's imprisonment. More outspoken. More… involved.

Lars stammered more excuses, but the king was no longer listening. In one swift motion, he unsheathed the rapier from the guard at his side and swung the blade.

I flinched as blood squirted into the air and the man's head rolled across the floor, coming to a stop at Soren's boots. The blood drained from the boy's face as he stepped back from the severed head.

The king turned around the room in a circle, holding the blade before him like a madman. "This does not leave this room! My son was killed after volunteering to be in a contest on Mt. Malus. The people will know nothing else."

He handed the sword back to his guard and barked, "Someone clean this mess up. AND GET THE HELL OUT OF MY COUNCIL CHAMBERS!"

He stormed from the room, slamming the connecting door closed behind him.

I exhaled slowly, some of the other servants around me doing the same, as we moved to exit the room.

This isn't over yet. Sterling won't be safe. If only I could get to Iyra... but I don't know how.

Thirty-Five

Too Late

* * *

Teigan

In the wee hours of the morning, I loaded the borrowed horse with supplies raided from the Oasis's storeroom, recalling Remmy's reasons for entering the contest. I could only hope it would be enough to tide the children over until I could visit again. Remmy was an amazing person, and I was one of the last people to see her alive. It left me with a sense of duty to look after her loved ones. I hoped to be able to deliver the news to them myself, but it may have already spread to the small villages. The courier may have even sent them a notice like we had received for Koretta.

Perhaps I can find a place for them to stay here.

My mind drifted to the father, and I wondered if he would step up now that his eldest daughter was gone. I couldn't understand a father not providing for his children. Remmy said he was a disabled drunkard.

He might not even be with them anymore.

"Here, boy, take these with you." Maggie emerged from the Oasis and held out a brown paper package for me. "Cakes for the children. If they're as bad off as you say, a treat will do them good."

"Thank you, Maggie. I will return as quickly as I can."

"Don't you forget what the Phoenix said. Proceed with caution in respect to the Fire."

I nodded seriously, understanding the reference to recruiting.

Rebel leaders were sometimes given code names to protect their identities when speaking in public. The king had spies everywhere, and caution was imperative.

The rear door to the pub swung open, and Deidre flew out, catapulting herself into my arms.

"Oh, Teigan! Can't I come with you? You'll be gone for so long. What am I to do here by myself?" She wailed.

I chuckled, thinking back to how shy the girl had been when we had met. She had opened up significantly in the short period of time, her affection for me growing daily.

"Well, your training, of course. You're a part of the Fire now, Deidre." I lowered my voice, speaking in a hushed tone, wary of any ears that could be listening from the darkness.

"Oh, Deidre, leave the boy alone. You have work to do inside. The boarders will wake soon, and breakfast must be started. Dauton is here already." Maggie swooshed her arms, motioning for Deidre to get inside.

Deidre's nose wrinkled at the mention of the grimy cook, and I chuckled, leaning down to kiss her forehead. "I won't be gone long.

Stay out of trouble."

Her face fell at my words, and a frown creased her brow. She shoved back from my embrace. "You treat me like a little sister."

I inhaled through my nose and pasted a smile on my face.

This is not the time for this conversation.

"Of course I do. You're the little sister I always wanted. Now be good, and I will see you in a few days' time." I pulled myself into the saddle and, without a wave, nudged the horse forward.

"I'll see you soon!" I called behind me as I spurred the horse faster, setting off through the city as the sun began to crest in the distance.

I rode for Merda with haste, stopping only for a few hours of rest and water for the horse, making the trip in record time. My body ached with bone-deep fatigue as I arrived in the small village mid-afternoon on the second day.

I made my way inside a bakery on the outskirts. A plump older woman with kind eyes and flour on her apron greeted me as I entered.

"Good afternoon! I haven't seen you around before. Just passing through?" She smiled warmly as she spoke.

"Yes, ma'am. Can you please give me directions to the Silva home, some biscuits, and a loaf of your finest sourdough?"

The woman's face tightened at my request, and her eyes traveled down my body, taking in my dusty but new attire. Maggie was now paying me a full wage, and I had used my savings, after learning of my parents' murder, to buy myself a few things, including the fine linen tunic I wore.

Her gaze returned to my face. "From Lunestair, I presume?"

I nodded politely, and she continued speaking as she began to package the bread I had requested. "Forgive my rudeness, but what business have you with the Silvas?"

I swallowed and responded quietly, a hollowness in my voice. "I was a friend of Remmy's."

I glanced down at the floor and then met her hardened gaze again to find tears welling in the old woman's eyes. "I've brought some supplies to her family."

She gave a low nod.

"I wish she hadn't gone." She whispered, confirming my fear that the courier had come. She cleared her throat and spoke louder. "The Silva home is on the far side. You'll need to pass all the way through town. You'll know it when you come to the border of trees. It is a small wooden shack with a painted blue door."

She handed me my goods, and I took out a silver coin, placing it on the counter.

The old lady shook her head, sliding the coin back across the counter to me. "I'll take no money from you. Only promise you'll look after those children."

"I will do whatever is within my power, ma'am."

I made my way through town, tiny purple valerian flowers lining the roads, and passed by a massive stone home fenced in with wooden posts. A girl with caramel skin, a few years younger than me, stood in front of the home screaming at what I assumed was a household servant.

"You cannot keep me here! I order you to release me immediately. I must go to her!"

"I am sorry, miss, but your father has ordered us to keep you within the estate."

"I don't care what that stupid oaf ordered!" She stormed, making for the gate as I tried to hurry past the home. The servant's face paled as he followed after her persistently.

I shook my head as I continued, nearing the edge of town.

I urged the horse along, coming to a small gravel path at the edge of town. The valerian was more sparse here, but patches of it appeared in spots along the way, a pop of color in an otherwise gray scene.

The gravel dead-ended at a run-down shack with a blue door, just as the old baker had described it.

Two small children screamed as the boy chased the girl through a sparse garden on the side of the old cabin. The plants were withered and covered with brown spots, some appearing worse than others.

Remmy mentioned a blight of some kind. But I didn't notice it on any of the other plants coming through town..? How odd.

The children did not notice me as I approached and rapped my knuckles sharply against the rickety door.

A moment later, the door swung open, revealing the most mesmerizing girl I'd ever encountered. Her large golden eyes were puffy and bloodshot, and long red hair cascaded down her back in gentle waves. Her luscious pink lips were turned down in a small frown, and her perfectly freckled nose was red from crying.

Thirty-Six

Stories and Reflections

* * *

Teigan

I stared at her, forgetting to breathe, until she addressed me curtly. "May I help you? Or would you prefer to stand there letting all the cold air in?"

I cleared my throat, my mind stuttering. "Oh! I'm sorry, it's only that I thought… what I mean is that—"

The girl cut me off, seemingly perturbed by my idiocy.

Who can blame her? I just stood here gawking at her for the last few moments. Come on, Teigan. Get a hold of yourself.

"Who are you?"

"I'm sorry. Let me start again. My name is Teigan Berger. I've come from Lunestair. I was… friends… with your sister, Remmy."

The girl's mouth dropped open.

"You knew my sister? How?" She lifted both hands to her heart. "Oh! Please, do come in."

She moved aside, allowing me to enter the small abode.

Poking her head out the door, she yelled to the children. "Eri! Echo! Come tie up this gentleman's horse and get it some water."

The children stopped their play, noticing me for the first time, and groaned at their sister's request.

They moved to do her bidding, taking my horse by the reins, and the girl closed the door and moved to place another log on the fire.

A middle-aged man with dark hair and vacant eyes rocked in a chair near the hearth, seemingly unaware of my presence. I stood awkwardly in the center of the room until she motioned to a table near some wooden chairs.

"Please take a seat. I'm Emerie. Tell me how you knew my sister."

Her words reminded me of my reason for coming here, and I stood back up quickly. The girl was startled by my sudden movement, so I rushed to explain.

"I will tell you all you wish to know, but first, I have forgotten why I came here. I have some supplies for you on my horse."

Emerie's brows raised in surprise, but she followed me out the door to the spot where the two children were feeding grain to my horse.

"I must apologize, but we have very little with which to feed your horse." There was a hint of embarrassment in her voice, but she held her head high as we walked.

"No need to worry. I've got plenty in my saddlebags for the horse, but I must ask you for accommodations for the night."

It was nearing dinner now, and I was too haggard to think of returning to Lunestair before at least one night's rest.

"Of course! I'll prepare a bed for you in the store room."

When we came to the horse, the boy whom Emerie had called Eri approached me.

"Your horse is real nice, sir. Wishing we had a horse like this."

"Be quiet, Eri. Poor people don't have horses." His twin scolded him. "We haven't got any money for a horse, have we, Emmy?"

Emerie released a puff of breath and smiled forlornly at me. She wrangled her siblings and sent them into the house to sit with their father.

"I'm sorry about them. We don't get many visitors besides my friend Inara and Alice, the baker."

"I don't mind; I've always wanted siblings."

I smiled at her as I unstrapped the saddlebags and shouldered the supplies, my muscles straining against the fabric of my shirt under the weight of the food.

Lifting the flap on one of the bags, I grabbed an apple and tossed it to the ground for my horse.

Turning to Emerie, I grinned widely and said, "I hope you have use for some meat, vegetables, apples, and bread. I've brought you as much as the horse could carry. I think there are some biscuits in here, too, as well as some ginger cakes for the children."

A flush, starting at her graceful neck, rose up the girl's face, tinting her cheeks a rosy pink. She swallowed visibly before responding, her voice barely a whisper, tears glistening in her captivating eyes. "Thank you for your kindness."

She sniffed and cleared her throat, her voice still raw with emotion. "Let's go in. The children will be so excited, and I want to hear about how you met Remmy."

I followed the girl inside, my heart aching at her response to the supplies I had brought.

They must be getting low on resources. If their father is not working, I doubt they have any income now with Remmy gone.

Inside the tiny home, I unpacked the food and launched into the story of meeting their sister, explaining how I had heard her scream from the road and rushed into the Cushing, pulling her from the water. The two young children sat on the floor, listening with rapt attention, while Emerie sat in the chair beside me, silent tears streaming down her still pink cheeks. Even their father had turned in his chair, listening as my story unfolded.

Echo looked up at me, her little face serious. "Our sister is dead. But Emmy said she is in Lumess with the goddess, and we should not mourn for her, because she would want us to be happy. But I miss her anyway." She shrugged her little shoulders.

"She gave the best hugs." Eridian piped up.

"I think your sister is right. Remmy gave her life for her family. You must honor that sacrifice by living happily, but never forgetting her. She loved you all very much. During our time together, she talked about you frequently. So much that I feel as if we are already the best of friends." I ruffled Eridian's hair, and he grinned up at me.

"Can you tell us more stories about Remmy?"

"I will, but for now, I think it's time to prepare dinner." I turned to Emerie, and she grinned shyly at me, wiping the tears from her rosy cheeks. "I'm going to help your sister prepare the most tastiest stew you've ever eaten!"

The children cheered enthusiastically, and Emerie laughed, rising to usher them outside for chores.

Closing the door behind the energetic children, she turned back to me. "The garden is almost pointless at this point, but it gets them out of the way when I need to prepare meals."

I smiled and rose to help her, beginning to chop vegetables for the pot.

"I must speak with you about something urgent, Emerie."

* * *

Remmy

I struggled to open my eyes; my body felt as though it were floating, suspended on air. The prince… he was carrying me?

We walked late into the evening as I drifted in and out of consciousness, wrapped in his strong arms. The arduous journey, many battles, and assault exacted a heavy price from my worn body.

I woke once, asking him to place me down and let me walk, but he refused, knowing I couldn't.

Surely his back is throbbing, I mused in one moment of lucidity. *Yet, he carries me as if I am more important than resting his own aching body. I'm not worth such kindness.*

"Your back…" I whispered, my voice gravelly. Sterling did not look down as he continued trekking through the darkened forest, holding me tightly against his firm body.

"Shhh. You're safe now, Rem. I've got you." I closed my eyes again, letting my head fall against his strong chest, resting in the security and warmth. The steady *thump, thump, thump* of his heartbeat lulled me into a peaceful rest, the scent of mint and smoke embracing me like a snug cocoon.

What are we going to do when we get to Lunestair? If Sterling can't shift... and the king wants to kill us... what about my family? I must convince Sterling to practice shifting. There's... there's no other way... we must survive.

Time crawled on uncertainly, until eventually, the prince stopped, laying me gently on the ground and dropping my pack beside me.

Deftly, he fished out the blankets and made me a bed in the grass.

Then, with all the gentleness of a mother cradling her newborn, he laid me within the fur, brushing back my hair from my face and tending to the cuts on my arm and chest.

Before drifting back into the darkness, I saw him raise a hand and spark a fire, lighting up the night sky.

Thirty-Seven

I Cannot Be Your Savior

* * *

Teigan

As promised, the lovely Emerie prepared me a bed of blankets in the bare storeroom, which was nothing more than a broom closet. I rose early the next morning, after securing her vow to join our cause, promising to return with more supplies in a fortnight.

When I had broached the subject of the rebellion, her soft, honey eyes had flashed, a storm brewing in them.

Her answer had been instantaneous, though she refused to do anything that endangered the twins or took her away from them.

I heard the door of the cabin creak open; the sound breaking the stillness of the dawn as I secured my saddlebag.

Emerie approached in a simple cornflower blue dress that made her red hair appear even more vibrant. A stray curl brushed her face gently. She stroked my horse's muzzle as she smiled timidly at me, a pale blush tinting her lightly freckled cheeks. "You've done so much for us, Teigan. How can we ever repay you?"

"Your sister was a great friend to me; that is payment enough. I will visit you whenever I can. Please tell the children goodbye for me."

"They will look forward to seeing you again. They thoroughly enjoyed your stories of Remmy's exploits."

I stepped closer to her, my fingers barely brushing hers as I stroked the horse's nose. "And you? Will you enjoy seeing me again as well?" I asked, my voice low and gruff.

The blush in her cheeks turned to crimson as it rose to her hairline, and I smiled charmingly at her.

"Yes," She responded in a whisper. "I look forward to your return."

I took her hand in mine and brought it slowly to my lips, my eyes never leaving her flushed face.

"Until then," I said and mounted my horse as she stepped away.

Emerie offered a gentle wave as I turned the steed onto the gravel path.

"Until then." Her soft voice echoed my words, stirring something deep within me.

* * *

Remmy

I woke before dawn, the night still and quiet. My fur was stretched beneath a tall evergreen, and Sterling slept peacefully on his stomach beneath my wool blanket beside me.

A tiny ball of fur was burrowed into my side, and I smiled as I stroked Ember. The little fox stretched lazily and peeked at me through curious black eyes. I was happy he had stayed with us after the attack. My wounds twinged as I moved to survey our surroundings sleepily.

Turning toward Sterling, my chest tightened.

He must have carried me for hours... why? Why would he do that for me? His face... when that guard had tried to take me... I've never seen him so angry. He burned them from the inside out.

Looking away from the sleeping prince, I realized we were not on the mountain anymore.

Silvery moonlight cast eerie shadows upon a lake with waters as black as night, tendrils of steam reaching like ghostly fingers toward the star-flecked sky.

The Black Lake. I've seen this on Father's map.

Leaving Ember snuggled within the blanket, I rose, slowly making my way to where Sterling had dropped my pack and weapons.

Finding the last of the morsious salve, I crept to where he slept.

Gently, I tugged up the back of his black shirt, the fabric sticking in the blood from his injuries.

I covered my mouth with a hand to quiet the cry that wanted to slip from my lips, my heart clenching again inside my chest.

Those murderous bastards!

The claw marks were gaping punctures in his back, marring the beautiful tattoo that graced his spine, blood oozing from them in clumps.

I forced down the bile that rose in my throat and dipped my fingers in the morsious. As carefully as possible, I slathered the salve into the wounds. The prince moaned and shifted his head, attempting to rise.

"Hush now. I'm just tending your wounds. Lie still." I placed a hand on his shoulder, gently nudging him back down.

"There is no need. I will heal." He mumbled, his voice husky and laced with the remnants of sleep.

The sound of it sent a chill coursing through me, which I promptly ignored.

I cleared my throat to rid myself of the forbidden desire welling up in my convoluted thoughts. The prince was still as frustrating as ever and still determined not to marry me, though I was starting to believe him when he said the king would never fulfill his promise. He was trying to kill us after all.

What are we going to do?

As I finished rubbing the salve into the wounds, I pulled the shirt over his chiseled back muscles, chiding myself for staring.

Why did he have to be so bloody alluring?

"How are you feeling… after last night?" His silver eyes bore into mine, requesting an honest answer. My mind flashed to the assault and how hard Sterling had fought to protect me.

He must care for me a little if he would fight for me like that.

I looked away from him and sighed deeply. I was undeserving of such concern.

"I'm so sorry, Sterling."

"What could you possibly have to be sorry for?"

I gestured to his wounds. "This is my fault. If you hadn't needed to rescue me… if only I had been… had been strong enough to defend myself, this wouldn't have happened to you."

Sterling rolled onto his side and took my hands, holding them tenderly. "Remmy, even the strongest people need saving sometimes. Besides, these are nothing. They will heal before the day is over." His thumb was drawing lazy circles across my skin, causing my throat to tighten. I swallowed nervously.

"What are we going to do, Sterling? Your father is not going to let us go, is he?"

The prince sat up, elbows resting on his knees, and raked a hand through his thick, dark hair. The slow, careless motion sent a shiver through me, heat curling low in my stomach. Waves of inky hair flopped down on his forehead, and he blew out a weighted breath, scratching the stubble on his chin. "No, he is going to try to kill us. Which is why we must be cautious and remain hidden."

"You're hardly concealable. You're the Crown Prince, for Skotos' sake! The entire kingdom knows your face."

"I am not worried about myself. I'll keep to the shadows when we get to town. Cyrus will want your head because you know the secret of the temple, and the Blood Guard… they will try to take liberties because they can. When we get to Lunestair, I'll rent a safe place for you to stay for a few days. Once you are ready for the journey, I'll get you a horse so you can return to your family in Merda."

"Sterling, you don't understand. When I entered this contest, I had to sign my name and list my hometown on a waiver. Cyrus knows where I am from. If he does not want anyone to know… he'll come after me… and my family!"

"By the hair of Lunaire!" He cursed, jaw clenching. "Why did you not tell me this before?"

"I… I didn't realize…"

He cursed colorfully again and chewed the inside of his cheek.

"You need to shift."

"I cannot! I have told you time and again. I have no control over it."

"You must learn! Practice! You are the only hope we have. We must de—"

He jumped to his feet furiously and strolled away, pacing the ground, his face red and his brows knit together.

Ember leaped up and hovered near my feet protectively.

"Don't! Don't say it! You don't know what you are asking of me." The prince snarled.

"What I am asking is that you save us! You are the only one who can!" I pleaded with him, my voice breaking.

"I'm not what you think I am!"

"What I think is that you are the first dragon shifter in a millennium! I think that you are the most powerful being to walk Amengor in a thousand years. I think you're the heir to the throne of Valeria. I think you are the hope THIS KINGDOM NEEDS!"

I waved my hands enthusiastically as though to encompass all of Valeria.

"Stop it, Remmy!" He roared. "I cannot be your savior. You don't know what you're asking."

Angry tears streamed down my splotchy face. "Why are you denying it? Why else would this happen now, if not to save us? Why would the gods grant you this power if you are not meant to be our king?" I yelled back at him, jamming my fingers into his chest, shoving him back.

The sun was rising now, and a golden aura surrounded Sterling, catching in his tousled hair, gilding the strands in molten light. Shadows carved their way along the sharp lines of his stubbled jaw and the bare skin where his shirt had fallen open. He looked like something sculpted by the gods as he loomed over me, his usually bright eyes now dark and stormy like a tempestuous sea.

My breath caught in my throat at the fearsome beauty of the raging prince as I backed away slowly. My back hit a knob on the trunk of a tall evergreen, and I winced.

The prince extended both arms, grabbed my hips, and pulled me to him in one swift, gruff motion. He stared at me intently for a moment while I held my breath, and then his mouth crashed into mine, fireworks exploding through the recesses of my mind, a desperate need overtaking me.

One hand slid into my hair as he held my head against his mouth, tasting and exploring, the other holding firmly to my waist.

Hot, angry tears streamed down my face, the salt mixing with the smoky, mint taste of his lips. Yet, my arms slid hesitantly around his waist, drawing him closer to my body, as my anger drifted away like a feather on the breeze.

His tongue pushed against my lips, imploring and desperate, and I parted them with ease, giving in to what I hadn't believed was possible. What I hadn't dared to dream of.

Curse him for being so blasted handsome!

The prince drew back, breaking the kiss.

Panting, he gently rested his forehead against mine, inhaling deeply. My breath came in ragged gasps as I took in the scent of him that I'd come to know so well, the smell of it intoxicating, seeping into every part of my existence.

I placed two fingers on my lips, where his had been only a moment before. I could still feel the warmth of his kiss lingering there. A shiver coursed up my spine.

"I've wanted to do that since we met," Sterling whispered hoarsely.

"I thought you hated me," I responded softly, still shocked from the passion in his kiss.

"I could never hate you." He brushed back a strand of hair from my face, but then stopped, turning away from me abruptly.

"I shouldn't have done that. I'm sorry." He said. He ran his fingers through his hair.

"Why?" I touched the back of his shoulder gently, but he jerked away from me.

"Don't you see?!" He threw his hands up in frustration. "It doesn't matter! Nothing we feel matters. I'm a dead man, Remmy. This can lead nowhere. He will kill you the same way he did Isolde."

He put his head in his hands, rubbing them up and down his face, as he relived the death of his former lover. A part of me wanted to take that pain from him and bear it myself.

"We must fight, Sterling. You have to learn how to shift. Your dragon is the only way we can defeat him. I will help you however I can, but we cannot allow him to win. I did not come this far to die at the hands of a tyrannical maniac."

Sterling turned from me in agitation, ready to walk away again, but I reached for his hand, stopping him.

He spun back, his face stricken. I stepped closer to him and cautiously wrapped my arms around his neck.

"I believe in you," I whispered in his ear before lifting onto my tiptoes to reach his towering height, and brushing my lips against his full, warm ones—soft and tentative.

I could feel his resistance slipping as he circled my waist, gruffly pulling me closer to him, his lips demanding. He pressed his hips firmly against mine as he held me.

"You have undone me." He growled, and a thrill rushed through me as I melted into him, finally giving over to the desire that had been steadily building between us since we met.

Thirty-Eight

Leave Me To Die

* * *

Sterling

I *should never have kissed her. My father will use this against me, and I don't know how to protect her. Blast it! What have I done?*

Remmy had gone to freshen up, and I shifted impatiently on the evergreen root I had planted myself on.

The fox sat beside me, eyeing me warily. I couldn't blame him; I was wondering about myself as well. I had acted on impulse and given in, not once but twice, to foolish desires.

This is only going to make it more difficult to send her away. But I have to. I must send her and her family into hiding until I can... figure out what to do about my father.

My stomach rumbled, and I glanced toward the trees. I didn't want Remmy hunting on her own, but we were going to starve only a day's walk from Lunestair. I scratched my head, deep in thought, as Remmy resurfaced from the woods.

"What is it?" She questioned as she sat beside me.

I cleared my throat and motioned to the onyx waters of the lake. "We should see if there are any fish in this sludge."

"Isn't this the Black Lake? I doubt anything edible resides in these waters."

"Well, we have got to try. I'd prefer not to starve to death when we are only a day from the city."

Remmy's brows raised.

"Only a day?" She glanced around, nose scrunched thoughtfully. "I hadn't realized we were so close."

"We should be there by tomorrow morning, but we will need to stay off the main road once we reach the other side of the lake. There is not much foot traffic on this side, but we could easily be spotted once we hit the main stretch. My father will no doubt have guards searching for us."

I stood and stretched my back, feeling a twinge in the puncture wounds there. They were healing quickly, but they still throbbed.

A cool breeze whistled through the trees, and I was grateful for the fire blazing in my veins.

"I could try hunting?" Remmy suggested from the ground beside me, pointing to her bow, near our blankets.

I shook my head stubbornly. "These woods are dangerous, and anything or anyone could be lurking in them. Let's give the lake a try first. Hunting will be easier once we cross into the Stardust District." I grabbed the fishing net from her supply pack as I spoke.

Remmy rolled her eyes but moved to follow me as I made my way to the mysterious lake. I stopped where the water lapped at the shore and stooped to roll the legs of my pants up. Remmy chuckled beside me.

"What?"

"If your goal is to not get wet, you'll end up needing to take your pants off completely. We have to go in too deep for that to matter."

"You'd like that, wouldn't you, Rem?" The porcelain skin of her neck and cheeks flushed red, and she turned quickly away from me. I laughed.

"I've no particular thoughts on it, Your Highness. Are we fishing or not?" She didn't look at me as she waded deeper into the freezing water.

The fox skittered off, taking cover once again in Remmy's fur.

That thing sleeps a lot.

I smirked and joined her in the black water with the fishing net. "Why did you get in when we've only got one net?"

She snorted. "To teach you how to use it, of course!"

"Oh, I believe I know just fine how to—" A rippling in the water cut off my words, right as I intended to splash her, and I flashed back to the last time we were in the water together.

Remmy noticed my pause and followed my gaze. The opacity of the water made it difficult to see—but we didn't need to. We knew.

"Selkies." She croaked as she shuffled to my side.

The water rippled again as two dark figures emerged mere paces away, their fathomless black eyes staring straight through us. They swam forward, skimming the surface like water wraiths, as I hurried to pull Remmy toward the shore.

A rumbling noise shook the sediment beneath our feet. One large tentacle rose from the water, coming down with a resounding splash on the two Selkies.

A hundred paces away, the water stirred forcefully, sucking back from the shore, and leaving us standing in ankle-deep muck.

A four-headed creature of myth rose from the center of the lake, its flat teeth chomping in its massive mouths.

Remmy screamed, the sound ear-splitting.

"What is that thing?" A strangled sound came from one of the Selkies as it fought against the tentacle, trying to pull it closer to the great creature.

I grabbed Remmy's hand again, pulling her frantically from the water.

"That is the Baga."

"I thought the Baga only surfaced at night? Why is it awake now?!" She screeched as the giant heads of the beast towered above us. She tripped on her dress and stumbled, rolling her ankle as she tried to flee the water.

The fox awakened from his place in the blanket and started his frantic chatter, screeching and yapping.

Not helping, little guy.

"At night and when it senses fresh meat in the water, I guess!" I shouted above the roar of the creature.

We collapsed breathlessly on the shore, but only for a moment before Remmy was moving again toward our campsite, in a fearful attempt to escape.

I grabbed her wrist, stopping her, and she looked at me in confusion. "We will be safe here, as long as we stay out of reach of the tentacles. The Baga can't leave the water."

She nodded and sat on the bank beside me, her fox scurrying to her side. We watched in horror as the massive creature devoured the two Selkies that had been intent on eating us, splitting them between two of its giant heads.

"So much for fishing." She mumbled. "I'm not going back in there. Did you know it could surface during the day?"

I shook my head.

"Hunting it is!" I said, too jovially for the situation. "You stay here and rest. I'll take your bow and see what I can find."

Remmy huffed. "Why should you go and not I? It does happen to be my bow."

"It is safer for you to stay here."

"I don't need you to protect me!"

Her face reddened as I pointed to the deep cuts on her chest. "I know you can protect yourself, Remmy, but the man who did that to you escaped. He will go to my father. And my father will send more Blood Guard. You are *disposable* to them, and they won't hesitate to… to do much worse than that. So please. Just. Stay. Here."

I stood and snatched her bow from the ground, heading deeper into the woods, drowning out the sounds of her protest.

* * *

Remmy

I watched as Sterling sauntered off into the woods, quietly fuming, while brushing my hand over Ember's fur. The prince's words echoed through my mind, and I pictured his face when he had gestured to my wounds; the pain there. I placed a hand softly to my chest, careful not to touch the wounds, and released a deep breath.

He only wants to protect me. If he had not been able to tap into his fire magic... I let the thought trail off, not wanting to think about what would have happened. That Fae was intent on taking what was not his. He would have—if not for Sterling.

How can he care for me?

I'd never had anyone care for me like that. Fight for me. Cry for me. Burn for me.

He kissed me for Skotos' sake! A real kiss.

Like he truly wanted… me. Scarred and broken me. Though he hadn't spoken of it since.

I tugged my cloak around me. It was getting colder every day; the sun doing little to warm the earth.

I suppose winter comes earlier up here.

The trees here were colored with bright, vibrant leaves; I had barely noticed before. There was no color on Mt. Malus; the magic there devoid of life. This was the first I had seen of normal trees in quite some time. The wind whistled through the radiant leaves, and a chill went through me.

The cloak Rogard had given me was now torn and filled with holes. I tugged it tighter around me, mourning its forlorn condition, and moved to wrap my fur around myself when a sharp cramp gripped my stomach. I cried out, clenching my abdomen.

Ember's ears perked up, confusion and concern on his furry little face as he snuggled closer to me.

Oh no. This can't be! Not right now!

My monthly cycle was severe and often irregular due to frequent malnutrition, and I could not remember the last time it had happened.

Of course, this would happen now.

A wave of nausea slammed into me, and I moaned miserably.

I burrowed deeper into my fur, curling into a ball to wait for Sterling to return. Ember nuzzled my hand with his nose and weaseled under the blankets beside me, as a sharp pain lanced down my spine and my stomach churned uneasily. After weeks of barely eating, I couldn't believe this was happening at all.

How am I going to travel?

A short time later, footsteps crunched on the fallen leaves as the prince re-entered our campsite.

"What are you doing?" He dropped two rabbits into a pile near the fire, then knelt before my blanket, peering at me curiously.

I forced out a response through gritted teeth as another cramp wracked my body. "I am unwell."

"What do you mean? Are your wounds infected?" He reached for my chest, but I shrank back, batting away his hand.

"Not *that* kind of unwell." I beseeched him with my eyes, begging him not to make me say it; my face flushed from embarrassment and the sudden rush of heat coursing through me.

"Well, what kind of sick are you?" He furrowed his brow, staring at me cluelessly.

"I've started my monthly bleed!" I bit out.

Sterling's eyes widened, and his own face turned a bit pink as he stumbled back.

"Oh—I… uh… well, can you travel?"

"No, I cannot travel! Just leave me here to die." I moaned miserably, pulling the fur over my head.

I heard Sterling chortle as he shifted on his feet above me. "Surely, it can't be that—"

I whipped the blanket off my head, glaring at him fiercely. "Do. Not. Finish. That. Statement."

Ember chittered angrily beside me, indignant for me.

The prince bit the inside of his cheek, clearly holding back a grin.

"Aaggghhhh!" I flung the blanket back over my head and threw myself against the ground dramatically. "I am going to sleep. If I do not die first."

Another snicker came from outside the blanket as I curled back into a ball and shut my eyes tightly, praying for sleep to take me.

Thirty-Nine

War of Hearts

* * *

Remmy

For the next three days, we stayed there, while I alternated between sleeping, writhing in pain, and hurling my food.

Ember left a few times, I assumed in search of food, but he always returned before nightfall, and cuddled close to me, his warmth and presence a welcome addition to my miserable nights.

The Baga surfaced occasionally, chomping its massive teeth on whatever prey it could lure from within the lake. It even swiped its giant tentacle at us, at which point Sterling insisted we move our camp farther inland away from the onyx waters, abandoning the pine tree I'd grown to love.

Our kiss was never mentioned, and the prince kept his distance from me whenever possible. He hunted each day with my bow, returning with a fresh rabbit or small animal, forcing me to eat, whenever I could keep food in my churning stomach.

I warned him to leave the foxes alone, and he had rolled his eyes at my perceived foolishness. He spread the wool blanket a few paces from my fur every evening, and my heart sank as he resumed his previous aloofness.

Had it all been a mistake? Did he care nothing for me after all? Then why had he kissed me? Why did he promise to try? He let me kiss him a second time… he told me I had undone him. What did that even mean? My heart ached as the questions tumbled around in my addled brain.

On the morning of the second day, I opened my eyes to find Sterling leaning over a fire, roasting some meat he had acquired on one of his hunting trips.

He quirked a bit of a smile at me and held out my bowl. "Want some?"

The smell turned my uneasy stomach, but I sat up anyway, groaning in discomfort as I took the food he handed me. "This better not be fox."

The prince sighed heavily. "Aren't you ever going to let that go?"

Ember let out a snarl beside me, and I chuckled.

I'm pretty convinced at this point, he understands everything we are saying.

"Nope." I shrugged. "Are you going to try to shift today?" I pressed.

I'd asked him yesterday between naps, and he had waved me off, telling me that he was more concerned about food. If I had not been in so much pain, I would have understood his insistence, but all the food in Amengor would not matter if we could not defeat his father.

Sterling turned to me, and a shadow of something dark briefly passed across his handsome face.

I wish I knew how he felt about me. It seemed so clear the other day. But now?

Despite my current condition, I craved his touch. I was overcome with an innate desire to feel his powerful arms cradling me tightly, as they had before.

Is he only acting this way because I am on my monthly? Surely Fae have them too? His lover must have... right?

Shaking off the thoughts, I turned my attention to his answer.

"Yes, but how do you suppose I start?"

"Well—uhhh—" I stuttered. "Umm, when you shifted before, what was happening at the time?"

"The first time I shifted was when you went over the cliff. The second was when the dark magic at the Temple of Deliritas wanted me to kill you." His eyebrows rose with a challenge, as though daring me to understand the implications of my request.

"And when you accessed your fire magic… that Fae was trying to…" I trailed off, my voice fading to a whisper as realization set in. "I need to be in danger for your magic to respond?"

Maybe he does care for me? Then why be so cold? Why is he keeping his distance?

Sterling shrugged nonchalantly. "I guess my dragon has a protective nature."

"Okay. Maybe close your eyes and try to tap into what you were feeling during those... instances of... of fear... or umm... protectiveness. Try to uhhh—sense the dragon and call for it?"

The prince peeked at me through one eye as I tried to guess at what he needed to do to force the dragon to emerge.

"What?" I questioned. "I'm not exactly an expert in Fae clans. I'd never even met one before you, but you need to try something!"

He smirked and closed his eye again, appearing to do what I

suggested. "Why don't you, umm—move away from me a little in case this works?"

Sterling opened his eyes and rolled them, shuffling farther away.

"Is this good?" He called, arms stretched out to the sides.

"Yes. Oh! Maybe you should uummm… take off… your shirt, at least?" A flush crawled up my face as I made the suggestion. "I mean, in case it works, you will still have your clothes." I hurried to clarify.

A smug grin split the prince's face as he began to lift his tunic, revealing the tan sculpted muscles beneath.

I covered mine with my fur, hoping to hide the sultry thoughts that were no doubt written all over my face.

A moment later, I pulled the blanket down just below my eyes to see him turned away from me, discarding his black shirt on the ground, the muscles in his tattooed back stretching as he worked to undo his pants. The wounds from the guards' attack were scabbed over now, but still appeared gruesome.

My heart hammered against my ribs, trying to jump out of my chest. With a sharp intake of breath, that I hoped he hadn't heard, I pulled the cover back over my eyes and groaned, sinking into my bed—the temptation to watch him undress almost impossible to ignore.

What is wrong with me?

Ember burrowed under the blanket with me, planting a soft lick on my cheek.

"Were you a dog in another life?" I asked him with a smile.

It was silent outside the blanket for several minutes before I heard Sterling call out, "Remmy, this isn't working. I don't feel anything."

"Keep trying! Try to picture yourself in the events of last time."

"I am naked in the woods." He grumbled.

I groaned again.

Trust me, I know.

"Well, put a blanket on yourself, but keep trying! You have to figure this out."

I heard him exhale sharply, but he said nothing else, and as the woods became quiet again, I waited intently, praying to all the gods that still existed that he would figure this out.

He's our only hope.

* * *

Teigan

The bedroom door thudded shut behind me as I tossed my bags to the floor and sat on the edge of the bed to remove my boots. The old bed creaked and groaned under my weight as I shifted. I had snuck quietly into the Oasis to avoid being spotted by Deidre, who would no doubt want to talk. I'd only just returned from a meeting with the Thronfields. Ivor had wanted an update immediately, leaving me no time to recuperate from my arduous journey to Merda.

I explained to Xula and Ivor all the details I had discussed with Emerie, and Ivor had nodded in approval and proceeded to give me my next assignment. I leaned back on the bed, putting one leg across the other, thoughts rasping through my mind like boots on the cobblestone.

This mission was going to be far more dangerous than the weapons supply train. It would put us on the king's radar. Cyrus had written off the supply train incident as nothing more than raiders trying to make some easy coin. When we break into the Captain of the Guard's chambers... the king will know about the Dragon's Fire, and all this training I have learned in the last few weeks will have a real purpose. Ivor had told me to select two of my men, but I had only recently taken over this troop.

I don't know the soldiers well enough to know who would be best.

My chest deflated as I puffed out a breath.

I still have a week. Maybe I can talk to Rufus. Get a feel for who he thinks might be best and then choose.

I bit the inside of my cheek.

I'll need to do it tomorrow.

I decided to head out to the Olsen estate after my shift at the Oasis. Ivor was moving his office there along with several other branches and divisions, including training and reconnaissance. The sprawling grounds of the massive manor made an exceptional place for training and running exercises.

Ivor had offered me a room there, but I was not yet ready to give up my position at the Starlight Oasis. It afforded me the perfect opportunity to hear rumors, make friends with powerful people, and survey the Castle of Stars.

If I needed to get a message to the estate quickly, I could always pass it through the Drunken Dragon.

Plus, keeping an eye on the castle could be useful for this mission, since we were breaking into the Blood Guard's living quarters. The barracks were situated near the back of the castle in a separate annex. A rebel who works as a servant in the castle is going to smuggle us onto the grounds using an old underground sewage tunnel, and then we will be on our own from there.

Unfortunately, no one knew if there were any more underground tunnels or where they might lead, which was part of the reason for this mission. Any blueprints, maps, or plans would be with the Captain of the Blood Guard, Seely Bramwell.

I shuddered at the thought of the beastly phoenix captain. The man was nearly seven feet tall and a solid wall of muscle. I had never seen his clan form, but the fiery bird was supposedly the largest of its kind. The Bramwells were an ancient, powerful family line and had always been closely aligned with the Ericcsöns.

I learn a lot from drunken soldiers.

Seely didn't even have to try out for his position. It was passed down to him from his father. Certain members of the Blood Guard were furious about the nepotism, but would say nothing to oppose the fierce captain. He was the strongest of Fae, and no one with any sense dared cross him.

With that foreboding thought, I succumbed to the rest my body so badly craved.

* * *

Sterling

Remmy still slept, curled into a ball within her fur. I stared down at her sleeping form and fought the unbearable desire to lie down beside her and pull her close.

I must keep my distance. My father cannot know of my feelings for her, or he will use it against me. I should never have kissed her. This isn't fair to her. I should have let her keep on believing she was nothing more to me than the girl who released me from my prison. I must let her believe this kiss was a mistake. Establish distance between us once more. If only to convince her to flee.

I pulled my hands through my hair, my frustration palpable. I rolled my shoulders, trying to release some tension from my body.

Remmy shifted in her blanket, and I moved quickly away, not wanting to be caught watching her sleep. She remained asleep, so I grabbed the wool blanket she had given me and headed closer to the lake. Shedding my clothes, I sat on the shore near the sable waters, staring into their murky depths.

Recalling what she said yesterday, I closed my eyes, trying to sense my dragon, and relived the horrifying sensation of her being endangered. I sat there for well over an hour, torturing myself with the memories and even thinking back to being unable to save Isolde, but the dragon remained dormant, just out of reach. Warmth spread from the tips of my fingers and up my arms. I opened my eyes to reveal my fire coming alive.

The memories must have triggered it. But why not the dragon? No wonder they're extinct. They're difficult to control, temperamental beasts.

A shuffling behind me had me reaching for the blanket on the ground. I had no qualms about Remmy seeing me naked, but it seemed to make her uncomfortable.

Turning, I saw her sit up in the blanket, dark hair sticking out in all directions, like a crow had made a nest in it.

I faked a cough to cover my laugh. "Good morning."

She smiled sleepily at me and tugged a hand through her tousled waves. The fox poked its head up from beside her and grumbled noisily, yawning and yowling.

"Did I sleep late?"

"The sun has been up for three hours. How do you feel?" I was careful not to mention her bleed. She got flustered anytime I did.

"I don't feel quite as nauseated today."

Her eyes focused on the blanket wrapped around me, and a rosy hue tinted her pale cheeks, giving her a sun-kissed appearance. My heart beat faster at the sight of her. A part of me that I was suppressing longed to see her this way every morning—sun-kissed cheeks and disheveled hair, rubbing sleep from her bright, green eyes. To wake up beside her, tangled in the blankets from the night before. A night during which I worshiped her the way she deserved. My throat bobbed as I swallowed down the daydreams, knowing it was not to be.

"Why are you wrapped in a blanket? Were you trying to shift? Did it work?" She leaned forward, suddenly alert.

"Yes, I was trying. No, it did not. Are you hungry?" I asked, quickly changing the subject as a shadow of disappointment flicked across her features.

I can't stand to see her looking at me that way. Like I'm letting her down. I'll be failing her even more when I send her away. She'll never forgive me. Where am I even going to send her? Where will she be safe? I can't smuggle her and her family into Elysia. It's been closed off for years. Tangeer, then. It has to be Tangeer.

Her face lit up at the prospect of food, and she nodded her head at the suggestion. She had barely been able to eat over the last few days. I was not very familiar with human monthlies, but hers seemed severe. I hesitated to ask her about it, though, for fear of the intimacy it could cause. "Right, okay, I'll get dressed and we'll have some venison. I've already cooked it."

"I didn't know you shot a deer!" She exclaimed in surprise. "That's a lot of food!"

"You were sleeping."

She shrugged sheepishly.

I jogged over to the lake, picked up my discarded clothing, and began to dress.

I'll have to try again this afternoon.

Forty

"Can You Fly?"

* * *

Remmy

"I'm going to take a short walk around the lake."

Sterling opened his mouth to protest immediately, but I shushed him.

"I will stay within sight, but my back and legs are stiff from sitting for so long."

The prince had been attempting to shift for hours and had only just returned to the camp, claiming he needed a mental break.

I had no doubt it was taxing, but with my nausea subsiding and the weakness in my limbs fading, we would be on our way to Lunestair soon, and he had yet to shift.

Though the cramps still came in waves, they also lessened, and I needed to vent the frustration I was feeling. A walk seemed the safest way to do that; besides, I could use some exercise.

"Stay close!" He demanded as I dragged myself from my fur, into the chilly autumn air, and set off around the fog-enshrouded lake, Ember close on my heels. He was turning out to be quite the faithful companion. I didn't want to go too far anyway because I would risk running into another traveler the farther I got around the lake.

I inhaled deeply, the smell of magic and autumn leaves filling my nose. Autumn was a beautiful time, but in Merda, it simply meant the severity of winter was on the way.

I wonder how autumn will be in Lunestair? Rogard mentioned the weather was milder in the Stardust District. I wonder if that is true?

The sound of dead leaves crunching under my feet filled the quiet of the tree-ringed meadow as I walked, deep in thought.

This summer had been the most difficult of my life, desperately trying to survive with blight ravaging the crops. No one else in the village had experienced this blight, and I had been distraught trying to learn what I had done wrong. I had often thought the gods or the stars themselves were trying to curse our family. If I had guessed then where I would be now, I'd have sooner thought dead than on my way to Lunestair, trying to help the Prince of Valeria figure out how to kill his father, the king.

The magic was so strong around the Black Lake that the closer I got to the water, the less color the trees and shrubbery had. I chuckled to myself when I spotted the green and white leaves of laour plants crowding around the bank. No one would be bathing in this.

Fishing had been hazardous enough.

The Baga and Selkies were enough to keep most people out, and who knew what else resided in that lake.

A yell pierced the stillness, and I started, whirling toward the direction of our campsite.

Sterling!

Ignoring the stiffness in my joints, I raced toward the sound as more cries rang out, my heart heavy in my chest.

The king's men have found us!

Ember howled, following quickly behind me.

As I neared our camp, what met my eyes was not a sight of fear but one of joy, as I saw Sterling's hulking dragon form crouched on the ground, a glimmer of hope in his reptilian eyes.

"You did it!" I exclaimed as I rushed forward to meet him. A strange noise came from my furry companion, and he dove under our blanket, peeking out at Sterling fearfully. I chuckled and returned my gaze to Sterling.

He's bigger. This form seems larger than in the temple. Much larger.

I ran my hand over his snout, admiring the color of his scales, as a puff of smoke blew from his large nostrils. I giggled and waved it away with my hand, noticing something I had been unable to see in the dungeon of the temple. The dragon's scales were not just black. In the light of the full sun, they shimmered a deep midnight blue, having an almost ethereal quality.

"You're so beautiful," I murmured. "And huge! You grew!"

It was much easier to talk to him in dragon form. It felt like he was someone different altogether, and my shyness evaporated in his presence.

"Can you fly?" Excitement laced my words.

Sterling lowered himself to the ground, extending his wing in an invitation.

Without hesitation, I grasped his scales and began to climb up, seating myself on the huge dragon's shoulders and holding tightly to a rough scale. I leaned forward intently as Sterling took a few running steps forward and then launched himself into the sky.

I laughed aloud, throwing my hands into the air and gripping the great dragon's body with my thighs.

Unfortunately, I wasn't strong enough to hold on for long that way, and I was forced to grip the scales with my hands again, but it did not stop my heart from soaring, or my laughter from sounding as we circled above the Black Lake and Sterling dipped low, as though tempting the Baga. He stayed close to our campsite to avoid the risk of being spotted. His flight was slow on my behalf, and I appreciated it, for fear of falling off into the onyx waters below.

The landing was anything but smooth, and I slid off his back, crashing to the ground with a bout of laughter. I pulled myself upright, and the dragon nudged me away with his nose.

With a shudder and a low roar, the dragon began to morph into a man once more. Sterling lay on the ground curled into a ball, his body weakened from the transformation, but it had seemed easier this time, and he was able to do it on command, so that was a good sign. I rushed to him, throwing the blanket over his form.

"Sterling?" He moved a little and faced me, a small smile gracing his worn features.

"That really hurts." He muttered weakly.

"But you did it! And you shifted back on your own." I brushed back a lock of hair from his forehead, and he shivered.

"Oh, let me go grab your clothes!"

I glanced around the campsite searching for the prince's discarded wardrobe. Upon discovering it, I hurried back to his side and helped him stand, the blanket draped around his shoulders.

"Do you need help?" I asked hesitantly.

"No, it's all right. It weakens me somewhat, but it's getting easier." He took his clothes and began to dress.

Feeling hopeful, I returned to my fur beside the fire, holding Ember in my lap, and waited for Sterling to finish dressing.

Perhaps tomorrow morning we can start for Lunestair.

A few moments later, Sterling plopped onto the ground beside me with a loud exhale.

"How are you feeling?"

He shifted toward me, meeting my eyes. "Tired. Though this time did not hurt as much as the last."

I placed a hand gently on his arm, but he quickly pulled away from me, heading toward his own blanket. I sighed heavily.

What happened? I thought he... My frustrated thoughts staggered off as I watched him crawl into the wool blanket.

Maybe he is just exhausted.

I breathed a sigh of relief that he had finally managed to call his dragon. Our hope of defeating the king was restored.

"Sterling?" I called over to him, and he rolled in his blanket.

"Hmm?"

"I'll be ready to travel tomorrow morning."

The prince sat up in his blanket, his moon-drenched eyes boring into mine.

"You are well?" He asked hesitantly.

I nodded, my cheeks flushing slightly. "There is still some... lingering pain, but I am well enough to travel."

He gestured to the cuts on my chest. "And your wounds?"

His own injuries had healed now—the benefit of being a powerful Fae.

"Healing."

Sterling looked at me for a moment, then gave a brief nod. "We leave at nightfall."

"What? Why nightfall?"

"Because we are less likely to be spotted traveling under the cover of darkness. My father will have the Blood Guard patrolling the road from Mt. Malus to Lunestair. The night will conceal us, and then if we travel quickly, we can arrive in Lunestair before dawn."

"Oh," I muttered. It did make sense, but I didn't relish the idea. We were soon to cross into the Stardust District, but as it stood, we were still in Skotos's region, and the beasts roamed the night here. It was a terrifying concept to travel after dark. "How far from the region dividing line are we?"

"As soon as we get around the lake, we will enter the Stardust District. There is no cause for alarm. Try to get some extra rest, so that we may travel through the evening."

He lay back in his blanket and rolled over, facing away from me.

My stomach grumbled, and I seized some leftover meat from the pack, chewing it thoughtfully as I went over the plan for the evening in my head.

By this time tomorrow, I would be holed up at some inn in Lunestair, sleeping in a real bed.

With that blissful picture in mind, I laid back in my fur and closed my eyes, attempting to sleep.

* * *

Emerie

A quiet but insistent knocking sounded on the front door, jolting me from my slumber.

Who in the worlds would be out after dark? It is too dangerous!

Panic gripped me as I hurried to the door, wrapping my worn cloak tightly around me and sidestepping the creaky floorboard, careful not to wake Father or the children.

I opened the door only a crack and gasped in alarm when I saw Inara standing there, hair stuffed under a hood, tears streaming down her cheeks. Her dark eyes were ringed with even darker circles, her face stricken.

I opened the door and pulled her inside.

"Inara! What is it? What's wrong?"

She shoved a paper sack into my hands and paced about the living room. "He's done it! He's really done it!"

I grabbed my best friend's arm and forced her to look at me, keeping my voice low to avoid waking my family. "Who's done it, Inara? What are you talking about?"

She closed her eyes, and a tear slipped from beneath a lid, catching in her long lashes, as she inhaled deeply then released a shuddering breath. "My father. He's married me off to some overbearing noble in Lunestair."

I sucked in a gasp. "A Fae?" My hand subconsciously went to my chest, waiting for her whispered answer.

She nodded, her brown curls bouncing. "I'm to leave tomorrow morning."

"Tomorrow morning!" My voice rose, and I struggled to lower it again. "But that is so soon! Have you even met this… this Fae? What is his name? When will I see you again? Oh goddess!"

We were both crying now as we gripped each other tightly in a fierce hug.

"His name is Bramwell. Something Bramwell. He's… he's the

Captain of the Blood Guard!" She gasped, emitting a strangled sob. "I can't do it. I won't be married off like some pawn in a game of politics. I'm going to run. I've heard stories of him from my father's friends. He is… vile. Oh, Skotos, Emerie! He's perfectly vile!"

I jerked away from her quickly and grasped her shoulders tightly. "You cannot! It isn't safe. Where would you even go? You know your brothers won't help you."

My mind briefly went to Teigan Berger, and I wondered if he could help her escape if she went with Bramwell to Lunestair, but I couldn't ask that of him. I only just met the man. That would not be fair.

Still, it was not fair for Inara to be subjected to such cruelty. "You must go, Inara. It is the only way to remain safe. You must play the perfect housewife and do everything your husband asks. And then we will find a way. I will come to Lunestair, and we will find a way to get you out. But please do not do anything rash." Inara hung her head, refusing to look at me or answer, so I shook her shoulders. "Inara! Promise me you will not run! He will kill you. Or the beasts of the night will."

Finally, she raised her head and met my eyes. "I will not run."

"How did you get here? It isn't safe at night."

"Horseback. I brought the stable hand, Jax, with me."

The poor boy must be alone outside with the horses.

"You must return home immediately. Ride quickly and stay safe. We will figure this out. I promise you. We will."

I don't know how. But somehow, I will figure this out for her.

I gave her another tight squeeze, and she disappeared out the creaky door into the blackness of night. I prayed Skotos would call off his beasts long enough to allow her and the stable hand to make it home, as I opened the paper sack she had shoved into my hands.

Dried venison. Gods bless her.

I placed it on the counter in the kitchen and hurried back to the warmth of the bed I shared with the twins.

* * *

Vincent

Cyrus slammed both fists down onto the desk, sending papers flying into the air. "WHERE ARE THEY?!"

In Sterling's absence, the king had appointed me to be his manservant, dismissing Vaughn to the kitchens. I surmised it was to keep an eye on me and watch for signs that I was in contact with the prince. Captain Bramwell winced at the king's tirade.

"It is but a common farm girl and a clanless prince! They cannot be that hard to locate!"

"Your Majesty, my men are scouring the woods from Lunestair to the Darkhelm. We will find them, I assure you."

"Why haven't you found them already?!" Cyrus's arms flew into the air as his retractable claws shot from his hands.

The captain was easily a foot taller than the king, but still, he flinched at the lion's outrage. "I'm not certain, Your Highness. We believe they must be in hiding somewhere and not on the move."

The king's face turned pensive. "Could they have already made it into the city?"

"I'm having men search the local pubs and any potential rebels' homes."

"See that it's done." Cyrus waved his hand to dismiss the Captain, and Bramwell stalked out of the room, throwing me a sneer as he passed.

The king scrubbed a hand down his wearied face and let out a rough sigh as he slumped into his desk chair. "That bloody prophecy will be my damnation," he muttered.

"Vincent!"

I hurried to stand in front of his desk, bowing low.

"You know my son. You have been his servant for a long time, yes?"

"Yes, Sire." My mind scrambled.

"Where would he go in the city if he needed some place to lie low?"

He was testing my loyalty. I knew it. I could only hope that he did not know that I knew it.

I must give him something real enough to throw off suspicion without leading him to Sterling and Remmy.

"There is a pub… with an inn on the westside of town that he frequents sometimes. The name is… The Black Phoenix, I believe."

The king scratched his stubble, deep in thought. "Hmm. The Black Phoenix, you say? Isn't that the Bramwell's pub?"

"I believe so, Your Majesty."

"Send a message to my former Captain. I'd need to see where the Bramwell loyalties lie."

I nodded once and bowed again, taking my leave and praying to Lunaire that Sterling was safe at the Starlight Oasis.

Forty-One

What Should Have Been

* * *

Sterling

The spires of Lunestair greeted us as the horizon became a blazing fire of red and orange, the morning sun rising with the dawn. I pulled the hood of Remmy's old capote over my head as we entered the sprawling city, wishing it were black.

This light color makes me feel conspicuous.

We had narrowly avoided a late patrol as we crossed into the Stardust District. From what I'd overheard, they were searching for us. Fortunately, darkness had been on our side, and they passed without detecting our hiding spot. Remmy had managed to keep the fox shushed long enough that we could. That creature was constantly chattering about something.

I abhorred the idea of hiding instead of fighting, but I had only succeeded at shifting on my own once, and Remmy was worn from weeks of constant battles and nightmares. I wanted only to shield her from any more traumatic experiences.

I looked down at her and smiled at the wonder reflecting on her face. Lunestair was enthralling, possessing its own unique charm. I couldn't imagine what seeing it for the first time was like for someone who had grown up in the villages. Her eyes gleamed despite the dark circles beneath them, and she craned her neck every which direction, taking in the tall buildings, gardens, and fountains dotting the city streets. The market would soon be filled with vendors and street performers.

With the rising of the sun, the city would awaken, and that meant we needed to get inside. No doubt, my father had already doubled his efforts in searching for us.

Remmy needed a few days' rest, and I needed to make preparations to get her and her family to Tangeer.

I'll send a message to Vincent as soon as we get to the Oasis.

I led Remmy through the quiet streets of Market Square, making my way to the pub where I hoped she would be safe for a few days.

It was early yet, but the pub also served as an inn; therefore, the doors were always open. A few patrons were already seated about the bar, consuming hearty breakfasts, and I adjusted my hood farther down, the smell of venison, sausage, and eggs wafting out from the kitchen.

A tall, red-haired woman with a protruding tooth emerged from the storage room as Remmy and I approached the bar.

I racked my brain trying to remember her name.

Maggie... I think.

I'd had quite a few conversations with her on my previous visits to the pub. Her eyes grew wide as saucers when she spotted me, and she opened her mouth to say something, but I quickly held up my hand, hoping to silence her.

"P—P—Prince Sterling!" Her voice was hoarse as she whispered, a hand going to her forehead. "We thought you were dead! The king announced you had been killed in a quest on Mt. Malus."

"It's Maggie, isn't it?" The gigantic woman nodded her head quickly. "As you can see, I am not dead." I gestured down my body. "I hope I am correct in assuming that I can trust you to keep this quiet?"

Maggie's face paled, and she glanced around the pub as though searching for someone or something. She leaned across the bar, her voice low as her eyes scanned the room. "I can hide you, but I cannot promise your safety. This is a favorite hangout of the Blood Guard. You know that. You must stay in your room during the day."

I nodded and motioned to Remmy, who was patiently waiting beside me, the little red fox curled up in her arms. "This is—"

"Remmy?!" A male voice exclaimed incredulously, as a loud crash peeled through the quiet pub.

Remmy turned toward the voice, her nose turning red as her eyes filled with tears.

Ember perked up and scurried around her neck, sitting there like a furry scarf. "Teigan! Is it really you?"

Maggie hurried to hush a young blond man as he stepped quickly over the crate he had dropped and enveloped Remmy in his arms.

A wave of jealousy shot through me as I studied the man. He was almost as tall as I was, but he could not have been more than nineteen or twenty.

This realization calmed my jealous rage. He was just a boy. Perhaps a brother or a cousin. The young man's hair fell in waves over deep brown, honest eyes, and a smattering of freckles dotted the bridge of his nose.

He touched Remmy's sunken cheeks, looking her over as if assuring himself that she was alive, running a thumb over her scars.

As though she suddenly remembered I was there, Remmy turned to me and motioned me closer. "Teigan, I'd like you to meet someone. This is Crown Prince Sterling Ericcsön."

The man's brows arched.

"They told us you were dead." He extended a hand. "I am honored to meet you. The name is Teigan Berger."

I was grateful he refrained from bowing and attracting any more unwanted attention than he already had. He seemed genuine in his statement, though, so I clasped his hand tightly, giving it a firm shake.

Maggie appeared beside us, and I was suddenly made aware that several guests were staring. Thankfully, my hood was covering my face enough that I was certain I wouldn't be recognized.

I turned pleading eyes to Maggie, and she spoke quietly to Teigan. "Teigan, take them to your room to speak. It is not safe here, as you well know." She placed a key in his hand, and he nodded fervently. "I've given them the empty room across the hall from you. Go now."

Empty room. Only one.

I glanced at Remmy to see if she noticed, but her face revealed nothing.

It was not that I did not want to share a bed with her. Goddess, I wanted to share everything with her. I had refrained from mentioning the kiss in an effort to quell our feelings, hoping it would hurt less when I sent her away with her family.

It was a foolish hope.

Remembering that I needed to summon Vincent, I turned back to Maggie before reaching the stairs and placed a hand on her shoulder.

"I need my manservant, Vincent. Is there anyone you trust to get a message inside the Castle of Stars?"

Her face turned thoughtful for a moment, but she responded with a nod. "I'll see it done, Your Highness." She started to return to the bar, but then turned back to me. "And Prince Sterling… we're *all* glad you're alive."

I nodded my head solemnly and followed Teigan and Remmy up the dingy, smoke-filled stairs.

* * *

Emerie

I promised Teigan that I would begin to spread the seed of rebellion among the villagers, and I decided the first place to start was with the person I trusted most. After setting out some oatcakes for the children's breakfast, I dressed hurriedly and made my way to the Beck estate, as the colors of dawn were brightening the night sky.

I pushed through the huge iron gate, preparing to make my way to the back of the house and knock on Inara's bedroom window.

Before I could make it all the way there, the sound of a muffled sob coming from the stables stopped me in my tracks. What if one of the stable hands was injured?

Hesitantly, I approached the door of the barn and peeked inside, ready to call for help if need be. What I saw instead was Inara locked in a desperate embrace with a man, who was placing tender kisses down her neck and throat.

I gasped softly, placing a hand over my mouth to stifle the noise. I'd only met him a few times; his name was Jax. Inara had mentioned that she was with the stable hand when she came to my house last night. I hadn't realized.

She loves him? She never told me…

I began to back away slowly, not meaning to intrude on their private moment, when my foot snagged on something in the hay and I fell through the doors with a crash.

"Emerie?" Inara ran to help me stand, jerking me inside the barn and shutting the doors quickly, as I hastily brushed the hay from the front of my frock.

"What are you doing here?" She glanced at Jax, a look of guilt on her face.

"I'm sorry, I only wished to say goodbye. Surely your father won't deny us that."

She started to speak when the sound of an angry yell came from outside the barn.

"Inara!"

Her eyes widened in horror, and she grasped my arm tightly, shoving me into a horse stall.

"Hurry! You must hide before he sees you. You don't know my father. He's much worse than you believe. I'm not supposed to see you. Get in! Get in!"

The dutch doors swung shut on their hinges, and she raced to the stall housing her prize horse, Baldur. I ducked lower in the corner of the horse stall, confused by Inara's reaction. Her father was severe, but she was acting as though he would kill us.

The stable hand frantically grabbed a pitchfork and busied himself throwing hay in a pen at the far end of the hall, as the large barn doors slammed open and Viktor Beck stormed in, flanked by several servants and his personal guards.

Being the wealthiest man in the villages had its dangers, but Viktor was a force on his own. He was an imposing figure, having an aura of darkness about him. He towered almost a foot above Inara, who was at least several inches taller than me.

Two men dragged a red-faced woman inside the barn, who was crying and apologizing for something I couldn't quite make out.

A servant.

"I'm sorry. I'm so sorry." She stammered over and over again.

What in Amengor is going on?

"What's wrong, Father?" Inara emerged from the pen where she was brushing her horse, her eyes flicking briefly to my hiding spot, then returning to her father with a wary and confused smile.

Ignoring his daughter, Mr. Beck jerked his head toward Jax, and a guard converged on the boy, holding his arm. Jax didn't fight the guard. He hung his head low, as though he already knew they had been found out.

"What are you doing, Father?"

"Did you think I would not find out, Inara?" He boomed, his voice jeering. "The servants report everything to me!"

"W-w-what is wrong? Find out what, Father?" Inara stuttered fearfully, her brow furrowed.

Viktor's back was to me now, and I rose slightly from my place in the corner, my eyes meeting Inara's briefly. I wanted to help my friend. To hold her hand. She gave a small shake of her head, her brown eyes imploring me to stay where I was.

I sank back into my corner, listening from the hay as Viktor Beck pivoted, facing the hysterical servant.

"Don't play a fool with me, girl. Mrs. Goodman already told me about your little lover." Viktor motioned his guard to bring Jax forward, and Inara's eyes widened in horror.

"Father, no! It's not what you think. Jax and I… we are only friends. That's all."

Mr. Beck turned eyes as black as midnight on his now frantic daughter. "I will not be made a mockery. And you will not defy me again! Your mother's soft heart has allowed you to be unbridled for far too long. You will learn your lesson today, my spirited daughter. I'll not have you carrying on with common stable hands when you're to be wed."

He motioned for the guard to pass him his sword.

Inara screamed and threw herself at her father, clutching his arm and pulling on his sleeve. "No! Father, no! I'm leaving. I'll go with Captain Bramwell! Don't hurt him! Please!"

Hurt him?

Would Mr. Beck actually hurt Jax… for loving his daughter?

"Yes, my daughter, you will go with Captain Bramwell." He tossed her off with ease, and she fell to the barn floor in a heap, landing in the hay.

It happened so fast, Inara didn't even have time to scramble to her feet before the blade plunged through the boy's chest, and he slumped forward, his face contorted in agony. He had not even fought—resigned to his gruesome fate.

Hot, angry tears streamed down my face as Inara's scream rent the fabric of the universe. I'd never heard a more sorrowful sound in all my life. I gripped my chest as she collapsed to her knees beside Jax's lifeless body, his blood staining her satin gown. Her sobs consumed her, and I had to fight against every instinct to run to her, lest I be the next body at the end of Viktor Beck's sword.

Viktor bent over his forlorn daughter, his face hard and cold. "Dry your tears. Line your eyes. And for Skotos's sake, have someone get you a suitable dress. You're to be a proper wife now, and this deal is going to gain me a lot of clout with the king. I won't have you sabotaging it. I've sent a letter to your worthless excuses for brothers, that you will be arriving in Lunestair soon. They're to greet you. Bramwell will be here in an hour, and I expect you to be ready by then."

He handed the blade back to his guard and, dragging the sobbing Mrs. Goodman behind them, they strode from the barn, leaving Inara stretched prone over the body of her lover.

As soon as the barn doors closed, I ran from the horse stall and knelt beside my grief-stricken friend.

She sat up, and I wrapped my arms around her heaving shoulders. Inara buried her head in the crook of my neck, and together we mourned what could have been. What should have been.

Forty-Two

Conflicting Thoughts

* * *

Sterling

I walked the halls of the once-abandoned manse with the rebel leader, Ivor Thronfeld. The building was buzzing with life, as chatter and noise echoed from every corner and crevice of the grand estate.

The dark man moved quickly, stopping only to point out certain rooms and the purpose they served. After hours spent catching up with Remmy, Teigan had informed me of the Dragon's Fire, and I'd requested a meeting with their leader immediately.

My mind swam with uncertain thoughts.

Surely it couldn't be more than a few people?

There had never been a resistance in Valeria before.

Why had they put their trust in me?

Maggie was the only one I knew, and even then, only in passing, brief, drunken encounters at her tavern as I tried to numb the pain of my father's wrath. Why had they chosen a clanless prince as their beacon of hope?

What could these people possibly see in me?

I'd left Remmy slumbering in our room. She'd fallen asleep before the sun had even sunk below the horizon. After Teigan vacated the room, we stared at the bed awkwardly for a few moments before she valiantly offered to take the floor.

That, I had told her, was out of the question. She looked like she would argue for a moment, but the fight had gone out of her tired eyes, and she had fallen into the bed, asleep in minutes.

I'd stayed there in the chair across the room watching the rise and fall of her chest, as the golden sun had painted shadows across her lightly scarred face, fighting the desperate desire to crawl into bed beside her and shield her from the coming heartbreak.

I'd done her wrong—kissing her and then shutting her out, but there was no place for her here. I would not see the king snuff out her radiance. I would not see him take her life. I'd rather live a thousand years without her. I'd rather have her hate me than see her dead at his hand.

As the silver moon had risen over the City of Stars, I'd left the room, following Teigan out to the edge of Lunestair to meet the rebels.

Upon arriving at the Olsen estate, Teigan had split off to meet with his men for an operation brief, leaving me alone with the leader of the Dragon's Fire. The tall man was quiet and stoic as we walked, and again I wondered what had made him believe that I could be their savior. What did they see in me that I could not see in myself?

* * *

Remmy

I remained quiet as the door swung softly shut behind Sterling, my heart threatening to leap from my chest and follow him.

What had changed?

He acted as though he barely knew me, let alone expressed his desire for me a few days ago. Did he suddenly remember I was a commoner and therefore beneath him?

He refused to share the bed with such vehemence; it was as if I repulsed him. Maybe I did? Perhaps he'd been out of his mind with hunger when he'd kissed me. Or driven mad with lust and... and loneliness...?

I closed my eyes, and I could almost taste the smoke of his lips against mine.

Instinctively, I put my hand to my chest, trying to ease the pain of my throbbing heart.

Ember nuzzled closer to me, and I relished the warmth of his little body. He was warmer than the hearth.

My head pounded as I shifted beneath the covers of the musty-smelling bed. It was the first real bed I'd slept on in weeks, but I could hardly get comfortable enough to fall back to sleep. I felt weak and unstable.

The smell of mildew and mirthwood tickled my nose. How had Teigan lived here so long?

Perhaps he's gone nose blind to it. Maybe I will too if we stay here long enough.

We had not discussed a plan since we left the Black Lake, and I had no idea what the prince's intentions were. He had only shifted once in those three days, but his dragon's size had grown exponentially with the shift.

How big will he get before he stops growing?

The first time I had seen his dragon in the Temple of Deliritas, he had been larger than most normal animals, but still small by dragon standards, if the ancient texts were to be believed. I didn't know much about clan forms, but from what little I had learned in the tomes I had access to in Merda, dragons and wyverns were the only clans that continued growing after adulthood. I supposed because they were so large and they grew slowly.

Wyverns were extinct, though, and dragons had been as well… until Sterling, therefore, most of the information we had on these clans was well outdated. Even Sterling himself knew very little about the dragon clan.

What was his mother's clan? I can't recall it ever being mentioned.

Most information about the former Queen of Valeria had been snuffed out of existence. It was as though Cyrus wanted the country to forget we ever had a queen at all. And most of us had.

When Sterling returned from wherever he had gone, we would discuss the next steps. He couldn't force me to go back to Merda now, knowing that his father knew my hometown. We had to send for my family.

And put them where? We cannot all crowd into this dingy inn, right under the king's nose. It's risky enough for Sterling and me to stay here. Where will we send them?

I let out a frustrated sigh, questions swirling unanswered in my mind, and sat up abruptly, slamming my hands onto the mattress beside me. Ember yowled and nearly jumped a foot.

"I'm sorry, little one." I soothed his fur, patting his head softly as he settled back into the covers.

I'll go see Teigan.

Perhaps talking it out with someone would make me feel better until Sterling came back.

A wave of nausea hit me, and my stomach lurched. I regretted eating the food the pub owner had brought to our room. After weeks of eating leaves, berries from the forest, and tasteless dried meat, the rich fare was not sitting well in my fragile stomach. This might be a grimy tavern, but the food was incredible, and I had devoured way too much of it.

I shot from the bed, stumbling hastily toward the bathing chamber, and for once, I was grateful Sterling was not here.

Returning to the bed a while later, after my stomach had emptied its contents, I decided it would be best not to seek out Teigan. My body needed rest after the last few weeks.

Groaning, I slid under the heavy covers, Ember pressed against my side, and thanked the gods for warm blankets before sliding off into a thankfully dreamless sleep.

III

Part Three

Forty-Three

Maps, Plans, Contacts, and Torture

* * *

PART THREE
Teigan

At one point in time, meeting the Crown Prince of Valeria would have seemed an incredible feat.

Now? It's just another day. Though I am glad he's alive, and even more glad that Remmy is.

Prince Sterling had asked for word to be sent to his manservant to get in touch with Remmy's family. I would go myself if not for this mission. I wasn't sure how this situation would affect my chances of seeing Emerie again. What would Remmy think, I wonder, if I courted her sister?

Will Emerie even want to be courted by me?

Her shy smile and vibrant honey eyes had not left my mind since I'd returned to Lunestair. I rounded the hall corner, heading to the small office I'd been given.

Spotting Dante, I asked that he send the soldiers I had selected for this mission to my office. Being the owner of the Drunken Dragon and an integral part of the resistance, Dante had hired a manager for the pub and spent his time rotating between facilities.

Sitting down at my desk, I let out a heavy exhale. I had barely had a moment alone to process the events of today—the realization that my friend was alive. That the rebellion had its savior back. The death of the prince had poured fuel on an already raging Fire; his reemergence would either fan it or suffocate it.

There'd been an odd look on the prince's face when I had told him about the Dragon's Fire. Uncertainty and confusion had flashed briefly in his eyes before they shuttered, concealing his conflicting emotions. I hoped he could be the man the people of Valeria needed.

I fidgeted with the pile of parchment on my desk. Flyer after flyer of information to help plan this mission. I sighed.

Maps. Dates. Times. Contacts.

Sifting through them one by one, I went over the details, preparing to brief my men on what to expect.

I still had to stop at the storage closet after this meeting to acquire some clothing for Remmy and Sterling. They would have to stay hidden during the day, and the prince needed a cloak.

How did I get here?

A few months ago, I was nothing but a fisher boy working in pubs and robbing the elite in a fruitless attempt to save my parents.

Now I was a man, in charge of a squadron of soldiers, helping to lead a rebellion.

By Lunaire's hair, this is the first rebellion the entire continent has seen since the war.

I tugged at my ear and shifted the papers on my desk.

Would my parents be proud of me? Would they admire the man I've become?

For a while after their deaths, I was empty. A hollow shell of the person I had once been. Meeting Maggie, Deidre, Ivor, Xula, Rufus, and even little Gretchen, who now resided permanently at the Olsen estate, boosting the morale of the soldiers, had given me a purpose. A desire to live again. A desire to fight. A desire to avenge my parents and Koretta.

A heavy rapping sounded on my door, informing me that the men had arrived for their briefing.

I cleared my throat and called out with as much confidence as I could muster, "Come in!"

* * *

Sterling

"The Magpie informed us you needed to get a message to your manservant. Unfortunately, our spies in the palace have reported that Vincent Larssön has been made personal servant to the king in your absence. We suspect it's so that Cyrus may keep an eye on him and monitor any potential communications with you."

I swore under my breath and raked a hand through my thick hair, leaning forward to rest my elbows on my knees.

Ivor watched me intently, gauging my reaction to this new information.

Probably already wondering if he made a mistake trusting me.

"The girl. The one who rescued me. I need a way to get her and her family out of the country. Can you help?"

"Where are you hoping to send them? Surely not Rothton? Your uncle is as ruthless as Cyrus. He'd slaughter them at merely a whisper of their identity."

"How difficult would it be to smuggle them across the border into Tangeer?"

"It wouldn't be easy—"

A knock sounded at the door, and a woman with piercing light eyes and ash hair stuck her head in. "Ivor, I—oh! I'm sorry. I didn't realize you were in a… by the hair of Lunaire… Prince Sterling!" Her head whipped to Ivor, where he was sitting behind a large oak desk, and then back to me. "You're alive!"

"Xula, my love, come in here and shut the door quickly."

The woman did as she was told, all the while staring at me, her face as pale as death. The air around the woman shimmered oddly, as though she were cloaked in magic. She went to stand beside Ivor, placing a hand on his shoulder, still staring with eyes wider than soup bowls.

"Your Highness, this is my wife, Xula. She handles recruitment to the Dragon's Fire."

She bowed low beside her husband. "I am humbled to meet you, and grateful that the news of your death was… incorrect."

"Yes, the rumors of my death are… greatly exaggerated. Please, stand. There is no need for formalities here." I gestured for her to stand up. "I am honored to meet you both and to learn about the operation you are running. Surprised beyond belief, but honored, nonetheless. I was just discussing with your husband a plan for getting my savior and her family across the border into Tangeer. The need for secrecy is paramount, you see, as my father tried to have us both slaughtered on the mountain."

I returned my gaze to Ivor, meeting his dark eyes. "She was forced to fill out a document when she entered this absurd contest; therefore, he knows where her family resides. We must get them out. She knows too much, and he will stop at nothing to get to her, in an effort to control me."

Ivor nodded his head as he responded. "The man who dropped you off, Teigan Berger, is a leader in our reconnaissance department, and he visited her family nearly a week ago. He rode to Merda in less than two days. It will take longer with children, but perhaps we can get them here in four or five."

He turned to his wife. "Send for Ravii. Wake him if you must. We need to know if he has any contacts in Tangeer that can help us smuggle the children and the woman across. Also, have Axel Bolton come to my office. We will send him with a note from Remmy Silva to bring the children here until we can get them out of the country."

The leader of the Dragon's Fire turned his attention back to me. "Have your friend write a note to her sister, so that she knows it is safe to come with our man. They may all stay here until we hear from our Tangeerian contacts and can orchestrate the best plan for their escape. Does this meet with your approval?"

I nodded thoughtfully. "This Axel Bolten… he is trustworthy?"

"He's one of our best soldiers."

"Good. I will speak with Remmy in the morning, and have Teigan bring the note to you immediately. I can't risk being recognized."

Ivor motioned to his wife to leave, and she gave his shoulder a gentle squeeze before exiting the room quietly, the essence of magic leaving with her.

I shook off the weird feeling and reverted my attention back to the rebel leader. "That brings me to the next thing I wanted to discuss with you. While we were… traversing the mountain, my clan form emerged."

Something hopeful flashed in Ivor's eyes, and I charged on quickly, "Unfortunately, it's a rather difficult clan, and I have yet to master shifting. This estate is large enough and far enough from the other villas that I am assuming there is a place sufficient for me to practice? It'll need to be… rather large… and secluded."

The rebel leader's dark brows knitted together, but he did not ask the question I was hoping to avoid. Though if anyone lingered about during the nighttime hours, they were all bound to find out soon enough.

"Yes, of course. This home belongs to a distant cousin of yours, and it is heavily warded to remain unseen, so our recruits may train here safely."

My brows arched toward my hairline.

What distant cousin? I thought I was aware of all the Ericcsön family branches.

Ivor continued, "Her family was quite affluent, and the grounds are extensive. Several places are used as training courtyards, but there is plenty of space for you to do whatever it is you need to do. Would you like a tour of the grounds now?"

I rose from my seat. "Yes, thank you."

* * *

Sterling

After several hours of trying to shift, I slipped into our room at the Oasis, closing the door quietly behind me. It was after midnight, and the pale soft glow of the moon dimly lit the room enough for me to find my blanket. I eased myself onto the floor and slid under it, briefly noting that Remmy had thrown another blanket onto it.

I looked to where she lay. The little red fox nuzzled into her chest, and she stirred, slowly turning those deep green eyes on me. My heart bounded into my throat, and neither one of us said anything for a few moments.

Finally, she broke the silence. "Can we talk?"

Her voice was laced with sleep, and it was obvious she was still exhausted and worn.

"It's late, Rem. You should go back to sleep. We'll talk in the morning."

I knew what she wanted to talk about, and I didn't have it in me to discuss it now. Not in the middle of the night. Not when she was so beaten down, and not when I had just put my body through two rigorous shiftings and countless experiments with my magic. I'd almost lit the grounds on fire trying to direct the aim. If the estate wasn't heavily warded, I'm certain those fires could have been seen for miles. Ivor and Teigan had patiently put out fire after fire for hours before I sent them away to practice shifting. I was not ready to share my clan form with them yet.

Again, she stared at me, eyes seeming to pierce through to the very essence of my soul. She was quiet for several long minutes before speaking again.

"It's cold. Won't you come get into the bed with me? We can put a pillow between us if you're worried about that."

She thinks I'm worried about being close to her? I'd give my very life breath to be close to her. I just wish I could... ughhh... tell her. This is killing me.

I dragged my hands through my hair and let out a breath of frustration. I didn't know how to keep her at arm's length. I didn't know how to not love her.

Before I could sort out my thoughts to answer, she asked, "Is it because of *her*... because of Isolde?" She rushed on, "We can forget what happened. It doesn't have to mean anything; we can pretend it didn't and be... be friends. Friends who are part of a rebellion. A rebellion that you're the figurehead of. And I am just a random member. That's your friend. Your random member rebellion friend." Her pale skin flushed a deep crimson at her own ramblings as she kept talking to try to cover the awkwardness of the situation. I'd never seen her so flustered.

Tomorrow, I'd ask Maggie, whom Ivor had informed me was my cousin, if another room had opened up.

"Remmy." She didn't meet my eyes, her gaze fixated on her hands as she wrung them back and forth.

For Skoto's sake. I literally can't do this.

"It's not about Isolde." And I realized that for once, it wasn't about Isolde. I had not thought of her for several days. My mind had been utterly consumed with keeping Remmy safe. Somewhere along the way, I had fallen deeply in love with her, and I could think of nothing else. It was so easy to love her. Admitting that it wasn't a betrayal to Isolde had been the hardest part.

"If I get in that bed, will you stop rambling and go to sleep?"

I hadn't thought her face could flush any redder. I was wrong. She was practically purple now, but she nodded her head, still not meeting my eyes, and shifted closer to the wall, making room for me to slide in.

I gathered the blankets from the floor, spread them over top of the ones already on the bed, and laid down beside her.

Ember growled and grumbled, crawling over Remmy to sleep between her and the wall.

The old bed creaked and groaned under my weight as I adjusted, keeping a distance between Remmy and me, my back to her.

"Goodnight, Prince Sterling." I winced as she used my title, establishing a distance between us despite the physical closeness.

I said nothing, and soon the sound of her soft rhythmic breathing filled my ears as she drifted off to sleep behind me.

Why did it have to be her who rescued me?

Lunaire was torturing me. Or perhaps this was the work of Skotos.

Forty-Four

Venison and Kitchens

* * *

Emerie

I cursed as the deer startled, and my arrow thunked into a tree where the animal had just stood.

"By the hair of Lunaire," I muttered as I stalked to the Sessile Oak and yanked the bolt from the tough bark. I cursed again and stamped my foot when I saw that it had split. What was I going to do? This was the second arrow to split since I had taken up Remmy's bow. I was already teaching myself to hunt; now I had to learn how to make arrows, too?

There certainly isn't money to buy them.

I'd barely harvested five potatoes to sell at the weekend market.

Five.

The supplies Teigan Berger had brought would run out, and I had no idea if he would keep his word and return with more. I could not rely on someone else to provide for my family. Now that Remmy was gone, it had to be me.

I could marry.

I shoved away the foolish thought with a modicum of frustration. No one would want to marry a woman already saddled with a family. Even Lukas Vik had ceased his flirtations when the news of Remmy's death had reached the town. Anyone interested in marrying me would have to provide not only for me, but my two siblings and father as well. That was not a responsibility most men would want. I resigned myself to always being alone. To never having the love I dreamed of.

I took a deep breath, inhaling the crisp autumn wind. The earthy scent of pine and damp leaves filled my lungs. The vivid leaves of orange and crimson danced around me as the cool breeze whisked through the wood. Sunlight filtered through the canopy above, casting dappled shadows on the forest floor, where moss was clinging to the base of the ancient oaks that grew in this part of the forest.

I had perhaps a month to teach myself how to hunt successfully before winter would descend, the garden would die, and our only food source would be whatever I could stock up on and the bread Alice brought by.

Tightening my resolve, I dropped the split arrow into the quiver and withdrew another one. My breath was steady, though my heart hammered wildly in my chest.

Alone, this deep in the dense woods, the silence was both soothing and unnerving. The only sounds were the occasional rustle of leaves, the far-off call of a bird, and the low rhythmic thud of my boots echoing off the forest floor as I moved slowly between the multicolor trees.

I sucked in my breath as I spotted my target.

There.

Fifty paces away, unfazed by the noise of my boots, a deer stood grazing on the grass in the shadow of a tall Elm.

I nocked a bolt, pulling it taut against the bowstring, my frail arms trembling from the exertion. For a moment, I stood there, my muscles strained and my arms shaking ever so slightly as I held my aim. The world around me stilled as my fingers brushed the smooth shaft of Remmy's arrow, imbuing it with a prayer. I exhaled slowly, then pulled back the string a little farther.

A gust of wind stirred as I released it. It whistled through the air like a deadly song before landing with a thump as it found its mark. I dropped my bow in amazement and whooped, my shout resounding through the quiet forest.

I ran forward and stood staring down at the small deer. A wave of guilt rushed over me, but I pushed it aside. Echo and Eridian were more important. Kneeling beside the dying animal, I asked a blessing from Lunaire on its soul and then stood.

Now... how do I get it back?

It took me over an hour to drag the deer home through the forest. It had to weigh as much as I did. By the time I arrived, I was drenched in sweat, despite the cool temperature, and covered in blood and dirt.

When the cabin came into view, I dropped the animal with an exaggerated huff and collapsed into the dirt on my knees.

Next time, I will take a knife so I can cut it and dress it there. Should be easier to carry in chunks.

Why hadn't I thought of that before? My shoulders and back ached from the effort of dragging the heavy animal this far, and my fingers were red from gripping its legs. Tears gathered in my eyes, and I brushed them angrily away.

A shout rang out as Eridian came flying out into the yard. My legs trembled weakly as I stood and stepped forward to greet the boy.

"Emmy! Emmy! Are you okay? You caught a deer!" I smiled tiredly as the boy threw himself at me in a reassuring hug, wrapping his small arms around my waist. My shoulders screamed as I returned the embrace. My admiration for Remmy grew by the minute.

"I'm okay, Eri. Can you go inside and bring one of Remmy's knives out to me? We are going to learn how to dress a deer together."

The child's eyes sparkled at the morbid suggestion.

"And Echo can't come?"

I exhaled slowly, debating whether or not to ask Echo to help.

Deciding it was better if she learned now, rather than end up like me someday, I told Eridian to call her outside, stating it was a job for the three of us.

Disappointment flitted briefly across his face before he ran to call his sister and collect a knife.

"Do not run with the knife, Eridian!"

* * *

Inara

The Captain barely spoke to me on the ride from Merda to Lunestair. He sat across the carriage from me now, his great, hulking form slumped over in sleep. I studied him carefully as I debated the things Emerie and I had discussed.

A rebellion?

Truthfully, the king's ruthlessness had not affected me personally, but it had destroyed my best friend's life and taken so much from many others. A storm had been brewing in the people of Valeria since long before I was born.

And so had my father taken from others and destroyed in his quest to amass more power and wealth. That was the whole point of this marriage. That was why he had slaughtered Jax. My love. He wouldn't even get a ceremony in his death, for he had no family. No one to bury him. No one to mourn him but me. I blinked back the tears threatening to descend.

I clenched my fists at my sides at the memory of the boy I loved being slaughtered. I had no personal vendetta against the King of Valeria, but I would do anything to ruin my father after what he had done. Whatever it took. I would bring him to his knees and violently rip the rug out from under him.

Power. This marriage cements his foothold in the king's court. Or so he believes. I wonder what the king will think of his Captain marrying a lowly human girl?

The king barely tolerated humans, and my father, in his wealth, was no exception.

He thinks I will be at his beck and call. That my presence in the king's court will be a positive reflection on him; that he will gain information and standing from me. He is sorely mistaken.

He'd arranged for me to meet with my brothers, but they had done nothing to help me escape our father. I could hardly remember them anyway.

I will meet with them and gauge their intentions. See where their loyalties lie... then I will seek out this Teigan Berger, Emerie told me of. Hopefully, it will be easy enough to get away from Bramwell.

I turned my attention back to the Captain, his head now lolled to one side, bouncing up and down as the carriage rolled down the cobblestone streets. He would be devilishly handsome if not for his fearsome reputation. Lines of tattoos peeked out from the sleeves of his shirt, extending across the back of both hands. A jagged scar cut down his left cheekbone, giving him an even more terrifyingly striking appearance.

Without thinking, I leaned closer, studying the cut of his jaw. It was strong, lined with closely trimmed facial hair.

All at once, his golden eyes popped open, and I sprang back in my seat as my breath caught in my throat.

The man smiled, but it was more menacing than friendly. "See something interesting?"

"N-no, sir, I am sorry. I was just... ummm... going to ask if we were close, but I wasn't sure if I should wake you."

He had not laid hands on me yet, but there was nothing to say he wouldn't if he deemed me insolent.

A wife, for some men, was nothing more than a whipping girl.

My hands were shaking as I answered his taunting, so I shoved them beneath the folds of my now travel-worn silk dress.

Mrs. Goodman had chosen a gown with phoenix feathers woven into the silk, creating the image of a great fiery phoenix, to honor my new husband's clan. The gown was nothing extraordinary, just plain black silk with orange feathers sewn into the bodice, but it was meant to signify my commitment to him. If the rumors were correct, Captain Bramwell was the largest phoenix to emerge in one hundred years.

His eyes had darkened when he had taken in my dress, but he had said nothing of it, instructing me gruffly to get into the carriage.

There had been no ceremony, just my father signing some documents while my mother sobbed in the background, clutching me tightly. I loved my mother dearly, but she did everything my father demanded of her.

Viktor. He is my father no longer. His name is Viktor Beck, and I despise him. I will ruin him.

"We are arriving now." The captain's deep voice shook me out of my darkening thoughts, and I surveyed the city around me.

A row of neat houses lined the cobblestone, each one a muted color, with tiny vibrant gardens and flower pots adorning the lawns. Fountains dotted the streets, with moon lilies and lanterns floating in their crystal waters. I'd been to Lunestair many times on my father's journeys, and while it was a beautiful city, I'd never paid much attention before.

The homes the carriage stopped in front of were smaller than one wing of the house I had grown up in. I had honestly figured that the Captain of the Guard received a greater stipend than these homes implied. The carriage door swung open, and I scooted forward on the seat to look out the door as Bramwell descended.

Wordlessly, he reached inside and, placing one hand on either side of my waist, lifted me out of the carriage and plopped me onto the ground. Heat rose to my face as his hands lingered on my body for a moment longer than necessary. His fiery eyes bore into mine before he spun on his heel and entered one of the townhomes.

I looked around me helplessly, unsure if I should follow him or try to wrangle my belongings. A flowerpot with a dying plant hung on one side of the door, and a fireless lantern on the other. I'd briefly heard mention of quilldust from Emerie when her father worked in the mines, but I was under the impression that only the elite Fae had access to this type of magic, though I supposed, being Captain of The Blood Guard, made one elite enough.

"The driver will handle your luggage." He called behind him as he disappeared into the small home.

Quickly gathering my skirts, I followed him through the doorway, up the sturdy staircase, and down the narrow hall. The giant of a Fae stopped in front of a door near the end of the hall and swung it open, motioning me inside.

"This will be your room."

My room? We aren't to share? Where does he sleep? Is he to call on me like some paid night worker?

I cringed. I knew I would have to… do my wifely duties eventually, but I had tried not to think of it for fear I might vomit or pass out from sheer terror. I shuddered visibly at the thought, and the man's dark brow furrowed.

"Is it not to your liking?" He asked sharply.

"Oh!" I gasped, looking around me hastily. A bed with a canopy was centered in the room; the blankets adorning it were light and flowery. Underneath the window was a small writing desk, supplied with quill, parchment, and an oil lamp.

No quilldust for me.

To the right of the desk was a large wooden bookcase lined with dusty tomes. Excitement rose in me at the sight of it.

Books!

Viktor hardly let me read, claiming it was a silly pastime for women. Across from the bed, a fire blazed in a great stone fireplace, warming the room against the autumn chill.

"It's quite lovely! Thank you."

I smiled up at him, and the smile was genuine. I could barely contain my desire to snatch a novel from the shelf and curl up in the cozy bed for hours.

He jerked his head in a brief nod. "Follow me."

I scurried to do as requested, trailing him back down the stairs. At the bottom of the steps, the carriage driver was pulling my luggage into the entryway, preparing to take it up to my room.

Bramwell ignored him and turned, going past the staircase and pushing open a door, passing through the sitting room. I barely had time to glance around before the captain ushered me inside to the kitchen.

"There are no servants here, only my driver. It will be your responsibility to upkeep the home, the yard outside, and prepare the meals."

Prepare the meals? Oh, Lunaire.

I'd never set foot in a kitchen. Viktor never allowed me in the servants' quarters. I had no remote idea of how to cook anything.

Panic welled up in me as he continued speaking, his towering form looming like an imposing warrior in the doorframe. I'd never seen a man so tall, and Viktor was tall for a human.

"There is meat in the cooling box, and everything you will need is spread throughout the cupboards. I expect dinner promptly at seven, nightly." He nodded his head again and made to move out of the room, ducking low to fit beneath the door frame. "I'll leave you to it then."

The sun had been starting to set when we came in. I searched around the kitchen frantically for a timepiece. Six o'clock. I cursed. I had one hour to change and figure out how to cook.

I cursed again as I exited the kitchen, looking warily around for Bramwell. Not seeing him, I darted up the stairs to my new room and began to rifle through my luggage, searching for something more appropriate to cook in.

Finding a plain tan linen gown, I donned it, glancing wistfully at the books in the corner. I breathed a heavy sigh as I resolutely shut the door and found my way back to the kitchen. I stared dumbly around me, trying to remember what he had said about a cooling box, and wondered if he would beat me should I screw up dinner.

I can do this. It's just food. And fire...

Forty-Five

Nightmares

* * *

Sterling

Remmy had nightmares.

I'd learned this early in our journey, when she had made me a tincture for the ones that haunted my evenings.

Tonight they plagued her ruthlessly, and she thrashed about in the bed. Ember chittered and leaped out of the bed, curling into a ball beside the hearth, glancing at Remmy warily.

"Traitor," I muttered.

I've got to get him some food tomorrow. Wonder if Maggie has any mice running around the kitchen?

I slid from the bed and rummaged through our supplies searching for something to help Remmy's nightmares, but I was not skilled with herbs and plants as she was.

A small vial rolled out from a pocket, and I opened it up, lifting it to my nose.

The odor was sharp and pungent, with a metallic undertone. I jerked it away from my nose and glanced back at the bed where Remmy slept.

Poison?

Something about it was familiar, and I took in the pale yellow liquid thoughtfully. Then it struck me.

Vesper.

She had been carrying Vesper venom with her.

Did she plan to poison me? Or the king?

I swiveled back to the bed as Remmy let out a sharp, piercing cry. The agonized sound had me rushing to her side.

Ember chattered frantically from his place by the fire as if yelling at me to help her. Even if she had planned to kill me, I still wanted nothing more than to save her from this pain.

Sweat pooled in tiny beads on her brow, and teardrops slipped from the corner of her eyes, yet they remained closed.

"Remmy!" I sat on the bed beside her and shook her shoulders gently, trying unsuccessfully to rouse her.

Her arms swung wildly about, and one fist glanced off the side of my jaw as she fought an imaginary demon in her slumber.

The sound of her cry was so anguished that something inside me cracked. What nightmares had she endured on her journey to rescue me? What had her life been like before she found me? What horrors had she witnessed to cause such terror in slumber?

"Remmy, Adhará, you must wake!"

I shook her shoulders again, and her eyelids fluttered violently, then flew open, panic on her pale face as she stared at me without recognition.

After a moment, her eyes cleared, and she swallowed, licking her lips before speaking, her voice scratchy. "Sterling? What is it?"

"You were having night terrors."

"Oh. I'm sorry to have woken you."

"I tried to find something in your bag, but it seems you're out of valerian root." I gestured as nonchalantly as possible to our supplies in the corner of the room. "You do seem to have some Vesper venom, though."

Remmy chuckled lowly. "I hope you weren't planning to give me that for night terrors."

"What were *you* going to use it for?" I tried to leave the accusation out of my voice, but her flinch was enough to know I hadn't succeeded well enough.

"I didn't know what I would encounter on this trip. I'm sorry that I forgot it when the Blood Guard attacked us, but the sight of you burning that Fae's ass was not something I would have wanted to miss."

Her laughter warmed my heart, drawing an unbidden smile to my lips.

Ember resumed his spot on the bed, and she stroked his fur thoughtfully, her face serious.

She suddenly glanced around the darkened room as though she were expecting something to leap from the shadows. The moonlight bathed her face in a silvery glow as she lay back in the mounds of blankets and looked at me questioningly.

"What is it?"

"Will you hold me?" She whispered. "It doesn't have to mean anything. Just... just until I fall asleep?" She fidgeted with the blankets as she posed the question, clearly terrified of going back to sleep alone.

I nodded, hesitating only a moment, my resolve to keep her at bay dissolving by the hour. I would deal with the consequences tomorrow.

I slid into the blankets beside her, and she curled into my side, clinging to me for warmth or comfort. I didn't care which. Her honeysuckle scent was slightly masked from days without a bath, but I didn't mind.

I'm sure I smell worse than she does.

We had both been too exhausted to bathe, committing to doing it in the morning, when we would be confined to our room anyway.

"What were you dreaming?" The question popped out before I could stop it, my desire to know more about her overruling my common sense.

Remmy stared out the moonlit window, her expression pensive, before shifting her gaze to meet my eyes. "In the Cave of Beithir… there were a lot of mental battles… hallucinations or visions. I'm not sure which. One time, it was as though I were waking up from sleep, and I found you dead on the floor. I didn't even know you then, but somehow I knew it was you. You were so pale, and the blood… there was so much of it. I laid on the floor beside you and prayed for the beasts to take me."

Her body tensed as she returned to staring out the window.

"Another time, Skotos himself appeared to me and dragged me to the Netherworld."

She shuddered and took a deep breath. "It was like he put me into a trance to make me fall in love with him. He was beautiful. Like nothing I've ever seen. He was carved from muscle and walked on flames, fire shooting from his limbs, like yours… but blue. As he was moments from throwing me into the portal to the Netherworld,

I woke from the trance and tried to fight him… but he was too strong. He threw me in… but it wasn't the portal. I woke in another hallucination. I was so terrified that he had thrown me into the Netherworld and I would never see my family again." Her eyes shuttered as she tilted her head up to look at me. "I would never abandon them."

Instinctively, I reached out to brush a lock of hair behind her ear. "I'm sorry you had to go through that. I'll do everything in my power to ensure you and your family are safe."

Remmy nodded thoughtfully and pleaded, "Tell me a story. Something happy from your childhood. Your best memory."

I thought for a moment.

Something happy?

I had few happy memories, but one suddenly sparked in the recesses of my mind. "One of the last memories I have of my mother is when she introduced me to the library in the Castle of Stars. I was barely six years old and just learning to read. I remember the excitement on her face as she swung open the great wooden doors and pulled me inside. I haven't thought about her in so long, I'd almost forgotten. Her hair was dark as night, braided and coiled tightly into a crown around her head. She swept me into her arms, going from aisle to aisle. It seemed as though the shelves of books towered to the sky."

I put my free arm behind my head as I recounted the memory of wandering the great castle library with the mother I could hardly remember. It wasn't long before I realized I was talking to myself as sleep had claimed Remmy once more. She was peaceful this time, though her face was tense as she lay nestled into my side. I stroked her hair softly, whispering words of the magical library that I dreamed of showing her, until I drifted off to sleep as well, my slumber for once free of nightmares.

* * *

Remmy

The smell of smoke and something warm and earthy wrapped around me, pulling me gently from slumber. Sunlight streamed in through the murky window, and it suddenly occurred to me that my ear was hurting.

Why does my ear hurt? And why is my pillow moving?

My eyes popped open.

I'm lying on Sterling.

My first thought was to roll off of him and pretend it hadn't happened, but I didn't want to. I wanted to be close to him, and he either was not awake yet or was trying not to wake me. Judging by the even rise and fall of his chest beneath my head, I assumed the first was correct. His hand was tangled in my hair, and I remembered him stroking it last night, as I fell asleep.

I don't want to move.

My thoughts were at war with themselves, telling me that he didn't love me, while still hoping there was some explanation for his strange behavior the last week.

What if this was the last time he ever held me like this? What if he really didn't care for me at all?

If we defeated the king, then his contest would be invalid, and the prince would be free of his marriage to me. The last time we'd spoken of it, he'd refused it anyway.

Maybe it was selfish of me, but I decided that if he truly did not love me, then I would take advantage of this moment before saying goodbye, and I pressed my body closer to his, reveling in the feel of his skin against my face. I tried to keep the tears at bay, scolding myself for my blatant stupidity.

For falling in love with the Crown Prince of all people. The prince, who had hated me mere weeks ago. The prince, who had kissed me like the stars would surely fall if my lips were not against his. None of it made sense.

What part of him is real? Can passion like that be faked?

So maybe he didn't love me… but then why would he kiss me like that? He claimed I had undone him. What did that even mean? He must still be in love with Isolde. Or maybe he'd suddenly realized that he could never be with a low-born human girl. The haughty prince of Valeria returned, and I was not good enough for him. That didn't seem like the real Sterling.

Maybe the kiss meant nothing; he'd been mad from hunger and the constant fighting. It didn't change how I felt about him. It didn't change the love that had blossomed from the shared trauma of our time together. The pull to him was magnetic. I couldn't refuse to love him, even if I wanted to. There was something primal and magical about it that drew me to him even against my own weak will. Like the stars or Lunaire in her divine goodness had sanctioned it.

When did I begin to love him?

Was it that first joke he'd cracked in the cave when his smile had outshone the very sun above? Was it when he'd gruffly taught me how to maneuver my sword using a carrot? Or when he had chased after the Banshee that captured me in the Darkhelm? Or maybe when he had fought so vehemently to defend me against the Blood Guard? The look on his face had said he would burn the world to ashes, leaving nothing but smoldering embers in his wake, to save me from that fate. He had been deadly and beautiful in his rage. The smoke and fire had roiled off his body, painting him like a savage god of old.

I closed my eyes and inhaled deeply, hoping he would sleep for hours more, so that I could enjoy this embrace, however brief. My hopes were dashed as he stirred, and I heard him yawn.

I decided not to feign embarrassment this time as I met his eyes, and my heart jumped into my throat uninvited. They were like bottled moonlight. They glistened now as he stared at me sleepily through thick, dark lashes.

His chest rumbled as he spoke, untangling his hand from my hair. "Hey, there."

I quickly sat up, suddenly self-conscious of my filthy appearance.

"Hey." I ran my fingers through my tangled waves, grimacing at the greasy mess that was my hair.

The prince stretched and grinned at me, his white teeth gleaming.

So white. Why are they so white?

My brain stuttered for a moment, unable to think clearly, and I cursed myself again.

Who has teeth that white? Stop looking at his teeth, you imbecile.

"Did you sleep better?"

"Huh?" I asked, aware that I was still staring at his starkly white teeth.

He smirked and repeated, "Did you sleep better? After your nightmare last night?"

He knew I was staring at him, and he enjoyed it.

"Oh! Yes, I did." I fidgeted with my hair some more, sitting cross-legged beside him on the narrow bed, my knee pressing into his muscled thigh. "Um, thank you for… talking to me, and staying with me."

Stop looking at his teeth. Holy gods, I'm still staring at his teeth.

"I didn't mind. Your snoring was a grand symphony to fall asleep to."

"Ooh!" I huffed and smacked his arm before standing and leaping over him, bounding off the rickety old bed, and heading toward the bathing room.

The sudden motion woke Ember, and the little fox protested loudly before quickly leaping out of the bed and curling up beside the fire and drifting back to sleep.

Sterling roared with laughter as I climbed over him. His demeanor quickly changed as I sauntered over to the door leading to the small bathing room.

A wave of dizziness hit me, and I stopped for a moment, gripping the wall to steady myself.

"I need you to pen a quick note to your eldest sister. The rebel leader is sending a soldier to retrieve your family. We are bringing them here until we can arrange a plan to get them out, but we want to make sure she feels secure going with him. You must warn her that he works at the palace, so she isn't afraid."

My heart beat faster at his words, and I hurried to the small desk in the corner and dipped the quill in ink. My hand shook as I wrote, but I quickly finished and handed the note to him.

I was filled with excitement at the idea of seeing my family again.

Sterling took the note and rose from the bed. I felt heat rising to my cheeks as I was suddenly face-to-face with his bare, muscled chest again.

He smiled at me, and my thoughts turned fuzzy. "I'll take the note over to Teigan and have him get it to Ivor immediately."

Trying and failing to get my mouth to work again, I nodded my head and resumed walking to the bathing room, when I noticed a pile of garments on the floor beside our things.

"What's this?" I pointed at the pile, turning to face him. His arms were behind his head as he stretched, and I could barely see the edges of his tattoo wrapping around his neck. He looked like a deity, his muscles rippling as he shifted to see what I was pointing at.

He could rival Skotos for the most beautiful thing I've ever laid eyes on.

"Teigan sent those last night. Fresh clothes for both of us. Should be a few pairs."

"Thank the goddess!"

I couldn't wait to bathe and slide into a clean dress. I had never been so long without a bath. I wasn't sure how Sterling could stand to share a space with me, though he reeked as much as I did. His usual intoxicating scent was masked with dirt, sweat, and grime.

I bent over and began picking through the stack of clothes. There were no dresses. Not one.

They expect me to wear trousers?

I had seen plenty of women wear them, but I was not accustomed to it. It was not common in Merda, and I had only ever seen foreign travelers wear them. I held up a pair that were noticeably smaller than the others. They were tan suede, and I ran my fingers over the soft material. I had never owned anything so nice. Except for the now-torn cloak Rogard had given me.

These probably would have helped me immensely on Mt. Malus. Not only would I have avoided being encumbered by the dress, but it would have made it easier to climb.

I glanced down at the thin cotton dress I had been wearing for weeks.

I will not be sorry to say goodbye to this old thing.

Resolutely, I folded the trousers over my arm and selected a long beige tunic. It came about to my knees, and I guessed it would make the transition to wearing pants easier. I sorted through the remainder of the garments, searching desperately for some underthings.

Nothing.

The old panties I had were barely holding together, and I wouldn't be able to wear my shift with a tunic and pants. I cringed inwardly at the thought of asking Teigan to get me underclothing. I decided to wash the ones I was wearing and ask whoever brought breakfast to send for Maggie, the tavern owner. Surely she or her daughter could procure me some female underthings.

With a deep sigh, I slid into the scalding water of the bath, my self-discipline and strength slipping away on the steam as it curled in the morning air.

The exhaustion was bone-deep. My skin was red from the heat of the water, but I hardly noticed. Weeks of chaos and pain pressed in on me, and I slipped further below the surface of the water, dipping my chin in it. My thoughts became clouded and hazy as I soaked, the trauma of the last few months pressing in on me from all sides.

I glanced down at myself in the murky water, scanning the brutal scars that now graced my body. Scars everywhere. No wonder Sterling didn't love me. I'd been merely an average-looking girl before. My hand went to the Imp scars lining my cheek. Now... now I was hideous. Covered in scars and wounds, reminiscent of battle after battle. My body was as torn and broken as my mind was now becoming.

Without knowing why, I suddenly felt an urgent need to scrub my skin. Looking hastily around the rim of the tub, I spotted a bottle of laour lather on the other side of the bath. I leaned forward and grabbed it. Squirting a big glob onto the cloth, I began frantically rubbing my skin, trying to scrape off weeks' worth of dirt and grime. Of blood. Of monster bits. Of demon ichor. Of pain. Of filthy Fae hands trying to tear the clothes from my body. Cutting me. Touching me. Trying to take from me. I scrubbed harder and harder, my skin becoming raw from the frantic motions. I didn't realize I was yelling until the door burst open and Sterling flew into the bathing room, fire suspended in the palms of both hands, his moon-drenched eyes blazing with unbridled fury.

"What?! What is it?"

The fire went out when he saw me submerged in the tub, rubbing my arms raw with soap. I looked at him through blurred eyes that were unable to focus.

"I can't get it off!" I sobbed, my breath coming in short, ragged gasps.

"I can't get it off me!" I practically screamed the words, still rubbing frenziedly at the same spot on my right arm. "I can't get him off me!"

Sterling moved slowly to the tub and knelt beside it, his eyes never leaving my face. Never straying to what he knew I wouldn't want him to see. Never taking advantage of what was right in front of him.

Gently, he removed the rag from my hand and placed it on the side of the tub, those softened eyes still resting on my red, tear-stained face.

I let him take it, my arms falling limply into the cloudy water, my breath still coming in shallow wheezes. The water was so dirty that he wouldn't be able to see my body even if he tried. He cradled my face in his hands with more gentleness than I knew was possible, and stroked my cheeks, wiping the tears away with the pad of his calloused thumb. He looked at me like I was the only thing in Amengor.

But how can he hate me so, when he looks at me like this?

"Remmy, I want you to listen to me very closely, okay?"

I nodded as much as his hands would allow me to. His eyes bore into mine, and I noticed something I had never seen before. They weren't just silver. They were flecked with tiny specks of swirling gold. Like a whole galaxy was looking back at me. The thought calmed me enough to focus on his words, and I took a deep, ragged breath.

"You're safe. Okay?"

I swallowed slowly, trying to steady my breathing, and nodded again.

He continued, "You're safe, and there is nothing to get off your skin. You're not tainted. You're not ruined. You're perfect. Your body is perfect. You're beautiful and brighter than all of the stars in Valeria. They envy you. Their light is dimmer in your presence as though even they know no beauty could ever compare to yours." His fingers caressed my face, stroking my scars, as his voice rumbled through me, deep and resonant.

What is he saying?

"Do you hear me, Remmy?"

Again, I nodded, heart pounding.

He released my face. "I'll be right back." The prince disappeared back out the door he had burst through and returned a moment later holding a small bottle.

"Maggie sent this up for you with breakfast a few moments ago. Jasmine and honeysuckle."

He motioned for me to lean forward, and I did as directed. A shiver coursed up my spine as his hands weaved into my hair. He massaged the hair oil in, rubbing my scalp with such care, I nearly fell asleep.

If I had been lucid enough, I would have been mortified for him to find me this way, but as it was, I was just grateful that he was here.

He had seen me in all my worst moments.

What's this compared to all the things we have endured the last few weeks? It barely matters.

The prince produced a pitcher from somewhere and tilted my head back. With a gentleness I didn't know he possessed, he rinsed my hair, then laid a towel on the edge of the small tub.

He said nothing as he left the bathing room, shutting the door softly behind him, and I cried again, my whole body trembling. Sinking low into the water, I let it wash the pain away beneath its murky depths.

Forty-Six

Whispered Confessions

* * *

Sterling

My hands shook as I poured coffee from the breakfast tray into a mug. The Starlight Oasis didn't offer room service, but Maggie was making an exception for the Crown Prince and his rescuer. I couldn't risk being seen during daylight hours, so she sent the meal up.

Remmy wouldn't be recognized, of course, but I refused to let her go out without me. The city wasn't safe for a woman alone. The beautiful city of my birth had a dark side. The western quadrant was all slums, and the Blood Guard marched at noon every day, setting out on random patrols after their march. If even a whisper of her name slipped out on the wind, it could reach my father's ears, and the Guard would snatch her before I knew what had happened.

I'd inquired if another room was available, but had been told this was the nicest room in the inn and one of only three with a private bathing chamber. None of the others were available.

But that had been before. Before I'd heard Remmy screaming in her bath and rushed in to find her trying to scrub her skin off.

Her face had been broken. She'd looked so lost. I could barely stand the pain I saw etched into the facets of her gemstone eyes. With every fiber of my being, I had wanted to pull her close to me and hold her.

I scrubbed a hand over my face and exhaled. There was something resilient about this woman. Some deep-rooted strength that drew me to her. A defiance in the face of all odds—one that she wielded better than the sharpest sword. She was a force of nature all her own. Every scar that marred her skin told a story that I wished to hear. It was a testament to the resilience and unyielding strength residing within her. Seeing her break that way… I wanted to burn the world to ashes for the pain it inflicted on her. She was beautiful. So very beautiful.

I'm only adding to the pain she is enduring by keeping her in the dark. Will she ever forgive me?

I tipped back the scalding hot coffee, letting it burn its way down my throat, and stared out the dingy window. The sun was high in the sky, but there was no timepiece in this room. I guessed it to be around noon, and our breakfast still sat untouched on the tray by the door.

Reaching for it, I lifted some roasted venison from a plate and tossed it over to Ember. The fox nosed it a few times before gobbling it up and looking up for more.

"No more, you little leech."

He growled at me and then leaped back up onto the bed, building a nest in the blankets. I was starting to appreciate the little guy for the comfort he provided to Remmy.

If Remmy did not come out of that bathing room soon, I was going back in and I would carry her out of the tub myself. I ran my hands through my hair, impatience muddling my thoughts.

How am I supposed to remain locked up in this room all day, every day? I need to talk to Ivor. See if he has a plan for Remmy and her family. Once they safely reach Tangeer, I can move forward with plans to defeat my father. I need to develop some plans. I have no idea what I am doing. I don't have any plans. I don't have any bloody plans.

I heaved a sigh of frustration.

The resistance was growing every day, according to Teigan, and within a few weeks, I expected to be able to master shifting into my dragon form.

I need to talk to Ivor, I thought again, irritably eyeing the cloak and scarf Teigan had dropped off for me. I was running over the pros and cons of donning them and setting off for the estate in daylight hours when the door to the bathing room cracked open slowly, and Remmy emerged. She was dressed in the tunic and suede pants she had plucked from the pile of clothing, and her drenched hair hung in ringlets cascading over her shoulders, forming wet spots on the material. She was deathly pale, and her eyes appeared glassy. I took a step forward just as she collapsed, her knees giving way beneath her.

"Remmy!"

I caught her in my arms and gently lifted her, hurrying to the bed. As carefully as possible, I placed her between the covers, beside Ember, who was barking noisily and nuzzling her, and rushed out into the hallway and down the stairs to the pub below.

I shouted for someone to send for a healer, and the grimy man behind the counter jolted, eyes widening in alarm. Without a second glance, he ripped off his apron and bolted out the back door into the alley.

If he recognized me, I couldn't tell. I only prayed he was on his way to locate a healer and not the Guard. There was no sign of Maggie or her daughter anywhere, and Teigan had yet to return from delivering the note from Remmy.

Racing back upstairs, I knelt beside the small bed and took Remmy's slender hand in mine, holding it tightly. It was cold, despite recently surfacing from a warm bath. I stroked it gently.

"You're going to be okay, my Adhará," I whispered it over and over as I waited with bated breath for some sign that it was true.

Of all the things I had studied in the palace, healing was not one of them, and I cursed myself for it now.

I looked up in panic as the man from downstairs rushed into the room, an older man with a healer's bag following quickly behind him.

The old man came over to the bed and shooed me away.

Reluctantly, I released Remmy's hand and stood.

"What happened?" He questioned without taking his eyes off Remmy's pale form. He laid a hand on her head and felt her wrist.

"I don't know, she just collapsed! She was bathing, and then she was upset, and then she came out and... she... she just collapsed!" I knew I wasn't making sense, but I had no idea what had happened. I ran my hands through my dirty hair and scrubbed them down my face.

The old healer turned from Remmy to me. "I need you to calm down, Prince Sterling."

My eyes hardened and shot to the man from downstairs as a new kind of panic tore through me. I felt my blood begin to boil as the flames rose at my command. I would kill both of them before I let them leave this room and carry news back to my father that would harm Remmy.

The tavern worker quickly closed the door and held up both hands. "We work for the Phoenix."

What in Amengor?

I stared at him blankly, trying to discern what he meant, before I remembered my talk with Ivor last night.

The Dragon's Fire. Ivor is the Phoenix. These men are rebels.

My gaze shot back to the healer, who still sat on the bed beside Remmy. His eyes were kind and wise as he surveyed the fire still sparking from the center of my palms. I quickly shook them, dousing the flames.

The healer nodded and spoke again. "Now, please tell me the events leading up to this, so I can accurately help your friend."

I quickly ran through what little I knew of Remmy's journey before she reached the peak of Mt Malus, and the events that had occurred since, ending with her frantic bath and collapse.

The healer turned back to Remmy and examined her once more. "Your friend is human?"

"Yes, she's human."

Why does he ask this? Fae, human, Dwarf, Elf... it doesn't matter. She's clearly ill.

I tried to keep the irritation out of my voice, barely succeeding.

Looking around me, the healer spoke to the man guarding the door, whose name I still had not asked. "Go fetch some broth and boil a pot of tea."

When he had gone, the healer turned his gaze back to me. "Your Highness, your friend is going to be fine. She is suffering from malnourishment and exhaustion. Unfortunately, we humans do not heal as quickly as Fae, but with a few days of rest and proper nutrition, she will recover."

My shoulders sagged visibly with relief at his words.

"Thank Lunaire." I shook the old man's hand as he stood. "Uh—I am sorry... about the umm... fire. I need to keep my presence here as quiet as possible."

"The entire kingdom is aware of what your father has done. You have more support than you know. Please send for me again should the girl's condition decline." He patted my arm and took his leave just as the other man returned with broth and tea.

The healer turned back to me before departing. "Try to get some broth and tea into her, but otherwise, let her sleep."

I nodded my thanks to them and returned to Remmy's side, sitting gently on the bed beside her, as the door to our room softly thunked closed. I took her hand in mine and rubbed my thumb in soft circles.

"Remmy, come back to me, my Northern Star—my Adhará. I need you."

Forty-Seven

Stained Parchment and Bloody Plans

* * *

Inara

The captain grimaced as he bit into the mincemeat pie I had prepared for dinner.

Goddess save me, he hates it.

I flinched for the blow, but it never came. When I opened my eyes, the captain was staring darkly at me.

"What are you doing?"

I scrambled for an explanation for my odd behavior. Viktor would have slapped the nose off my face if he were displeased with my food. I couldn't prove it, but I was convinced he killed our cook from my childhood.

“I—uhhh—was just thanking Lunaire for the blessing that is this meal.”

I'm not nearly that devout, but he doesn't need to know.

Bramwell's eyes shuttered, and he shoved another bite of the tasteless pie in his mouth. It really was bland. What had I done wrong?

To be honest, I'm surprised the pies even held together. I wasn't sure what to put in the crusts.

I sneaked a peek back at the captain.

He's still staring at me.

It was completely unnerving.

What do I do?

Finally, he spoke. “You don't cook often, do you?”

I shook my head. “I'm sorry if it's not satisfactory.”

Again, I flinched, my reaction involuntary.

“Why do you keep doing that?” He stormed, slamming the fork down beside his plate with a scowl.

“I—I'm sorry—what... what am I doing wrong?”

“You wince every time I speak to you!”

“I'm sorry, Captain Bramwell... uumm, sir. I—uhhh, it won't happen again.” I worked hard to keep my face neutral and not flinch, but my heart had nearly left my chest when he slammed his fork down.

“Seely.”

“Sir?”

The captain's eyes darkened again, a storm brewing in their murky depths. “This is a marriage, and it will not do to have my wife calling me ‘Captain Bramwell’. People will think I have taken a hostage as opposed to a wife.”

“Yes, Cap-uhh-sir... Seely.” I winced again at my bumble, but the captain only sighed and rubbed a finger on his temple.

He's going to lash me.

"Your father has sent for your brothers to visit you in the morning. After they leave, go next door to Mrs. Elderwood and tell her I've sent you. She will give you some… tips for cooking." He pushed back from the table and stood, his pie half finished, striding over to the door.

I let out a sigh of relief. His voice startled me as he turned back.

"And Inara?"

"Yes?"

"The spices are in the cupboards. Use them."

He swung the kitchen door open and thundered from the room like a dark tempest, his boots echoing off the stone floors.

I collapsed against the table, burying my head in my shaking hands, and sobbed. For my lost love. For my lost life. And for the girl I had once been.

* * *

Emerie

Hunting was proving to be harder than Remmy had made it seem. Though the meat from the deer would last a while, I had wanted to stock up the storeroom with dried meats, so I wouldn't have to worry about it, but it seemed that first kill was merely beginner's luck.

Sometimes I sat in the woods for hours, squandering time I could be at market selling what little I could harvest, and came home with nothing, as I did today.

I rounded to the front of our tiny cabin and stopped when I saw a horse munching flowers in the gravel.

Drawing back my bow as tightly as I could, I proceeded slowly into the house. A golden-skinned man with dark hair stood chatting amiably with the children.

"Who are you?" I demanded, the bow drawn, arrow aimed at his chest. The children recoiled in fear at my aggression and scampered away from the man as he held up his hands in a show of peace, a glimmer in his eyes.

"I am not here to harm you. I have a letter you'll want to see." He reached into the pocket of his tan and gold tunic, withdrawing a small folded piece of parchment. I glanced warily at the lion crest on his pocket before lowering the bow slightly to snatch the letter from his outstretched hand. I unfolded the parchment, and my knees became weak as I saw my sister's handwriting staring back at me.

"My dearest Emerie,
I am alive. I'm sorry for the pain this has caused you, and my darling Echo and Eridian. A man comes to you now, wearing the crest of Cyrus. Worry not, for he is a friend. Go with him, and he will bring you to me. We will be reunited soon, sister!
Burn this letter and leave no traces. Cyrus will send his men to search the house. I will explain everything when you are here with me. I will see you soon.
May Lunaire guide your journey.

All My Love,
Remmy"

Remmy. She's alive?! My sister is alive.

My vision blurred as I stared at the parchment, my hands trembling. I stared, even as the words began to smudge from the teardrops dripping onto the letter, causing the ink to run.

"Emerie?" Echo rarely called me anything but Emmy. You could see the fear and questions in her bright blue eyes as she took my hand in her small one.

These children had been through so much. Growing up without their mother, Father abandoning them, Remmy dying… you could see it all reflected in her wise young eyes.

Their seventh birthday was tomorrow, and I had made barely enough from the market to purchase some flour to make a pastry.

This would make a much better gift than a pastry. I looked down at her and smiled wider than I had in many months. I knelt beside the girl and placed my hands on her small shoulders.

"You and Eridan must go and gather all your most precious possessions. We're going on a trip." The little girl's eyes lit up, and she looked to her brother, and they both looked to the man in our living room, then back to me in wonder and amazement.

"Really?" They asked in unison.

I nodded and stood, clapping my hands in front of me to usher them into motion. "Quickly now."

The children rushed to our bedroom in a flurry of excitement, and I turned back to the man waiting patiently.

"I am Emerie, and those are my siblings, Echo and Eridian. Tell me what we must do."

I said the words with more authority than I had ever used for anyone but the children, but the man in my living room just smiled congenially at me.

"We will leave at dusk. We cannot risk being captured. Word will soon spread that your sister and the prince are alive, and the king will send the Blood Guard to patrol the streets."

"But it is not safe to travel in the Therion Region at night! We'll all be killed!"

"You'll be safe, I assure you."

I was not certain he understood the dangers of the region, but Remmy had said this man was trustworthy.

I moved to throw the parchment into the fire, and the man spoke again. "My name is Axel, by the way. Axel Bolten. I am a guard at the Castle of Stars, but I am a friend to the prince."

I nodded, my mind racing. "You must ensure the children are safe on this trip, no matter what. Promise me we will be safe."

The man reached forward and placed a hand on my shoulder, squeezing it lightly. "You and your siblings will be safe with us. I swear on the goddess herself."

I nodded and swallowed, and the man dropped his hand.

Breathing a sigh, I tried to think of what must be done first, processing the information that my sister was indeed not dead.

The man had said the prince was alive, also. What hope this would be for the rebellion movement.

I wonder if Teigan knows?

"Oh! I have forgotten. My father," I motioned to where he rocked in his chair unawares, "—he must go with us."

He may not be in there any longer, but he was still my father, and I would not leave him behind to die at the hands of the ruthless guard.

The man called Axel swiveled his head toward Father. "He wasn't mentioned. The plans don't include him."

"I will not leave him."

His nose twitched, and he raised a hand to clasp the bun of hair that sat atop his head. "Very well then. We have a few hours yet until dark. Pack your things. I must go into town and meet with our contact to procure a carriage. I'll return before dusk."

He bowed slightly and then ducked to fit his large frame through the small doorway of the cabin. Was he Fae? He certainly was intimidating enough.

I watched as he mounted his horse and trotted off, then I closed the door firmly.

Striding over to where Father rocked in his chair, I knelt before him and placed my hands on his knees, searching his green eyes for any sign of the man I had once known. A small glimmer shone there—the only indication he had heard anything that had been said.

"Father, we are going on a trip. And we are never coming back."

* * *

Sterling

I stood in the meeting room at the estate on the outskirts of town and paced the small space, my hands occasionally running through my hair.

I had almost refused to leave Remmy's side, but I needed to work on shifting and lay out an attack plan with the rebels. Teigan and Deidre had assured me that she was well cared for.

My thoughts drifted to Soren as the rebel leaders argued the logistics of the ideas we had discussed thus far. My brother was remarkably resilient, and I was certain he was handling this all well, though I longed to protect him from Cyrus's brutality. I'd asked Ivor to get a message to him at the palace, full well knowing the risk, and doing it anyway. He deserved to know I was alive. Ivor had assured me the servant would be discreet in delivering the message, but I had still refrained from mentioning my location, only confirming that I was alive and a plan was afoot.

A plan. What bloody plan?

The truth was, we didn't have one. Charge into the palace in dragon form and burn everything to the ground? Ludicrous. Storm the castle with the Dragon's Fire? Too many innocent deaths.

I shook my head vigorously, trying to clear the thoughts that relentlessly charged through my mind in quick succession, turning back to the table where the disagreements raged.

It seemed wrong to be developing these plans without Teigan, but one of us needed to be with Remmy in case she woke or, gods forbid, her condition worsened.

"We cannot charge the castle! It would be suicide." Aldric, the weapons instructor, bellowed. "Our trainees simply are not ready, and our numbers are not great enough to have the advantage over the Guard!"

"Well, what do you suggest we do then?" Aubern shouted back. "So far, you have not presented one viable plan. All you have offered us is opposition to every idea suggested!"

"Don't take that tone with me, girl. I trained you, and I have more years of experience than you have years of life."

The old man slammed his hand down on the sessile oak table.

"My father trained me, old man, and I am not a girl." The woman's eyes flashed, and her warded ears peeked through the illusion, as though her fury dampened the magic concealing her heritage from the world.

I wonder who did her wards?

Rufus rolled his eyes at the outburst, but Ivor Thronfeld was surprisingly quiet, his dark eyes taking in the table with seeming disinterest.

Maggie, who I had learned was code-named The Magpie for rebel operations, slowly turned her leader coin over and over in her hand. I'd come to know the woman well enough in our short time together to recognize the storm brewing in the lion shifter's mind.

"What are you thinking, Maggie?" I asked my cousin, speaking for the first time since this meeting began.

Her gaze shifted up to mine, and finally she spoke, still flipping her coin in her hand. "We draw out the Blood Guard… outside of the city… leaving the palace partially exposed. Cyrus will still have some guards at the castle, of course, but with the majority of his forces focused on our army, we could lead a small team in, using the tunnels under the city to take out the remainder of the Guard and assassinate the king. Taking the battle outside of the city concentrates the loss of life to the Blood Guard and leaves the king vulnerable, because we know he will not leave the Castle of Stars to join us on the battlefield. That's not his style."

The room was silent for a moment, everyone contemplating this plan, before Xula nodded and broke the silence.

"It'll work."

She glanced at her husband, who in turn looked at me, brows raised, subtly deferring to me.

All eyes turned as I glanced down at the maps spread about the table. We would still need several months to prepare. Gather supplies. Sort out details.

Before the meeting, Ivor had informed me that the battle would not ensue until a rescue mission was performed. He claimed the prisoner we were rescuing would be essential in defeating Cyrus, but had yet to tell me who this important prisoner was. Teigan's next operation was stealing the blueprints for the dungeon so this rescue could be executed effectively.

I nodded to Maggie. "It's a good plan, but we need to discuss some things before we go any further with it."

My eyes met Ivor's across the table, and from the look on his face, I surmised he knew what was coming next.

"The prisoner… who is it?" I knew of most of the prisoners brought into the palace dungeons before my exile to Mt. Malus, and I could not think of a single person who would be crucial to this war we were plotting. Most of them were common Fae accused of not paying taxes, inter-species marriages, or the simple crime of being in the wrong place at the wrong time.

Very few Elves still resided in Valeria, as my father had an affinity for arresting them for perceived wrongdoings, which is why those who remained generally warded their ears and passed off as Fae as much as possible. Cyrus hated Elves, Dwarves were best as servants, and the Mer-people… well, gods forbid they leave the water. I hadn't even heard rumors of more than a few Selkies in the last decade, including the ones Remmy and I had encountered.

Ivor released a heavy sigh. "I don't know all the details, Your Highness. We have a man in the palace we have been working with since the dawning of the Dragon's Fire." He motioned across the table to me. "Your manservant, actually."

Vincent? Vincent is working with the resistance? For all this time... he never told me...

"He came to us after your father killed Ivanna and Boris. Their death was a spectacle for all of Lunestair."

I remembered hearing about it. At the time, I was recovering from one of Cyrus and Captain Rathe's very particular forms of punishment, and could do nothing to prevent the travesty.

Ivor continued with his story. "He approached in the days following, with an offer to be our source of intel within the castle walls as long as it did nothing to endanger his daughter. Vincent sent word before we even knew you lived that he had found the location of a very important individual who would be instrumental to our cause. He never told me who it was, only that he could do nothing to help them without risking his wife and daughter."

Thalia.

The girl was practically a sister to Soren and me, though as Cyrus grew more brutal, Vincent kept her away from the palace more often than not.

"The prisoner is located in ancient dungeons that are situated below the known castle dungeons. Very few know of their existence, which is why we need all of the blueprints that exist. Vincent could not tell us how to access them without risk of exposure."

Ancient dungeons beneath the dungeons?

I'd never heard of any such thing, but I did trust Vincent. I rubbed two fingers against my temple.

"It would make sense. The Castle of Stars was built by the Vanta long before my family came to rule. A lower dungeon would have been an ideal place for the Vanta to keep special prisoners."

I wonder how my father found out about it? And why did I never find the access as a child? Does Soren know about them?

He had always been given more freedom than I when we were children.

"I am assuming this prisoner has been down there for some time?"

"Vincent implied that it had been a very long time, indeed." Ivor nodded.

"So he will need to rest and recover before offering any benefit to our cause. If this prisoner is Dwarven or human, it could be months before he is well enough to go to battle."

Xula spoke up at my reflection. "We have many herbalists and healers amongst our ranks, creating salves and healing potions for the battle. We will have them start working on extra morsious, willowroot, and even some sleeping tonics to aid in the prisoner's recovery."

I puffed out a sigh and nodded in her direction, satisfied with this answer, before remembering the vial I had found in Remmy's pack.

"Would these herbalists have any need for Vesper venom?"

Someone in the room gasped, "You have Vesper venom?! Uhh—Your Highness?" The question came from Rufus Dinkle.

I shook my head. "No, but Remmy does. I am sure when she wakes, she will not mind donating it to the cause, if there can be a use for it."

Dante Ariti, who had been silent for the course of the entire meeting, cleared his throat and spoke up.

"We could use it to make a potent poison for the team going into the castle. It could disable some of the guards or even dispose of the king himself."

Several of the members around the table nodded their approval at this suggestion.

Xula's eyes glowed as she addressed me, and once again I noticed the shimmer of magic around her form.

"Sire, when Remmy is recovered, please bring it by so we can get started on crafting a poison for the assassination team."

"And what pray tell, will we do, should the girl not wake?" Aldric asked impetuously.

Fire immediately rose to my palms at the insinuation, and the room went quiet around me. Tension roiled through every being present.

I fought to control my anger as I responded to the swords-master, my eyes glaring daggers into his skull. I was beginning to not care for the man.

"Remmy will wake. For if she does not, poison will not be necessary, as I will raze this kingdom to the ground and build a new one upon the ashes of its bones."

I let my answer hang in the hushed silence like an impending storm. The old man's face paled, and he gulped.

Returning my gaze to Ivor and Xula, I spoke again, this time in a calmer voice.

"That brings me to the next topic I wish to discuss with you all."

The rebel leaders listened with bated breath as I told them of my clan form and how I would contribute to our war plan.

Forty-Eight

Bad Plans and Worse Plans

* * *

Sterling

The Dragon's Fire had received a response from the palace, its envelope sealed with my father's crest. Ivor looked at me, a dark expression on his face as he handed it over.

"Where are you?"

There was no name, but I recognized my brother's messy scrawl. The message struck me as odd. Surely he was at least glad to hear from me? He should have known that I could not tell him where I was. I raised my head from the crinkled parchment, looking back up at Ivor.

"This is it?"

He nodded his head solemnly. "Are you sure this message is from your brother?"

I scrubbed a hand through my thick hair. "Yes, it's his handwriting."

"Could your father have found out and forced him to try to find you?"

I blew out a long, slow breath. "I'm not sure, but I don't think Soren would betray me."

"Regardless, you cannot reveal your location. It would not only endanger you and Remmy but also risk exposing the Fire."

"I'm aware. Send no response, and ensure your messenger was not followed."

"We have taken precautions."

"Good. Have you made any progress on the plan to get Remmy's family into Tangeer?"

"Our man Ravii Basu has made contact with his cousin in Aspara. Valeria's trade agreements with Tangeer make it possible to travel since the end of the war, but we still need to forge travel documents and arrange for passage. The trip will be arduous. Are you sure this is what you desire for them?"

"I can't send them to Rothton. You know this, and Valerians tend to go missing when trying to cross to Elysia. Tangeer is the only option, unless I wish to send them across the ocean and have them leave Amengor altogether."

For a moment, Ivor looked like that might not be a disastrous idea.

"Absolutely not. It's out of the question. The Broken Sea is treacherous, and the closest isle off the southern coast is Tenebriss, which is shrouded in darkness and inhabited by more beasts than the Therion Region. Traveling to the west through the Deserted Forest is a suicide journey as well. Tangeer is the safest option."

Ivor nodded his head in understanding. "I will send word when the documents have been fabricated."

I stood to leave, and the rebel leader stooped low in a gesture of respect as I exited into the halls of the Olsen mansion.

The world might slumber, but the headquarters of the rebellion were abuzz with recruits training for the field and people running about plotting and planning for the next strike.

I didn't participate in most of it, though Teigan and Ivor tried to sway me into more involvement. They kept me updated on all new information and frequently requested opinions, but I tended to think of myself more as a figurehead than a rebel leader. Though I knew they saw it differently. Recruits would stop me in the hall requesting permission to move classes or take leave.

Someday soon, I would have to accept my place within their ranks.

I exited the stately building, heading to the courtyard where I had been practicing, and quickly shifted into my dragon form. After so many repeated shifts, the process was now smooth and painless, and I took to the skies, flying into the cover of the clouds before the wards wore off, making me visible to the nearby city. I wasn't sure how far up the wards extended, but I was not interested in finding out.

My dragon had grown with every shift, and I took up nearly the entire courtyard now. I'd come a long way from the dragon that fit in the temple basement, and I knew I could best my father in one fell swoop, but we needed to stick to the plan for the safety of everyone involved.

A dragon soaring through Lunestair after thousands of years of extinction would lead to mass panic. I wasn't even certain I could land anywhere in the city. My size was now comparable to a full wing of the castle.

I rose above the clouds, as high as I had ever dared to fly, and stretched my massive wings.

The bright moon and billions of stars that dotted the night sky of the so-named Stardust District seemed to recharge my body and soul like fuel to my fire.

I've had so many conflicting thoughts since my clan emerged. I was the only one of my clan, which could hardly be called a clan at this rate, and the most powerful shifter in all of Amengor.

But I didn't feel like it. Mere months ago, I had been victim to my father's claws and Rathe's daggers. The two of them loved to shift and lord their clans over me. I may have been taller, stronger, and faster than the average human, but without a clan and at the mercy of an over-sized lion or wolf, I was no different from human.

With the emergence of my clan form and magic, my body had grown swifter and more powerful, making me a force to be reckoned with. It was the way of the clans. Your clan determined your strength and agility, and mine was an apex predator.

How can I be a clan that has been extinct for so long? It doesn't make sense.

I glided above the clouds for a while longer before the call to return to Remmy's side was too strong, and I landed in the courtyard with a thud, quickly shuffling back into my clothes.

* * *

Teigan

We'd decided that traveling separately was less conspicuous. Gendore rode on horseback, Pahlee traveled on foot, and I drove a wagon loaded with fake supplies. We were to convene at the entrance to the sewers, on the other side of which, Ravii would be waiting to let us through the sewer grate onto the castle grounds.

Axel Bolten, who had weaseled his way into a low-ranking position on the guard, had informed Ivor that the captain would be at home this evening with his new bride, rather than staying in the barracks where he spent most of his evenings. It was an opportunity we could not pass up.

We had only been given a week's notice to plan, so I raked over every detail nervously, praying to the gods that we had not missed anything.

My nineteenth birthday had come and passed, and I barely noticed it. Mother not being alive to bake me her traditional spiced cake left me despondent. She had made it for every birthday, including Father's and her own. My heart ached as I thought of them, but I shoved it down, hoping they would be proud of me, and focused on the cart I was trying to direct on the dark road leading into Lunestair.

I was not overly familiar with driving a cart, but we each had our cover stories for the return trip, if we made it out alive, and the cart was part of mine.

Pahlee was a lowly servant returning home from a late night of work, and Gendore was returning to his wife in labor after fetching a healer in town. The story was that the healer was traveling separately and not far behind him, and I was a merchant peddling my wares. Merchants tended to travel at all hours, making the story perfectly viable.

I had found it hard to leave after learning of Remmy's condition, but the healer had assured us that she would make a full recovery. Sterling and I took turns staying with her, drizzling broth and tea down her throat. Sterling refused to leave for any other reason than practicing his shift or meeting with the rebels. The fear of seeing her so weakened had inspired him to master his clan form. I still couldn't believe what he was.

A dragon.

I shook my head in amazement. This would change the tides of the war. I had not been able to attend the meeting where he had informed the rest of the leaders, but he had filled me in on everything discussed.

It wasn't long before the lights of the city greeted me. It was lovely, despite the raging underbelly.

Castillo no longer felt like home to me as I worked every day to build a life in Lunestair that would be worth living.

It was barely dinnertime, and the city was still bustling with peddlers, dancers in the streets, and denizens out for a bite to eat or returning home from work.

I watched it all in quiet thought, replaying every possible scenario of this mission in my mind over and over, until the one scenario I had not thought of actually happened.

There was a rustling in the wagon behind me.

What... or who is in my cart?

I could not afford to be delayed. Ravii had but a few minutes that he could open the grate for us before he would have to return to his station. He was taking a great risk for us, and I would not let it be in vain. I couldn't allow my first mission as a leader in the Dragon's Fire to be botched. A deeply rooted part of me still needed to prove to myself that I was worthy of this position.

I steered the cart down a narrow side alley and pulled over, withdrawing a knife from the scabbard at my side. Turning back to see what was going on, I let out a startled shout as a figure poked up out of the back of the wagon.

"Deidre!" I yelled, my mind blank with rage. "Get out! Get out of this cart right now!"

The girl's eyes widened, tears pooling instantly. It seemed as though she cried every time we spoke these days, our easy friendship dissolving into strained awkwardness.

"But it's dark… and we are in Schooner Alley."

My mind cleared, and I looked around to see where I had pulled off. Sure enough, we were in Schooner Alley, a hotspot on the westside for crathe dealers and traffickers.

Blast. Blast it all. Of course, she does this to me again, and of course, it isn't safe for me to send her home.

I turned back to face her, fury lacing my voice. "For the love of the gods, Deidre! Do you have any idea what you have done?"

"Why are you so mad? You should have picked me to help you. I'm a part of this, too, and no one ever lets me do anything!" She sobbed dramatically, drawing in a ragged breath, her brown hair sticking in the tears on her cheeks.

"Maybe that's because you're a child, Deidre, and you're not fit to be here." I snarled at her. "Do not say a word. Lie down in the back of this wagon under the blanket and do not speak. Do not move. Do not even breathe heavily until I return." I kept my voice low and tried not to say anything damning lest anyone be close by.

"I'm never allowed to speak to you! Every time I try, you shut me out or turn me away. What is wrong? I thought you cared about me?"

"I do care about you, Deidre. As a little sister. And nothing more. There is nothing else between us. You are a child, and you should be at home. You have to stop sneaking around and following me. You have potentially ruined this entire operation."

Her face turned redder than a beet, and she opened her mouth to protest, but I held up a hand demanding silence.

"Do as I have said. Get back under that blanket and stay there for the next few hours, and don't let me hear you. Do not let anyone hear you. Your life depends on it."

She bit her lip and sank sullenly beneath the burlap blanket covering my fake wares.

I urged the horse forward, pulling out of Schooner Alley and back onto the main thoroughfare into Market Square. If she jeopardized this mission because of her idiotic obsession with me, I was going to kill her.

* * *

Teigan

I pulled the wagon to the prearranged location—a member's bakery, right outside of Market Square. The smell of saffron and cinnamon floated out from the bakery as I parked the cart, hopped down, and hurried to the back. I gently lifted the blanket and peered at Deidre.

"I expect to find you here, right like that, when I return. Do you understand me, Deidre? It is imperative that you DO NOT leave this cart."

Lunestair was beautiful, but like any large city, it wasn't safe for a young girl to be out alone after dark. Maggie would kill me, and I would never forgive myself if anything happened to her.

"Can I not come with you?" The girl whined. I pinched my nose. The mood swings of girls her age were exasperating. One moment, she was far too wise for her age, and the next, she was whining in the back of a wagon she had stolen away to in the middle of the night.

"No." I sighed, exasperated. "You cannot. Go to sleep or something."

I pulled the blanket back into place, drowning out the sound of Deidre's huffing, and double-checked my weapons. I would go on foot from here and meet Pahlee and Gendore at the entrance to the sewers near the castle.

I quickly made my way the few blocks through the darkened streets, the sounds of rowdy music from the pubs and drunken revelers filling my ears.

Finally, I turned down an abandoned street, and at the end, hidden beneath layers of grime and discarded refuse, a gate of blackened iron marked the entrance to the tunnels leading into the sewers. Deep grooves scratched into the stone around it, and a faint, unsettling hum emanated from the darkness beyond. The air hung heavy and cold, reeking foully.

Gendore waited for me, hidden in the shadows near the iron grate.

"Pahlee isn't here yet?"

It would take longer for Pahlee to make the trip from the villa, but he had left before the two of us so that we would all arrive around the same time.

Gendore shook his head, and a worried frown creased my brow.

Stepping into the shadows with the soldier, I leaned against the cold stone, waiting silently. We could only allow a few minutes to wait for him before we would have to enter the sewers without him. A rat skittered across the top of my boot, and I suppressed a shudder.

I hate rats. This sewer is going to be a nightmare from the Netherworld.

I could have sent my men alone on this mission, but I didn't join the rebellion to sit behind a desk doing paperwork. I would lead my men into the sewers, and we would fight this battle together. I'd never be the type of leader who would let his soldiers do all the dirty work. Regardless of how much I hated rats.

The hollow sound of footsteps echoed off the cobblestone, and I stiffened. Gendore's hand lingered near the hilt of the dagger at his side as a shadowy figure emerged from the darkness, stepping into the dim glow of the streetlight.

I breathed a shallow sigh of relief when Pahlee appeared before us, his olive skin barely visible in the low light. I stepped forward and grasped his forearm, patting him on the shoulder with my other hand.

"We were starting to get worried. Did you run into any trouble?"

"Nothing I couldn't handle. Just some crathe dealers looking to pick a fight."

I noticed a trickle of blood at the corner of his mouth, but said nothing. He was an excellent fighter; if he said he had things handled, I believed him.

"Right then. Let's be off."

Gendore was already swinging open the iron gate leading to the tunnel under the granite hillside.

Ivor had managed to procure some quilldust lanterns, so that we didn't have to rely on fire to see, and I lit one now, holding it up as we slipped into the eerie tunnel, leaving the gate open behind us. If anyone was wandering this part of the slums tonight, it would be too dark or they too drunk to notice the open gate, its blackened iron disappearing against the mountain of onyx granite.

It was only a few paces before we found the grate in the floor leading down into the sewers. Gendore lowered himself first, stepping carefully onto the first rung of the ladder as I passed the lantern to him. Slowly, Pahlee and I followed, descending into the sewers with a resounding splash.

"Ugh!" I swallowed a gag at the vile stench while Pahlee hacked and coughed behind me.

Gendore remained silent as usual, but the lantern revealed his face twisted in a grimace. The air was putrid and stale, clinging to our skin and hair like a thick, filthy blanket.

I tried to hold my breath as we sloshed through dank sewage, but could only do it for so long, so I settled for plugging my nose with my free hand.

We trudged forward in silent agony for what seemed like forever before a low rumbling echoed through the darkness of the tunnel, bringing forth the first words from Gendore.

"The creatures of Skotos are confined to the Therion Region, are they not?"

"They're supposed to be, but who knows how far these tunnels extend or where they go?" Pahlee responded in a hushed tone. "Would the barrier extend underground?"

My mind whirled. He was right, of course. The sewage tunnels were largely unexplored since the building of the city several millennia ago. No one would truly know if the magical barrier confining Skotos's beasts extended this far under the earth.

Splashing sounded from behind us in the direction from which we had come.

"Dim the lantern."

Gendore hurried to comply.

The sounds had come from deep within the tunnels, so perhaps whatever it was would stay far from us.

"Stay close together and keep quiet. Ravii said we would come to a three-way intersection. We are to take the middle tunnel, and it will lead us straight onto the castle grounds."

The men nodded, and we pressed on, alert and ready for whatever had made those noises. It wasn't long before we came to the three tunnels and proceeded down the middle one. The passage became so narrow that we had to walk single file.

Gendore led, still carrying our only lantern.

My stomach roiled from the stench as I followed closely behind him. The walls were practically closing in on us now, our shoulders scraping against the wet stone as we climbed through the sludge and sewage.

Thank the gods I bought another pair of boots. This entire outfit will need to be burned.

I continued listening for the sound of another growl or splashing from behind us, but the only noises were the scuttling of cockroaches and rats, and our heavy breathing as we made our way down the cramped tunnel.

A rat leaped from the wall into the sewage in front of Gendore, splashing him with sludge.

Grunting in displeasure, he swung his foot, kicking at the vile creature as it swam through the muck. I was on the verge of shushing the warrior when a faint sliver of light caught my eye, streaming down from the ceiling a few feet ahead.

"Up ahead! Look! Is that the grate?"

Gendore quickened his pace, and Pahlee and I hurried after him.

A rusty iron ladder stuck out from the stone wall, leading up to a steel grate cut into the rock.

Ravii bent over the opening, his bright quilldust lantern casting shadows on us as we shimmied up the rungs.

"You're late."

Forty-Nine

Espionage

* * *

Teigan

Disabling a few guards had been easy enough, but hiding their unclothed bodies had proven to be a little harder. The one I was currently trying to stow kept falling out of the corner I was stuffing him into.

We'd met no one as we crept through the castle grounds, making our way toward the guard barracks. The gardens were lit with low-light quilldust lanterns, moon lilies dotted the surface of every fountain of water, and flame moths danced through the flowers, their glowing bodies lighting up the verdant grounds. It was unbelievable that none of the nobles spent their evenings strolling the grounds.

The first guard had spotted us as we left the gardens and crossed to the back of the barracks. Pahlee had easily discharged him before he could yell a warning, and we'd hidden the body in a large astera bush. The massive star-shaped leaves and thick branches of the flower made it easy to conceal him. We'd doused him with valerian root to keep him sedated for a while before continuing around to the back of the large black building.

The next three were exiting the barracks through the door at the back. In the darkness, they didn't see us until we overtook them, sliding our blades cleanly through their tough Fae skin.

Now, as I pulled at the too-tight uniform, I'd stripped off my mark, we tried to conceal the bodies well enough to give us time to locate the captain's office and steal the plans we'd come for. The knife wounds were precisely placed to avoid loss of life, and their Fae healing would kick in soon enough. When war came, I would be ready to kill, but for now, I was not interested in assassinations.

Fire lanterns faintly lit the stone hall as we made our way inside the building.

Curious. They don't use quilldust in the barracks.

Shadows danced off the stone walls, and raucous laughter from the dining hall peeled through the otherwise quiet evening.

We proceeded past the common area where off-duty guards lounged in various states of undress, playing chess and warming by the fire.

Turning the corner, I whispered to my men, "Ravii said the captain's quarters are after the main sleeping hall, at the end of the building."

A man exited the barracks room as we passed, and I averted my eyes to avoid contact. If anyone suspected we weren't Fae, we would be found out. I knew Gendore was a sphinx, but I was unsure of Pahlee's race, and my mundane eyes were decidedly human.

Blood Guard members were distinctly elite Fae—the best of the best, supposedly. The thought made me chuckle at how easily we had dispatched four of them already tonight.

Near the end of the hall, a door appeared on the left, a name etched into the oak: "Captain Seely Bramwell, Commanding Officer of the King's Royal Guard."

'Blood Guard' was the nickname the Royal Guard earned from instilling fear with their bloody tactics; they embraced the name wholeheartedly.

Gendore made his way a few paces down the hall, and I kept watch at Pahlee's back while he worked the lock. If anyone passed, Gendore would mimic a phoenix call, alerting us to the danger.

After a few tense moments, Pahlee had the door open, and I grabbed a torch from the wall as we rushed inside. We shut the door behind us, locking it firmly.

"I don't know how long we may have, so make quick work."

I handed the torch to Pahlee.

Gendore, who still carried the lantern, quickly began searching the other side of the room. I headed for the desk, awash in light from the moon, and began searching for anything useful.

The captain was organized.

Very organized.

Correspondence, weapons orders, patrol schedules, and recruitment rosters were all separated neatly into individual stacks. All of this could be potentially useful to the Dragon's Fire, but we had only come for the dungeon plans. Stealing all of this would be too noticeable.

A thought suddenly crossed my mind, and I began opening the drawers of the large cedar desk, searching for blank parchment.

Finding none, I turned to where Pahlee was searching the large shelf stacked with books.

"Is there any blank parchment over there?"

Scanning over each shelf with a quick pass, he found a stack and quickly brought it to the desk. "What did you find?"

"Patrol schedules, recruitment rosters, and weapons info—everything except the blueprints." I glanced up to where Gendore was rifling through a big trunk in the corner. "Anything?"

"I think there's a false bottom here."

Handing the parchment to Pahlee, I instructed him to copy down the patrol information and schedules, and made my way over to Gendore.

A clicking noise sounded as I approached, and Gendore lifted the bottom of the trunk.

"Lumess!"

"What is it?" Pahlee called from the desk, where he was frantically scribbling down intel.

My eyes lit up as I answered. "What we came here for. Have you finished?"

With a flourish and a wave of the quill, he rolled up the parchments and stuffed them into his cloak.

"I have now."

"Let's get out of here."

Gendore finished reassembling the hidden compartment and divided the maps between the three of us, each stuffing them into our cloaks. With a peek into the hallway, we exited the captain's office and took off into the night.

We made our way anxiously through the grounds, ditching the torch in the shadows, and found our way back to the sewer grate.

As we approached the dark entrance, a shout rang out through the courtyard.

"The guards must be awake."

Pahlee's face was pale as we hurried to move the iron grate, and he scrambled down first. I quickly followed, and Gendore filed in last.

Ravii was not there to replace the grate, so he handed me the lantern and struggled from within to move it back into place, not wanting to bring attention to the tunnel entrance.

The commotion from above us grew louder as more guards frantically scrambled about in an attempt to locate the intruders.

Sorry to ruin your wedding night, captain.

I turned the quilldust lantern to the lowest setting as we shimmed down the ladder and into the muck below.

* * *

Sterling

Two days.

That's how long she had been unconscious. Two of the longest days of my life. I rubbed a finger on my temple as I stared down at Remmy's pale body, her fox protectively curled beside her. He tended to panic when anything went wrong, but I could see his bond with Remmy growing stronger each day since she had found him in the Darkhelm.

Maybe someday he'll be a fighter.

He seemed very young, though I wasn't sure how to tell the age of a fox. There had been times when I suspected he was a Fae living in his clan form that would one day transform back and profess his love for Remmy, but his animal eyes were much too mundane to be Fae.

I stood from my chair beside the bed and stretched my sore muscles. I finally had the hang of shifting into my dragon form, having done it over and over the last two evenings while Teigan stayed with Remmy.

Though I had revealed my clan to the rebel leaders, we had determined it best to keep it from the soldiers until closer to the time of battle. We could not risk word reaching my father or his guards. The wards prevented any spying eyes from witnessing my shift.

The repeated shifting had taken a toll on my muscles, and my body ached with each movement. Refusing to succumb to the weakness, I trained in our room while Remmy remained unconscious on the bed.

Ember had expressed his discontent with me several times, but usually opted for curling up by the fire or nestling into Remmy's ribs.

I sauntered over to the window, looking out at the city below.

My city.

The Oasis was centered right in the heart of Market Square, the hub of Lunestair. The Stardust District pulsed with the sounds of music and laughter, the last of the night's pleasure seekers dancing in the faintly lit streets.

Our room was at the back of the building, so I could not see the castle, but I knew if I could, I would see two members of my father's guard looking out at the revelers with a mixture of distaste and jealousy.

No doubt after shift rotation, those same guards would be sitting in the bar below where I now stood. The pub was crawling with them nightly. It would be so easy to pick them off one by one, but I had no desire to become like my father. So I let them live and drink beneath my feet, knowing that most of them would kill me on sight if given the order.

I sighed heavily and rested my head on the dingy windowpane, thinking of the battle that lay ahead.

A noise from the bed broke me out of my reverie, and I turned in time to see Remmy attempting to rise from the bed. I almost collapsed with relief.

She's awake.

My heart felt as though it might burst from my chest as I hurried to the side of the bed and gently eased her back down onto the edge of it.

"Steady now. You've been out for a long time."

"Out? What is wrong with me? What happened?"

I turned to the pitcher of water on the table and poured a glass, handing it to her. "Exhaustion and lack of proper nourishment—according to the healer. You passed out."

"How long was I asleep?"

"Two days."

"Two days?!"

Her jaw dropped, and she tried again to rise from the bed, no doubt ready to jump into action, but she swayed unsteadily, her hand going to her head.

I grabbed her elbow, steadying her on her feet. Her large eyes met mine, and my blood turned to molten lava in my veins, warmth pooling in my gut. For a brief moment, I wished I could get lost in their clear depths and drown in the essence of her. Her scent. Her body. Everything about her drove me mad.

She spoke again, and the soft lilt of her voice drew me back to stark reality.

"Did the messenger make it to my sister?"

I motioned for her to sit back on the bed, and she slowly complied.

Grabbing a chair from the table, I pulled it in front of her and plopped down.

"If he did not run into trouble, the man sent to fetch your sister should be arriving in Merda soon. We told him to ride hard and fast. Once he arrives, he will check in with one of our few contacts in the villages and procure a carriage for your family. It will take several days for them to arrive, as I imagine traveling with the young ones will slow them down a bit."

Our contact?

Every day, I was closer to accepting my role within this thing. I rubbed a hand on my temple and tried to smile reassuringly at Remmy.

It must not have been as reassuring as I thought because she reached across the open space and placed her shaky hand on my knee. A spark shot through me at her touch, and my fire reacted to the strong emotions warring within me. I fought to rein them in and quell the temperamental magic.

"Are you all right, Sterling? You seem tired."

Her pale face showed concern. The thin scars from the Imp attack were barely visible due to the lack of color in her skin.

I stood, suddenly desperate to distance myself from everything I saw in her eyes. Her brows raised at my abrupt change, but she said nothing.

"You need to eat. I'll go grab us some food, and then I need to meet with Ivor."

Without another glance, I strode from the room and stepped into the smoke-filled hall, releasing a breath I hadn't meant to hold.

How was I going to send her to Tangeer now? My desire for her transcended the physical. The sight of her in that bed had completely undone me. But I had to let her go. I wasn't worthy of her goodness. Of a soul that could sing on Mt. Malus.

Fifty

Adhará

* * *

Teigan

We raced through the darkened tunnels, sloshing through the muck as we made our way back to the inner city entrance.

As we grew closer, a harsh growl reverberated off the walls of the culvert, echoing like a sinister whisper. We stilled.

"It sounded like it came from the direction we are heading," Pahlee muttered nervously, as I quickly moved to turn off the quilldust lantern.

"Keep moving forward," I responded. It's the only way we know out of this underground maze. We had no other option. "Hopefully, whatever it is will mind its own. Do either of you have weapons still?"

Both men nodded, and my shoulders sagged in relief. With all three of us armed, we stood a decent chance, even if it was one of Skotos' beasts. I secretly hoped it was just a rabid dog, though I doubted a dog could make a noise like that.

We continued in silence, the darkness of the tunnels seeming to swallow us whole as they stretched endlessly ahead, their damp walls slick with moisture and covered in grime. The air was thick with the scent of decay, a mix of stagnant water and sewage. Our footsteps echoed eerily as we squelched through the filth, the distant drip of water seeping through the cracks in the stone the only other sound to be heard.

A snarl sounded a few paces behind us, and our footsteps stilled again.

How did the creature get behind us? Is there more than one?

I turned slowly, my hand instinctively going to the dagger sheathed on my hip, as I was greeted by a set of neon green eyes towering several feet above us.

Gods and goddesses, it must be ten feet tall!

There were not as many beasts in Castillo as in the other towns in the Therion Region, due to the population, but somehow I knew I was looking at a Lemian.

"Run." I hissed to the men beside me as I backed slowly away from the creature. It was still several paces away, and maybe... just maybe... that would give us time to escape.

Almost as one, the three of us spun and fled toward the tunnel entrance.

A low howl echoed through the cavern, the sound chilling me to the bone, before the beast gave chase.

A dim light from the city appeared ahead of us, and hope speared through me.

But what if the creature follows us out of the tunnels?

It was evening.

No. No, they can't cross the boundary into the Stardust District.

Lunaire made sure to contain Skotos' beasts to one region. But how was it in the tunnels if these tunnels were under the Stardust District? It didn't make sense for the boundary not to stretch underground.

Maybe it's weaker underground?

My breath was heaving as we neared the tunnel entrance. My foot collided with something heavy and firm in the water. I glanced down, intending to go around the obstruction, when the light from the city illuminated it.

A body.

A body was lying face down in the sewage. Horror gripped me as I recognized the faint pattern on the dress of the figure.

No! No, it can't be!

Frantically, I pawed at the body, struggling to roll it over as the Lemian raced toward me.

Gendore and Pahlee were already scrambling out of the iron gate as the moonlight shone on her pale face.

Blood dripped from the side of her mouth and soaked the bodice of her linen dress. Deep gashes resembling claw marks tore holes through the simple garment where her skin was ripped apart, and her left arm was twisted at an unnatural angle.

An inhumane sound ripped from my lips as I beheld Deidre's broken body.

My throat constricted, and hot tears scorched my face as I lifted her from the mire, pressing her body close to my chest as I ran.

The noise of the Lemian's snarling faded as I exited the tunnel and collapsed in a heap on the hard ground.

Pahlee and Gendore looked at me as I knelt in front of them, her body draped across my knees, their faces marked by grief.

"I told her to stay in the wagon." I sobbed, clutching her tightly against me.

* * *

Remmy

I'd heard everything when my body had been trying to heal itself. Every confession. Every whispered secret. Every passion-filled declaration of love. The love I hadn't dared to hope for, believing no one, especially him, could ever love me.

He'd called me Adhará. His Adhará. His "Northern Star" in the old language of the Fae, or depending on the translation, "Guiding Light."

I'd studied it briefly in one of Father's old tomes, but I was not fluent as the language was mostly dead following the years of the Vanta.

But I had also heard him say that he would send me away. He had no intention of allowing me to stay when the fighting began. He claimed he was trying to protect me from the king's rage, but he was too afraid to tell me. He gripped my hand and murmured the words softly as though voicing them to my unconscious form would give him the bravery he sought. I had fought to wake—to reassure him, but the darkness had pulled me back time and time again as though my body knew I would not survive if I didn't have the rest it demanded.

We'd eaten in silence, and then Sterling had left to meet with Ivor. I wanted to go with him, but he had begged me to rest a little while longer, and I didn't have the strength to deny him. Not when my heart still burned with his words—the ones I knew I didn't deserve.

How could he love someone so broken?

Perhaps this was why he had been withdrawn since our kiss. He was trying to distance himself from me so that it would be easier for him to send me away.

He was going to be sorely surprised when I utterly refused to go. I would not leave him, and I would not run like a coward. We were in this together, and if war was coming, I would dive into the fray with him without a second thought or kernel of remorse.

I might be his guiding star, but he was my galaxy, and I'd follow him unto the ends of Amengor and whatever lay beyond.

Sterling had asked me to sleep until morning, but I had been sleeping for over two days, and I knew my heart and mind would not rest until he was safely returned to me. I would speak to him in the morning—let him know I had heard his words and where my heart lay. No matter how unworthy I was of his love, I couldn't stand to be parted from him. Not now. Not after everything.

I rose from the bed, stroking Ember's soft fur as the creaking of the old springs cut through the silence of the room, and made my way on unsteady feet to the lavatory.

My gaze swiveled to the small tub where the hair oil the prince had massaged into my scalp still perched on the side. His words, as he had gripped my face, pierced my mind. *'You're beautiful and brighter than all the stars in Valeria.'*

How could he think me beautiful when I was so scarred? So thin from starvation? So tainted.

I hadn't been sane enough at the time to recognize what he was saying to me. Telling me he loved me without actually saying it.

I stared at the tub intently, the emotions of that bath crashing into me once again like a landslide.

A shiver went up my spine as I thought of that guard's hands on my body, tearing at my bodice, and what he planned to do to me. What he intended to take from me. My hand instinctively went to the wounds in my chest that his dagger had inflicted. Sleep and time had practically healed them, but some scabs remained as a persistent reminder of his intended defilement.

I used the chamber pot shakily, smiling at the novelty of having one after weeks of relieving myself outside, and then exited the bathing room, closing the door firmly behind me.

A searing pain shot through my skull, and I fell to my knees, the world going dark around me.

* * *

Sterling

I'd forgotten to grab the Vesper venom in my hurry to leave the oppression of the Oasis. I'd seen the pained look on Remmy's face as I had rushed from the pub, but my resolve had shattered completely when she had woken, and I needed Ivor's counsel to ground me and convince me to stick with the plan. It was for her safety. For the safety of her family. She couldn't be around when the fighting started, and every moment she was here with me in Lunestair, a target remained on her head.

I also hoped for an update on Teigan's mission. We needed those blueprints.

Several commanders and members had begun to gather in a meeting room, awaiting a report, when one of the soldiers who had been on Teigan's mission burst into the room. The man's face was ashen, his features twisted in an expression of mortified shock.

Xula rose from her chair, the blood draining from her face. "What is it? What's happened?"

"Someone fetch The Magpie!" He gasped.

A young girl left quickly and returned a moment later with Maggie in tow.

"What's all this about?" She bellowed, eyeing the young man suspiciously. "Has something happened to Teigan? You tell me right now, boy! Spit it out!"

Finally regaining his breath, the man started to speak again. "No, ma'am, it's—"

The door flew open, and Teigan stumbled in, followed quickly by the other soldier. In his straining arms, he held a limp, blood-soaked body. I strode quickly across the room and grasped his elbow, solemnly surveying the woman he carried.

Yet, it was no woman at all, but a child. Maggie's daughter.

Deidre. Lunaire, have mercy.

Great gashes resembling claw marks were torn down the girl's chest and abdomen, and her arm was bent and broken.

What in Amengor? Was she attacked by a shifter?

Teigan's face was drawn and pale, still wet from the tears he'd shed, and blood stained his filthy shirt.

A wail pierced the strained silence, as Maggie jerked me away from Teigan and beheld the body that he still clutched close.

"What have you done?! What have you done to my baby?! Deidre! She's supposed to be at home! Deidre, no! No!"

She took the girl's face in her hands and shook it, rubbing her dirt-smudged cheeks. She looked to Teigan, her eyes begging for some explanation. He said nothing, merely hanging his head in silence.

A roar left the large woman, and in seconds her clothing was shredded, and a great lion with a splash of red hair tore through the room and out the open door.

A sound resembling a sob left Teigan, and I hurried to him, gently removing Deidre's body from his arms and placing her on the floor.

I summoned the girl who had retrieved Maggie and asked her to procure a blanket from somewhere. A death veil would need to be located for the sacred rite to return her soul to Lunaire, but for now, a blanket would have to do. The rite could not be performed without the girl's closest kin.

Ivor stalked toward the door solemnly. "I will go after Maggie. Someone, please, escort Teigan home. We will get a report tomorrow and prepare for the ceremony."

He was the only one in the room besides me who was strong enough to calm down a raging lion. He shifted before he left the hall, his own clothes shredding, as the fire from his phoenix dimly lit the corridor.

The girl returned with a blanket and helped me cover Deidre's body. She also brought help with her to move the body to a holding location until the ceremony of rites.

I walked back over to where Xula now had her arms around Teigan, shushing him and patting his back like a mother would do, ignoring the stench of his clothing.

"Come, Teigan. A hug from Remmy will do you good."

His head lurched up. "She's awake?"

I smiled and grasped the boy's shoulder. In this moment, he was not the strong rebel leader I'd come to know, but a boy. A boy who'd lost most of the people he loved in less than a year.

"Yes, she woke a few hours ago. She asked for you."

Teigan didn't smile, but relief was evident in his eyes as he told Xula goodbye and spoke briefly with the two soldiers preparing Deidre's body for transport. A part of me wanted to stay behind and ask the soldiers what had happened on that mission, but a larger part of me saw Soren in Teigan. He needed me.

Dawn would be breaking soon, so we made our way to the Oasis quickly, while I filled Teigan in on Remmy's condition. He didn't speak of his mission beyond saying the blueprints were retrieved, but the events of the night haunted his stricken face the entire walk back.

Fifty-One

Ashes and Bloodlines

* * *

Teigan

Wearily, we climbed the dingy stairs to the second floor of the Starlight Oasis. This place had become home to me, but without Deidre… I decided I would finally take Ivor up on his offer of a room at the rebel estate.

Skotos, I'd rather stay at the Drunken Dragon than here.

Hopefully, Maggie would allow me to keep my job.

I'm not sure she will ever forgive me.

I clenched and unclenched my fists at my side, the sight of Deidre's mangled body ravaging my thoughts.

As we neared our rooms, I turned toward the prince. He'd been gracious enough to not mention the smell, and I was grateful for his company on the walk home.

"I'd like to clean up before seeing Remmy. I've just been traversing through a sewer—among other things."

Sterling nodded in understanding, his penetrating gaze more sympathetic than I could bear, and we turned toward our separate rooms.

I closed the door and slumped onto the bed, staring at the trunk of clothes on the floor. I prayed that wherever I landed next would have its own bathing room. Though I was sure no one would be in the public bath, I could barely muster the wherewithal to dig out my clothes and head over there.

I had just summoned the motivation to rise from the bed when a shout rang out from the room across the hall. I leaped to my feet and hurried toward my door. As I touched the handle, a powerful roar shook the ground.

Holy gods.

I jerked the door open and stumbled into the hall, the floor quaking beneath my feet. The door across the way was ajar, and I could see the profile of the prince as he stood in the center of the room, fire encasing his hands.

I pushed the door open slowly, the creak of the hinges alerting Sterling to my presence.

Remmy's fox sat on the messy bed, screeching noisily at him. Clothes were strewn all over the floor. The furniture was flipped on end, and the small lantern that hung in the corner was cracked, the flame illuminating the room in a low glow, as the colors of dawn began peaking through the dingy window pane.

"What the—"

He swung toward me, his face contorted in a mixture of rage and grief.

"She's gone."

A dull roar filled my ears as the blood pounded in my head. "She's—? She's gone?"

My mind swam, and I could barely make out the words that he was uttering as a wave of fear rolled over me.

Mother, Father, Koretta, Deidre... I couldn't lose Remmy, too. I had already lost her once.

"Cyrus found her. He's taken her. There's blood near the lavatory."

I tried to focus enough to concentrate on what the prince was saying. Remmy had been kidnapped. And the prince's entire body was now surrounded by raging flames.

Not good.

"I'm going to kill him! If he hurts her, I will burn this entire city to the ground! He probably has her stuffed in the dungeon. The guards will—" He trailed off, his face paling as his thoughts betrayed themselves.

No. I wouldn't allow that to happen to her. We had to get her back.

I neared Sterling, my hands outstretched in front of me, trying to signal him down.

"We will find her, okay?"

His face turned red again as he raged, "You don't understand! You don't know what she went through in that forest. When we got here, she was broken by what they had done to her. What they tried to do to her!"

"We'll get her back." I spoke with more conviction than I felt. "But we need to send for Ivor immediately. He's most likely making arrangements for Deidre's ceremony."

The prince's face softened slightly at the mention of Deidre, and the fire surrounding his body sputtered and went out.

"Teigan, I'm sorry. I'm so sorry about Deidre. But I can't lose Remmy. She doesn't even know. She doesn't know." He slumped onto the bed beside Ember, who curled soothingly at his side, resting his head on the prince's lap.

Sterling dropped his face into his hands. "I cannot lose my Adhará."

He whispered the words so softly I barely heard them. I was struck by how powerfully he loved my friend, the word of the old language ringing in my ears.

"Stay right here. We will get her back. I promise." I meant those words. I didn't love Remmy the way Sterling did, but I would fight just as hard to bring her home.

I stormed into the halls, which were now filled with fearful patrons questioning the earth-shattering roar that had awoken them from slumber.

"Please return to your rooms! Everything is under control."

The tenants of the Oasis looked at me warily but did as requested.

I rumbled down the stairs, making my way quickly into the kitchen, where I found Dauton, the greasy cook Deidre didn't like, who had summoned the healer for Remmy. The man cowered behind a barrel of whiskey. I snorted with derision, though I could hardly blame him. That roar would scare the bravest of men.

"Dauton, get up! I need you to fetch the Phoenix immediately."

The cook stared at me. I rummaged through my pockets, withdrawing my Dragon's Fire coin and flashing it at him. He straightened a little at the symbol of a commanding officer.

"What is it?" He questioned.

"The prince. He's going to reduce this city to ashes. Go now!"

The man's eyes widened, but he scrambled to his feet and bolted out the back door. I would string him from the rafters if he did not return with the rebel leader.

* * *

Remmy

A deep-aching cold gnawed at my bones, and my head pounded relentlessly. My eyes fluttered open as I woke with a shudder, curled in a ball against a cold stone floor. The sound of water slowly dripping somewhere in the distance reached my ears.

Drip. Drip. Drip.

I sat up with a groan, painfully pulling myself up against the damp moss-covered walls. My head spun, pain exploding through my skull.

Where am I? What happened?

I put a hand to the back of my head where the pain pulsed. I felt something warm and sticky, and I sucked in a gasp.

Blood.

My memory slammed through my already splitting skull.

Something hit me in the back of the head when I came out of the bathing room, and then nothing. A vague recollection of being carried…

I looked around frantically, trying to discern where I was, squinting in the dim light. The faint glow of a torch flickered beyond the bars, casting long jagged shadows against the dank walls. It was barely enough to see my surroundings—a cell. Crude iron bars and a corridor stretching into more darkness just beyond them.

No. NO!

Panic speared through me like one of the famous waves of the Broken Sea—colossal and raging. My heart slammed against my ribs as my fingers roved over the dungeon floor searching for something… anything to use as a weapon.

A dry cough came from outside my cell, and I froze.

I'm not alone.

But is it captor or prisoner? My question was soon answered by a female voice, gravelly and rusty from disuse.

"You won't find anything to help you, dear. He swept the cell before throwing you in."

"Who are you?" I demanded.

"A prisoner like yourself. My name is Iyra." She spoke with a soft, lilting accent that I couldn't place.

Iyra. Iyra.

Why was that name so familiar? I rolled the name over in my mind, trying to remember where I had heard it. It wasn't a common name.

"Why are you in here, Iyra?"

"For the crime of love, I believe."

She said this so easily, like that love was worth the untold horrors she had no doubt suffered in this gruesome place.

"Who took us, and where are we?"

"I was not taken by the same person as you. Your captor does not even know that I am here. He only recently discovered the entrance to these dungeons, and I could not reveal myself to him for fear of what kind of man he might be. You and I are the only ones down here. Far beneath the Castle of Stars."

The castle? The king has captured me. But if the king is not who captured her, then who did?

She coughed again, and the noise of a chain rattled as she raised a hand to cover her mouth. She had obviously been here a while without anyone to talk to.

I wonder how often they visit to feed and water her?

I pulled myself closer to the bars, trying to see in the low light.

Across the hall was another cell. A woman with greasy dark hair streaked with silver leaned against the bars.

She turned her face toward me, and I sucked in a breath. Her eyes glowed turquoise, and her cheeks were gaunt from starvation, but she was still stunningly beautiful. She looked to be around my mother's age, but she was Fae, so she could easily have been two hundred and fifty years.

"Since I am pretty certain that I was captured by the King's Blood Guard… who is holding you?"

"You were not captured by the king, my dear. Based on what I overheard, I am not even sure Cyrus knows that you are in here."

"Well, who then? Who did you see bring me in?"

Iyra released a heavy sigh, and her bright eyes mirrored the sadness I felt in my soul. "My son. Prince Soren of Valeria."

Fifty-Two

Wife

* * *

Inara

My brothers didn't show. I couldn't say I was surprised. I didn't know them well, but they certainly seemed the worthless sort.

At half past ten, I watered the dying plant by the front door and proceeded to head slowly toward the neighbor's house. Captain Bramwell had forgotten to specify which house belonged to Mrs. Elderwood. There were houses on both sides of his.

Ours, I guess. I live here now.

I sighed as I chose the house on the left side and leisurely made my way across the brown grass.

I suppose it can't hurt to meet both neighbors.

I pulled my shawl tighter around me as I approached the house and gently lifted the door knocker. Autumn seemed to be milder here in Lunestair, but there was still a definite chill in the air.

A giant of a Fae answered the door.

Wrong house.

I slapped on my most charming smile, praying to Lunaire and Skotos both that he would not decide to eat me or something. "Hi there! I'm Captain Bramwell's wife."

I blinked.

Did I just say that? Did I just bloody well say that?

It sounded strange, leaving a pungent taste in my mouth. For years, I had expected to run away to the mountains and be Mrs. Jax Fenwick. We just weren't given enough time to make the plans. Sorrow clenched my heart, and I struggled to finish what I was saying as the towering man in front of me looked me over curiously. "I'm… I'm looking for Mrs. Elderwood."

"I heard that Cap got himself a wife. I didn't believe it until now." He eyed me again. "A pretty little thing, ain't ya?"

My fear must have shown on my face because he gave a gruff chuckle.

"Don't worry, girl. I ain't brave enough to mess with the Captain's wife. Mrs. Elderwood is that house." He pointed at the house to the right of ours. I thanked him and hurried away, my skin crawling.

Wife. Wife. Wife. Wife.

The word haunted me all the way across the lawns.

* * *

Inara

Mrs. Elderwood was a kindly human woman, old enough to be my grandmother. I mentioned my surprise that she didn't reside in one of the villages, as she showed me how to knead dough. She informed me that Lunestair had always been her home and she would not cower to 'that dastardly king.'

I applauded her bravery, my mind turning to Teigan Berger.

I'd been in her kitchen all day while she did her best to teach me the basics of cooking. She elicited a promise from me to come back tomorrow, and I assured her I would, as I prepared to leave.

"Mrs. Elderwood?"

"Please call me Onia, dear."

I smiled. "Onia, can you tell me the best place to go if I need to locate someone?"

She brushed her hands on her apron and thought for a moment. "I'd say the pub at the center of Market Square." She tapped her temple with her finger. "Uhhh—the name is… the Starlight Oasis! The barkeeps there know everyone, or you can post a notice to the community board. My husband, Gene, sometimes posts his services on the board there."

"Thank you."

Onia drew closer to me and placed a gentle hand on my cheek. I froze, uncertain what the old woman was doing. She searched my face for the answer to some yet unspoken question before dropping her hands back to her side.

"How did you come to be married to the Captain, if you don't mind an old woman asking?"

I turned my gaze from her briefly and stared wistfully at the door for a moment.

"It was arranged."

Understanding flitted across her weathered face, and she gave me a sympathetic look.

"If you need anything... anything at all, child, just let me or Gene know."

"Thank you, Onia."

I glanced at the clock on the wall as I said goodbye. I had two hours to locate the Starlight Oasis and make it back home before the captain.

Fifty-Three

Deadly Loyalties

* * *

Vincent

I stood silently behind the king's desk as he chatted with his former Captain of the Guard. The Fae assured the king that he had not seen the Crown Prince, but if he did, he would report it immediately. I could hear the suspicion tainting the king's voice as he questioned Bramwell.

"How about your son?"

"I don't believe Seely and the prince are friends, Sire, but I assure you, Seely is loyal to you. The Bramwells have stood with the Ericcsöns for centuries, and we will continue to do so until our deaths. My son takes his vow as captain very seriously."

He placed a hand to his chest in salute.

I could almost hear Cyrus rolling his eyes at the man's hemming and hawing.

The king was becoming more maniacal every day, and the people whom he had abused were turning against him. Valeria was rallying. I'd received a coded message that the Dragon's Fire was planning a dungeon rescue, and fearing the fallout, I'd sent Ingrid and Thalia south to Feydore. A Dwarf I trusted lived there. Rogard would shelter them until it was safe to bring them home.

Thalia had cried, clinging to my jacket and demanding to be here when Sterling returned. She'd been heartbroken when word had come that he was dead. She had only agreed to go because Ingrid had begged her.

Ingrid was not Thalia's birth mother, my first wife having died in childbirth, but she was the only mother Thalia had known since she was eight years old, and the girl couldn't bear to cause her mother pain. She'd reluctantly packed a trunk and left under the care of a trusted friend.

"If you hear news of my heir, you will send word immediately."

The former captain took that as his dismissal and rose, bowing deeply to the king. "I will see it done, Your Highness."

As soon as the Fae left the room, Cyrus snapped, "Vincent!"

"Yes, Sire?"

"Have him followed."

I moved to do his bidding, but he spoke again. "Oh, and fetch me Soren. I need to see how my son fares in his new training with my captain."

Training with the captain?

I had not been aware that the prince was training with the Captain of the Guard, but Cyrus had been spending a great deal more time with Soren since Sterling had been imprisoned on Mt. Malus.

"Yes, Your Highness. Right away."

I hated showing deference to Cyrus, and as the years wore on, it became more difficult to play the loyal servant.

"One more thing, Vincent."

I wanted to roll my eyes at his demanding list, but the king had kept me occupied day and night since taking me into his service.

Today was no different than any other. In the days leading up to their departure, I had barely been able to see Ingrid and Thalia at all.

He suspected. It made it deadly to communicate with the resistance, leaving us to carefully coded messages and meetings in the sewers during the dead of night. I'd lain awake until after two in the morning to deliver the latest intel, which is when I learned of the planned rescue.

I was forced to leave Ravii, the Tangeerian, in my place should the king have woken. He would have been furious if he had. He demanded to be attended only by Valerians. Tangeerians and Rothtonians were allowed to work in the palace, but they could not be the king's attendants, as with Dwarves. Elves were not even allowed to work in the palace, and the king's hatred of them often led to their slaughter.

"Sire?"

"Bring me a quilldust lantern. I need to pay a visit to the dungeons."

Iyra. I must follow him. I have to ensure he isn't going to move her. Not this close to the rescue.

I'd only just discovered her prison after all these years.

"Yes, Your Highness."

* * *

Remmy

The queen. Lunaire's hair.

Sterling's mother had been trapped beneath his very feet for the last twenty years. A whirlwind of thoughts crashed through my head at once.

We must get out of here. Sterling needs to know his mother is alive. And his brother... his brother is a bloody traitor!

Sterling loved his little brother so much. This would break his heart. I stared dumbfounded at the Fae in the cell across the hall. She had said she was in here for the "crime" of love. Evidently, she did not love Cyrus. I wanted to ask her more, but I wasn't sure if I should pry.

Before I could decide, she spoke again.

"Tell me about yourself. I haven't had company in such a long time. What is your name?"

Queen Iyra coughed again, and I momentarily wished someone would come to bring her water, but thought better of it. I was here as a way to locate Sterling. I had no doubt that the guards would have their way with me if given the opportunity. The Blood Guard had already proven themselves to be ruthless murderers and rapists.

"My name is Remmy Silva, Your Majesty. I come from the village of Merda."

"Please, call me Iyra. I haven't been the queen in nearly two decades, and they've had these clan-suppressing chains on me for so long, I barely even count as Fae anymore. Merda, you say? I haven't met anyone from the villages in so long." She paused. "My son spoke of using you to locate my firstborn. Who is Sterling to you? Is he all right?"

I hesitated for a long moment before answering her. This was not how I had planned to meet my soulmate's mother. Trapped in a dungeon below the palace. Cold and damp, with blood dripping down the back of my pounding head.

"Remmy?"

"I love him," I whispered the words I'd not dared to speak aloud, to the mother of my heart's desire.

"Ah." I couldn't see her well in the dull light, but I could hear the smile in her voice. "And does my son love you in return?"

"Yes… I think… but… it's… complicated."

I vaguely saw her wave her arms in the air. "We have all the time in the world, darling." She chuckled at her crude joke. "Tell me. Please."

She deserved to know. With as much detail as I could bear to share, I recounted the details of the king's cruel proclamation, how I had met the Crown Prince, our journey together, and how I'd come to love him. I finished the story with my illness and Sterling's whispered words of love, as I had lain unconscious in our room.

"I don't deserve his love, but I must get out of here. If I don't… everything I have worked for… will be ashes around me," I said hoarsely, as I rested my sticky head on the cool dungeon wall.

"You are a strong woman, Remmy. I can see why my son loves you. I believe you will escape this prison, but in order to rise from the ashes—you first have to burn."

TO BE CONTINUED IN BOOK TWO OF THE VALERIAN CHRONICLES

Glossary/Pronunciation Guide

Gods:

Skotos- (SKOH-tos) The god of the Netherworld, of darkness, and death

Lunaire- (loo-NAIR) The goddess of Lumess, of light, love, and stars

Afrontis- (uh-FRON-tis) The god of earth

Ammadon-(AH-mah-don) The god of the sea

Characters:

Remmy Alina Silva (REH-mee)

Sterling Sage Ericcsön (STUR-ling)

Teigan Andor Berger (TEE-guhn)

Emerie Amora Silva (EH-muh-ree)

Inara Solene Beck (Ĭh-NAR-uh)

Echo Silva (EH-koh)

Eridian Silva (eh-RID-ee-uhn)

Rogard Blithinton (ROH-gard)

Ramilda Blithinton (rah-MIL-duh)

Isolde Meinaire (IZ-old)

Cyrus Ericcsön (*SYE-rus)*

Soren Vale Ericcsön (SO-ren)

Tyran Ericcsön (TEER-an)
Vincent Larsson (VIN-sent)
Xula Thronfeld (ZOO-lah)
Ivor Thronfeld (EYE-vor)
Gretchen Thronfeld (GREH-chən)
Maggie Olsen (MAG-ee)
Deidre Olsen (DEE-druh)
Rufus Dinkle (ROO-fus)
Aldric Ravnik (AHL-drik)
Axel Bolten (AK-suhl)
Gwendolyn Nova (GWEN-doh-lin)
Ravii Basu (rah-VEE)
Aubern Heil (AW-burn)
Dante Ariti (DAHN-tay)
Dauton (DAW-tən)
Seely Bramwell (SEE-lee)
Gene Elderwood (JEEN)
Onia Elderwood (OH-neye-uh)
Iyra Ericcsön (EYE-rah)
Dauton Greaves (DAW-tən)
Ione Silva (eye-OH-nee)
Klaus Silva (KLOWS)
Magette Vaneer (muh-GEET)

Locations:

Amengor (ah-MEN-gore)- Continent on which Valeria, Rothton, Elysia, & Tangeer are located

Valeria (vah-LEHR-ee-uh)- Home kingdom named after its vibrant purple valerian flowers

Elysia (ah-LIH-see-uh)- Closed off country to the North

Rothton (ROTH-tuhn)- Neighboring kingdom to the West ruled

by Cyrus' brother Tyran.

Tangeer (tan-JEER)- Neighboring kingdom to the East

Lunestair (LOO-neh-stair)- Capital of Valeria

Merda (MUHR-duh)- human village that is Remmy's hometown

Feydore (FAY-dor)- One of the mixed villages south of Lunestair (dwarves and humans reside)

Castillo (kah-STEE-yoh)- Tourist city on the southern coast of Valeria known for its white sand beaches and swaying palms; hometown of Teigan

Crenya (KREN-yuh)- human village south of Merda

Saxavall (SAK-sah-vahl)- Capital of Elysia

Aspara (ahs-pah-RAH)- Capital of Tangeer

Eirikstad (AIR-ik-stahd)- Capital of Rothton

Outis City (OW-tis)- Northern city on the border of Elysia

The Netherworld (NEH-thur-wurld)- The realm of death where Skotos reigns

Lumess (LOO-mess)- The realm of light where the gods and goddesses reside

The Stardust District- The region encompassing Lunestair, former home of the goddess

Lunaire

Therion Region (ther-EE-on) - The region of Skotos' beasts

The Sankot Desert (SAN-kot)- Large desert separating the villages from Lunestair

Cave of Beithir (BAY-thir)- Cave on Mt. Malus with a portal to the Netherworld

The Starlight Oasis- The most popular pub in Market Square, frequented by the Blood Guard

The Black Pheonix- Pub on the westside owned by the Bramwell family

The Drunken Dragon- The pub that serves as the rebellion

headquarters

Mt. Malus (MAL-us)- Treacherous mountain with a cave that has a portal to the Netherworld

Emerald Lake- Lake with green waters on Mt. Malus, home of the Thalkor

Highland Mountains- Mountain range on the northern & western borders of Valeria

Highland Pass- Mountainous pass leading to Mt. Malus from the south

The Black Lake- Lake with onyx waters between Lunestair and Mt. Malus; home of the Baga

The Darkhelm Forest (DARK-helm)- Forboding forest at the base of Mt. Malus

The Cushing River (KUSH-ing) River running through Valeria to the northern mountains, most popular home of the Selkies

The Broken Sea- Ocean off the southern coast of Valeria

Thalassian Ocean (thuh-LASS-ee-uhn) Ocean off the coast of Rothton

The Temple of Deliritas- (deh-LEER-ih-tahs) Secret temple on Mt. Malus, known only to the Ericcsön family and a few select Guards

Tenebriss- (TEN-eh-briss) Isle off the southern coast of Amengor, known to be controlled by monsters

Creatures:

Lemian (LEE-mee-uhn) Green green-eyed wolf-like creature. Kin to the Lycan, but

lacking the same level of intelligence.

Lycan (LYE-kan) Red-eyed wolf creature with human-level intelligence

Selkie (SELL-kee) Mer- people that reside in most water sources in the Therion Region.

They have black eyes & hair & sharp, pointed teeth. They love to eat humans & Fae. Not a

creature of Skotos.

Baga (BAH-guh) One of a kind creature that resides in the Black Lake. Similar to a worm

with four heads and dull teeth.

Thalkor (THAHL-kor)- Only one known in existence. Resides in the Emerald Lake. Large

dinosaur creature with spiked ridges and four legs on an elongated body.

Vesper (VES-per)- A viper native to Tangeer with venom that causes paralysis &

eventually death; known to prefer warm climates

The Faceless One - The ancient being that serves Skotos, guarding the Cave of Beithir

and the Temple of Deliritas

Phalynx (FAY-lingks) A Fae shifter with the body of a large cat, glowing sigils in the

forehead & translucent wings

Sphinx (sfingks)- A Fae shifter with the body of a lion, wings of an eagle, and the head of

a human

Flame Moths- Beautiful creatures resembling butterflies or moths with wings that glow

& tend to live near lush, verdant landscapes such as gardens, rivers, etc

Phoenix (FEE-niks)- A Fae shifter that is a large, beautiful, fiery bird.

Vanta (VAN-tuh) - Race of shifters that invaded Amengor from another realm

Wyvern- Extinct Fae shifter

Dragon- Extinct Fae shifter

Others:

Willowroot (WIL-oh-root)- A healing salve intended to treat minor injuries; lacks

stronger antibacterial properties that morsious contains.

Morsious (MORE-see-us)- A salve with strong healing properties

Dol (DOLL) - Plant the morsious salve is made from

Mirthwood (MURTH-wood)- Drug substance with hallucinogenic properties

Crathe (KRAY-th)- Harsh drug-like substance with addictive properties

Adhará (ADD-har-uh) - Sterling's nickname for Remmy, meaning "Northern Star" or

"Guiding Light"

Tilian Steel (TIL-ee-uhn)- One of the strongest metals in Amengor

Aster Bush (ASS-ter) - A large plant with star-shaped leaves

Laour Plant (LAA-oor)- A plant that lathers as soap

Quilldust *(KWIL-dust)* - Magical substance mined in Amengor. A remnant left behind by

the Vanta.

Valerian Flower (vuh-LEER-ee-uhn)- Vibrant purple flower that is common in Valeria, used for its herbal properties as a sleeping draught

About the Author

R.C. Perry lives in a mythical castle with a handsome broody Fae prince. They've been happily married for centuries and have two little furry Fae babies. When R.C isn't writing swoon worthy romances or whimsical tales of conquest, she's baking goods at her cottage bakery, sipping coffee in a corner cafe, soaking up the sun at the beach, traveling the world, or curled up in her cozy reading chair, exploring fantastical realms.

As an avid reader with interests spanning multiple genres, it's no surprise she has stories to tell.

Follow her @rcperrywrites on Tiktok and Instagram for updates on the next book in The Valerian Chronicles, and to find out what else she is working on!

You can connect with me on:

- https://www.instagram.com/rcperrywrites